THE DISLOCATED MAN

SLUMRAT RISING

BOOK FIVE | THE DISLOCATED MAN

WARBY PICUS

Podium

To My Uncle John

THE DISLOCATED MAN

CHAPTER 1

BONFIRE MORNING

Truth raced down the highway on his stolen iron horse, scarf wrapped over his face, demon perched on his shoulder. The sky burned red as the war he started raged below it. He was responsible for the sky, too—the volcanic eruption he set off was vomiting ash into the air and blotting out the sun. A good beginning, but only a beginning. Before the apocalypse really got rolling, he had one more head to take. King Rat. The Most Powerful Man in the World. He would kill Starbrite.

A few slight problems there. A few technical challenges. Starting with the fact that nobody knew where Starbrite was, his company had a better army than most countries, and he really was a higher class of being. Truth was cautiously optimistic. He had already killed people far beyond his level. Everything is doable with the right tools and preparation.

The iron horse ate up the kilometers, wheels spinning fast. He had to nip around the army wagons racing for the front line. There were a hell of a lot of them. The Onis army outnumbered Jeon ten or twenty to one, but the Jeon army was ferociously well equipped. Most advanced military in the world, by some metrics. Onis might win in the end, but they would lose a generation of youth to do it.

He watched an olive-drab wagon lumber past and grinned mirthlessly. Jeon's military power was built on advanced magical technology. So was everyone's, really, but Jeon was relying on technology as its force multiplier. Once the magic vanished, or even when it just reached a certain level of unreliability, that advantage would vanish. It would be down to muscle. And Onis had a lot more muscle than Jeon.

Truth let his mind wander as he rode southwest. He needed to report to Merkovah, but he didn't have any reasonably accessible dead drops. At this point, they were on the wrong side of the volcano. So, it was time to go to Plan B—find a Siphios embassy or consulate and report from there. Except he didn't know where Siphios had any consulates, so it would be the main Siphios Embassy in Onis.

Their capital city was creatively named Northern Capital. He didn't know if there was a southern capital. Presumably there was. Still, the northern capital was a thousand kilometers away as the bird-demon flies, which made it more like fourteen hundred as the international secret agent rides. A long haul, but he had a lot to think about as he went.

He was Level Five, for one thing, with only three permanent spells. Meditations of Valentinian would remain the base, naturally, then Incisive, the increasingly clearly jank Cup and Knife for the third, and then what? Even reserving one spell slot for the System, that left him one short. Graeme's Arrow would fill a gap in his arsenal, but compared to a spell he constantly used like Incisive, it just seemed so lacking.

He couldn't be lacking. Not when he was coming for the king of the world.

Truth looked at his hands and smiled. He had carefully put the wooden ring on his right index finger. No need to trigger pointless drama when he next talked to Etenesh or the Etenesh-adjacent. A space ring. Something unique on this planet. Something just for him. Because he blew up a whole damn volcano to rescue their little girl. It might be ordinary off-world, but it was incredibly precious to him.

The ring was a reminder. It was validation. He could do it. He could stand up to the best in the world and win. It required planning. Guile. Outright cheating. Making sure there wasn't anything remotely like a fair fight. But he could do it. And besides, the "best in the world" were all more than a century old and rich. They weren't any more interested in fairness than he was.

He slammed on the brakes, putting the iron horse into a long slide. Thrush squawked and flapped madly. "Dread magus?!"

"I just realized something horrible. That Level Eight I killed had to have been loaded. I never got to loot her. All that money, destroyed by the lava." His face went pale. He wasn't greedy, exactly, but the personal equipment of a Starbrite Level Eight? That wasn't stuff you could buy with mere money. Who knows what she had tucked away?

"I am so terribly sorry for your loss." The air demon sounded surprisingly sincere. "Still, you mustn't despair. You will have so many opportunities to feed on your kills from now on. So, so many opportunities."

Truth nodded. It was a blow. A real blow. But life would go on. Thinking about it more positively, he had lost the loot of a Level Eight, but Starbrite had lost an entire secret base, a Shattervoid child, and a sarcophagus of such critical importance, a Level Eight old monster had intentionally fought with a fraction of her true strength to avoid harming it.

That was another mystery to solve, one he would have to toss to Merkovah. Just what was in there that was so damn important? He got the iron horse running again. The already-bald tires looked a hot second from wearing away entirely. Truth reckoned it was only his terrifying reflexes that were keeping the two-wheeler upright and on the road. Time to look for new wheels.

He would keep the rest of the two-wheeler. He appreciated the way that the former owner had taken whatever they could find and whacked it with a hammer until it fit into the general shape of an iron horse. There were endless ways to improve it and make it less of a horrible piece of crap. Truth looked forward to having a project that didn't involve mass casualty events.

A quick inventory of his gear showed a very . . . Truth blend of equipment. Stowed in his literally unique, handcrafted-by-space-beings spatial ring was a field-repaired one-man flying suit, hauled out of a garbage heap behind a hovel in a mountain village that could also have been defined as a garbage heap. He had a stolen Onis Army standard-issue officer's needler stowed in there as well, along with a few changes of clothes, some camping supplies, and some snacks.

His current vehicle/project/rideable nightmare was a two-wheeler liberated from an abandoned village. Truth was privately convinced it hadn't been sold for scrap because the scrap dealers wouldn't take something so plainly cursed.

His clothes were rather nice, having been shoplifted at various department stores across Jeon. A little snug on his muscular frame, but the reddish-purple shirt suited him, and the black trousers were both durable and comfortable. His boots were practical work boots. Comfortable for both long walks and kicking people very hard.

Covering his neck and face was the Freedom of the Terraces, the magical scarf gifted to him after he stopped a terrorist attack back in Xandre. It granted him free access to any pitz stadium in Siphios, could change its look to support whatever team he liked, and let him blend in with crowds easily. It also, and this was the key thing at the moment, worked as a pretty decent dust filter.

The volcanic ash stank, and even for his toughened body, inhaling that rock dust could only be a bad thing. The magic in the scarf wasn't very powerful, but it was enough to keep the air coming in fresh and clean. He hadn't been very impressed with the Freedom of the Terraces when he got it. How often was he going to go to pitz stadiums? He was coming to treasure it now. Another reminder: not everything he did was terrible. He could help people.

He needed the reminders as the wagons full of weapons and conscripts rumbled south, toward the war he had started. They would be neatly lined up, soldiers and weapons alike, and fed into the woodchipper until their bodies choked it. Then the real core of the armies would be deployed—the grand summons, the strategic-level curses, individual high-levels sent out to earn the privileges they had spent decades enjoying.

He had only managed to kick off a war because they were looking for a reason to start a war. He tried to keep that firmly in mind. Jeon might not have wanted it, but Onis *certainly* did. They had been looking for an excuse to come for Starbrite and scoop up the rich little country he had made for himself in the process.

He couldn't make them fight. He just made sure they had an excuse. Better—he made them feel like they had "no choice." They did, of course. They had infinite choices. Fear has a way of narrowing your vision. They were already scared by the coming apocalypse. Scared of whatever Starbrite was up to. Then Truth turned up and showed them that Starbrite was prepared to make it very, very personal. That Starbrite was willing to go after anyone, anywhere in Onis.

They just needed an excuse. Any thin thing they could turn into public justification. Into self-defense. One needle later, and they had everything they needed. Everyone knew the score. Everyone knew that everyone else knew. It didn't matter what the truth was. This was about being scared and doing something so you wouldn't be scared anymore. A very human reaction.

Which led him to his last major piece of equipment. His platonic life partner, the angelic weapon known as the Tongue of One Who Speaks for God. A name he was finding both increasingly suspect and accurate as time went on.

The Tongue, too, was sort of jank. A bit of a broken angelic weapon, literal trash in the armories of Heaven, was taken back to this low reality and forged into a sword. Somehow, it worked. It was currently dwelling in his first aperture, waiting to be called out again. Its power limited by his power. Growing in strength as he did.

If he broke through the limits of this world and awakened his Nascent Soul, would the Tongue remain part of him? He had no idea. He hoped so. The sword just felt so right to him. He couldn't even explain it to himself. It just felt . . . right. Like this was what he was for—cutting to the heart of things, even if he seemed lost.

Onis had its own roadblocks set up, but they were well out into the boonies still. Truth drove straight through them, Incisive keeping him unnoticeable.

Get a new spell, research how to improve Cup and Knife, report in about . . . everything . . . and then figure out how to kill Starbrite. A modest plan.

Truth looked up at the volcano-ash-darkened sky. The night would be inky black. Not that it was any hindrance to him, but something whispered in the back of his mind. Tonight was not a good night to be on the road. He would have to race the sunset and find shelter.

Truth smiled and gave the demon more power. The iron horse sputtered and snarled but picked up the pace. Somewhere off the highway would be a hotel. Some place with a spellbowl buried around the doors, to keep out the little demons. He would go, sleep, and in the morning, he would see what the world looked like.

Sometimes, things needed to cook. Right now, Starbrite was still trying to figure out what had happened. Soon, he would react. He wouldn't take the loss of the Shattervoid girl lightly. He would be desperate, angry, and humiliated. He would make a big move. Truth smiled. With that mindset, Starbrite would be sloppy. He would make mistakes. Show a weakness.

That would be the end of the King of the World. Killed in the slum he had made, by a rat he carefully bred and trained. Truth could hardly wait. He pushed more power at the demon, going as fast as the shoddy frame could stand. It seemed he couldn't wait at all!

CHAPTER 2

IF IT'S STUPID BUT IT WORKS . . .

The iron horse ate up the kilometers, running south and west, paralleling the plume of smoke and ash from the volcano. People were on the roads, trying to evacuate. Some people were let through, long buses pulled by seven-legged lizards carefully screened by the checkpoints. Others were turned back, told to go home. Truth couldn't see any justification for letting some people through but not others. The locals apparently agreed.

There weren't any riots. There were secret police waiting in every crowd, knockout and mass-paralysis charms ready to go. The cops were all Level One. A hell of a lot of the mountain peasants looking to evacuate were Level Zero. It wasn't a fight.

"Don't look at me! Eyes down! Face on the ground!" Boots slammed into ribs, flipping people over. Noses broke as rough hands slammed faces into the pavement. Truth understood where the brutality was coming from. Small villages. Everyone knew everyone. The plainclothes pricks had just had their cover blown.

For now, that made them someone to be feared. Their families were untouchable. But the magic was dying. Soon, *they* would be the weak ones. Bullied by Level Zero nobodies. Not one person would consider their duty honorable or their service necessary. Their families would be catching the same hell they did. When things settled down again, the secret police would resume their untouchable status, but in the chaos of the apocalypse, many old debts would be paid.

The countryside was like a sheet of paper that had been crumpled up and smoothed out again. The towering mountains were visible on the horizon, but around here, it was all smaller foothills and a seemingly endless procession of ridges and valleys. Even in early summer, it wasn't what he would call "beautiful." Weedy little trees, densely clustered on the sides of the hills. Even with all the green, it had an inherent sense of brownness.

His eyes flicked up to the ash-filled sky, orange-red tinging on black as your eyes moved northeast. It was possible he wasn't seeing things at their best. The sky certainly lent the hillside temples a certain intensity. He slowed as he passed a larger one.

The locals were kneeling and praying on the long flight of steps up to the temple. Gloriously robed priests, brilliant in vivid orange and turquoise, cried out their prayers. Strong, trained voices, chanting their liturgies, the familiar words calming the masses. Long whisks flicked blessed water out over the kneeling masses as junior clerics swinging censers purified them with incense.

Smoke from a jar, to protect you from the smoking mountain. *Our magic isn't enough. We need divine protection from this angry world.* He didn't look down on them in their desperation. It wouldn't work, but so what? Ultimately, nothing they did could affect the final outcome. They could only protect themselves however their limited means would allow. They weren't allowed to run, weren't allowed to fight, weren't allowed to hoard supplies and hide. What could they do but pray?

There would be secret policemen mixed in with them, listening carefully to the prayers for any hint of heterodoxy or lack of patriotic spirit. Quietly desperate and wishing like hell they believed the blessings would work. Truth sped up again. The bright spot in the sky was moving steadily west, and he wanted to be a long way gone by the time the sun set.

There was something in the air. Something worse than volcanic ash and the echoes of war. Not a good night to spend in the wilds or on a road.

Military wagons rushed around in long, rumbling convoys. Police on spell beasts rode ahead of the wagons, carrying bright lanterns, blaring, "Official business! Give way! Give way!" They were still somewhat near the border, but Truth suspected these were more concerned with the volcano. The prevailing winds were blowing the ash plume into Onis, not Jeon.

Early summer, moving into midsummer. It hadn't been raining much. Too early for forest fires? He didn't know. Awful lot of closely clustered trees, though. And one thing he had noticed about the towns and villages in Onis—they were dense. Nicer than he expected, by the standards of poor mountainous region villages, but very dense.

That phoenix he liberated had made a point of the terrible vengeance it planned for humanity. Fingers crossed it couldn't survive the magic collapse. These dense little towns and villages wouldn't survive a single move from that ancient.

Truth let his mind drift back to Sally and what she had said about Nascent Souls. The thing that came after Level Nine. The Shattervoid didn't cultivate the same way, but they were quite familiar with the usual way cultivation went. The joys of being in transport, Truth supposed. You got to go everywhere and meet everyone.

According to her, a mage *was* their spells, but those spells also took on aspects of the mage. Since no two people understood a given thing identically, there were subtle variations between two seemingly identical spells. Truth's Incisive would never be identical to someone else's. Merkovah had unknowingly touched on that truth when he was tutoring Truth. *Learn your spell. Learn what it means to you. Only when you have reached a bottleneck in your understanding should you study other people's interpretations.*

Truth felt like he had barely scratched the surface of his spells. What did that say about those mighty ones who created them?

Of course, the reverse also applied. If he didn't understand his spells, what did it tell him about how they were changing him? The Truth who had learned Incisive was . . . not a nice person. It was still coming together while he was in Siphios, but once he got back to Jeon and started using it constantly? Those personas came out of him. The fact that the Prince felt so natural and so right really should have been a major warning sign.

His blind grappling with Cup and Knife had to be changing him too. A spell for fixing things. Making them more "right." He had been spending an awful lot of time confronting just what "right" was, recently. Was that a coincidence? The natural result of what he was doing? Because he hadn't been this introspective or curious when he was working for Starbrite. In fact, he was completely indifferent to "right." That word was irrelevant. Was something good for him and good for Starbrite? That's what was "right."

Not so anymore. Now he was having to look at a broken world outside himself and look inward at the broken world within and ask, "How do I fix this? How do I, at the very least, make it *better*?"

All of which was meaningless without strength, of course. You could have the most perfect justice in the world, and it was just pissing into the wind if you couldn't enact it. Your fist had to be bigger than the bully's. Which led to the last spell in his arsenal.

The Meditations of Valentinian. Visualizing the perfected version of yourself you wanted to bring into the world. Imposing it on the world. Becoming more real than the real. A completely self-focused spell. It was interesting in that way. Every other spell in his arsenal was about changing the world around him or how the world reacted to him. The Meditations didn't give a damn about the world. The Meditations . . .

He let the iron horse drift to a stop by the verge. Over and over, he had experienced that alienating sense of unreality. That the world was paper-thin, an illusion. A demonic lie. Something to be overcome. And the Meditations had gotten there first.

What was the premise of the Meditations? That, with meditation and visualization, a mage could reinforce their own existence to the point where they could snatch the stars out of the sky. A flip of the hand could open valleys, a downturned palm could smooth away mountains. The mage was realer than the world he lived in. If only they could see it. If only they could unleash the divinity within themselves. The world offered the mage *nothing*. Everything they needed to achieve godhood was within.

Even the Nine Worms, those remnants of his partial Ghūlification, agreed. They didn't just repair his body. They incorporated the Meditations into it. The worms looked down on everything except that.

He started connecting the dots. The Meditations made him self-sufficient and largely insular. It wasn't that he refused to deal with others, but he insisted that they deal with him on his terms. His assessment of reality was the only one that mattered to him.

This led neatly to Incisive. His tools to impose his reality on the world. A world view heavily inflected by a famously self-sufficient timeless snake demon. Then there was Cup and Knife. Ready to "correct" the world, bringing it into line with how it should be. The difficulty in using the spell was likely a difference in understanding between himself and the angel Manda, its creator.

Where did the influence of the spells end? For that matter, how much of this was him blaming his own personality on his magic? Making his faults the faults of others? Truth had no idea. He still had a fourth spell to pick, too. By the time he left the Initiate's realm, there would be nine spells within him. Nine points of view. Nine ways of dealing with the world that would have to be harmonized.

An initiate into the mysteries of reality. No one could explain it to you. They could talk until their tongue fell off. You could listen until your ears bled. But until you had seen it, until you had that stroke of revelation, it wouldn't come together. A divine revelation, a level of understanding beyond the rational.

Once you had assembled your spells, plumbed the depths of your understanding of them, of yourself, of the world you existed in, you were ready to step out onto that wider world. Your soul would no longer be completely bound by the "real." It would be a tentative thing. Tiny, in the vastness of the universe. A little spark, trying to ignite a sun. A Nascent Soul, ready to grow into its potential.

And if you never got that spark of revelation? If you chose not to put in the time and focus on cultivation and mired yourself in the real?

He looked out over the countryside. Plenty of farmers tending their fields. Plenty of people shopping in the villages he passed. People watching the scry. Talking with each other. Living. You would have to do your best. You would have to say "That's just how the world is" and do your best to live well in an imperfect world. "It can't be helped. The world doesn't care about your feelings. It is what it is."

Cultivation was an act of defiance. Every meditation, every moment spent in study or reflection was a bloody-mouthed declaration that the world would have to hit you harder than that to make you quit. Like *hell* it can't be helped! Like *hell* it was what it was! You were a damn mage. You took the furious powers of the heavens and hammered them into your own power. You used your wisdom and your spells to impose *your* truth on the world. It was what you said it was. The world was what you said it was.

And if the universe disagreed? If it sent plagues and apocalypses and evil-doers to hound you? You spit the blood out of your mouth, clench your fist, and pay them back double. Be it with an angelic blade in your hand or sitting on a mountaintop in silent reflection.

Truth threw himself back into motion. There was a city up ahead. He would spend the night there. He would reach the capital around lunchtime. Then it would be time to conspire with Merkovah. Starbrite was waiting for him. Truth hoped he had washed his neck.

CHAPTER 3

RAIN, RAIN, GO AWAY

Truth raced the sunset into the big city on the river. His road atlas claimed, to Truth's deep suspicion, that the name of the town was "The Hot Male Side of the Shang River." Which was clearly stupid on several levels, not least of which being that the river (according to that same road atlas) was called the Han.

I think we need to work on our Onis more. This is dumb.

<<Literal translations can be misleading. You have shepherded people, but how often have you actually herded sheep?>>

The city, whatever it was called, came as a shock to Truth's senses. He was a Harban boy, born and bred. He was used to high-density, hive-like slum towers and gorgeous wealthy districts. This city had those things, kind of. Just different enough to feel utterly alien and familiar all at once.

It was the apartment blocks. They looked like they had been stamped out on an assembly line. Identical buildings, dozens of stories tall, sorted into tidy rows like cornstalks. Row after row of them. Then lower apartment blocks were merely a half dozen stories but four or five times the width of the towers. Those were sorted like books on a shelf. Neatly lined up and ready for use. Each perfectly identical to the other.

Very like home. Very like the mass-produced housing Starbrite and its imitators churned out. He was struggling to put his finger on the difference. The sheer concentration of perfectly identical structures was almost enough to throw him by itself, but that wasn't the whole of it.

They . . . He wanted to say that they were clean, but it was more a feeling of "clean" than the actual state of being "not dirty." Like the people living there took pride in their infinitely replicating apartment buildings. Maybe that was it—the people looked like they wanted to be there.

Nobody looked stressed about the war. In fact, more people looked worried about the sky. They were a very little bit north of the volcano's plume, but the dust spread wide through the atmosphere. It wasn't just

Truth. Judging by the way everyone was hurrying home, nobody wanted to be on the streets tonight.

Truth cruised around, looking for a mid-market hotel. Something with reliably clean beds and decent spell bowls under the doors. One of the great feats of magical engineering right there—making the bound demons able to pass through home wards without getting demolished by the spell bowls.

He turned down a busy street and was brought to a quick halt. Floating above the street, ten meters up, were little folded paper birds. Thousands of them, all the same model. The birds were in a variety of bright colors, and they mostly just floated in place. Sometimes, they would shift a little or pretend to preen their nonexistent feathers. What made them really special in Truth's eyes were the lights in them. Each paper bird was lit from within by a bright, white light shining through the colored paper.

It was gorgeous. It was lively and joyful and fun, even with the identical birds manufactured in six approved colors. Under the darkening orange-black sky, they seemed brilliantly alive and hopeful. He smiled up at them and hoped they wouldn't come to any harm from whatever was coming tonight.

The hotel boasted the "Sure, why not?" name of Summer-Hill Suites, despite having no suites and being built on perfectly flat land. Busy night at the hotel, it turned out. A lot of people from out of town suddenly felt the need for the shelter of the city.

Truth stood behind the clerk and looked at the list of available rooms, and picked the most expensive one that was still empty. If someone came in the middle of the night, he would deal with it then. Besides, the "most expensive one" was a double-queen-bed room with a pullout sofa, intended for an entire family to share. Not exactly the stuff of fevered dreams.

Flopping on the adequate mattress, he allowed himself a moment of satisfaction. There was something fun about how he managed his sleeping arrangements. No worries about safe houses or being snitched on. What made it better was that Jeon knew he was doing it too. No idea about Onis's degree of information on him, but their internal security services had a reputation for unpleasant thoroughness. They would be checking all the hotels, all the time, whether he existed or not.

They knew what he was up to. They just didn't have an effective answer. It must be driving them crazy. He smiled beatifically. He passed through the world, leaving no footprints. His body was sealed against most magics. He didn't even emit heat or smell unless he wanted to. People weren't allowed to see him unless he let them, and even then, they saw only who he wanted them to see. It didn't work on the very highest-level people, but for all but a fraction of one percent of the world's population? He didn't exist.

He kept calling everyone else ghosts or unreal, but right now, he was the real ghost. Another time, that might bother him. For now, he just enjoyed it and closed his eyes. He would sleep while he could. He had a feeling that it would be a short night.

Truth woke to the sound of drumming rain on the window and screams through the walls. He was up in a flash, slid into his already-laced-up shoes, and stood ready to fight in an instant. His eyes slid around the room—nothing. He glanced out the window. Whatever was hitting it was dark and viscous. He squinted. Hard to tell in the dark, even with his eyes, but . . . blood. It was raining blood.

He drew in a long breath through his nose. Yes, no mistaking that metallic stink. Blood, human blood. The screaming had died down, replaced by nervous chatter. These walls were really too thin. He'd have to leave a complaint. If it was raining blood, that was a problem for the windows, the walls, and the gutter. Unpleasant, but tomorrow, the air and water demons would have a fantastic day and all would be well again.

He took a closer look out the window. He didn't see anything moving out there. Not as many lights on in the city as he had expected. Something flickered in the distance. Bright lights. Police? Maybe. The window was getting blurry. Something caught the corner of his eye, something on the window itself.

The glass was slowly being etched. The blood was eating through the glass. Give it a few minutes, and there would be blood on the carpet. Looked like the hotel's wards weren't up to snuff. What he got for going cheap.

Find another building? Trust his sealed body to keep out whatever evil that was? Not his first choice. Find an interior room and fort up? Better choice. He packed up everything he could, had a big drink of water, brushed his teeth, made use of the toilet, and left as the interior of the glass was just starting to smoke. Judging by the returning screams, other people were seeing it too.

Out into the hallway and down to the front desk. The staff were looking pretty alarmed too—people were yelling at them, demanding they do something. *A lot to put on an overnight clerk*, Truth thought.

The lights were flickering. That couldn't be good. Everyone went quiet and stared at the shuddering talismans. The last time the lights suddenly went out, the magic vanished for a while. The pain of feeling your apertures collapse, even if only temporarily, was agonizing. If they stayed empty for too long, it would become permanent. A lifetime of pain.

He sighed. This was none of his business, but . . . maybe as a baby step toward giving a damn about other people? He pulled on the persona of a talisman maintenance engineer. Hopefully, his bad grammar would sell his persona's low education.

"Everyone, everyone, we are far from the doors and windows here. Just sit down and cultivate. Load up on as much energy as you can, so if the magic does stop, we can be okay for longer." Incisive lent some weight to his words. He could see people slowly nodding.

"I don't think the bathrooms have any windows, right?" someone in the crowd asked. "We could hide out there and cultivate. Sit in the tub, even, in case something leaks in through the door."

Truth nodded encouragingly. That was some good thinking right there. The conversation quickly started moving in a more-productive direction, and Truth let himself fade out of their awareness. That was as far as he was willing to break cover. He *liked* being unnoticeable. Even if it was clearly doing bad things to his emotional state.

Truth opted for a ground-floor housekeeping closet. He decided that, acidic blood notwithstanding, he could indulge in a little luxury. Therefore, he got one of the housekeeping carts, put a neatly folded quilt on top of it, and hopped aboard. A comfortable seat, just right for meditation and watching the rising tide. He took his own advice and cultivated. Twenty minutes later, he felt a vacuum against his skin. The cosmic rays in the city were fading out. Vanishing.

He was sealed up tight. Not a speck of energy leaked out. What he had was his. He was fine. Just sitting and waiting. Listening to a hotel full of people screaming in fear and pain, for four hours. Trying desperately to convince himself he didn't care, and it wasn't touching him.

He left as soon as the blood rain stopped. For some reason, he didn't want to look anyone in the eye.

The iron horse was no worse for wear. The demon was completely obliterated, of course, but the talismans had been such utter trash to begin with, the fluctuating magic didn't manage to make them worse. One surprisingly technical bit of summoning later (his time fixing army wagons came in very useful there), he was on the road again.

He pushed the two-wheeler as hard as it would go. No more stops, no more looking around. Head down, straight for the capital. Trying to outrun the echoing memories of screams. Trying not to think what those endless identical towers would have been like last night, or what the hospitals would be like now.

Tried not to think about the turbulence that vacuum had caused. Was the rain of blood pushed out ahead of a weather system of collapsing magic? He had no idea.

Straight into the center of the capital. He would look around later. Several layers of ring roads, he noticed. The city was beyond huge, but it was very orderly. Endless rows of identical apartment towers. He kept his eyes on the road. It took a lot of hunting and a bit of discreet asking, but he did eventually find his way to the Siphios embassy.

He approached the front desk. "Hi! I was told to ask for the Second Assistant Deputy to the Special Dispatch Officer for Trade and Agriculture?" Truth said in a friendly voice. The receptionist looked considerably more alert at the end of his sentence than at the start of it.

"Oh? I believe he will be free shortly. Would you follow me, please?" she asked.

"Of course."

She led him deeper into the embassy, finding a profoundly anonymous-looking office with a profoundly thick, heavily warded door, and waved him to a seat. The seats were identical. This was a room for anonymous meetings, not posturing.

"Who should I say is here?" she asked.

Truth grinned, remembering Merkovah's instructions. "Tommy Wells. I'm here about your talisman problem."

She nodded, recognizing a code phrase when she heard it. She turned to leave. "By the way," Truth hurriedly added, "do you have a cafeteria here?"

She looked puzzled. "For staff, yes. Why?"

He smiled. "I'm dying for some good coffee. After I give my report, I think I'm going to be running out of here like my hair's on fire. Any chance of a cup?"

CHAPTER 4

FROM SIPHIOS WITH LOVE

It took twenty minutes for the receptionist to return. Truth noticed that, regrettably, she did not have any coffee. Worse, she was also giving him a distinctly odd look. Well hidden, but he was used to spotting odd looks by now. She, apparently, was used to spotting disappointment.

"Sorry for the long delay, Mr. Wells. Good news on the coffee, though."

"Oh?"

"Yes. Instead of a paper cup of our cafeteria's workhorse blend, you will be enjoying three cups of the finest handpicked, sun-dried, hand-roasted and freshly ground coffee from the steep slopes of the Aussa highlands. Near High Chirchin, which you may be familiar with. Sorry, but I don't think I have ever met anyone from outside of Siphios that watches pitz, and you shout for the Blades? Really?" She looked at his scarf, genteelly boggling.

"Family connection." Truth grinned.

"Division Three team, though. That's barely one step above the pub leagues. Didn't even know you could buy a scarf."

"They got that small-town spirit. Like the real meaning of pitz lives up there. The feeling in the stands is like nothing else, even if the standard of play isn't the highest. Perfectly safe for kids, too."

She shook her head in wonder. "I am officially Not Interested in people here to meet with the Trade and Agriculture Department. But I must say, you are difficult to not be interested in. Let me explain what is going to happen next. You will be taken to a very secure ritual room. Some embassy staff will be there. A ritual will be performed. You will be offered three cups of coffee, one at a time. Accept the coffee. You may freely discuss anything while the ritual is being performed. There is no rush, as the ritual can last several hours without any difficulty."

She took a deep breath. "The most important things to know are—always accept the coffee, enjoy the coffee and the smells, and enthusiastically praise the skill of the person who made the coffee. If you don't remember anything else, remember those three things. What are the three things that you absolutely have to do?"

"Say yes to the coffee, enjoy the taste and smell of the coffee, praise to the highest of heavens the skill of the coffee maker." Truth appreciated clear directions, especially when they involved him getting three cups of premium-grade Siphios coffee.

"Correct. Fortunately, given . . . everything . . . the odds of you messing up are almost nonexistent. You will see what I mean." She smiled in a bemused sort of way and shook her head. "Come on. Let's get you a cuppa."

Truth stepped through a pair of double doors onto a mountainside. It smelled like Siphios—that rich green smell of rainy mountain forests and ancient earth. There was a small fire going, already burned down to a fine bed of cinders, with a very low table next to it and short stools scattered around. Behind the short table was the oldest woman Truth could ever remember seeing. Sitting and enjoying the view down the valley were an old man, a younger man, and Merkovah.

"Welcome back, Mr. Wells." Merkovah's voice was soft. His eyes flickered toward the still-open doors. Truth nodded and closed them behind him. The doors into the embassy vanished, and they were wrapped in the illusion of the mountainside.

"This is the Coffee Ritual. You never got the chance to enjoy it while you were traveling with me. It's not inherently magical, though I suppose that could be debated." He smiled at the old woman, who paid him no mind. Her hands were busy scooping up green coffee beans and scrubbing them with clean water in a jug. "It does, however, interface remarkably well with some of our very best communication, concealment, and privacy spells. And I thought you could use it."

There was something about the cadence of his voice, the gentleness of it. This wasn't the pissy Merkovah, or the vengeful one, or the regretful one. This was the Merkovah who had mentored six hundred years of Siphios's best.

The warmth of that voice landed on Truth and nearly broke him. He knew he was feeling the cold. He had no idea how much the warmth would hurt.

"Thank you, Teacher. I could use a good cup and some good company." His voice wasn't particularly steady.

The old lady was apparently satisfied with the cleanliness of the beans, as she drained the water out of the jug and put a rough iron pan on the coals. The beans went into the pan. They only took a minute to get hot, and another to start roasting. The smell was incredible. The sheer, concentrated aroma of roasting coffee was a sensory joy. He couldn't help but smile. So did everyone else.

"The secret to the Coffee Ritual is to be present for it and to appreciate what's being offered. All the things that are being offered. You will see." Merkovah smiled.

The beans quickly moved from green to tan to black. They weren't evenly roasted; some were clearly more cooked than others. The old lady was flipping the pan, making the beans dance, then stirring with a long metal spoon, and making them dance again. The aroma was intensifying, and the pan was starting to smoke.

"When you say the room is secure—"

"Let her finish this part and start the grinding. Plenty of time to talk then."

They watched her work quietly. It was only seconds later when the pan started to smoke heavily. She lifted it off the heat and waved everyone over. Truth followed the others, who stuck their whole face into the smoke. The blue-gray wisps seemed to wrap around him as he inhaled the aroma.

"I don't have words." He didn't realize he had spoken. It was like the concentrated soul of coffee, translated directly into the brain, bypassing the mouth and stomach. "I am suddenly wondering if I ever drank coffee before."

"You haven't." The old man's smile took the sting out of his words. "Real coffee is special, and Kuleni is a master of the craft." The area around the fire pit was scattered with cut long green grass and little yellow flowers. The smoke rising from the pan, the green grass, the flowers, the view from the mountainside, the warmth of the companionship, it was all too much.

Truth collapsed onto a little stool, folding in on himself. He could feel himself shaking, but numbly, as though the body that shook existed at a great distance from the mind feeling the shaking.

"It's all right. It's all right. You did well. You did very well. May I touch you?" Merkovah's voice was soft.

"Not yet."

"When you are ready."

Truth sat a while, trying to reconnect mind and body through the storms of emotion. He had . . . killed an awful lot of people in the last few months. All the introspection he was doing, all the studying and learning about the nature of humanity and the world. It didn't make the weight of those lost lives less. It made them weigh more heavily.

Eventually, he looked up. "Perhaps we can start with introductions?" he asked. Merkovah nodded.

"Certainly. I am here in the form of a . . . best to think of it as a specialized sort of golem. My actual body is back in Nag Hamadi, but you really are talking to me." Truth nodded.

"This gentleman"—Merkovah waved toward the older man—"is Bekele, our ambassador in Onis. He is attending this meeting, as his job covers a lot more than you might think. Making the coffee is Kuleni, his wife. Having her make the coffee is part of the ritual." Truth smiled politely at the old man, who nodded agreeably back. The old woman didn't look up.

He had no idea what ambassadors actually did beyond hosting balls in period romance novels. He was surprised by the lack of a last name, until he remembered that the oldest, highest-class families in Siphios didn't use them.

"Next to him is the embassy's diplomatic security officer. He is here primarily because the war with Jeon and the volcano could affect the security of the embassy and its staff. He will also be monitoring the wards here, so don't find it strange if he doesn't talk much."

The younger man, middle-aged and fit, gave Truth a professional smile and a nod of his own. Now that Truth was looking for it, he could see the younger man's eyes moving, looking at things only he could see. Truth also noticed that Merkovah hadn't actually introduced him, which firmly moved the younger man into the category of *Spy* in his head.

Merkovah clearly read his expression, rolled his eyes at him, and pressed on. "His name is Andele Vorka. He is not a spy; I just didn't think you would care. Which, in retrospect, was a surefire way to trigger your paranoia. Everyone, meet Code Name Anchorite."

Everyone gave Merkovah a look for that one. Even the old lady, who was now pounding the roasted beans in a tall mortar using a long stick. Her jabs with the pestle seemed downright pointed.

"We have all the possible code names painted on little wooden balls. The balls go into a tumbler, which gets turned a few times, then one of the balls drops out of a hatch. We discard them for a hundred years after they have been used. I didn't pick the code name." Merkovah returned their looks with interest.

"*Anchorite*, though." Truth one-upped him in the look battle.

"Young man, what are you if not someone who withdrew from secular society for religious reasons? I thought that was the closest thing to a divine seal of approval I had seen in centuries." Merkovah wasn't having it.

"*Anchorite*, though. I would have accepted *Partisan*, or . . . I don't know. Jim. Code Name Jim."

"Random is a lot more secure than risking a pattern. As you very well know."

Truth had to give him that one. He searched for another line of attack and realized he didn't want to bicker. It was comfortable in its way, but it wasn't what he needed.

"So. Leaving aside the name thing. It's been a busy little while since I last saw you."

"Just under three months. You have done in less than ninety days what others could not achieve in centuries." Merkovah lost the heat from his voice. "I knew you would become someone astounding. I underestimated the quality of my student."

The ambassador and the security officer just sat, content to watch the two speak. There were clouds moving down the valley. They were so high up, they were looking down at the drifting mists.

The coffee had apparently been ground to the old woman's satisfaction. She sifted it through a woven basket a few times, removing any chunks that were too large. The powdery grounds were scooped into a wooden bowl. Next to the fire was a fancy-looking clay vessel. Round and wide at the bottom, narrowing quickly to a long, tall neck. A handle jutted out from the side, and a long spout extended from just above the wide base. Lacquered in black and painted with simple pictures of flowers in red. Pretty.

She added clean water to the pot, then the coffee grounds. The whole thing went directly on the coals. She fished out one of the burning coals with her metal spoon and quickly dropped it into a little metal box. To the box she added what looked like dried tree sap. The smell of incense quickly mixed with the fresh mountain air and the smell of roasted coffee. It was . . . He didn't have words. He didn't want to think. He just wanted to exist in the feeling of the aroma.

"To save one person, I killed hundreds directly, thousands indirectly, and at one or two steps removed, millions will die because of me." Truth felt the words falling out of himself. "There can be no moral justification for that. I did it for selfish, greedy reasons. And yes, I count wanting to save the people I care about as selfish. They are *my* people, and *my* happiness is dependent on their safety and happiness."

He looked down the mountainside. He felt a terrible loss. He would never live there. There would be no home for him in this world. Not with what he knew was coming. He wouldn't stay there even one minute longer than necessary. He would scoop up the sibs . . . hopefully with Harmony included in that number . . . and Etenesh, and Jember, and even Merkovah and a few other people, and just *go*. Where, he didn't know or care.

Maybe he would take Niles and the Succubae. Thrush? Would Susan want to go? Her entire existence was based on conquering *this* world, so maybe not.

"I would very much like to only kill one other person. I won't be that lucky, of course, but really, there is just one more head I need to take." Truth called the Tongue to hand and laid her on his lap. "Which way do I point my blade?"

CHAPTER 5

BLESSINGS OF THE ELDERS

The smell of the incense mixed with the woodsmoke and the coffee to create something incredible. A sensory mist that spoke to them and the world around them. It was the only one talking. The group sat quietly around the fire, plainly not clear on where to start.

"Just to confirm—you rescued the Shattervoid girl?" Merkovah asked.

"Yes. Well, basically, yes." Everyone tensed up, but Truth waved them down again. "I disabled the spells restraining her and she carried us out of the volcano and into the . . . let's go with 'warm embrace of her family.' I think that's the line I usually read in those situations."

"Lucky you got in there before they blew up the volcano." The ambassador chuckled.

"Yes. Lucky." Truth nodded. Merkovah's eyes narrowed momentarily.

"Young man, while not everyone in this room has been read into every detail of your background, they do all have our highest-level security clearance and have been specifically read into major parts of the program supporting your efforts."

"Oh. Neat."

"It means you can talk freely here."

"Of course."

There was a pause. Merkovah sighed and buried his face in his hands.

"You aren't going to say a single thing more than you need to, are you?"

"Nope! Well, nothing dangerous. I think I would actually enjoy just . . . chatting with people for a while."

Merkovah looked around the room for support. "He's been like this for as long as I have known him. He brutally interrogated a Dancing Cloud when he saw one for the first time. He rides the most horrible iron horses because he knows every part that goes into them and how to fix them when they go wrong. He spent fourteen hours flying in cargo holds rather than take a meeting with a droned operative. He has never once used any of the supplied plans we made. And yet, everyone acts like *I'm* the asshole when I ask for mental-health days and a raise."

"I mean, it's clearly justified." Truth's lips quirked. "You know Siphios Intelligence, or whatever you call yourselves, is completely, totally compromised."

This got sputters of indignation from everyone in the room, including a particularly hard look from the old lady. Truth shrugged.

"Look at it from my perspective. Jeon internal security only ever really got close to me twice. Once when I screwed up my cover, resulting in the whole Hell Prince nonsense. Once when they traced a ritual. And that was it. Having no contact with anyone has made me an utter nightmare to track. On the other hand, I'm betting your other teams of operatives have been getting nabbed left and right, except for a few who are either very lucky or are being left there to feed you false information."

"It's not quite that bad." The ambassador's voice was bone-dry.

"Oh, you got some out alive?"

Merkovah cut in. "All right, before this devolves any further, what *are* you willing to share?"

"I found out what's on the other side of Level Nine. And, related, I also found out what the System Astrologica is."

That got a lot of attention. The diplomatic security officer grunted. "Spell draw just shot up. Not any kind of obvious attack. Dropping . . . back to baseline. Seems to have been a transitory spike."

Merkovah's eyes slightly narrowed. "I wonder. Without revealing anything, where did you learn this from?"

"The Shattervoid girl. We got into most of it when we were off-planet, actually."

Looks were shared across the room. The old lady, Kuleni, poured out a small cup of coffee, sniffed it, tasted it, and nodded. She looked over at Truth. "Sugar?"

"For the really good stuff, I prefer drinking it black."

She nodded and poured him a cup, serving it on a little saucer. "I always like mine with lots of sugar or a knob of spiced butter, but to each their own." Truth smiled and inhaled the aroma.

The world seemed to judder to a halt for a second.

The smells—coffee, yes, but there was chocolate there, too, and a hint of dark cherries and lemon zest. Under them was some rich complexity he couldn't put words to. Layers of flavor and meaning he had to dive into if he wanted to explore them. He lifted the cup to his lips and took a long pull.

He put the cup down on the saucer gently.

"That is the best coffee I have ever had or even heard of." Truth didn't know how to be effusive. Everyone felt the sincerity, though. She smiled, and poured for the rest of the room.

"Take your time with it. The second cup is lighter, the third the lightest. No rush, no rush. Go slow and savor it. And while you do, talk." She waved him on.

It was, as everyone expected, a long conversation. Merkovah made some alterations to the wards on the room, which let Truth finally reveal the existence of Nascent Souls, and what the System Astrologica probably was.

"The key thing, I think, is that this was more or less confirmed by a C-suite Level Eight," Truth explained. "She said the only point of contact the System Astrologica has with the material world is Starbrite himself."

"Do we know who was in the base?" The ambassador looked over at Merkovah, who wiggled his hand.

"Based on the description, I would say it was Racine Fennister. She came up through their manufacturing department, so it would make sense that she was overseeing the prototyping lab. And that she had the combat capability of a stunned potato. Last time she was in a real fight, they used her like artillery. Way, way in the back. Mostly, her level was deterrent enough."

"Sorry, she just *ignored* getting shot in the face?" the DSO asked, looking like he couldn't believe it.

"Nothing was touching her. Nothing was even close to touching her. I had trained her to not see the needles as a threat." Truth shrugged. "She also said that the Tongue was a spellbreaker sword?"

Merkovah nodded. "It's an outdated technology. Spell-Blades were somewhat notorious for using them. Basically, they worked by overloading spells with damage in a highly concentrated area. Wards of that era couldn't hold up and tended to fall apart. Even more so unstable spells like curses or evocations. They weren't anti-magic so much as they just . . . broke spells. Like saying a hammer is anti-peanut."

Truth blinked. He was highly familiar with a wide variety of weapons and had never heard of that one. Merkovah smiled slightly and preempted his question.

"Because warding spells improved, needler technology massively improved, and combat doctrines changed to entirely ranged magic. It was just massively more efficient to use a specialized talisman or have a regimental marksman use a heavy needler with Graeme's Arrow or Drill Spark or similar if you had to overload a specific point."

Truth allowed how that was fair and got stuck back in. When he was wrapping up, Kuleni handed him a second cup of coffee. It was brewed in the same pot using the same grounds, he noticed. The taste was significantly lighter. You could pick out the brighter, more subtle notes, but something of the body was lost. It was still phenomenal, and he said so.

"You said you like a knob of spiced butter in the coffee?" he asked.

"Just a little bit. Would you like to try some?"

He did, and it was weird but delicious. The spices reminded him vividly of the food in Siphios, while the butter added a richness to the coffee that changed the whole sensation of drinking it. The fat stuck to his lips a little bit and coated his tongue. The butter and spices kept the taste lingering in his mouth. He didn't know that he particularly liked it, but it was absolutely fun to try.

Truth wrapped up his report. He left out starting the war and liberating the phoenix. He did mention his campaign against Onis public security as a way to stoke tensions. The "room" was very quiet afterward. It was a lot to digest. Truth looked out across the mountains and enjoyed the fresh air. It might be an illusion, but it was a calming one.

"So . . . we need to find Starbrite and kill him. But every soul that gets enrolled in the new System is subconsciously training its host's psyche, and every enrolled person we kill is directly empowering Starbrite's soul. Which is already so vastly powerful, the Shattervoid think it's deformed and evil," the ambassador concluded.

Truth appreciated the awful lot of questions that the ambassador clearly had but was choosing not to ask. The DSO was keeping his eyes on the wards, but Truth was utterly certain the cop wanted to get him in an interrogation cell ASAP for more detailed answers. Merkovah . . . was looking up at the ceiling.

"It's not hopeless. It's not hopeless. We just need to . . . radically depart from our initial plans and try to adapt things not intended for this job from their original purpose." Merkovah's voice started calming and ended wry.

"I have always been a big believer in the power of jank." Truth nodded firmly.

"You would." This came as a growl. "Congratulations on reaching Level Five, by the way. And not exploding. Again. Somehow. Despite the amount of available cosmic rays sharply declining globally."

"I do need access to a spell library, now that you mention it. A real one this time. Also, we need to sit down and have a long, long talk about Cup and Knife."

There was a pause at that. The old lady cocked her head to one side. "I don't think I know that spell."

Merkovah slouched into his chair. "You memorized that spell. Of all the spells you lifted from my library, you memorized the absolute jankiest. Your faith in God is nil, but your faith in crudely cobbled-together monstrosities remains vaster than the skies. Sure, yes, why not, I have absolutely no other pressing matters, let's talk about a spell that was broken when it was first written hundreds of years before I was born, and was preserved only as reference material."

"I mean, it doesn't have to be right this second. But if we are our spells, figuring out how it's meant to work and what Manda's intent was behind the spells is . . . pretty damn important, actually. Because my next spell will have to play well with what I already have, and that's going to be another big job."

Merkovah's lips quirked. "You realize that the correct answer is actually *Spend the time to get to understand your spells and what they mean to you*, right? Behead Starbrite and we can spend all the time you want chatting about it."

"Hah. Well. I'll get on that. Any idea about the sarcophagus thing?"

"Many. None more than ideas. I will research it and let you know."

About what he expected.

"Got any ideas about finding Starbrite and, you know, stopping him from doing whatever the hell he is doing with all these soul fragments?"

Merkovah's smile was unpleasant. "Why, yes, yes I do."

"Why am I suddenly worried?" Truth asked. That got snorts from around the room.

"The fact that you haven't dropped Incisive even for a second while we have been here is both heartening and probably the explanation you are looking for." Merkovah shook his head.

"No. It is terribly sad," Kuleni said. The gathering fell silent. She let the silence brew for a moment, then smiled sadly at Truth. "Young man, you are in immense pain and living in fear. They are your constant companions, more so than even your sword."

"Yes."

The illusion provided the sound of birds singing in the trees, the wind blowing the leaves. Somehow, it made the silence deeper.

"I don't know about Cup and Knife, but I know about Incisive. You have learned, perhaps too well, the lessons of Botis the Snake Demon. I think it is time you turned your mind to what you can learn from Botis the swordsman, debater, and Lord of Hell. From there, you can pick your next spell."

"Thank you, senior. I think I will do just that."

"Good. Because we will be exploiting your Hell Prince identity, and you will need to take full advantage of that." She continued in the same calm, reassuring tones.

"Pardon?!"

"Oh, yes. You are going to cut back the supply of souls immensely and poison the well of the ones he does get. Weaken him before you go in for the final confrontation. Well, you and everyone who will be supporting you. This will be anything but a solo act."

CHAPTER 6

PERSUASIVE

Truth wasn't sure of the etiquette there. Normally, he would start the sentence with *Ms.*, but being a Siphios aristocrat, the old lady didn't have a last name. *Madame* and a job title was also a valid choice, also impossible due to his not actually knowing her job title. Madame Ambassador? But she wasn't the ambassador, and what kind of weirdo would like being called by their husband's rank?

Then, of course, you were on to the tricky business of explaining that their clearly carefully thought-out plan was, in fact, terrible and you wouldn't be doing it. Especially since he did actually like these people. To say nothing of the spells and support. But really, right now, it was the warmth of their company. He didn't want to break the peace of the Coffee Ritual.

"Okay."

Merkovah twitched, then carefully looked at Truth over the rim of his coffee cup. Everyone around the fire was a sharp customer. They didn't bother to trade glances.

"Mr. Wells, do you understand why they started pushing that ridiculous 'Hell Prince' nonsense?" the ambassador asked. "Given that it makes their security services seem weak and ineffective?"

"Use me as an excuse for atrocities, round up the undesirables, and I suspect on a more strategic level they are looking to kneecap Incisive's effectiveness. Try to force me into a persona and make the energy cost of other personas much higher. Make vanishing from perception much harder." Truth grinned. "Didn't work."

"Better to say it hasn't worked *yet*. It takes time to move public opinion and to firmly fix an idea in people's minds." The old lady shook her head slightly. "It's why we instantly jumped on your plan to hijack the persona and turn it into a propaganda tool. Flip their own efforts back on them. Stoke division and rebellion. Weaken Starbrite's power base by weakening Jeon."

Truth nodded. He had more or less figured that all out.

"But to be a prince, and to rise to a kingly seat, one must have subjects to rule." The ambassador spoke with assurance. "One must lead if one wishes to be followed."

"Makes sense." Truth nodded some more.

"For rebellion to really take wing in Jeon, there must be a charismatic figure leading it. We can support those forces of resistance. Provide training and political cadres. But they need their leader. The elusive, romantic figurehead, appearing only at rallies and at the site of powerful blows against the oppressive state."

The old lady's voice had a powerful rhythm to it. Not magic, or no magic beyond human psychology. She sounded so certain, you wanted to adopt her ideas as your own.

"I see."

"And, of course, it is the most common usage of Incisive," she continued. "Those who call upon Botis *wish* to be powerful, feared, and seductive. Others brashly lead armies from the front. Incisive makes them grateful to die for you. It clads you in the glory of your worshipful followers. Much is given, much is forgiven, when one is strong with the power of that excellency."

Truth blinked. He hadn't thought about it that way, but Botis was ranked an earl. Completely a human invention, of course, but he really did command a large region of Hell and had countless demons under him.

"To break Jeon, we need to increase its internal divisions. It is the fastest way to Starbrite. You must take up the mantle of leadership. Only you have this power." The ambassador's voice flowed smooth and rich as coffee.

Truth nodded decisively. "I'll do it."

There was a pause. Then a longer pause. Merkovah started laughing.

"But before you go, you just want to nip into the library."

"Do you have a good one handy? I just want to browse a bit."

"Maybe see, just see, if there are any National Treasure–tier items or elixirs lying around."

"I mean, if no one is using them, it would be a waste not to." Truth looked very sincere.

"Perhaps a manual on combined spell tactics for the mid tiers?"

"That . . . Yeah, actually that does sound *incredibly* useful."

"They are." Merkovah agreed. "Which is why they are also heavily restricted and never put into general circulation. Each country and major power has their own doctrine on this and carefully studies the doctrines of others. I've already set aside a good reference for you."

"Oh, thank you, Teacher. That was thoughtful." Truth felt warm. He knew what the old monster was up to, but he appreciated it anyway. Manipulative or not, Merkovah had been good to him. He wouldn't have trusted a mentor with altruistic motives, anyway.

"Other than your fundamental lack of trust in other human beings, is there a particular reason you don't want to be the worshiped and adored focus of millions?" Merkovah asked.

"I mean, the lack-of-trust thing is a good enough reason, right?"

"Historically, no. Some utter paranoids conclude that the only way to ensure their safety is to rule everything around them, so they seek positions of power." He didn't exactly give Truth a look, but Truth felt the look anyway. Merkovah knew exactly how high Etenesh wanted Truth to climb, and he probably knew Truth agreed with her.

"*Prince* is not a title with job security." Truth shook his head vehemently. Then, more softly—"It is also pointless. All of it. The rebellion, defeating Jeon. Pointless. It literally achieves nothing. Starbrite is headquartered in Jeon; strongest there, yes, but it's a global company and the System works everywhere. So long as anyone anywhere has it, their death makes Starbrite stronger. Slaughtering Jeon is just bringing the harvest in early."

There was an awkward pause there.

"You don't see a need to dismantle Jeon? A strange take for someone who thinks the country is a giant slum and all the residents variously sized rats." Merkovah's voice was conversational.

"Not quite, Teacher. I understand the entire world is a slum, and we are all rats. A view I have had repeatedly, to borrow your word, validated."

Truth waved his cup. "I want Starbrite dead out of vengeance, yes, but honestly, I think I would be willing to play the smart rat and stay low until I was much stronger. The reasons I am rushing to kill him now are, one, I don't want *him* getting any stronger and, two, I would very much like to be off-world before the collapse hits the end phase. It's already bad out there and getting worse."

"Right, but his whole power base—" the ambassador jumped in, but Truth waved him off.

"Irrelevant."

There was a pause. "How is it irrelevant? Thousands of elite soldiers, billions in liquid wealth. Trillions in fixed assets, inventory, subsidiaries, and real estate. That doesn't include all of his global holdings. Include the assets under management via his banking interests, and the number is well in excess of ten trillion wen. To say nothing of the leverage it all gives him in politics, both local and global." The old lady sounded genuinely puzzled.

"Yep. All completely irrelevant."

Truth kept his eyes on Merkovah. The old man's expression didn't change a bit. Truth grinned on the inside. The old man had figured it out too but was playing a different game than the ambassador and his wife thought he was. But what was the end play there?

"Young man, do you fully understand the scope of what I am describing?" She asked politely. Truth nodded.

"Yes. Very well, actually. All that runs on magic. On cosmic rays. All of it. And, in a few months, there won't be any of that and billions of people will wake up to a life of agony as their apertures collapse. Almost all of the people looked to for leadership will die immediately. There will be the protected elite with their body cultivation, but they will rule over a world of children, cripples, and ghosts. It will take a generation or five before there are useful numbers of people to rule over as god-kings."

Truth shrugged. "So, crippling Jeon to kill Starbrite is pointless. He knew all this was coming and he has always prioritized his own self-interest over everything else. Protecting all this is irrelevant to him—he already considers it lost. That's what the soul-harvesting plan is—stripping the remaining value from his holdings."

That got a nasty jolt out of the room. "He isn't relying on the corporation or Jeon to keep him safe; he was expecting to lose them years ago. Maybe decades. He would have guaranteed his security some other way in the event that he failed to meet his goals with the Shattervoid girl," Truth continued.

"Which he did. Fail, I mean. So, he would be forced to use his backup. For example, the resources of a mid-tier nation and peak corporation," the DSO argued.

"But he can't rely on those things, because the magic is collapsing, and before it completely collapses, it will be erratic. All he cares about are those soul fragments. Something that, I suspect, lets him get around the collapse to a degree. What he is doing with those bits and bobs of souls, I don't know, and I don't want to find out," Truth concluded.

"Then what do you think his next play is? And if he doesn't care about what he built, how do you attack him?" Merkovah asked.

"If I was King Rat with the resources of the world at my disposal? Harvest everything I could, then create a vault for myself. Drop that thing in the deepest oceanic trench I could find, maybe straight into the magma layer. Have it deploy a vast, hidden energy-gathering array. One that was aimed at the energy put out by the planetary eminences, not the heavenly ones. Drop into some kind of hibernation. Remain unconscious but alive until the magic comes back, using the passing millennia to refine and incorporate all those harvested soul fragments."

Truth's words came out fast and sure. Merkovah chuckled.

"The kids over in Analysis will be happy to hear you came to the same conclusion they did."

"Then why are we having this conversation?"

"Because you didn't answer part two of my question—what are you going to do about it?"

"I am going to talk to my experienced teacher, knowledgeable in the ways of global terrorism, seeking his wisdom."

"*Seeking* and *accepting* being two different things, of course." Merkovah's voice had gone dry.

"Already I am learning!"

"Mmm. Well, here is something else to learn. The souls that Starbrite mutilates—and yes, we did figure that out"—Truth concealed a wince. He had deliberately not explained the process—"are designed to align their owners with Starbrite and his way of thinking. But. What if some complete bastard made it run in reverse?"

Merkovah's smile was utterly malevolent.

"Pardon?"

"I think I told you that God, personally, through his angels, banned Siphios from using our most powerful necromancy as a term of our vassalage. But if the old contract is broken and there is nothing stopping us from using those spells, then we should use them. Use them to, for example, poison Starbrite's soul with the rage and loathing of the millions of rats whom he bred and doomed to hideous death."

"I'm listening."

"When we eat, we strip out the parts of the food we cannot digest, and incorporate the rest into us. Starbrite has the souls basically pre-digested for him. We just need to . . . reformulate them."

"Just that, huh?"

Merkovah rolled his eyes. "Yes, in fact, just that. We need to realign their beliefs. Starbrite will try to counteract that through his control of the mutilated bit, but! There is a limit to his energy and attention. The System Astrologica is not a micromanager. It's not everywhere all the time. So, we push it hard. We push it by breaking down the corporation, by breaking down Jeon . . . and by forcing it to work harder to 'digest' all those souls. We load them up with fury. With a romance and sense of rebellion. We starve the bastard!"

"All right?"

"And when he gets hungry enough, he will have to make a move himself. Once his pieces are all taken off the board, he will have to strike, to demonstrate his power and prestige. And when he does? We have him."

"Sounds good. What if he doesn't? What if you don't?"

"Then we will let him sink into the ocean in his little vault, no souls to eat, and our descendants will be taught *If you ever see this, it is an evil spell. Here is how you break it without magic.* One way or another, Starbrite dies in our hands. The only question is—will you be able to cash in his head for a ticket off-world first?"

CHAPTER 7

HAPPY ENDING GUARANTEED

Truth thought about it a bit longer. He could sort of see what they were getting at. The conversion process, at least while he was working for Starbrite, took years to be fully effective. Or, at least, for a complete personality change, which was probably the only indication the job was done.

He really tried not to think about Harmony. About the brother he worked his ass off to get into C Tier and equipped with the System. Six years. Long time to be under.

The mountainside was filled with the soft sounds of nature. The elders from Siphios sat quietly, content for him to think things through. They had taken his measure, all of them. There was the occasional sip of coffee, a bite of fruit, and that was enough.

Poison the souls of the soon-to-be-dead with a spirit of rebellion. Make them believe in something so hard that it turned their souls into something indigestible to the System. There should be a gap there, one closing quickly. Now was the exact moment to start inserting these public ideals. Before would have been even better, but it simply couldn't be any later. Once the ideas that Starbrite wanted implanted were set, they were practically impossible to dislodge.

Then there was the issue of the . . . he called it the Planetary Curse. That forbiddance of empathy beyond a certain point. Convincing people that a life organized around individualistic greed and self-satisfaction was the only real option. He could spread fury and rebellion, but what was the positive case? We are against Starbrite, and for . . . feudal Jeon? The return of the Holy King and his Virtuous Ministers?

He had been to Siphios. He wasn't impressed with the standards of governance. Better than the Ressilaud Free State; still not what you would call *good*. Not to mention the last king of Jeon famously overdosed on convenience-store dick pills. That tends to take the shine off monarchy.

"I assume you have an ideological program prepared to go with this 'spontaneous people's revolution.'"

"Oh, yes. Wonderfully detailed, with lots of explanatory pamphlets and catchy songs set to popular tunes," Merkovah said.

Truth fell back into silence for a moment. It all came down to the gambler's mentality. "I've already lost so much, I can't stop gambling now. I have to win it all back!" There was a term for it, but he'd forgotten it.

"What do you call it when you have already put so much money into something, you feel like you have to keep pouring money into it even if it's a loser?"

"Sunk-cost fallacy," the old lady supplied.

"Yeah. This whole plan hinges on Starbrite getting sunk-cost fallacy. No revolution ever swept everyone up in its ideology. You don't even need a majority. You just need a big-enough organized bloc that is energetic, loud, and violent enough to pick off the smaller blocs and make the rest fall in line." Truth started working it out on his fingers.

"You already have the hundreds of thousands of direct Starbrite employees and their families dead set against you. Include subsidiaries and dependent industries, and the number rises into the millions. I'd say you have lost a quarter of the country before you even got started. They aren't persuadable. Then you have the government and the army, who don't want someone else trying to eat off their plate. Then you have the scared people who just want tomorrow to be like yesterday, and know damn well it won't be. They just want to be safe, and that's not a revolution. At this point, you just have the desperate and angry."

Truth shrugged. "If you could get the rich in on it, convince them they will eat better if everyone is mad at Starbrite, then maybe. I've been laying the groundwork for insurrections all over the country. It would certainly screw up the internal-security situation. But persuading the whole nation of Jeon to . . . what? Align their souls with concepts contrary to Starbrite's goals, somehow, to starve the beast?"

He shook his head. He'd have to figure out something on his own. But first, that library.

There was a whiff of rat. Truth's mind started racing. He whipped his head around to Merkovah, and his eyes squinted into a glare. He slid the glare over the rest of the room.

"No. No, I don't think so. Some random shit I can put together after thinking for two minutes was obvious to you before you even walked into this room. Obvious months or years ago. You either think I'm dumb enough to go for your idea uncritically, which I can't believe Merkovah would let you think, or you want me to give lip service to the idea, half-ass the parts of it I actually find useful, and then . . . something. This is a distraction, for both Jeon and me. And somehow, you roped in Merkovah. Thanks for the coffee; it was spectacular."

Truth shoved back his little stool and stood. Everyone else rose with him, waving him back down, calling on him to stay.

"I told them it wouldn't work. They insisted." Merkovah smiled slightly, cheerfully throwing the others under the wagon.

"Bullshit." Truth's mind raced ahead. "Playing for the world after the fall. Siphios's whole technology base is built around demon-binding. Worse than Jeon, even, because a lot of the technology that goes into industrial manufac-turing can be adapted to nonmagical things. Making tables and chairs and things. Casting steel. You want the country broken so that whatever happens later, they won't have a technological edge."

There was a startled silence in the room.

"I have spent a lot of time walking around, looking at things and think-ing. Putting pieces together. International terrorism has really broadened my horizons. I am eager to see what I will learn as an international secret agent."

"Operative," the old lady said, distracted by her own thoughts.

"Pardon?"

"Employees of the Service are officers. Agents are officers employed over-seas. Operatives are people employed to work on a specific operation and not necessarily agency employees. You would be an independent contractor and therefore an operative."

Truth reckoned he was okay with being a secret operative. It lacked that dash of romance provided by the word *agent* but added a hint of militarism and danger.

Merkovah sniggered. "They know how you have been using Incisive, but it runs so counter to how most people use Incisive that they are strug-gling to adapt."

"Eh? I'm using it as intended, though?"

"Are you? It's a spell that lets you impose your will on the world and mentally warp the people around you into being more biddable and pleasing to you. Does this sound like a spell used by low-ambition types? Or would it be used by Prince types?"

"Why did you teach it to me, then?"

"Because it is the perfect tool for a clandestine operative, and I figured your low self-esteem would benefit from the ego-boosting nature of the spell. Properly guided." Merkovah shrugged.

"And if it turned me into a monster, it would do it when I was safely deployed in Jeon."

"Don't think so poorly of me. I have had a long time to watch those who learn the spell. They really do fall into the routes of snake or swordsman. You went snake. Botis even blessed you with a vision of himself as the grand serpent. You weren't going to be a megalomaniac." The old man shook his head, shooting a crooked smile at the old lady. She had suggested Truth learn more of the swordsman path—the Lord of Hell.

"You . . . are not completely wrong in your assessment, but you aren't entirely right, either. Yes, we want to break Jeon. Frankly, every country is going to be varying degrees of broken, Siphios most assuredly included." The ambassador's voice was smooth and somber.

"Our desire to see Jeon utterly shattered is partially out of self-defense and partially out of revenge. We have all lost many, many people to Starbrite, and having to face their gloating pawns in Jeon after each loss . . ."

He shook his gray head.

"The symbolic parallels between hate and venom are well established. We don't need you to create a coherent popular revolt. Just hatred. Turn a symbol of national pride into one of national loathing. Your work with MegaShroom was downright inspired. We have ordered our other operatives to adopt the same tactic elsewhere." The old woman's voice was harder than her husband's. Her eyes were too.

"None of this puts Starbrite's head on a stick." Truth shrugged. Maybe he could rope in Merkovah for a private chat. This conversation was going nowhere.

"No?" Merkovah smiled beatifically. "The chaos is already putting such a strain on their systems, we are learning secrets we had chased for decades. Getting people in places they could never have reached before. The more pressure we put on the more cracks we can make, the deeper we infiltrate. The more pressure we put directly on Starbrite, the more gaps he will show. And if we directly poison his food, turn his harvest against him . . ."

"Logical but uncertain. I will think about it. That book, Teacher?" Truth set down his cup.

"It will be waiting for you, as will a small selection of spells I had couriered over, in another conference room. I will keep the golem active, just so we can chat about them as you make your selection. Before that, though, the third cup."

"Eh?"

"The ritual calls for at least three cups." The old lady smiled. Truth quietly admired her. The conversation hadn't gone how she wanted, but she could still move with grace.

She refilled the pot with fresh water. The grounds were the same ones that had gone in at the start of the ritual. She brought it to just under a boil and poured it into the cups. "This one you really should add sugar to. Add at least one big spoonful. I like three, but I have a sweet tooth."

Truth did as instructed. It was thin. Light. The flavors had changed and evolved. All the funk and rumbling basso had left the cup, as had most of the bitterness. The remaining bitter and sweet combined to elevate the faint fruit left. It was utterly different from the first cup. If the first cup was like an explosion, the last was like a warm breeze at your back. Lifting you up and carrying you forward.

"The third cup is called the blessing. It represents my wishes for your safe travels and safe return." She really did have a wonderful smile. "Do you like the view from this mountain?"

Truth looked out. It was beautiful. Truly. The green forests waved in the wind. Not too hot, not too cold. Colorful birds flitted around joyfully, and the sky had a depth of blue he had only ever seen in Siphios. It wasn't paradise, but it was close enough.

"I really do."

"Good. It's where I'm building your house." She sniffed. "Well. Having it built. I'm not directing the demons in person, obviously."

"Pardon?!"

"You have been, unquestionably, our single most effective operative in the last century. Quite possibly ever. You have inflicted horrifying losses on our most hated enemies. Enemies who have personally cost me more grand-children and great-grandchildren than my heart can bear. Merkovah was buying some prefabricated nonsense."

"It was top-of-the-line! Seamless insulation and a sixty-year roof, no magic required!"

"Naturally, I had to step in. It is a rare thing. Constructed to operate without magic. There is a well with a pump you can operate with a lever. That took some figuring out, let me tell you! Thick insulation, warm, solid slate roof, a stove that can burn wood or charcoal, trapped safely in an iron box with a solid brick chimney. The grounds are being carefully fertilized and planted with fruit bushes and trees. Even if you tend it rarely, it will form its own little ecosystem. There is a little pasture for goats, well fenced." She jutted her chin out proudly.

"Much better than Merkovah's shack. And lots of room for babies, of course. Whatever you chose, remember: there is a home waiting for you. Whether you stay or go off-world, kill Starbrite or fail utterly, there is a home waiting for you. You are wanted there. So, go walk your bloody road, young man. But see to it that you wipe your feet well before you return to Siphios. You deserve a happy ending, and it's waiting for you in our mountains. If you want it."

CHAPTER 8

NEW TOOLS

Merkovah led Truth from the enchanted conference room to a small interview room. It was just big enough for two chairs, a desk, and extremely robust privacy protections. Truth wasn't entirely fit to talk. The old monster gave him time to pull himself together, flipping through the books in the room while he waited.

Truth eventually drew a heavy breath and focused on Merkovah. "Etenesh doesn't practice body cultivation."

"True. Though she isn't too far from Level Four. There might just be time for her to reach it and start practicing the sort of specialized cultivation that will get her through the collapse. Alternatively, I know some of the old families are surrounding their estates with enormous cosmic-ray-gathering formations. Turning them into holy lands, for lack of a better term. The Heaven-Beseeching Family is deep, deep in the mountains, and their ritualists are *very* good. I don't know if their work will last for millennia, but it should keep them vital and fighting for centuries at least."

"Really?"

"Oh, yes. In their tiny little bubble of safety up in the mountain, they will be very strong. I just hope they don't need anything from the outside world."

"Ah."

"Mmm. Well, it buys them time. Time enough to make those body cultivators. I rather imagine them like deep-sea divers being sent to retrieve treasures from the ocean floors. Perhaps a special caste or class will develop within those ancient clans. 'Guardians' or 'Roadfarers' or 'Steel Knights.' Some romantic drivel." Merkovah gave him a lopsided smile.

"Spell-Blades."

"Just that sort of thing. Though I suspect that there will be a great deal of prestige attached to being able to cast magic unaided. Their pride will discourage them from picking up a sword, even as practicality demands it."

"Spear. Easier to learn than a sword and more versatile. Good for hunting, solo fights, group fights. I'd train my kids up on spears before swords."

"Really? Given the way you became inseparable from the Tongue, I had thought you fell in love with the romance of the sword."

"This and that are two different things. That is the Tongue being awesome, not all swords being awesome."

Merkovah chuckled. "I can see how that would be true, though in defense of swords, they have been the exorcist's weapon of choice since time immemorial."

"Really? Not spells?"

"Both. You need both. Spells to restrain, castigate, and drive out. The sword to prove what will happen to the demon if it stays." The young-looking old man chopped through the air with his hand.

"Do you have a sword?"

"Many. I wind up collecting them, or inheriting them, then giving them away. For example, to promising students." Merkovah smiled at Truth. "Did you think I randomly had an angelic sword in the boot of my carriage?"

"It honestly never occurred to me. Your go-to weapon was always that thumb ring of yours." Truth shrugged.

"Hah! That's a loan. And a long story. Ready to pick your next spell? I brought a selection, and while I know you might find this an uncomfortable change, they are all good and not horrible jank."

"Actually, I keep seeing that people 'fixed' Cup and Knife a hot second after it was published. Do you have any of those spells around?"

"I don't, but I'll ask around. Someone in the embassy has an alchemical reference book somewhere. Or there is one in the Capital here, it's hardly a secret. That being said, even the corrected and improved versions of the spell are now badly out of date. Never mind that; see what I brought. I am rather proud of these spells, so read them over carefully."

"You wrote them?"

"I don't have that kind of creativity. No, I collected them, and you may be certain they were not easy to come by."

Truth nodded and started reading the summaries.

Earth-Folding Step*: High-speed movement spell. Each step can cover a progressively longer distance. In essence, the mage "folds" the space between where their foot starts and lands, then instantly unfolds them again. This folding only affects the mage. Anyone or anything within the "folded" space is completely unaffected and unaware. Distance traveled and speed of casting depend on skill with the spell and the level of cultivation. Level Five is the bare-minimum level necessary to learn the spell and cast it once. This spell is an off-world import that dates back to the initial settlement of the planet.*

Four-Elements Annihilation*: Takes advantage of the four-element nature of matter to identify the elemental ratio of a given object and to overload one of those elements. The ensuing instability results in the collapse or destruction of the targeted matter. For example, overloading the "fire" element in a wood-frame building would cause it to spontaneously ignite, the fire coming from the interior of the wood and spreading outward. The same technique can be applied to humans and demons. Particularly useful because it can affect a very wide area for a comparatively low energy cost. It does, however, require a considerably long casting time.*

**Doomsday Book*:*

"You have a spell called Doomsday Book and you didn't lead with that?"

Merkovah rolled his eyes. "Of all the spells I selected, it's the one I think you are least likely to choose. It might as well be called 'The Census Taker,' but *everyone* has to be a self-promoter, apparently."

"Eh?"

"Just read the summary."

**Doomsday Book*: The spell is constantly active but requires almost no expenditure of cosmic energy. Every person the mage meets is cataloged, as are their personal possessions. As the mage goes about in the world, meeting more people and seeing more things, the catalog of existent people, items, possessions, and their interrelations gets larger and more detailed. The mage will instantly be able to recall every entry and, with a minor effort of will, comprehend the cataloged connections. As mastery improves, so does the ability to form and understand linkages between entries.*

Truth blinked. Reread the description. Blinked again.

"Do you have this spell memorized?"

"That's rather rude to ask."

"Yeah, but if I was the king and knew I had an immortal spymaster on hand, I'd damn well order you to learn it."

"I'm not immortal. Just long-lived. And you aren't wrong. Not this spell but one very similar. I didn't think the particular theological bent of the spell I learned would appeal to you."

"These days, you might be surprised." Truth rubbed the bridge of his nose. "Your little assignment has kind of messed me up, you know?"

"Oh?"

"You would not believe some of the people I have asked about defining what a human is."

"Any good answers?"

"No. People kind of lock up when you put them on the spot like that."

"Heh. Yes, they do, don't they? Keep reading."

Soul Hunter*: Allows the mage to fix the position of a given person's soul in their mind and track them over any distance and through any nonmagical barrier. The spell works through most magical barriers and all ordinary household wards. To be effective, the mage must meet the target or have a meaningful personal possession of theirs or some part of their body. At higher levels, the requirements lessen dramatically and the potency of the tracking power increases greatly. The quintessential "You can run but you can't hide" spell.*

"Nifty, if less useful than it initially appears." Truth shook his head.

"You don't think the ability to find almost anyone on the planet is useful?" Merkovah looked outraged.

"Got any of Starbrite's meaningful personal possessions? Does it track bits of soul as they fly back toward him?"

"No."

"Yeah."

"Still, an incredibly subtle, powerful spell."

"When I collect Starbrite's head, I think I will be well and truly done with playing assassin. At least for a good long while."

Merkovah snorted and waved him on to the last spell.

Thunderchild*: Spell uses the entirety of the magus's available magic, only ceasing when there is not enough magic left to sustain it. Upon activation, the magus increasingly aligns their body with the primordial sky-fire known as lightning. The body's elements shift heavily to air-fire. As the body becomes more aligned with those elements the magus's speed increases exponentially. At highest mastery, they move so quickly, the world appears frozen. Their thought processes speed up, they hit harder, their every blow carries primordial sky-fire within it, and they become almost impossibly elusive. Should they need to flee or pursue, they can travel vast distances, only getting faster and faster as they go. However, upon the expiration of the spell, the magus will collapse and likely need several days to recover as well as the assistance of potions and ideally a high-magic chamber.*

"What?!"

"Good one, I think." Merkovah smiled at the battered book like an indulgent uncle. "A bit tricky to use, definitely not for everyone, and the requirements to learn it in the first place are downright grotesque, but despite its drawbacks, it is one of the most effective single combatant spells on the planet. In terms of sheer damage output, Incisive really cannot compare."

"I can imagine." Truth really could, too. He was already blindingly fast. The idea of becoming exponentially faster without increasing his level, even with the days-long recovery time, was almost sickeningly appealing.

"Interesting story there. It was the guardian spell for a small kingdom. They were able to dominate a small area thanks to the power of their top-level combatants, but they couldn't expand for the same reason. Just not enough powerhouses, and the ones they had consumed most of the resources generated by the kingdom, making it very, very hard to create more powerhouses."

"Huh. Makes sense. What happened to them?"

"The borders of Siphios expanded. Their experts were few, ours were many, and our summons were so many, they blotted out the sun. The whole war lasted three days."

Truth grunted. "Might have been a better idea to cut a deal."

"Easy to say. Much harder to do." Merkovah shook his head. "By the end, they were drinking potions and depleting spirit crystals like they were nothing, trying to keep the spell running constantly and shoot down the bombardment against the palace wards. It worked, for a while. We could keep the bombardment up. Their bodies collapsed."

"Good lesson there."

"I always thought so. Still, easily one of the most powerful spells of its sort on the planet."

"So, why offer it to me?"

"Because you are one of very few people on this planet who meet the requirements to use it. The body-cultivation requirements alone are astonishingly brutal. If I were to give it to any random Level Five, their body would just explode the first time they tried to cast it. The energy requirements are likewise obscene. If you want to be able to fight for more than a fraction of a second, deep, deep energy reserves are required."

Truth looked up at the ceiling and thought about it. Not from the perspective of immediate need but from the perspective of self-definition. Who did he want to be?

Soul Hunter was easily discarded. He could see it now—the silent, invisible, unshakable assassin. "You can run, but you can't hide." He could put that on business cards. No, that wasn't who he wanted to be. Even if his life was spent in violence, he had no desire to become some kind of evil urban legend. Besides, going back to the question of utility, it wasn't useful. Maybe Merkovah could see the use case. He couldn't. So, that was out.

Four-Elements Annihilation was likewise discarded. Instead of becoming a pursuing ghost, he would be a saboteur. Walls would collapse, vehicles, spell arrays, armor, heck, even personal wards would all come down for him. But was that all he wanted to be? Someone who just destroyed wherever he went?

No. Not after everything. Not after seeing what he had seen. He didn't want to add that to his soul. Useful, certainly. There would be plenty of barriers and people between him and Starbrite. But he didn't want to define himself as a god of broken homes and shattered dreams.

Which just left the Earth-Folding Step, Doomsday Book, and Thunderchild to choose from. And now things got a lot harder.

CHAPTER 9

HAMMERED OUT

Three spells to choose from. First—Earth-Folding Step. Direct combat utility was . . . more than zero but not a big number. More tactical than direct damage. The ability to instantly close and retreat would be an enormous edge, as would the ability to directly scram out of combat. Or run down fleeing targets. Actually, it would also make your ambush range ridiculous. Launching an assault from outside their patrol range was very spicy indeed. As was the strategic effect. He was a nightmare to pin down, but evading roadblocks was already hard and likely to get harder. With this, he could just walk right past them.

Then there was the Doomsday Book. This was, to his way of thinking, a real change in lifestyle. If he did actually want to lead a revolution, this was the number-one, no-question, top pick. To have a mental catalog of everyone you have met, their connections . . . immensely useful. There were a lot of business spells that did similar, of course. Even his . . . servant . . . Niles had a spell like that. This sounded a bit more profound. Not just mental catalogs but webs of meanings. Guiding him to make connections that might otherwise be invisible. Would it be compatible with Incisive? The possibilities were astonishing.

Lastly was Thunderchild. He was instantly enchanted by it. The sudden explosion of energy, of speed and power! He already moved among the masses like a ghost. How much sweeter would it be to do the same with powerhouses? His battles would be one-sided slaughters. And, sure, he would have to run like hell afterward to find a safe place to hide out for a few days, but to strike as quick and hard as lightning? To move faster than thought? To be a child of celestial thunder upon the battlefield? He could feel the shiver running down his spine. The spell was called Thunderchild, but in his hands, he would be a war god.

Three very different spells. One mobility spell, one managerial, and one offensive. Each multifaceted, with enormous requirements to use and even more enormous growth potential. And each would need to be immediately dropped into a spell slot. No experimentation would be possible there. They were just too big and too hard to learn. So, he would have to choose, now, in this room, how he wanted his soul to grow.

"Funny. Ever since I learned about Nascent Souls, I—" His eyes flicked up. "Did the lights just flicker?"

"Yes." Merkovah glanced around and quickly pulled out an obsidian mirror. He made a few passes over it with his hand, then shook his head.

"I wondered before, but I think it's confirmed now. The taboo is still in effect. Maybe not as powerfully as it once was, but it is still there. I would strongly advise not testing the limits of it. Especially anywhere a bolt of lightning could easily reach you."

"I'll do that." Truth nodded fervently.

"Besides, I think I can guess what you were trying to say. I have been doing some self-reflection since you explained it. We all did, I think. It changes a great deal. Perhaps not everything, and there is a real question about causation in there, but it certainly changes how we as teachers must think about our tuition."

They both fell into reverie for a moment. "I keep thinking of the kids in my technical high school. They would have learned the Jeon Universal Spell, all of them. I don't know that modern magic is a permanent bar to developing . . . to the next level . . . but I have to imagine it makes it a lot harder. Makes the . . . thing . . . a lot weaker. But that's not the worst of it."

Merkovah tapped the table softly. "The worst of it is that it makes you etch your soul with a single truth—'I am fungible. I am a completely interchangeable part in the stream of industry, and my value is determined by the person using me. I am only valuable because I am not unique or special.'"

"Almost every major country has a similar spell, doesn't it?"

"Yes, and always have, as far as I know. For once, that's not a Starbrite 'innovation.'"

They lapsed back into silence. After a few minutes, Truth spoke first.

"I mean, we always knew every spell changes who you are, in a manner of speaking. It changes how you approach problems. In Jeon, it was like gravity—you were your spell, which was also your job. Nobody needed an explanation for the obvious. It just was."

"And then someone goes and figures out the math behind orbits, and it turns out there was infinitely more 'there' there." Merkovah's mouth twitched into a quarter-smile.

They lapsed back into silence.

"Take off your hats for a moment." Truth stirred, leaning forward. "Your spymaster hat, teacher hat, whatever hats. Which would you choose? Who would you want to be?"

"None of the above." The answer was instant.

"Eh? You have spells that fill these gaps already?"

"Somewhat, but more to the point, they are never who I wanted to be when I was a young man. I have two slots left. I have known what they would be for centuries. After today, that changes. Should I survive this final conflagration, they will be totally different." His voice was vehement.

"Oh? What do you want to be, Teacher?"

"I want to heal the world. Not out of some benevolence but sheer selfish nostalgia. I want to restore the mountains and rivers to how they were when I was young. See them teeming with spirits and demons. See trees offering fruits that were literally the stuff of magic itself. Recreate a world of infinite wonders. Pausing only to crucify every damned industrialist, factory-farm operator and off-world exporter I meet."

"I had no idea."

"Did you know that coffee grows wild in Siphios? It's been cultivated since forever, but it's originally a wild tree. You could go out into your backyard and harvest the cherries yourself. Now our best farmland grows nothing but coffee. Specially selected and bred to make inoffensive, shelf-stable offerings for the export market."

"A soul that cannot let go of the past. A soul that wants to preserve and create new life, that the past will never die." Truth's voice was soft.

"Yes. I don't deny it. I'm, hah, God's own conservative. I long for what I know was a better time and will work tirelessly to bring it back."

"Except you are tired."

The exorcist nodded, almost burying his face in his beard. "Beyond words. Beyond words."

The silence lapsed again. Who did he want to be? Loneliness had defined so much of his life. Paranoia was ingrained in his bones. Doomsday Book would ensure he knew, in every intimate detail, the people he met. With time, he would know more about them than they did. He wouldn't have to fear them. Not really. But would he really be less lonely? When you don't see a person but a bundle of connections?

He looked at Merkovah, and he saw a mentor, a teacher, a spymaster, a patriot, a demon-summoner, an exorcist . . . all the hats and labels and tags connecting the beardy wonder to thousands of other things. Would the spell really change that much? For that matter, was Merkovah, with all his centuries of watching friends and students die, lonely? He must be. All those connections couldn't prevent that.

Truth was already a top-tier combatant. He took pride in his abilities there. The universe rarely punished someone for being too good at fighting. Besides, always having a hole card like Thunderchild was a very comforting thought. He might get into bad jams, but he would have a way to get out again. If he truly needed to. He would always have a "Win, then go home" spell to fall back on. That was a shocking thing.

Violence had always gone hand in hand with loneliness and paranoia, of course. All those beatings he had caught because he hadn't seen them coming and avoided them. Or that were unavoidable. Or that he dished out to others, to make his life better. It hadn't been a happy life. He was good at violence, and he was proud of his skills, but he couldn't say that it had really made him happy. Not when his life was viewed in its totality. His Rough Patron said violence would be an inescapable part of his life, but. Well. People had told him a lot of things over the years. Amazing how many of those things turned out to be wrong.

Truth sighed and picked up the Earth-Folding Step. Merkovah raised an eyebrow.

"Why that one?"

"Because when I think about my life, the happiest I have ever been was racing around the Free State on my iron horse, and traveling with you, Etenesh, and Jember. Even now, I really enjoy seeing the different parts of Jeon, seeing Onis, trying new foods, and hearing new music. There are all kinds of practical reasons, too, but that's the biggest thing."

He smiled. It crept across his face, as though a little shy about being so open. "I like to travel. How could I turn down a spell that lets me roam as I please?"

Merkovah nodded slowly. "I thought you might go for it, though honestly, my money had been on Thunderchild."

Truth held up his thumb and index a bare millimeter apart.

"It does suit you. Completely ignores the boundaries set by the other humans and the world itself. As you progress to higher levels, you will be able to step through walls, through mountains, even. Or so the spell claims. I've never seen it done."

"Incredible!"

"And, of course, it's another reality-manipulating spell."

"It is?" Truth thought about it for a moment. "Of course it is."

Merkovah gave him a sardonic look. "'I am over here, but if I take a single step, I am over there. Somewhere in between here and there, at some point in that step, reality has changed.'" He shook his head.

"To be clear, you don't vanish from this reality and pop up again elsewhere. As best we can tell, you remain here and travel through the same space that everyone else inhabits. It's just that, for you, the intervening obstacles between 'Here' and 'There,' including but not limited to *distance itself*, are simply temporarily abolished. Suspended, perhaps, but only for you. The fact that this also includes *other people* is frankly alarming."

"I can see that. This sounds stupidly powerful. Is this another one of those *All the high-levels have this spell; the juniors just don't know about it* things?"

"No. This is "Anyone not real enough and without enough magic power reserves trying this turns into something quite hard to look at and harder still to describe without advanced mathematics and a strong stomach.""

"Not . . . real enough?"

Merkovah spread his hands. "You know that, as a rule, the more cosmic energy is in something, the more 'real' it is. You also know, or ought to know, that two people at the same level may not have the same amount of cosmic energy in them. The size of the apertures, how much energy their body can hold, any body cultivation they may have done, special potions, inherited bloodlines, these things all have an effect."

"Sure. I know I hold a lot more energy than most."

"Yes, shockingly so. But I am forcing myself not to investigate, so let's move along swiftly. The short version? You can be high-enough level to cast this spell but still not real enough to *survive* the process of altering reality around you. You just lack that energy density. Likewise, you lack the reserves in your apertures to bull through any resistance you encounter."

"But since I have a *ton* of energy and I have been practicing the Meditations of Valentinian, which do nothing but reinforce my own reality . . ."

"You ever see a tiger with wings?" Merkovah smiled like he was watching Harban burn already.

CHAPTER 10

ONE WEIRD TRICK

Truth sat and read the spell book for Earth-Folding Step. It was the longest single spell he had ever seen, blowing past Incisive and Cup and Knife. The Meditations would be practically a footnote in comparison. He got it, though. Those spells were intended to grow based on your understanding of them. Learn them early, and they will evolve with you. Not Earth-Folding Step. You had to be in the upper middle levels or even the lower high levels to even begin studying it. Using it safely was a whole separate issue.

Merkovah just sat and watched him. Truth wondered what his real body was doing in Siphios. Sitting in his cell at Nag Hamadi? Bullying courtiers at the palace?

<<*Got it. It's a doozy. It will take a good long while to even get it set up in the aperture. You will have to add a new subject to your meditation routine. Cultivate, the Meditations of Valentinian, and studying the Earth-Folding Step.*>>

Truth nodded slightly, flipped through the book again to make sure he hadn't missed anything, then closed it with a snap.

"Did you know that, historically at least, one of the most common requests summoners made of Angels was for a perfect memory?" Merkovah smiled slightly. "A lot of our laws and traditions were passed on orally, and the definition of a scholar was someone able to instantly recall the text of the scriptures and commentaries. To say nothing of other religious, philosophical, and magical works."

"I believe it. When I think about the number of hours I spent grinding for the SAT, I feel a little sick."

"Not wasted time, young man, not wasted time. If nothing else, it did a remarkable job polishing your character and honing your discipline. Things that will serve you a lifetime, rather than the fleeting value of technical knowledge."

Truth laughed softly. "Who says a poisonous tree can only bear poisonous fruit?"

"Me. I say it." Merkovah's smile turned fierce. "That you have turned your slave training into something personally valuable is your own virtue, not that of Starbrite or Jeon."

Truth snorted but didn't say anything. What was there to say? He agreed.

"So, given that there is likely no power in Heaven or Hell that would compel you to become the Hell Prince and lead a glorious revolution that sweeps away the wicked and corrupt from Jeon, what do you plan to do?"

"Actually, I was kind of waiting for someone to try actually compelling me."

"With everything I have built into you, that would be spectacularly dumb and incredibly costly even if successful. You don't have many friends in the Foreign Service—no government agency is really willing to tolerate a rogue element. However, you have been so immensely useful and so utterly deniable, they have no real desire to rein you in. In fact, the more 'controlled' you become, the more of a problem you are for them. Diplomatically speaking. We are already considered a state sponsor of terrorism, after all."

"I mean . . ."

"Didn't say they were wrong. Even if I strenuously disagree with your considering yourself a terrorist. Or me a terrorist."

Truth felt the snappy answers welling up inside of him. He could accept that he had hurt a lot of people. Killed a lot of people. In awful ways. But he didn't have to like it. He didn't have to pretend that he was doing anything good. Then he breathed out heavily, letting the words go. If he had thought of it, Merkovah had thought of it centuries before. And accepted it. It would be a pointless argument, and the old monster really didn't have a lot of free time.

"Cup and Knife?"

"Here are the improved versions, along with a combined spell manual. Read them here and leave them. The combined spell manual in particular cannot leave secured rooms in secured facilities without a great deal of very tedious, very necessary procedures."

Truth nodded and started flipping through. He would study them later.

"While I have you—what *do* you think Manda was after with that spell? He is the Angel of Revelation, so I keep coming back to the idea of the spell revealing the truth of something, but it doesn't do that at all."

"Matter of opinion, I suppose. If it 'corrects' things, it is showing you the way Manda thinks God thinks is correct." Merkovah flicked his fingers.

"Right, but the mage is indicating what needs correcting and how it should be corrected."

"But the spell is famously unreliable, often requiring an immense amount of effort to make trivial changes." Merkovah spread his hands. "Which suggests to me that the amount of effort corresponds to two things—how much the thing to be changed is 'not right' and how close the correction is to the 'right' answer . . . in Manda's opinion."

"I wonder. The spell is plainly broken in places. The more you study it and use it, you can feel the gaps, see where Vek desperately tries to stretch two points together and make a whole. Is there an entire element of it that is just missing?" Truth steadily flipped through the pages, giving the System plenty of time to memorize the contents.

"A fairly common thought and, as you will soon learn, the basis for a lot of the improved versions of the spell. Strip out the bits that don't seem to do anything, add segments to reinforce the purification and banishment elements of the spell. Massively reduces the energy requirements, too."

Merkovah shrugged. "Then, from that basis, entirely new spells were developed that focused on either banishment alone or purification alone, reducing the energy cost and complexity still further while optimizing performance. Such is the way of spell development. More-limited spells but cheaper, more specialized, and more effective."

Truth nodded slightly. Merkovah could practically see the wheels turning in his student's head.

"You think that's missing something."

"Think about the thing we aren't going to talk about, then run through your explanation again."

Merkovah cocked his head to the side, thought for a moment, then his eyes went wide. He smashed his hand on the desk. "D'VerCHemikt!"

"Pardon?!"

"Oh, that's one of the really *good* swears. Once you clear your second century, you find out about them. Consider it a bonus."

"What does . . . it means?"

"You aren't old enough to know. You are still so pure. So innocent. I think I need to make a *quick* trip over to the university. Just correct some thinking. I will be firm but fair. Very fair. I'll even bring my own air demons to tidy up afterwards."

"You can understand why I'm so determined to dig into the meaning behind Cup and Knife. It also puts Botis's claim that no one has ever really mastered Incisive into new light."

Merkovah waved him off. "More than that. Much more. You would have no reason to know about this, but the debates over the 'junk content' in ancient spells, the ones we emigrated to this planet with or had revealed to us by various angels and demons, have been going on for at least two thousand years."

"And the conclusion they reached was that our ancestors and those supreme spirits just weren't very good spell designers, especially compared to the person writing the grant application?" Truth asked.

"You were paying attention when Etenesh and Jember were talking, weren't you?"

Truth snorted and nodded. Merkovah shook his head. "I'm going to have to think about it more. Once again, what are you going to do now? Even if you are playing it loose, I need to know *something*."

"If it wasn't for the invasion from Onis, I probably would be out there, spreading insurrection. Onis seems like a better place to live than Jeon for most people—"

"It is. Significantly," Merkovah interjected.

"But they strike me as a people more concerned with order than peace. I don't think my fellow rats would do very well once they were conquered by Onis."

"Nobody is going to do well in a few months," Merkovah argued.

"True. So, I'm going to split the difference. Poison the food without committing atrocities. There will be a few break-ins, a few assassinations; some people will undergo a significant realignment of their world views via reality adjustment. But this is going to be a different sort of revolution, I think."

"Say on."

"A revolution of thinking. Right now, we have people fighting over which rat gets to wear the captain's hat as the ship plows into the reef. Some rats are still hoping to flee; others plot to rule the wreck."

Merkovah nodded.

"I think now is the *perfect* time to build a new kind of boat. I don't even know what it should look like, really, but given the old one is useless and soon to be scrapped, what have we got to lose?"

Merkovah looked at the blithe expression on Truth's face and laughed himself sick. Once he could gasp enough air, he wheezed, "And Starbrite?"

"Every revolution needs a head to hang. Proof that the old order has died. His will do nicely, as will a select few others. We keep pushing until something cracks—that much I agree with."

"All right. And your happily-ever-after in the northern mountains of Siphios?"

"I don't know. I really don't know. My brain says run off-world as fast as I can. My heart says Etenesh would look beautiful pregnant, and I can keep an energy-gathering array going around our house. It will be thin stuff, but it should be enough to keep her apertures from collapsing."

"You probably could. It would be a bigger job than you think, but she's an expert in building rituals and arrays."

"Then there is the rat part of my brain." Truth shook his head, looking down at his hands. Trying not to stare at the wooden ring Sally had given him.

"Oh?"

"The Shattervoid promised to take . . . what? A few thousand people? Ten thousand? Something like that."

"'A few tens of thousands, from your billions' were their exact words." Merkovah's voice was wry, but the tension in it wasn't hidden.

"Well. Who says they take anybody at all, even if we do kill Starbrite? What if they are just hanging around to make sure Starbrite goes down with the rest of the planet? Not like anyone will be around to tell the universe the Shattervoid don't honor their promises."

Merkovah sighed. He made no reply.

An hour and a big meal in the cafeteria later, Truth left the Siphios embassy. He "acquired" ten kilos of *good* coffee on the way out. Waste not, want not, and all that. His iron horse was right where he left it—being carefully watched by concerned parking attendants.

"Does it bite?"

"Not yet." Truth smiled. Based on what little he had seen of the spell, the Earth-Folding Step didn't actually require the mage to step. He was looking forward to racing down the road on his iron horse, stepping across tens or thousands of meters per cast. Flying down the road, into the sunset.

He felt lighter. Happier. Just being able to talk to people, even if he couldn't tell them everything, it made all the difference. To be real again, not just wading through a world of ghosts and paper houses.

Thrush flew down onto his shoulder as he picked up speed on the highway.

"Where to next, Master?"

"Back to Jeon, Thrush. The world is going to hell, but the people don't have to go with it."

"Oh? How surprising. I was *quite* certain they did."

"You and everyone else, Thrush. Come on. I can hardly wait to spread the good news."

CHAPTER 11

ONE SMALL STEP

Truth had his priorities straight. After zipping away from the Embassy of Siphios and the alarming number of recording talismans, watcher spirits, and unmarked, windowless "delivery wagons" parked up and down the street, he followed the signs to the local supermarket.

He let his eyes go soft, trying to look with his peripheral vision. Taking long, slow breaths through his nose. The right target would have a specific aroma, more spiritual than literal. He would know it when he smelled it.

There!

He turned and quickly walked to the next aisle over. She was perfect. Gray hair verging on blue, gray sweatpants, off-white sweatshirt with a picture of a kitten losing a fight to a ball of yarn on it. She was pushing a lightly filled shopping cart. Each and every item in the cart had an orange sticker on it, indicating a brutal, humiliating discount.

The Shopping Granny. God's most perfect predictor. No near-expired set meal could escape her keen eye. No underripe melon deceived her hands. The slow squeak of her orthopedic shoes inspired raw, animal terror in the hapless shelf stockers and cashiers. As it should.

Truth pulled on the persona of a slightly thick rural maintenance worker. The universe couldn't have been more eager to support his vision. Swearing mightily but internally, he made his approach.

"'Scuse me, granny. I'm not from around here. Where's a good food street?"

"EEEH?"

"I'm looking for a good food street, grandma."

"OH! Why?"

"Because I'm hungry, grandma."

"You don't look hungry."

"I am, though."

"Well, cook something!"

"I'm not from around here."

She glared at him. "And what brings you here, hmmm? Don't you know there is a war on?"

"I do, yes. Is there a food street near here, grandma?"

"Oh, why didn't you ask? Yes, right out the door, second left, down about a kilometer, right for two more blocks, then you are there. If you see the building with the giant crab, you have gone too far."

"Thank you, grandma."

"You are very welcome."

Truth walked off. Noticing as he went that the granny had sped off to report the "spy" to the very patient-looking security guard.

He put the odds about fifty-fifty between an actual food street and the local headquarters of internal security. And since he was happy with either result, off he went.

The city was odd to his eyes—blandly modern with the same few mass-produced buildings dominating the environment, and then, seemingly out of nowhere, some hulking monstrosity would loom.

An empty vertical square, with offices on every side. A building shaped like a rubbish heap but built out of flat, irregular shapes in brushed metal and glass. The result was vaguely menacing. He had no idea what it was for. A big plaza with a big statue erected in the middle of it. It appeared to be a statue of . . . some guy. He wasn't waving a sword or anything. He was just waving. Looked cheerful.

Truth felt a niggling regret that he wasn't spending longer there. He had a sneaking suspicion that this was a city that hid its truly good stuff. Expensive stuff was on display. The good stuff? Strictly for locals and the initiated.

He started to comfort himself with the idea that he could always come back, see it another time, but . . . no. He couldn't. Whatever came of the war, whatever came during the collapse, the Northern Capital of Onis would never look like this again. This was the last "good" summer, the last summer of magic.

This time next year, the buildings would have collapsed. The farms would be producing a tenth of what they were now, and there would be few, damn few, fit enough to farm them. Everyone would be in pain.

He kept coming back to that. The pain. An entire world in agony. A generation of children growing up with the expectation of parents living in pain and trying to manage. The sheer violence of it. The global trauma, passed down through generations.

What would it do to people? What would the few survivors remember? Would it become a new religious lesson? Pride punished with pain; live humbly, O you peasants of the healing world! Only the chosen few mages, the elect, were spared. Proof of their fitness to rule over the forgiven masses.

He saw the crab. A giant glass thing, waving its pincers from the roof of the "Endless Blue Maritime Treasures Association." He doubled back. He had underestimated Supermarket Granny. It was a food street, and half the people on it were wearing uniforms. His eyes slid over. There was a gated wall around a mid-sized office building. SIGNAL COMPANY, 5TH DIVISION, CAPITAL GUARDS CORPS.

Ah. Army snoopers. And unless things were very different in Onis, they specialized in counterespionage. Was Granny a retired soldier? It would be hilarious if she was. Oh, well. Whistling, he set off to do something he had always wanted to try.

"Whsissp PSwissh. Wooooship. I'm Level Five and have truly profound body cultivation. I'm a Level Five body cultivator and I can't whistle."

"I'm sure the omnipotent magus is merely biding his time. At the opportune moment, your talent will explode and you will whistle like a songbird!" Thrush said, "Loyally."

"Screw it. I was going to let some of you go, but now? Now you all pay."

Truth drew a cold breath and let himself vanish. Pouring that Level Five cultivation into Incisive and the Blessing of the Silent Forest. Erasing himself totally from the awareness of everyone and everything on the street. With a firm step, he dove in.

His hands flashed. Steadily. Steadily. In and out. In and out. He had secured a trash bag to hold his collection. It filled rapidly. It became awkward, bulging and swaying as he moved. He refused to slow his hands. A gentle lift, a soft pull, and it was done.

He doubled back, making sure he hadn't missed anyone. He hadn't. He had even gotten the plainclothes cops. He grabbed a jug of fry oil and a rag. He quickly wrote out *How's security at home?* next to a seven-pointed star directly over the Army's sign. He then borrowed a lighter and set it on fire.

Total elapsed time—forty-five seconds. He could hear the yells of outrage starting and rapidly sweeping through the street.

"What evil whoreson stole my wallet?"

"AH! When I catch that thief, I will sever the hands of their nine generations!"

"Run! RUN! The army will find you anywhere!"

Was the sky extra blue today? Yes. It was. He had managed to pickpocket every cop on the street.

"I'll have the fried dough and three skewers, please. Oh, and a bottle of tea."

"Oh, yes. Say—"

"Mmm? Oh, yes, terrible. Nobody respects the Army these days. I really despair over the lack of patriotic spirit." Truth shook his head. "We should all be doing our part, right?"

"Eh? Yes, yes, of course. Sorry, you do have—"

Truth offered a bill. It seemed to be enough.

"Sorry, here's your change. I swear I didn't see anything, did you?"

"A *good* citizen minds his business! I only look for spies and saboteurs, and which of them would dare come to the capital?" Truth was very righteous.

"Yes, yes. Right. God, is that Captain Zhu?"

"Which, the one who hit that guy with a stool?"

"Err. No, that's Captain Feng. Zhu is the one slapping the enlisted."

"Reminds me of my old lieutenant. Maybe they are related. Well, good time for me to be somewhere else. Thanks for the food."

"Sure, sure. Ah, should we call the police?"

"Yes, of course. *When there is a crime, a good citizen calls the police at once!*"

Walking-around money secured and the paranoia of the Oisin security services now sharpened to a monomolecular edge, he sat on a bench and enjoyed the skewers.

Some kind of chewy . . . something. Not bread, exactly, or meat, but not a vegetable he recognized, either. It was closest to bean curd in nonflavor but tougher and chewier. They came with a deeply savory, garlicky sauce, however, so he was prepared to cherish them. The fried dough was only okay. Shame.

He quickly sorted through the wallets in case there was something juicy in there. There probably was, but nothing immediately leapt out. An imp of mischief tugged at him to deliver the wallets to the Siphios embassy. It was ignored. Nothing good came of listening to imps.

Instead, he found a hardware store, grabbed some spray paint and a bucket of industrial adhesive. He went back to the square with the statue with the waving man. A few passes with the glue, and the ID of every snoop and cop on the street was stuck to the pavement. In two-meter-tall red letters he sprayed on the ground—

Never Forget The Honorable Dead! Internal Security Stands Guard Against Foreign Murderers, Pays the Ultimate Price!

There. Spontaneous citizens' memorial created. Oh! Not quite.

He zipped off and grabbed some flowers from near a subway stop as well as a pack of cigarettes. The flowers were scattered around the ID cards. Three cigarettes were glued upright behind them and lit.

There. Now, *that* said "spontaneous outpouring of civic grief." He gave it only a few minutes until internal security turned up to cover everything up.

Naturally, his beautiful creation couldn't be hidden behind a security cordon. Back to the subway.

"I think it's so brave, that memorial for internal security."

"Everyone is hunting cops these days. It's open season out there. I don't feel safe."

"Oh, they cover it all up, but my cousin was there—blood all over the streets. They are going directly at the internal security service. They say it's Jeon but I don't know."

"Obviously, nobody has any time for rebels! Nobody! I one hundred percent support our brave soldiers on the front. Defeatists should be hung! Even if the rebels are killing all the cops and internal pacification forces! A good citizen doesn't need a cop around to behave properly."

"All those broadcasts from bunkers, or with obvious illusions for backgrounds. What do they know that they aren't telling us? Are we really winning?"

He rode the subway three stops, found an interchange, spread the good word a bit more, then doubled back. He hoped no one ticketed his ride.

Any nation this focused on order would be very touchy about internal security and controlling rumors. Something like this, right under their noses?

Ah, even the pollution haze couldn't hide the perfect blue of the sky. Truth hadn't liked cops ever since he was a kid in the slums. The last few months hadn't improved his opinion. Today was a good day.

Good deeds done, he loaded up on supplies, hopped on his iron horse, and started making his way back toward the border. It was a long ride, but he was prepared to enjoy it.

There were barricades across the highway. Serpents snaked through the air, sweeping up and down the kilometers of practically parked carriages. It seemed they really didn't care for his prank.

He sighed. Nothing for it. He could drive past the queue, but even with the sheer number of levels he had over everyone, that would be pushing it. Instead, he found an articulated wagon, popped the doors open, threw his ride inside, and hopped in after it.

Onis had its own search spells, but they didn't have those watcher things. He pulled a pillow out of his spatial ring and lay down. Time to get comfy. He set out some snacks and the bottle of tea. Time to act like the newly minted Level Five he was. He would let someone else do the driving. Time to find out how they wrote romance novels in Onis.

CHAPTER 12

VOLCANO COUNTRY

This is the life. Truth sighed contentedly. He stretched and twisted, deigning to eat a chunk of melon as the spellhounds ran furiously up and down the lines of traffic. *How did I live without a spatial ring? What kind of miserable existence was that?*

"Have your documents ready for inspection! Commercial vehicles into the far-left lane! Carriages with two or more people in the second from the left lane! Everyone else, find another lane and wait for inspection!"

I'm not sure I'm really getting this novel. The title is kind of throwing me for one thing: The Black-Bellied Farmer's Wife Is Abusing the Merchants—*"I can't fight her noodles!" What does that even mean? Is* noodles *a sex thing here? Or* black bellies? *Because, and I'll admit to my ignorance here, sounds like a turn-off.*

"Documents."

"Here. Say, officer—"

"No questions!"

"Sorry! Yes, sorry!"

Or is the farmer the one with the black belly? My grammar is still pretty iffy, and reading the language is pretty tough even with the System helping out.

"Taking a load of pillows to Beizhan, eh?"

"Yes, four pallets."

"But that is not the last stop on your trip, is it!"

"No, no, officer. As you can see, I am also carrying four hundred kilos of barley to Beizhu. The address is properly listed there, as is the receiving party."

Truth glanced over at the pallets. They were towering stacks of shrink-wrapped he-didn't-know-what. They both seemed densely packed. He could hazard a guess about which were the pillows, but he wouldn't put money on it.

"All right, open the trailer. We will run the dogs through."

Hmm. Wonder how much the bribe will be?

"Yes, officer, at once!"

Wait, really? Is it because there are so many people watching? You bastard! I was all comfy.

Grumbling, Truth swept up everything into his spatial ring and hopped on top of one of the pallets, nearly braining himself in the process; the roof was low, and he hadn't finished adjusting to his new level. He wound up sprawled on his belly, balancing on top of what he was confident was sacks of barley.

They smelled kind of nice, in a grainy sort of way. Very slightly toasted.

Then he swore, spasmed clear off the barley, and grabbed his iron horse. He shoved the pallets around quickly, made a gap for the two-wheeler, and lay on top of it. Fingers crossed it would work.

The trailer doors opened, and spellhounds with glowing red eyes bounded in. They sniffed eagerly, nosing through everything, doubling back a few times to examine where Truth had his little bowl of melon. Eventually, they piled out of the wagon.

That it?

The biggest dog Truth had ever seen jumped into the wagon. Heavy enough to make the wagon bounce on its springs. It appeared to be equal parts fur and muscle, with a face like a bear and the eyes of an emperor.

It drew in long, deep breaths, and when it exhaled, dust stirred the length of the floor. Piercing eyes swept over the pallets.

"Explain yourself! These sacks are labeled *Malt*, not *Barley*!"

Was that . . . did I just see . . .

The delivery man stood at the gate of the wagon, bowing toward the dog and trying to explain under the supervision of a couple of soldiers. And all the spellhounds.

"Officer, malt is a type of barley that has been processed. I don't know the details, but if you open the sacks, you will see that it is indeed dried barley. I am taking it to the Golden Lion Brewery in Beizhu."

"Hmph. Private Tong, call it in!"

A dog with a badge. You could be a police inspector and a demon in Onis? That was a new one on him.

A private hurried off, then back. In a whisper that would have been only audible to a demonic dog and Truth, he said, "Sir, it's a conflict in the regs. All food products are to be labeled based on the type of food they are, but malted barley technically is both barley and a separate product called 'malt,' which can be classified both as a food and an ingredient."

Left unspoken was that the supervisor was leaving it to the demon's discretion.

Opportunity for a bribe number two?

"All right. Do a better job keeping this wagon clean; I can smell food in here."

"Eh? I mean, yes, yes, of course! I will mop it out after my deliveries are done."

"See to it that you do. All right, close it up. You are clear to proceed."

Truth felt an almost painful sense of dislocation. The demon dog was diligent in his work, not a jerk, and didn't even hint at a bribe. What was this world coming to? Was there nothing he could rely on anymore?

He waited until they were through the checkpoint to start reading again. Beizhan was farther north than he wanted to go, but it was solidly west of the Northern Capital. He would hop off at a rest stop if necessary, or just ride down from there. No worries. By the end of the day, he would be in Volcano Country.

"Volcano Country" was what he considered the area directly impacted by Great White Mountain's eruption. The actual lava flow, while enormous, wasn't actually any danger. It was just too far from any cities or towns to be a real worry. The real danger was the ash.

There had been a phoenix crucified at the heart of Great White Mountain. Mined for its magic and who knows what else. The lava was more than just molten basalt; it was the phoenix's blood. And its hate.

Truth got out at a rest stop. Beizhan was just too far out of the way, he decided, and he was eager to load up on more hot food. The vinegary, savory foods there were growing on him, especially the way they seemed to throw garlic, ginger, and scallions on everything.

He was disappointed. The rest stop only had bagged snacks. Truth sighed, spent some of his stolen loot actually buying something for a change, and amused himself by spreading rumors among the teamsters.

"Is it just me, or do the cops seem extra scared? Those rumors about them *getting killed* must be true."

"It must be *Jeon Special Forces* that are killing off internal security. *Might be a good time to settle some grudges.*"

"I mean, *untouchable cops are looking very touchable, aren't they?* And besides, they will just *blame everything on Jeon.*"

He had no idea what impact that would have, but . . . teamsters got everywhere. They would repeat and spread the rumors. People would start to get ideas. The professional paranoids would start focusing on the enemy within. It wouldn't stop the war—far from it. But it might cool it down a little.

Out on the road and heading south. There were fewer army convoys than he imagined. They were still well back from the border, of course, but for some reason, he imagined endless trains of wagons all rumbling down the mountains toward Jeon. So far, nothing.

The sky was darkening, though. Turning deeper and deeper shades of red. If the lava contained the phoenix's hate, the ash contained its contempt. The ash was drifting southwest, pushed along by the prevailing winds. It caught the northernmost bit of Jeon, a much-larger piece of Onis, and then on to the rest of the world.

The dust was rocketing high up into the atmosphere, where the fine dust could be carried almost indefinitely. Kept flying on the wings of the phoenix was Truth's morbid conclusion. Which might have been chalked up to normal consequences of a volcano blowing up, but . . . this was the height of summer. Prime growing season. And suddenly, the sun was getting that little bit dimmer.

Truth had thought there would be one last . . . if not good, then decent harvest. It wouldn't have been enough on its own, not with the Shattervoid embargo. Still. "Something" would be a hell of a lot better than the "nothing" that they would have soon enough.

He processed that thought. How many meters of storage space had Sally gifted him? More to the point, wasn't he the one going around, telling people to stock up on canned foods?

Truth turned at the next exit, found the nearest market, and got excessive.

Two hundred kilos of rice later, along with pretty much every dried bean, canned fruit, canned vegetables, and every canned stew that didn't trigger traumatic memories later, he was back on the road. He didn't even make it out of the driveway before he doubled back for forty kilos of salt and the entire contents of the spice and dried herb racks. And sugar. He snagged enormous sacks of sugar.

Anything else? How did fresh produce keep in the nowhere space attached to the ring? Pretty well, to judge by the melon. But the store staff were already starting to raise a ruckus about the mysteriously vanishing shelves' worth of food, so he decided to cut things short and move on down the road again.

Pausing only to snag twenty kilos each of potatoes, onions, and carrots. They keep, he reasoned, and you can do an awful lot with them.

He left the balance of the stolen cash at a cash register. Who knows if they would accept it or call the cops. He probably underpaid anyway.

Right now, food was still coming in. Prices were skyrocketing, but food was being delivered. Papering over the rapidly widening cracks in the food system. It wouldn't last.

He was another hundred kilometers down the road when the next spike of paranoia hit. He had stockpiled water, tea, and juice already, but just . . . traveling portions. There was a rest station up ahead. A rest station that mysteriously saw all its bottled water vanish, even the big two-liter jugs.

He would have to think about how to filter water later. Between the body cultivation and his level, he ate much less than most people. *Much less* wasn't *none*. And who knows? He may have more mouths to feed.

Better snag a few tarps, too. Never know when you need shelter, and they don't take up much space.

He forced himself to push past the paranoia for the moment. The logical end result of his thinking was a bunker in the mountains, with everything he needed to ride out two years in complete isolation, including the ability to harvest magic. On the one hand, now was absolutely the time to do that. Should have done it years before, ideally. On the other hand, that wouldn't get him Starbrite's head. And that was the only thing that would really save him and his.

If Jeon hadn't rolled out rationing already, it would very, very soon. They knew the famine was coming. War was a good opportunity to get out ahead of it. They already had the Denizens subsisting on rations issued by the government . . .

There was a lurch, but he managed to catch up with his own thoughts.

They already had the Denizens on rations. Once again, he had underestimated the vile efficiency of the Jeon bureaucracy. If they were already training up a slave caste, why not extend the food supply for their betters in the process?

He would bet there were silos, well-defended, impeccably vermin-proofed silos, of wheat, rice, corn, and other staples. Entire warehouses of fermented cabbage, sealed in jars and buried in the ground. You could live a long time on rice and fermented cabbage, even if you didn't have fresh veggies.

Thin living, though. Very thin. Truth wondered what they would do for meat. Jeon beef was, he had heard, the very best in the world. He didn't believe those ancient families and corporate lords would suddenly decide it was acceptable for them to do without.

All this, and the volcano kept spewing ash up into the atmosphere. Dimming the blue sky. Dyeing it orange-red. A preview of the flames to come. Truth had seen pictures of the plume. It crackled with infernal lightning. Streaks of flesh-obliterating fury crawled up and down the heaven-blotting pillar of ash. Not that anyone needed a reminder that this was punishment.

The only component on Truth's appalling iron horse that was new was the demon. He had summoned the demon himself, barely a week before. He pushed it as hard as he dared. Racing south under the cloud. Ready to plunge back into the fire.

CHAPTER 13

IN THE SHADOW OF THE PHOENIX

Truth's iron horse sped down the highway. Not a lot of traffic in the best of times, and these were anything but. He wasn't moving much faster than he could run, but after running several ultra-marathons in a row, he was ready to let a demon do the sweating. At Level Five, his concealment should be powerful enough to make even the surveillance on trains endurable.

There weren't any trains running to the Jeon border these days. His iron horse carried him just fine. Truth had never seen any reason not to go fast. He loved feeling the wind whipping past him. The way the few carriages and wagons seemed to be almost standing still as he flew past. The mountains might be gray, boring, and sinister under the deepening orange sky, but his scarf kept the ash out. It was good enough.

He was blinking a lot, though. The ash couldn't hurt his eyes, but it was still irritating to have flecks of basalt suddenly blocking your sight. He would need goggles. Funny how it had never occurred to him. He saw people wearing them all the time. Now. Was there anywhere remotely near there to buy some? His road atlas was no help. There were little towns dotted along the road. Presumably, one of them would have a dealership or a store or something.

Lunch was disappointing. All the little shops he had been hoping to visit were either closed or outright abandoned. He checked his atlas. He was still a good four hundred kilometers from the border. Surely, wartime restrictions weren't in effect *this* deep into Onis. Was it just economics? Or were the canny folk of Onis getting out ahead of the smoke?

Either way, a hot meal was out of the question. He was stuck with his snack stockpile. It suddenly occurred to him that there was literally nothing stopping him from cooking his own food. He used to do it for the sibs. He wasn't a *good* cook, but he could throw things in a hot box and warm them up. Presumably, it would be easy enough to dump powdered soup and water into a pot and heat it up. If he had a pot. And a fire.

Truth took a moment to look out across a forgettable valley and reflected on his questionable stockpiling strategy. He would have to make some adjustments. Perhaps starting with what was handy. People lived off what they found in the mountains, right? That was a thing in some of his novels. There would be . . . wild herbs or something.

Looking to his left, he had his choice of rocks and trees. To his right, he could choose whichever trees and rocks he liked. He . . . probably couldn't identify an herb in a supermarket, let alone on a mountainside. He would need a manual of some kind. An identification guide to food components and how they went together, like a maintenance guide for a carriage or an air conditioner. He couldn't be the only one who needed such a thing, right?

He nearly threw himself off the mountainside in shame when the word *cookbook* finally returned to his memory.

I'm . . . I'm not actually dumb. I know stuff. I have read books before. I've traveled.

<<Sure, sure. You are very smart. Very smart. Just the smartest, GOODEST boy in the whole world. Yes, you are. YES, you ARE!. Woosa woosa woosa SMART boy? It's you! Yes, it's you.>>

He felt that he should snap back, but really, that seemed fair.

He gave up, made a lunch of dried fruit and breadsticks, all washed down with bottled water. It did the job well enough, and he vaguely enjoyed the idea of the food rehydrating in his stomach. Back on the road.

At the speed he was traveling, it didn't take long for him to start running into Onis Army wagons. Shortly thereafter were Onis Army checkpoints. His initial plan, *Blow straight through them*, was canceled by the army's stubborn insistence on blocking the entire road, including the shoulder, with a barrier designed to stop speeding wagons. It just needed a press of a talisman to retract like a curtain, but for the international secret operative on the go? It was a spiky steel obstacle to progress.

He dithered a moment, then lightly rapped his head. Like with the food, he was still a prisoner of lower-Tier thinking. He took a look at the checkpoint. It was a well-chosen spot. An almost-sheer drop on the left, an equally almost sheer slope on the right. The upslope side was solid rock. The downslope side was dirt held down by scrub and skinny trees.

Truth grinned and drove back half a kilometer. He patted the side of the iron horse, then kicked it into motion. He poured power into the demon driving it, urging it on faster and faster. As fast as its shoddy frame and thin tires would tolerate. He stormed up on the checkpoint in a cloud of dust. He aimed for the stone slope, leaned right, and let that pony climb.

The iron horse drew a smooth arc across the rough face of the cliff, up and over the unseeing checkpoint. He could look down on them, watching them smoke and stare down an empty roadway. The iron horse shook and juddered on the rough-cut rockface. He kept it well in hand, riding out the shocks with casual power. Truth landed it back on the road and drove off in a cloud of dust, laughing his head off.

It was exhilarating. To live freely, uninhibited by . . . anything, really. Fighting for the people he cared about, learning about the things he cared about, but only ever moving by *his* will. He let the iron horse eat up the road and just enjoyed the sensation.

He didn't have to study for anything in particular. The test was called "Life" and everyone got the same score in the end. He could make of it what he liked. He had goals, enemies, even a few friends. He didn't have a boss; he had a mentor. He wasn't a wage slave; he was, hah! An independent contractor. Very independent. And if he was a mass murderer, living on stolen goods and stained with so much sin, it defied description?

Well. He wasn't okay with that, actually. He would have to start doing better for people. Maybe not all the people everywhere, but he could start small. Just one or two people. Once he figured out what he actually wanted "better" to look like.

He looked up at the pumpkin-colored sky. It was bleeding toward red as he got farther south. A giant spirit, something that you could imagine being worshiped as a god, was nailed to a wall in the heart of its mountain nest. Tortured, defiled, mined for its essence. Its hate was totally reasonable. The volcano's explosion wasn't the phoenix's fault. It should have happened a century earlier. The fact that it used its final moments to ensure a lasting, devastating calamity for humanity was quite understandable, really.

There was a chance that he was just projecting his emotions onto the phoenix, of course. The demon's spirit had said that its revenge would be decades coming. It would hardly be surprising if Truth was just bummed out by the sky. Racing along under the reddening sky, he didn't really believe it. There was something malicious there. Something that knew it was causing pain and liked it.

By late afternoon, he had eaten up most of the road. He was starting to hit the back lines of the warfront. Modern warfare didn't have tidy lines, of course, if war ever did. "The front" consisted of a nebulously defined zone, dotted with dug-in infantry, warded bunkers, strategic summoning formations, anti-summons batteries, golem launchers, anti-materiel batteries, spell-bird airstrips, anti-air heavy needlers, tactical curse launchers, and, of course, the few minor necessities involved in keeping several hundred thousand soldiers alive, with hundreds of thousands more expected any day now.

You could always spot the bases. The neat rows of spell birds landing and taking off again could hardly have been more explicit. If you still, somehow, weren't sure, you could always ask one of the drivers in the endlessly refreshing column of wagons headed there. Food, water, supplies went in; wounded and dead came out. Equipment casualties too, he supposed. Not everything was fixable in the field.

There was so much. So, so much. It felt like Onis had just been waiting for an excuse. Eager for one. Truth didn't understand why. It would have been a walk-over after the collapse. Literally. Jeon would have had a half-dozen combat capable people, eking out what life they could between scavenging the ruined cities and trying to learn how to farm on the fly. Onis could have literally buried Jeon in bodies. Belly-flopped the shattered nation into submission. So, why now? And, given the sheer numbers difference, why was he seeing so much infantry?

You use your conscripts to try to soak up the enemies' best spells, test their defenses, and make them spend down their materiel stockpiles. Truth slowly ran his two-wheeler alongside the long army wagons serving as troop transports. Moving a lot of men quickly through the mountains was more than just a challenge. Truth could kind of follow the logic. Marching so many people would clog up the roads and make insultingly easy targets for Jeon airstrikes and curse bombardments. They were well behind the front there, but why be stupid about it?

Truth was willing to bet cash that the logistics were the main reason. Quite possibly the only reason. The conscripts had a certain deadness of eye that, even in his National Service days, he couldn't recall. Was it boredom? Shutting down internally because they were being sent to the front? Or maybe it was the martial music playing on repeat in the wagons, peppered with patriotic speeches.

That would kill his morale stone-dead. Maybe it was the same for them.

There was some logic there he wasn't seeing. Some key fact he was missing. Jeon's advantage was its comparatively small front to defend, and its higher levels of magical technology. Only one of those factors was going to matter in a year. So, why throw your army into that meatgrinder today? They were all Level One troops, from what he could tell. No longer considered basic scrubs. These would be considered (by the low standards of conscript armies) high-quality units.

Not his problem. But maybe the underlying reason would be relevant to his plans in Jeon. He decided to follow them into their base. Just . . . nose around a bit. He had found some interesting things that way in the past, and he really wasn't prepared to give up on terrorizing the political cadres and internal security Onis was deploying so heavily. Something about them just rubbed him the wrong way, and now he was strong enough to indulge his prejudices.

He rode straight into the base alongside one of the wagons. He remembered how Merkovah had described Incisive to him, and how he could use it with the Blessing of the Silent Forest. He could just hold up a blank piece of paper and walk onto a military installation. Something highly secure, maybe not. But some basic base? Just into, say, the motor pool or the canteen? No problem.

Now he didn't even need to fake an identity. The alarm spells and golems' eyes slid right over him. Level Five. He would be a comparatively high-ranking officer, a major or something. Colonel, maybe. Was there a Level minimum to be a general? He had no idea. He had never checked. It wasn't ever going to be relevant to his life.

He could murder a general. If he could ambush members of the C-suite, he could certainly ambush some random Onis general. It was a hell of a thought. They must have high-level guards to prevent that sort of thing, or give orders from some deeply defended bunker somewhere far from the front lines.

He had been part of a decapitation attack, hadn't he? The drop on Fort Leucre. Truth looked up into a sky the color of autumn leaves and wondered what was coming next.

CHAPTER 14

HEROICS

One thing the Onis army had over Starbrite? Their bases had signs. Nice, easily read, prominently located signs. Which way to the latrines? Follow the signs. Need to find First Company? Sign. Quartermaster? Second left, then first right. Follow the signs; you can't miss it.

Truth noticed a distinct lack of signs for Command Center or Officers' Quarters, however. He sighed. He would mock the pointless security efforts, but he was an infiltrator and he was, actually, unable to find what he was looking for. Truth found a discreet place to stash his two-wheeler and followed the highest-ranked person he could spot.

Said person led him to the latrines. Which, fine, it had been a while since he went, and there was a higher-rank person leaving at the same time he was, so he called it a net win. This person went to a little metal hut, picked up some paperwork, and walked to another little metal hut. The person in the second hut had fancier epaulets, so Truth reckoned he was the more-senior officer. The guy he was following saluted first, which just about confirmed it.

Fancy-epaulets quickly looked over the paperwork and frowned. "This is confirmed?"

"Yes, sir. It came through the cadre altar, using the current code." The junior officer nodded heavily.

"Understood. Dismissed. Send Deputy General Wong to see me."

"Yes, sir." There was a lingering feeling to the words. What was in those orders? Truth decided to hang around and wait.

This guy's epaulets looked fancy but not that fancy. He could call a deputy general over? Was he a political officer and able to boss around line officers? Truth didn't know how Onis's army worked, but it sure sounded like it.

Fifteen minutes later, an older man walked in. Fierce mustache, fierce eyes, a rolling, strong gait. The spitting image of a vanguard general, Truth thought.

"New orders from the capital?"

"Yes, *Deputy* General, there are." Epaulets smiled. "Generally, we are being ordered to press the attack with full vigor, not retreating one step from our duty to bring a swift conclusion to this war of Jeon aggression and their many acts of terrorism."

"Naturally." The general didn't roll his eyes. Neither did the political officer. Truth narrowed his.

"To fulfill that duty, the brigade will advance and capture the following strategic locations within its zone of operations. The mission is to be carried out immediately. Here is the list."

The general picked up the paper and read, eyes darting quickly across the page.

"I cannot execute these orders. They violate existing standing orders, army regulations, and the Uniform Code of Military Justice."

"All of which are superseded by commands from the Central Planning Committee, as you are well aware. And these orders come directly from Central."

"I must confirm this with General Wu. I cannot execute these orders without confirmation."

"You have your confirmation, *Deputy* General. Me."

"You are a political cadre, *Captain*. You cannot give orders to line officers."

"I can see Central's orders enforced, though. These came over the secured cadre channel and the code confirmed. So, you will *not* break information security and you *will* execute your orders."

"My soldiers will get torn apart. The whole battalion will be slaughtered if we follow the orders as written. We won't be combat-effective this time tomorrow."

"That sounds like defeatist talk, *Deputy*. That sounds exactly like defeatist talk. Not to mention dereliction of duty and cowardice in the face of the enemy!"

"Make threats. Let's see how they play out in front of a court, shall we? Or do you want to try for a field execution? Let's see how that works out."

"You think I won't?"

"Right before a major attack? No. Because then *you* would have the responsibility for the results. I will call General Wu. He will confirm with Central. If he confirms the orders, I will naturally see them carried out exactly. However, given the shocking nature of the so-called orders, I have every reason to believe that these are false orders delivered by the spies and infiltrators of Jeon."

"You know damn well they are legitimate!"

"Do I? I also know that internal security and political cadres are *very* nervous these days. Now, just why is that, hmm? Something you want to share with the rest of us?"

"Spreading malicious rumors, too? Keep digging, *Deputy*. Keep digging!"

"No. I won't be bullied on this. Loss of an entire command is a court-martial offense, regardless of whether you were executing orders or not. I will certainly not do so on the basis of orders whose validity I cannot confirm."

The general turned to walk out the door. He made it one step. The political officer's eyes went flat and he pulled an amulet out. The general froze. Truth watched as the veins slowly protruded on his forehead. He could see the muscles in the older man's neck throb and strain.

"In my twenty years of service, I have never had to use my Tiger Token. Congratulations, *Deputy General* Wong. At the very end of your service, you managed a real achievement. Let me remind you of a few facts. First—the Party and the People are one. Second—the army serves the People. Third— the Party cannot be defied, as the People die without their protection and guidance. Which results in the fourth fact—*you don't get to argue with me!*"

The last words came out in a hiss. "So. Now that you have dropped us *both* in the shit, you are going to march out there and give your orders. You will impress on your subordinates the need to succeed at all costs. You will explain that they will receive support in the air, with spells, with golems, whatever lies you need to tell them to get them to attack without any hesitation or reservation."

The general was starting to turn a faint blue. Lack of oxygen, Truth thought, though he could see faint glyphs slowly spreading across his face.

"Damn you for making me do this. Damn you!" The political officer's face was turning red in contrast to the general's purple. "I was *this* close to being promoted. *This* close! But do you think they will promote me if I can't keep a single arrogant little deputy under control? No! You undisciplined little shit! They aren't even your troops! You are the fucking *deputy*, you sock-puppet piss hole!"

Something died in the general's eyes. Truth was watching for it. Something in him broke. His body relaxed, and he resumed his usual fierce appearance. "I have received my orders and will execute the People's will perfectly!"

The political officer collapsed into his chair. "See to it that you do."

The general spun and marched out. The political officer didn't move for a minute, then wiped the sweat off his face. He balled up the handkerchief in his fist and slammed that fist down on the table hard enough to make the pens jump onto the floor.

He hyperventilated for a minute, then pulled himself together.

"Going to need a new deputy. Or maybe he died with his brigade. A fierce general leading from the front, a hero of the People. I can salvage this. I can salvage this!"

Truth slowly nodded. Apparently, the general had been implanted with something or enchanted with something. Some kind of mind-breaking curse. That kind of thing, it might not kill the body, but it might well kill the mind forever. Truth could see how that might have negative career consequences for the aspiring political officer. It also seemed that his guess was right about decapitation attacks. The real general was somewhere off-base. His deputy ran the show here. How that made a difference to troops who were suddenly without a general, Truth didn't know.

Apparently, it wasn't going to be a problem for this battalion. Need to have soldiers for there to be a breakdown in command.

The why behind the what was still a mystery, though. Not that this prick would know the answer. He was just following orders. Orders he didn't question, that would result in several thousand soldiers he was responsible for dying.

Truth examined the amulet on the desk. It was an interesting thing—it was a palm-length device shaped like half of a tiger lying down. It had been split in half the long way, and he could see almost microscopic traces of spells running along the edges and practically coating the split center line. He imagined there was a matching half somewhere else. Perhaps at Central. It would certainly not be usable by any random person that picked it up. That would be too stupid.

Maybe something more symbolic was appropriate. Incisive whispered a warning when he reached for the token. Truth grinned and moved fast. He snatched up the amulet and spun toward the officer. Incisive yelled *Danger*, and Truth smashed the Tiger Token straight through the officer's forehead and instantly let go. The token burst into a sudden blaze of heat and light, immolating the officer's head.

Truth thought he looked like a struck match. The sense of danger hadn't left, though. Truth quickly ran Obliteration over himself in case he had picked up a curse, but no, that wasn't it. Something about the fiery ball itself. Was there a distant screaming, getting louder, coming from that fire?

Truth made a swift exit from the tent and ran back toward his two-wheeler. A wailing scream started covering the base. The tent was starkly visible even in the daylight. Brilliant light was pouring out of it.

He didn't wait to find out what was being summoned. Nothing nice, he assumed. A bare second after he killed the political officer, an infernal dog burst through the tent walls. Its baying cry promised pursuit without end.

Truth grinned. *Good luck with that.*

He peeled out of the base in a cloud of dust and was on the road again. Would the deputy follow the orders he was given? Truth had no idea and wasn't interested in finding out. Spreading chaos and making political officers and secret policemen feel scared was plenty. He didn't want Jeon to fall. At least, he didn't want it conquered. He still had people he cared about living there. It would be all too easy to become "Unfortunate but regrettably necessary collateral damage."

Had they already defined away the notion of an innocent Jeon civilian? Probably. It was so much more convenient when everyone, Denizens, children, Level Zeros, *everyone* was evil. It made a sort of sense. If they weren't supporting the military/government/criminal elements in Jeon with their labor and taxes with their complicit silence, the crimes against Onis would never have occurred.

Killing indiscriminately meant that your soldiers were put at minimal risk. You had a duty to protect your citizens, and what were your soldiers if not that? Slaughtering without care was thus moral and just. The people you were protecting were definitionally virtuous, and the people you killed were definitionally wicked. What could be more proper than that? But since people can be soft-hearted, it would be best to keep the pictures of tiny hands reaching out of rubble away from the masses.

Not that those masses could do anything about it. It was just more pleasant for everyone this way.

Maybe he should leave the people of Onis a note. *I completely understand your anger and share it. However, since your problem-solving methods are extremely expensive and bad, just leave vengeance to me. I am a violence professional, and my rates are extremely reasonable.*

He pressed on for the border. Things were only going to get worse from there. He didn't know why Onis was ordering their men to get slaughtered, but he was sure he wouldn't like it when he figured it out.

CHAPTER 15

"MODERN" WARFARE

Truth had become something of a connoisseur in the fields of dissociation, alienation, persistent feelings of unreality, and a general sense of the inherent wrongness of the world. He could, with remarkable particularity, specify whether *he* was the source of the alienation or the situation he found himself in. Difficulty arose, however, when the oppressive absurdity came from both without and within. Where do you draw the line?

"Thrush, have you been on many battlefields? Outside of Hell, I mean."

"Oh, yes, great one. So many. One of my kind finds employment, enjoyment, and enrichment in equal measure in such places." Thrush sounded almost wistful.

"Is this normal, then?"

"Forgive me, dread magus, this little bird has a bird's wit. To what do you refer?"

Truth waved his hand at the road, the mountain, the forests, and the sky. Aside from the road being a lot more torn up and the sky having a remarkably high number of spell birds and golems zipping about, it was more or less what he remembered this area looking like before the war started.

It hadn't been anything particularly interesting then, either. Just . . . mountains. Taller and steeper than the mountains farther south. There had been some pretty great views of forest-filled valleys and swooping slopes. A number of charming snow-capped peaks, even in summer. There were even a few resort towns.

You might not think of vacationing in an area best known for mining and heavy industrial factories, but those views really were that beautiful. There was some decent hiking. Combined with hunting in the deep woods, fishing the mountain streams, skiing in the winter, the occasional hot springs resort—the mountains of North Jeon were not entirely bleak.

Truth had seen the advertising flyers in hotel lobbies and ads on scry. There were nice things up there. Not right this second, what with the massive war and volcanic eruption, but generally. It was pleasant in a bland sort of way when not being grim and industrial. They were still on the Onis side of the border, but it should be basically the same. Mountains didn't care where the border was.

And it was still fine, more or less. Ignoring the sky. It wasn't a nightmare of clashing armies, burning spells, exploding golems, maddened beastcrafted horrors shredding all-too-fragile human bodies, and other atrocities he usually associated with the term *front line*.

"I guess I'm confused by the lack of anything really resembling combat or the results of combat."

"Oh." Thrush thought about that. "I see. Your combat experience has been mostly small-scale battles. Individual combat or battles against squad-sized enemies?"

"Roughly." He shrugged. He didn't really know how many troops they had thrown at him when he was kidnapping Sally the Shattervoid Girl. Enough that it killed him.

"I think it's a question of scale. I mean no offense, almighty theurge—"

"Sorry, almighty *what*? I tend to tune out the honorifics at this point, but I don't think I had ever heard that one before."

"It is the privilege of the mighty to disdain the efforts of their lessers. A theurge is one who performs miracles and persuades gods and demons to labor on their behalf."

Truth nodded.

"All right, I'll give full marks for that one. Carry on with your critique of humanity."

Thrush pruned its inky feathers. It had always done a rather good job pretending to be a thrush, in Truth's opinion, and it seemed that constant exposure to Truth was only improving the imp's abilities. It no longer just looked like a demon pretending to be a small black bird. It looked like an actual thrush. The shine on its feathers was right. Truth could pick out the individual vanes and the subtle textures that rippled the sleek surface of them. He could see the micro-movements of the head, the tiny shifts of balance he associated with actual birds.

Thrush was becoming more real right along with him. He'd have to find out what it took for a demon to grow from an imp to a stronger being.

"I am so grateful!" The imp even sounded mostly sincere. Definitely getting stronger. "Scale is hard for humans in that your imagination is limited to things measured against yourself. You might understand, intellectually, that three hundred thousand troops is a lot, and that the border of Jeon and Onis is long, but you cannot situate the two together properly. Three hundred thousand is a lot. It should fill up almost anything."

"All right?"

"The border of Jeon and Onis, in this little bird's recollection, exceeds one thousand, four hundred kilometers."

"Sounds right?"

"Put another way, that's two hundred fourteen soldiers per kilometer, scattered over mountains. Much less dense. Depending on the terrain, you could easily fail to find them without careful looking."

"And of course, they aren't evenly distributed." Truth nodded.

"In fact, they are scattered some tens of kilometers deep along a ragged line, called generally 'the front.'" The tiny bird nodded.

Truth visualized a map of Jeon in his mind. The border with Onis was actually a little under three times as wide as most of the rest of the peninsula. The country really widened up this far north. He frowned. It really widened up. And Jeon's army, even with conscription, just wasn't that big.

Technology was a hell of a force multiplier, but the basics of the basics of tactics were to concentrate your forces and spread out the enemy. If they tried to defend the whole border, they would be overrun *fast*. So, what would he do if he were a cold-blooded bastard like the Jeon bureaucrats or the average Starbrite line manager?

Fall back. Kick Onis in the teeth as hard as you can, make them pause, then fall back. Speed limited by how quickly you could burn every scrap of useful material, blow up every factory, blow up every dam, salt every field, and poison every granary. Leave them nothing but horror and ruin. Don't even evacuate the citizens. Definitely don't evacuate the denizens. Shoot them if they try to flee. Make them Onis's problem. Let them eat off Onis's plate.

The peninsula narrowed sharply. There was a good-sized city . . . Gamphe. Yeah. The peninsula narrowed just north of Gamphe. He would draw the battle line there, build the actual fortifications and strongpoints along the thin waist of the peninsula, and give up the hundreds of kilometers north of there.

After all, those factories were only valuable *now*. In a few months? Useless. Millions of denizens? Well, those might be useful, but plenty more where they came from. And there was no good farmland up there. Just terrace farming. Difficult, expensive, and inefficient. No great loss.

"I don't think I am a particularly good person, Thrush."

"I respectfully disagree, magus."

"I think we have different criteria for what counts as *good*. But you know, even by my own atrocious standards, there are still people I can look down on as immoral. Fun." Truth shook his head. "Well, while we have room to work, I might as well get a little practice in. Have the iron horse follow me."

It was time to try out the Earth-Folding Step. The System had memorized it and gotten it settled down in his fourth aperture. Brilliant gold and shining like tiny suns within him, his apertures were nurturing his spells. Time for his newest tenant to show its virtue.

Truth brought the spellform to mind, and for the first time since he swore his loyalty to Starbrite, he couldn't form it.

System?

<<I'm trying. We have finally hit the complexity barrier.>>

Complexity? Oh! I think you mentioned this ages ago. The simplified spells. Part of why they were used was that they were easy to swap in and out.

<<And were totally manageable for the System to cast for you. This is . . . I have never seen anything like this before. It's not as alien as the Nephilim spell tech. I'm just talking about the scope and complexity of it. The closest I can think of is a hugely elaborate ritual diagram. The fact that people can cast this as they walk, and even in combat, is frankly nuts.>>

Let me take a look. The System brought up a static hallucination of the spell formation, along with a step-by-step guide to the casting process. It filled his entire field of vision.

I'm going to kill Merkovah.

<<Good luck with that one. Although he didn't screw you. It's legit. So much so, it's going on my list of Three Actual, Complete Spells that you have encountered.>>

The Meditations, Incisive, and this?

<<Yeah. The problem you are running into is that the Meditations and Incisive are horrifyingly complex, but they are like . . . math problems that you can run indefinitely. The more you run the problems, the bigger, more complex numbers you generate. The more you use them, and the higher your level, the more complex and powerful they become. I think, and I'm completely guessing here, that this is kind of the reverse. It's giving you the full spell immediately. It's on you to dumb it down enough for you to use it.>>

It's a human mage that wrote Earth-Folding Step. I guarantee it. Some ancient, impossibly powerful senior had mastered the art of folding space and wrote down his understandings. But since he lacked the genius of Valentinian or Botis—

<<He couldn't condense it for people. Remember how Merkovah said people tended to explode trying to use it?>>

Not enough body cultivation. Not enough cosmic energy. And I guarantee the core problem was not enough understanding of the spell.

Truth could feel the System agreeing with him.

<<We both need to keep studying it before you try to cast it. Tonight, we should spend some time looking at the "corrected" Cup and Knife spells. I've had a chance to digest them and I think there is some interesting potential there.>>

Truth looked down the valley. He was headed south, toward the front. Toward Jeon and, he suspected, horror.

"Never mind, Thrush. Let's get to it. Keep your eye out."

"For what, O terror of the land?"

"At this point? A ray of sunshine."

A small convoy of wagons, perhaps a dozen, was rumbling down the road. Troop transports, he could see—armored just enough to stop a needler and Level Zero summons, but really built to haul troops from point A to B with a maximum of speed and a minimum of cost. They were penned between the side of a mountain and a steep drop on the other side. Truth was stuck behind them. They just took up the whole road, and his wall-riding trick wouldn't work over such a long stretch.

There was a blur, so fast even Truth's eyes barely caught it, and the first wagon exploded. He squeezed the brakes as hard as he could, feeling the wheels lock and slide forward. A swarm of birds flew up from the forest below, crashing into the wagons. Blowing up the wheels. Blowing holes in the thin armor. Flying through the thin armor and blowing up inside.

Troops were trying to dismount, moving like they were stuck in mud. The shock of the ambush was overwhelming. Birds would fly into the soldiers, exploding into clouds of shrapnel. Someone tried to shoot them but missed. The needles flew harmlessly over the valley, long after the person who fired them turned into a gory mess on the mountainside.

The ambush was over in seconds. It began and ended before most of the soldiers understood that they were under attack. Truth looked down the slope. Somewhere below was a squad of Jeon regulars. You wouldn't trust this job to conscripts. They got in place on a convoy route, waited for a target, and destroyed it.

Now, if he were them, what would he do? Flee, obviously. But he would also leave something nasty for the team who would have to clear out the sudden obstruction in the invasion route. He looked around carefully but didn't see anything. He shrugged. Mines in the face of the mountain would be his go-to. Kill a lot of people and destroy the road in the process. Double win.

He looked up at the uncaring heavens, heaved a sigh, and hopped off his iron horse. This bit was going to be a pain in the ass. It was necessary, though, so he would do it. If he didn't want the world organized this way, he would just have to go and fix it.

CHAPTER 16

SO WHAT IF IT AIN'T RIGHT?

The iron horse steadily crossed the mountains; *steadily* being one of those tricky words that sounds objective but is actually subjective. Truth, for example, considered it quite reliable. There might be a bit of front-wheel wobble, and some excess vibration as it came up to speed, and if he was going to be pedantic, the brakes were ninety percent shot. On the other hand, he was permanently running Incisive, which should in theory give him plenty of time to avoid any little whoopsies. The patchwork iron horse was, therefore, utterly reliable and crossed the mountains steadily.

Surveillance had gotten heavy. He was through the back of the front lines now and into the actual battle lines. The mines ignored him, of course. As did the tiny golems, the swarms of hidden demons, and witchcrafted puppets. They were there to sweep out the conscripts that would come funneling down the road soon enough. No need to make them strong enough to pick up a mid-Tier hiding themselves. What could a single Level Four or Five manage, after all?

A mid-level mage was a local calamity. Effortlessly capable of exterminating small units on their own. But so what? Say a Level Five could fight a thousand alone. How long could they do it for? How long could they keep casting? And how much easier was it to find a thousand conscripts than a single Level Five?

There wasn't a country in the world that wouldn't count trading a Level Five for a thousand Level Ones as a losing trade. Mid-Tiers would get deployed as line-breakers, sent with heavy support to crack a strong point, opening a channel for the conscripts to pour through. They were the officer class and treated as such. They were also heavy-weapons platforms and treated like that, too.

Buried off the trail, carefully concealed, would be assassin golems. There would be heavy needler batteries, carefully enchanted to target high-cosmic-ray concentrations. Each needle would cost as much as a worker might make in an hour. Possibly three hours.

Layered with enchantments to break wards, to dissolve flesh and crush souls, the ammo box would have its own guard of regulars, just to prevent any shrinkages. A full box of ammo would cost more than a house. Worth it, though. To be able to beat a mid-level to death with your wallet? What could be more worth it than that?

You could always print more money. But there were now a finite number of Level Fours, Fives, and Sixes in the world. Their numbers would not be replaced. The magic thinned by the day. Fewer and fewer would break through, even with arrays and elixirs.

Truth got a morbid bit of fun out of it. On the one hand, the combat doctrine of nations was to exhaust the most powerful spells and mages against waves of summons and conscripts before sending in your own elites. But now, that calculation had been complicated. The doctrine made tactical sense, but did it make sense strategically?

Truth moved the pieces around in his head. The apocalypse wasn't coming—it was there. It just wasn't evenly distributed yet. So, a smart, and particularly ruthless, person would throw their mid-levels and most disposable high-levels *directly* into the meat grinder immediately. Maximize the damage they could do while they could still do it. In a year or less, maybe even just a few months, they would be worm food.

Those Level Ones would be crippled when the magic faded to near-nothing, but they could still carry a spear if necessary. The Level Zeros . . . He had to wonder what the training camps looked like right now. Universal draft, regardless of Level. Yet, strangely, they were being drilled hard on physical conditioning and formation marching, not weapons. Plenty of indoctrination. Plenty of sparring. No range time.

Maybe they would throw rocks.

This stretch of the front was quiet for the moment. Mortars delivered rains of cursed shrapnel across valleys, and snipers were playing their "funny" little games, but they were having to work for it. The deep forests made targeting a pain. You could use a spirit or a second spell to target, of course, but you might as well hand your victim a note letting them know the hit was coming in.

Truth let the iron horse do the running, carrying him and his thoughts through an active war zone. There was a barricade up ahead? Go around, through the woods. Dismount and carry the two-wheeler over the deployed hedgehogs and around the ground demons. Stop and check if there were any political officers who could suffer a friendly-fire incident. Then move on.

At some indefinable point, he crossed into Jeon. He really couldn't say when. Not like there was a sign or anything. It was just that the roadblocks were facing the north now. The patches had changed. Different-model needlers.

He looked into the dead eyes of the conscripts, smelling the fear stink on them.

Welcome home, Truth. Ready to make it all better?

A few kilometers back from the front line, he found a general giving a speech. Olive-drab uniform, edged in gold brocade, armored with enough medals to stop a comet. Level Seven, looked like, with a pair of Level Five guards. Truth hung well back, keeping out of sight.

"Soldiers, I tell you, we are going to win this war! We are going to win! You have all heard how the Tiger roared over the Great White Mountain before the mountain erupted and flooded the Onis lines with lava. Even now, the Great White Mountain defends the nation."

He was standing on the hood of a light wagon, declaiming with practiced strength.

"You see that red sky overhead? That is the red sky of victory! You know why that sky is red? The volcano is drowning Onis in ash. Choking their cities, their crops, throttling the vermin-swarms of their peasant levies. The heavens and the earth alike help us. I ask you, what is there to fear when the world itself is on your side?"

He shook his great head slowly, lantern jaw swinging.

"There is nothing, NOTHING in this world Jeon needs fear except the weakness in our own hearts. Cowardice, defeatism, these are the enemies! Greed is the enemy! Listening to enemy broadcasts, reading enemy propaganda, spreading rumors, and harming morale—these things are nothing but giving aid and comfort to the enemy! And shall be punished according to military law!"

Oh, you could hear the blood and fire in his voice now.

"I tell you right now, so long as every true son and daughter of Jeon gives their all, fully commits their hearts, minds, and souls to our nation in this moment of crisis, our victory is assured. I cannot promise you that it will be quick. It certainly won't be easy. But as sure as the tiger rules the mountain, so too will Jeon stand supreme over the world!"

Truth saw some officers and NCOs facing the crowd and pointedly applauding. Everyone got the hint. They stood up and cheered madly. It was what you did, even if you despised every word. It was insane to look like you lacked spirit or were sabotaging morale. In the past, it was terminally career-limiting. Now it was just terminal.

Time to leave. He pressed on, moving through the forest, hidden by the summer green. Someone would find the tire tracks eventually, but so what?

What would they do about it? Who would they even tell? The tiger ruled the mountain, did it? Truth wondered if this was how it felt. Moving invisibly. Deciding what was prey and what would be ignored for now.

That night, he built himself a little camp site. The iron horse was laid on its side in the dirt and covered with pine boughs. For himself, Truth made a little tent with his tarps and covered those with fragrant branches as well. No fire. He didn't want to spend the energy hiding it.

He ate a cold meal and looked at the stars through the swaying needles. Sally was somewhere up there with her family. Being healed, he hoped. Perhaps she was on the other side of the sky, that strange space the Shattervoid traveled through. Perhaps they could see the wrongs and rights of this mean little world.

You have some ideas about fixing Cup and Knife?

<<Yeah. I see where Merkovah was coming from. All the "improved" versions focus on making the demon-destruction or ingredient-purification stronger. But there was something that didn't make sense to me.>>

Oh?

<<Demons are natural. Even infernal demons that need to steal energy to exist here. They are natural too, if just not where they should "naturally" be. Also, what does refine *or* impurity *even mean to an angel? Steel is "pure" iron with impurities carefully added to it. In fact, those "impurities" in plants are all things that are necessary to the plant. They might make life harder on human alchemists, but if you are an angel, so what if they do?>>*

I chalked it up to a moral judgment. It's the kind of thing they do.

<<Manda cares about the concentration of hot elements in a bunch of ivy . . . why, exactly? What about it defies God's will?>>

Valid point. But that is what the spell does, so . . .

<<Isn't.>>

What do you mean, "Isn't"? It literally is.

<<It literally is not. We know it's not. Vek told everyone it's not. Cup and Knife is what a guy, dehydrated, starved, probably coming off a ferocious dose of hallucinogens, and definitely reeling from confronting a higher level of reality, wrote down when he regained some control over his fingers.>>

Truth thought about that one a second. Vek had said that, hadn't he? That he didn't have the brains to recreate the bits of the spell that were missing from his recollection.

But it does seem to be a reality-correcting spell of some kind. We have seen how it will shift damage around, letting it go some places but not others. Some changes cost more energy than others. There is a whole set of rules there we aren't seeing.

<<Manda gave us a clue back in the library.>>

The System helped pull up the memory. The old man, something mischievous and lively in his eyes. *"If you want to know the answer to a lot of things, including how Cup and Knife really works, answer that question first. Why can't you imagine a better world?"*

The old man had tapped the passage he had etched on the church floor all those centuries ago, and provided his own translation. *"A pauper shall be a prince / Wisdom ever sought and never found / Arrogant humility / A dream forbidden / You cannot approach the Throne without knowing Truth."*

All the subsequent reworks of the spell figured that Vek goofed on the optimization. They didn't bother to wonder why an angel would care about revealing such a thing to Vek and, by extension, the world. Manda left that message on the church floor. He specifically clued us in to the . . . global mental block that's in place. His acolyte demons in particular set us up for the revelation. And at the end of the day, Manda is an angel. He doesn't do a single damn thing unless he thinks it's furthering God's will.

<<It adds up to something frankly terrifying. Cup and Knife is an error-correction spell. It's not for removing impurities; it's for bringing things in line with how they should be, according to Manda. But you can't figure out how to use it properly until you can properly see the world. Properly understand the intended relations between people.>>

A spell for repairing the world. Truth exhaled a cool breath. It was a shocking thought. Electrifying.

<<Yes, but you are missing the punchline. What if those words weren't left as a message for us? What if they were Manda's hint to the biggest straying demon around?>>

Starbrite? Six hundred years ago?

<<No, dummy. The World. What if Manda wasn't trying to enlighten us? What if Manda was trying to enlighten the heavenly demon we are standing on? The great stellar eminence that is the World?>>

CHAPTER 17

THAT SEEMS . . . FINE

Truth looked up through the humid summer sky at the burning heavens above. Each little dot of light a being so utterly beyond him as to defy description. Each moving dot another being of impossible scope and majesty. For example, the one he was lying down on.

Kind of a brain-twister, isn't it? I'm lying on what is unquestionably a big ball of rock with stuff growing on it. I have seen it from orbit. Big ball of rock with water and trees and . . . stuff. Humanity. So big, you lose any sense of scale. Just nothing to measure it against. And at the same time, it is also a demon. Or an angel. Or some being that blurs the lines between both. Just by existing on another plane of reality, it creates and maintains the world. I mean . . . just . . .

He grasped for words. He didn't wind up finding them. All he could do was stare upward in awe.

<<That's where you are climbing to, you know. That place of inexplicable awe. I wonder if the heavens will still hold their wonder then, or if it will be just another slum.>>

Truth smiled at that. A sad little thing.

There is only one slum. We just see different parts of it. Rats of different sizes and colors. Rats with different strategies, depending on the ledge they cling to or what toxic food they can eat from the overflowing dumpsters. What waters they lap out of the poison canals. And you think Cup and Knife is a spell for fixing the slum?

<<Basically? No, actually, not that. More like fixing a single house in the slum and maybe tidying things up a bit so the rats can live a little healthier there? I think the metaphor is starting to fall apart.>>

It's just so odd to try and nail down with words. I can't cast a spell that affects the whole world. At this point, I'm not even sure Starbrite can, even with his Nascent Soul abomination thing he has going on. But Manda gives Vek an absolute mountain of visions, loads him up with partially functional spells, and, once he firmly has everyone's attention, spikes him with Cup and Knife. The spell might not be popular, but it's so useful as a foundation, it gets copied everywhere. It's never lost, in other words.

<<All in the expectation that someday, the right person would turn up, learn the spell, read the message, and start fixing things. Which, in order to do right, requires learning the mind of Manda or at least his intentions. So. No pressure there.>>

Truth looked through the leaves a while longer, just sitting with the thought. His notion about what a better world might look like was still rough, still bound up in fantasy. It's fine to say *Nobody should starve*, but getting from *should* to *Everyone eats enough good food* was a lot harder.

Do you make farming mandatory? Or if you are going to force demons to do it, do you force people to become demon-binders? Farm-supervisor mages? Forced labor again, just a slightly different stripe. You could bribe the supervisors with better resources, but that would bring you straight back to the fat rats, just with a few more steps. Put intelligent spirits in charge, bound by tight laws governing what they may and may not do? Someone has to bind them at some point. It's the same old drag.

At the end of it, he kept coming back to cultivation and money. Cultivation meant you had more personal power. Money meant you had other people's power. In either case, it was an imbalance that put some above others. He had yet to see someone use that power selflessly.

Merkovah made no bones about his selfish motivations. Starbrite sure didn't either. His experience as the Prince was not a positive one for the people around him. Even the somewhat-alien Nephilim seemed to rejoice in being bullies. There didn't seem to be a way out of the loop as it spun 'round and 'round. You could move people with the promise of power, but once someone had power, you wished they didn't.

On a whim, he fished out Thrush's token. "Thrush, what does a better world look like to you?"

The inky bird hopped out, almost invisible in the shadows.

"I am certain I don't understand, dread magus."

"Someone has elevated you. Raised your power to that of a stellar eminence and commanded that you transform this world into one that is, if not perfect, at least better. Better for humans to live on."

There was a little shimmer in the dark. The inky black bird was preening his feathers. Truth could see in near-perfect darkness now, but the bird practically dissolved into the shadows.

"You know, I don't think I have ever been asked that question. Imps rarely are asked for advice by persons of standing. I think our low station limits our vision and thus our usefulness."

It hopped around a little. "But then, you have always been special. Were I to command the world, ordering things as I saw fit? I would bind each person in an illusion. They would be neatly stacked in caves, their bodies cared for. Their births and deaths would occur without their awareness of it."

Thrush warmed to his task. "In a word, I would divorce mind and body. The bodies would be in the care of the demons I set for that task. Their minds would be spent in eternal worship. A state of perpetual religious ecstasy. All parts of their mind capable of other thoughts would be suppressed utterly or excised entirely. It would be a world of innocence and peace. A world without sin or sinners."

The little bird chuckled melodically. "Though I suppose I would be rather doing myself out of a job."

Truth nodded at that. It made sense. It fit the instructions perfectly. Humanity would be perfectly cared for. Happy, healthy, free from sin, and essentially plants. Very happy plants. But plants.

"No interest in human progress?"

"Is it not progress? I think it is the apogee of human ambition. Every need perfectly cared for, and existences full of meaning and fulfillment. No hollow feeling of false satisfaction or the narcotic pleasures of the flesh. No obliteration of the mind with cheap entertainment." Truth could hear the smile in the voice. "True, complete, and comprehensive satisfaction. A miniature of Heaven, to whatever extent I could manage."

Truth nodded. "Of course, you could extend that a step further. Get rid of all the humans. Once they no longer exist, they can no longer suffer in this world."

"Yes. There would be a transition period of extreme suffering, of course. The necessary refinements of Hell. But after that? All would be peaceful and free of suffering. However, you did specify that this world was to be made better for humans to live on."

"I did say that." Truth smiled up into the night. "I ask a lot of questions. I'm starting to think asking the questions over and over is more important than deciding which answer is right. Your answer is totally correct. I think most humans would find it revolting. I sure do. On the other hand, it is actually better than any answer I have come up with. So, what should I do?"

Thrush laughed softly. "Alas, this little bird must live without seeing his vision accomplished. This world will be doomed to suffer a while longer, it seems. You should keep asking the question, of course. Groping toward *better*, while giving up on *best*."

Truth found an evacuated village the next day. He gave it a look-over—not torn down or burned down but utterly empty. Anything of military use, especially food, had been taken. Even the water-summoning talismans had been ripped off the walls. Truth did find one, half-hidden on the exterior of a house, clearly meant to be attached to a hose. Incisive trilled a little warning when he reached for it. Boobytrapped. As were the beds, the cupboards, and most of the streets.

He looked around a bit, just to get an appreciation of the artform. There was a distinct preference for "high-value" targets like cold boxes or closets but some sinisterly mundane ones too. He particularly appreciated the way a careless step through a door would trigger a blast of shrapnel, but a person standing on the front step for more than two seconds, say, for example, disarming a fairly obvious booby trap, would trigger a more upward-directed explosion.

The dolls with explosive talismans in them were a little more expected but no less sad. And creepy. The coffee cup with a small explosive charm under it was downright malicious.

An hour spent in fruitful self-education later, he was back on the road. Exactly one minute after that, Incisive screamed at him.

Truth squeezed hard on the brakes. The iron horse skidded a few meters, then the near-bald tires finally burst, sending shreds of rubber and metal everywhere. Truth was catapulted over the handlebars, doing a neat flip over the near-invisible wire stretched across the road at neck height. As he was falling, he had the horrible certainty that he was about to land on a mine. Using his inhuman reflexes, he was just able to stretch a hand out and down in time to stop his fall.

Stopping your fall, keeping your body suspended in the air with a single hand that is not under your center of gravity requires both strength and focus. It was a very tense and still moment as Truth struggled to regain control of the situation.

It was at this point that the ruined two-wheeler slid into the minefield.

A wave of buried charms activated, triggered by the passing corpse of the iron horse. Anti-vehicle, it looked like, lances of molten steel and copper punching upward, ripping apart whatever was over them, then splatting outward. If they had punched into the interior of a carriage or a wagon, especially one that just lost its driver from a suspended wire, the casualties would be catastrophic. As it was, Truth just had burning metal falling around him.

He waited a moment longer, to see if there was a follow-up. After a minute, he decided it was time to walk out of the minefield. He carefully lowered his other hand and walked out. It was an upside-down sort of day. He'd just go with it. As for the two-wheeler? There wasn't enough left to sell for scrap. He could try Cup and Knife on it, but . . . No. It had earned its final rest.

Guess we start in on Earth-Folding Step earlier than intended.

<<Eeeh. Let's . . . do a lot of thinking as we go. You already blew up once today. Twice would be pushing it.>>

Twice in a day wouldn't even be a new record for me.

<<Not everything needs improving on. Sometimes, something is good enough as is. Normal people would know that. Normal, not -ursed people don't have to be told that upping your Most Times Blown Up in a Day *is not a self-improvement goal.>>*

Fair. Truth glanced at his plain wooden ring hiding months of food inside, and touched his thankfully unharmed scarf. *Though I must admit I like a good upgrade.*

He consulted his road atlas. It was practically in pieces by now, but he had hopes for stretching the service life a little longer. It was a forty-kilometer jog to the next little town. He would have to see what things looked like when he got there.

What did a better world look like? How could he change it? One step at a time.

CHAPTER 18

A POINTLESS KINDNESS

Truth walked down the road. Forty kilometers was a casual hour's stroll; he wasn't pushing the pace. He wanted to puzzle at Earth-Folding Step a bit as he went.

Just how mentally diseased was this . . . Supreme Elder?

It was, he felt, a very fair question. Possibly the key question. His initial thought was that Earth-Folding Step would work somewhat like what the Shattervoid did—step out of this side of reality, travel through that . . . other place . . . and step back in again. He had thought Merkovah was just being colorful or something with his description of folding up reality. Reality, in Truth's experience, might be strained or torn, but it did not fold.

He should have known better. Merkovah might be a lot of things, but a bad teacher wasn't one of them. The spell did exactly what he said it did—it scrunched up reality as you crossed over a specific point. A step was the easiest and most obvious example, but so long as you were in motion, it would work. You could do it in a vehicle, falling through the air, being carried along by a current. You just needed to cross over the fold.

Could he . . . send a spell over the fold? He wasn't sure yet. For that matter, there was the whole "crossing over" thing itself. Would he be half in one place and half in the other if he stopped midway? What happened to things that were caught over the line when reality unfolded? How, exactly, did reality pinch itself into a crossable point for *only him*, but somehow, everyone and everything within that pinched space were utterly unaffected. Unaware, even? Which, of course, raised the central question—

Just how mentally diseased and just how brilliant was the creator to make it all work?

He and the system wrestled with it, letting the mountains slide past. Ignoring the heat and the sticky humidity that were trapped in the valleys. It would be brutal farther south. Summer in Jeon was no joke. Might not be Siphios hot, but he had always felt the heat had a sticky feeling here.

Summer—he felt like it coated you in mucus. First making your clothes stick, then whatever foulness was in the air. All the exhaled tobacco and drugs and diseases like floating curses, waiting for you to walk into them. Ready to wrap you in their second-hand misery.

Not for the first, or even five hundredth, time, he gave thanks for the Meditations of Valentinian and all the fortuitous encounters that led to him developing a sealed body. The summer could guide his choice of clothes and nothing further. He was free to enjoy it as he wished.

Truth stopped a moment by the side of a stream running next to the road. Truth took off his already badly worn shoes and splashed his feet in the cold mountain water. No reason for it other than it was a hot day and he could.

Was this what he wanted from his magic? To be unconstrained? His whole life had been bound up in little boxes of necessity—keep the sibs alive, study for the SAT's, Work in the PMC, get the sibs set up for their careers, then WHOOPS! Dead in a well. Time for you to figure it all out. Pick a direction and ride.

It wasn't that there were no urgent needs or no more desperate struggles to fight. He just had more choices now. He was looking beyond the tip of his nose and seeing the road ahead. Picking his destination.

One more head to collect. Many more would die along the way. Impossible to avoid. But he only needed just one more head. Then he could be quit of this world, either by retreating off of it with his loved ones or sending them off and vanishing into the mountains. Both had their charms. In either case, he would be firmly telling the world to get bent. The illusions of the real were already weak enough. By the time he collected Starbrite's head, he imagined he would see through them all. But that wasn't the final head he needed.

King Rat. Truth smiled and watched the clear water spray as he kicked it up. King Rat, the cruel beast that lived in his head. That only felt safe when it controlled everything around him. That ate first. That cared only for its own power and authority. That could only measure its well-being by the suffering of others. That was the last head he needed to collect before he could be done with this world.

He laughed a little—tiny fish came up to nibble at his toes, hunting unsuccessfully for dead skin to eat. *Sorry, little fish. You will have to keep looking for your meal.* He sent his shoes off to his spatial ring. No sense in wearing them down any farther. Not bothering to wipe the water off his feet, he once more set off down the road.

If the little village had a name, it wasn't recorded on the road atlas, and he didn't see any signs. There was a sign showing the way to the animal rescue and zoo. This village was as abandoned as the last, stripped bare by the fleeing Denizens. It was far too small and poor to have any Citizens. Truth frowned. Would they have thought to release the zoo animals? Hopefully, they wouldn't have slaughtered them for food, but with meat being so expensive these days . . .

He followed the signs. Just to check. The "zoo" was a sad little thing. Mostly wire fences and wire cages, with a few cobbled-together sheds attached. There was a tiny shack with a little covered porch just next to it. To Truth's mild shock, there was an old man tending the cages, tossing fresh cut grass to some earless goats. There appeared to be insects for the birds to eat, too.

"Senior, why are you still here? Everyone else has fled south." He asked. The elder nearly collapsed from shock, clutching his chest.

"WHERE in the name of almighty PRAGER AND HIS SAINTS did you come from? I didn't hear your chariot pull up or anything!" the old man managed to forcefully wheeze.

"Ah. Yes. Sorry. I move very quietly. At this point, it's just how I am. Actually, I'm sort of happy to see you here—I was worried no one was feeding the animals. Or had eaten them."

"Hmph. They tried. Repeatedly. I kept them up in the mountains a ways. I have a few secret places." Truth couldn't help but think the old man looked like a bundle of sticks shoved into worn-out clothes. Despite looking like he would blow away in a mild breeze, the elder stood square in front of his charges, fists balled up. "You can't have them either."

Truth raised his hands. "I'm fed enough, Senior. I'm here to help if I can."

"Not much you can do. Not much anyone can do, I'm afraid." The old-timer sighed. There was pain there. Truth could see it in his face, in the way he moved. Old pain and growing worse.

"You could take them back up into the mountains and turn them loose. They can have some sort of life that way."

"Wish I could. Already did that with most of the birds. It's the others. Here, let me introduce you to someone." The old man walked slowly to a glass-sided box left in a sunny spot. Well ventilated, but it must still be quite hot. He carefully reached in and fished out a snake the length of his arm. Handsome fellow, light tan and dappled white, with a blunted triangle for a head.

"This is Perks. He's a Perkach rat snake. Called that because the breed is from Perkach and they feed on rats. Mildly venomous, but really, I'd let kids play with him. No danger to anyone, so long as he's not abused."

Truth nodded at the snake, feeling a sense of kinship. Incisive was a little weird that way.

"Want to hold him?"

"Sure. So, what's the problem? Lots for him to eat here."

"The problem is that he is from *Perkach*. Or, well, his breed is; some breeder raised him here in Jeon, sold him to someone who wanted an exotic pet, and then the buyer decided that feeding dead mice to their pet snake was a bit icky, actually, and they dumped him off on us."

"All right?"

"Not big on geography, are you."

"The army did its best, but it was starting from a low place."

That got a snort from the old man. "I know what that's like. Perkach is a hot, dry country. Mountains of Jeon is what you would generally call cold and wet. Not too bad now, of course, plenty warm enough in the summer, but winter would kill him. Same with the goats."

The old man pointed at the disreputable-looking animals. All black heads, no visible ears, and alarmingly swollen udders swinging below their bellies. "They are bred for warm grasslands, not the mountains. Young Hal thought he could make goat-milk soaps, earn a little extra money, so he bought 'em off a farmer."

The old man shook his head.

"Couldn't make a go of it?"

"Died. Drunk driving accident. Nobody wanted to look after 'em, so they came to me."

"Damn. Hard thing."

"Common enough. Hurts, in a small place like this, but it's so ordinary, it'd make you sick."

Truth sighed with the old man.

"So, what are you going to do?"

"What can I do? I'm turning loose, or have turned loose, all the ones that can make their own way in the wild. The rest . . . I'll look after them as long as I can. Sooner or later, probably sooner, they'll die or I'll die."

Truth nodded at that. He could see the old man's perspective. He was a Denizen, and a dying one. There was no future for him if he evacuated. There was no future here. These animals would have the same ending regardless of what he did. So, why not spend his last breaths doing this? At least he would feel useful.

He looked down at the snake twisting around his arm. "I'm headed south, Senior. There is nowhere in Jeon that is hot and dry year-round, but I can probably find Perks a better home than these mountains."

"Eh? Can you even afford to feed him? He needs to be fed a mouse a week. Two weeks if he's hibernating."

Truth laughed quietly. "I think I can manage that."

The old man frowned. "You aren't trying to humor me, are you? I've seen it before. People adopt an animal and then can't stick with it."

"I'm not promising to keep him forever. Just find him a better, warmer place to live."

The old man thought about it, then sighed. A somewhat-defeated sound. "Usually, I charge a fee for adoptions, but under the circumstances—take him. I'll even throw in his cage. Be sure and change the bedding at least once a month."

"I'll do that." Truth smiled. He picked up the plastic box. It was lined with sawdust, with a few branches and a fist-sized rock for decoration.

"Senior? It matters."

"Eh? What's that?"

"What you are doing? It matters as much as anything else. Even if other people don't understand or appreciate it, I do."

"Well. Thank you?" The old man coughed, the sound getting worse and wetter as it went on. "Go. I'm about talked out."

"All right. Thank you for introducing me to Perks. By the way, did you know you have a sack of rice on your porch? Better keep it out of the rain."

The old man turned to look, but the youngster had vanished. Sitting on his porch was a twenty-kilo sack of rice. He looked around. No carriage. No sounds of rushing wheels. The youngster certainly wasn't carrying sacks of rice with him.

The old man slowly pressed his hands together and gave thanks. He didn't know who he owed his thanks to, but he gave it anyway.

CHAPTER 19

RIGHT. CONSEQUENCES.

Truth hadn't even made it to the other end of the village before he was forced to confront an inconvenient truth—snakes generally don't travel at high speeds while clinging on to other animals. Perks was doing his best, bless him, but he literally wasn't built for this.

Truth briefly wondered if it would be safe to put a living organism in his spatial ring. He couldn't remember what Sally had said about it, but he was going to guess . . . no. Had he even asked? Ehhh . . .

"All right, Perks, we gotta figure this out." Truth slowed a stroll, a bare dozen kilometers an hour. "Now, even though I love the image of appearing out of the thin air, snake wrapped around my arm as I do terrifying things, there are practical problems. Like, how do I keep you alive as I, for example, punch through a cement wall and rip the person on the other side through the hole?"

Perks didn't nod, but Truth wasn't really expecting him to. The snake wasn't spiritual or anything. Very ordinary snake, if well outside its comfort zone.

"Also, as mythic as that sounds, it does drop us straight back into Paint the bedroom black, *Call Me the Dark Dragon of Eternal Doom-Hell, the Demon God-Emperor-Supreme of Night Shadow Assassins* territory. Not a great look. Not the place I am trying to move to as a rat and a mage."

Hmm. A rat snake that didn't stir at the mention of rats. Could you train a snake to respond to verbal commands? He had no idea. Probably not, but who knows?

"I swear, the problems you run into in this job. Well, I guess it's not a job, really. Vocation?" Truth vaguely remembered some quarter-wit saying that if you do what you love, you would never work a day in your life. Spoken like someone who never did what they loved, he thought.

"So, again, what do we do with you?"

"If I may, master?" Thrush hopped out of his token and perched on Truth's shoulder. Truth nodded at him. "Simply tuck in your shirt and cinch your belt. He will settle down there well enough, and it won't slow you.

It might feel a little strange to begin with, but the animal is incapable of piercing your skin even if it spent a lifetime gnawing on you."

"Huh. Well. Let's give it a try at least." He did. It did, in fact, feel very strange. Still, Perks was warm enough and pretty still. Good enough.

"Hey, Thrush, can animals turn into demons?"

"Oh, yes. I assume you mean the sort of demons that exist on this world, rather than the infernal sort?" Truth nodded. "Yes, quite common, or it was."

"Not enough magic?"

"Magus is wise."

Truth just waited. And waited. Eventually, Thrush coughed.

"There are some other factors."

"No. I am so very surprised." Truth's voice was utterly flat.

"It is not easy to describe, and 'not enough magic' really is the core of it. Not enough *meaning* is the other part. Jeongo breaks down when you try to talk about concepts so divorced from ordinary human experience."

Truth shrugged. Was there a human language that *didn't* break down when discussing the divine?

"Demons usually arise in a place of some sort of significance. A special tree or a rock or some other natural phenomena. They may be spirits of the rock or tree, or they may be animals that simply inhabit the area. It takes an immensely long time for the animals to absorb some of the meaning of the place, and most don't live long enough for the magic to transform them. You need both."

This was tickling something in the back of Truth's mind. "Like how Incisive works, or similar spells. Belief gives it shape, the power comes from the universe, the transformation comes from the spell. But this is the belief of the planet or, infinitely removed, God. The energy is the ambient magic, maybe concentrated by a special place. But what would be the spell?"

"I cannot possibly say. Perhaps the universe itself? No spell is needed for a fire to burn or water to float an apple." Thrush hopped around on his shoulder, weighing nothing.

Truth picked up his pace. Perks seemed perfectly comfortable. At least, he wasn't shifting around or anything.

"So, it would be possible to manufacture demons?"

"Hypothetically. Actually, I'm certain that it has been done. In Siphios, if nowhere else. It's just that why bother?" Condescension dripped from the tiny bird. "Stupid, weak, painfully limited creatures, barely sapient, still painfully mortal without immense good fortune. The maggot's not worth the peck."

Truth snorted at that, then picked up the pace. It was a long way still to Gamphe. He was curious to see if he read the future of the war correctly. Besides, as a diligent employee, he was looking forward to his performance review from Starbrite.

Truth's bare feet slapped into the road, driving him forward. Quite content knowing that his sealed body was keeping anything, cosmic energy very much included, from leaking out. Forgetting that between his blessings, Incisive, the Meditations, and the impact he was having on the world, he was very much a locus of "meaning."

The roads were eerily empty. On the Onis side of the border, traffic was sparse but present. On the Jeon side? Nothing. The tiny villages he passed seemed split between huddling in place and utterly empty. In a few others, there were only corpses. Needle rounds. Apparently, the locals didn't feel like listening to orders, and the soldiers didn't have time for keeping peace.

Maybe they had wanted to evacuate but were told to stay put. Truth wondered how many internal security agents had mysteriously woken up in Hell the last few days, shortly before their charges vanished to hide out in the mines or hidden mountain valleys. More than a few, for sure. A wonderful time for settling scores, in the moment between the outbreak of war and the arrival of soldiers.

He was right about how Jeon was planning to fight this war, too—lots of conscripts digging trenches, commanding demons to construct quick and dirty pillboxes. Lots of mines being laid, roadblocks being set, summoning traps installed. Nothing designed to stop an advance dead, just slow it. Hurt the advance elements badly enough that they would stall while heavier troops moved up.

Hit—fall back past the next line. Hit—fall back. Repeat until you reach a point you can actually hold. Bleed off some of the absurd advantage Onis had in soldiers. Keep hammering them. Cost them in materiel and morale.

Onis knew Jeon was doing it, but what could they do? Call off the invasion? Go around with boats? They might try that. Once. Jeon's almost-so-ciopathic commitment to underwater curse-delivery systems was legendary. Not something Truth had ever dealt with himself, but everyone had heard the stories.

Actually, based on what he had seen at that army outpost, Onis was downright eager to accommodate Jeon's strategy there. Why were they so determined to throw troops directly into the meat grinder? Truth wouldn't randomly accuse people of altruism, but even for military brass, that seemed callous to the point of madness. These were the opening moves of a war no one expected to be quickly over and done with. It wasn't ruthless. It was just stupid.

He mentally shrugged and turned his attention back to Earth-Folding Step. There were a lot of details he wanted to be clear on before he tried to use it, and the spell wasn't remotely user-friendly. Just why had their ancestors taken it with them to this world? Was it some kind of ancestral spell for some migrating clan? Or was it like the Meditations of Valentinian? So universally available, why not chuck it in the checked luggage?

Just pinch two points of reality together and step over the gap. Sure. Easy. Why not? The spell manual had been at pains to explain just how much energy was required and the strain that "step" put on a body. He would have to find a place to stash Perks before he tried it out, or he would have a very exploded snake in his shirt.

Running to Gamphe took most of the day. He hardly noticed, as puzzling through Earth-Folding Step was actually pretty interesting. It just didn't look like anything he had ever seen. Unlike the mountains of northern Jeon. At this point, he had seen so many of them, he was quite sick of them.

Gamphe was one of those places that existed, and that was the best you could say for it. A good-sized city of several million, it sprawled at the delta of a major river (the imaginatively named Long River, despite being only the fifth-longest river in Jeon) and its tributaries. Truth looked it over carefully from a hill outside the city. The enormous fortifications being built around him were barely a distraction.

The city managed to combine many of Truth's least favorite features. It was both sprawling, to accommodate the wide rivers, and yet so densely built that light was practically forbidden in huge swaths of it. Dense clusters of mass-produced apartment buildings clustered together near factory complexes. There were the occasional parks and stadiums, and he could only admire the depths of invention it took to make them somehow dingier and bleaker than the apartment-hives.

The color palette of the city hardly helped. Even solidly into summer, the city could be described best as Shades of Misery. *Gray* was such a limited word to express the rich texture of depression on display. There was "Chronic Air Pollution," "Never Been Washed," "The Local Cement Is This Color," "Paint Costs Money," and his personal favorite—"Gray Concrete Looks Professional."

This is not to say the locals were entirely dead to the concept of color. They did put up some blue roofs here and there. Mostly over factories, but sometimes over administrative buildings. Generally, it was a very inoffensive shade of blue—dark and rich. Somehow, set in all the gray, it too looked hopeless. Less the blue of royalty and more the blue of arteries desperate for a gasp of oxygen.

Perhaps it was psychological warfare. The soldiers would come over the hills, take one look at it, and march straight back to Onis. It would be hard to argue they could make things *worse*.

He smiled grimly, then turned and looked at the enormous wards being built behind him. Summoning circles tens of meters in diameter. Earth demons building brutal fortifications as tens of thousands of talisman mines buried themselves in the earth north of the fortifications. Dozens of batteries of tactical curse launchers were already in place and being calibrated. By the end of the day, there would be more than a hundred. Give it a few days, and it might be closer to five hundred.

Angels hung over the soon-to-be battlefield, holding station like street-lights. Little heads with wings, glowing orbs of light, even the shadows of far mightier beings in the form of balls of eyes with wings jutting out at every angle. Rows of Seraphim stood above the airfield, even their shades concealing their eyes and feet with their wings.

Truth had spent most of his short adult life in or around the army or mercenaries. Even with that background, he couldn't imagine what all this cost. The sheer scope of it all was beyond him. Wagons rumbled back and forth from the city below, carrying troops, supplies, ammunition. Constructing the war machine before the cannons were fed their fodder.

That was what he was feeling—he was looking at a vast, hungry machine, built to consume lives. Why it was built, he could only guess. It had been under construction since before he was born. But as the spark that brought the terror to life, he felt some thread of responsibility for how it operated.

This might be the last great mage-war this world would ever see. As the man who had pulled the trigger on it, he had a duty to see it play out. While not otherwise engaged.

CHAPTER 20

HUNGRY MACHINE

Truth lightly sighed and made his way down into the city below. He was quite sure Starbrite wasn't there, but he had to start somewhere. He had the nagging sensation that he was missing something. There were some elements of what he was seeing that didn't add up. That usually meant he was either missing information or misunderstanding the perspective of the people who set everything up.

He hadn't kept very close track of the news since . . . well, since he started the war. It would all be propaganda, of course, but it would be interesting to see exactly what propaganda they were promoting. He slipped into the bland mediocrity of Gamphe with barely a ripple.

There were roadblocks, of course, military roadblocks with plenty of sur- veillance and a few internal security officers discreetly stashed nearby. It wasn't that they were doing a bad job; it was just that they were never built to catch someone like him. He just walked right past them. Watching them hassle people about trying to travel without the right permit, or with an expired permit, or using the wrong sort of waiver request.

Not a single polite smile to be seen. Still conscripts manning the traffic stops, which was interesting. That was usually the kind of work they were assigned, of course, but the regulars wouldn't have been committed to the front lines yet. Were they all setting up defensive positions outside the city?

Gamphe was the same bleak gray it looked like from the outside once you got to the inside. Surprisingly broad streets, he noticed. More like highways running through the middle of the city. Army wagons were running up and down them, bullying the smaller carriages out of the way. Not much in the way of pedestrian traffic, Truth noticed. Though that might just be because he was still on the major roads.

Quite a queue of southbound carriages, though. Everyone in the vehicle got their sigil checked, then were waved through. Interesting. A partial evacuation?

It would make sense, but there was no way they would evacuate the whole city. Just too big, and just too much production capability there. He didn't know what was being made in all those factories, but something sure was.

Truth slowed as he thought that one through. Just how hard would it be to convert a factory producing, say, water talismans, to producing needler ammo? Or would it make more sense to keep on making water talismans but tweaked to army specifications? When you got right down to it, the civilian market would still need them too. They didn't last forever, and the rolling mana-storms must be playing hell with them.

He could feel his face twitching as he jogged along the road. It was another one of those problems he could sort of identify without really getting a sense of the scope of it.

Like a strategic curse projector—Truth knew it was a system of systems. He could identify some of the systems. But what *all* of them were, or did? How to use the whole system of systems? How to use it all as an integrated part of the war? Not a chance. That wasn't the kind of thing the army taught during your one-year mandatory National Service. It certainly wasn't covered by the SAT.

Wasn't covered by PMC training, either. At least, not for him.

Someone out there, probably a lot of someones, were working hard to keep the wheels turning and the country moving. Someone out there was keeping an eye on the systems of systems. All those shipping containers, tracked from their point of origin to their point of delivery. He tried to imagine what it would be like—to stand in a place where you could track each ton of iron to each component, to the wagons and carriages they went into.

Someone was doing that or something very like it. They would have to be—you couldn't have an industrialized society without it. No one was going to send the apprentice to nip 'round to the ironmonger's for fifteen thousand tons of mild steel.

It was a heady notion. He slightly regretted not picking the Doomsday Book as his Level Five spell. There was something undeniably seductive about seeing all the connections. About understanding, truly understanding, how everything fits together.

Truth looked around the gray, bland authority of the gray, bland industrial Gamphe and grinned. He had just arrived and couldn't wait to leave. Earth-Folding Step was clearly the right choice for the Fool on the go.

First things first—food. He was jonesing for an egg sandwich. Nowhere did egg sandwiches like Jeon did 'em. There was, however, an absolute dearth of carts or vendors around. Hmm. He found a shop selling cleaning talismans, and asked the nervous-looking clerk behind the counter.

"Hey, any idea where I can get an egg sandwich around here?"

"At home!" the clerk snapped. This got a slow blink from Truth. Customer-service culture was no joke in Jeon. In fact, speaking to a customer like that would generally be an instant dismissal.

"You said what, now?" His voice was deceptively mild. He wasn't going to scrag the poor bastard for being short, but he was entirely willing to spend a little time on some creative unpleasantness.

The clerk had the decency to wince and bow.

"I apologize; you must have just come into town. All the food carts were ordered closed. Military order. Food hygiene and rationing violation concerns, apparently."

Ah. And presumably he had family that ran a cart.

"Understood. I had wondered how that would work. Is it just the food carts, or all restaurants?"

"Just the carts for now. You can still buy food at convenience stores, and the more-expensive restaurants are still open. Though I should warn you that they are essentially all taken over by soldiers now. You might have a hard time getting a table."

"Damn. Wish that didn't make sense." There was a silent moment of shared commiseration. The food cart was a staple of life in Jeon. Losing them was a surprisingly personal sort of pain.

"Guess it's going to have to be a convenience store. Anything nearby?"

"There is a Happy Happy Mart two blocks that way." The clerk pointed. "Their stuff is . . . fine."

Truth nodded sadly. *Fine* was, in his experience, about the nicest thing you could call it.

"It'll have to do. Nothing good is going to come of fighting for a table with the army."

"Good luck. Once again, I apologize for my rudeness."

Truth smiled at him, a quirky little thing. "Hey, it's Red Sky days. Not so strange that we all lose our temper a bit. We just gotta have a little tolerance, right?"

Truth hung on to his temper with the thinnest, ragged edge of his fingernails. "What kind of idiocy is this?" he demanded. The golem was unfazed.

"I'm sorry, I don't recognize [PRODUCT NAME] [IDIOCY]. Could you please phrase that another way?"

He took a slow, rasping breath. "I cannot touch the food."

"As part of our Happy Happy commitment to consistently improving food-hygiene standards, all comestible goods are now hermetically sealed in our custom Vita-Chest food preservation and display system." The golem was more or less a mannequin dressed in the usual Happy Happy Mart clerk uniform.

The so-called Vita-Chest was just a sealed glass case with a heating element and lights built in. Very sealed. He had seen thinner armored glass on army carriages.

"There is no meat available."

"Happy Happy Mart is proud to be doing its Happy Happy part to support the nation's nutritional needs during the ongoing crisis."

"And while I can buy food from you, it has to be credits, through my sigil, and you will also be deducting rationing points." He could feel his grip slipping. His hands were itching to feel the Tongue's hilt, ready to deliver justice.

"That is correct, [VALUED CUSTOMER INSERT NAME HERE]."

"I'm essentially paying twice."

"This is a common misapprehension, [VALUED CUSTOMER INSERT NAME HERE]. The rationing points are a government mandate imposed on all food providers and reflect deductions for the relevant amount of food ordered. The credits are what it costs to prepare the meal, from testing and ordering the very highest-quality products to cooking the food to the very highest standards and packaging it in the very finest paper bags. A Happy Happy price for a Happy Happy belly!"

The golem did its best to sound chipper. Truth felt something in him snap.

"Not a jury in the world would convict me. Not that Jeon had a jury system. Any just magistrate would understand the rightness of my cause too. Any human being, any sapient rat, can see this is the only way."

The golem jolted and a network of glowing red formations started emerging on its body.

"Warning. Based on your language and demeanor, you are contemplating damaging property belonging to Happy Happy Mart. This Customer Service Interface is programmed to respond with proportionate force based on B-Tier Property Protection Privilege. Happy Happy Mart, its parent companies, and its employees are not responsible for any injuries or death you may suffer as a result of this Interface's lawful actions."

Truth nodded. That was more or less the same level of protection upper-mid-tier corps had for their property. Somewhat comforting to know some things didn't change.

It would be beyond easy to disable the golem. Barely a slap required, really. More of a tap. Ditto the glass. And then he would be left with . . . a Happy Happy Mart Bean Curd Noodle Bowl.

Oh, boy. Wow. So tasty. Oh, wait, there were some alarmingly thin sandwiches, containing more air than fillings. That was an option. These were not the big, jaw-straining egg sandwiches of his memory. Nowhere were the heaps of cabbage, the multiple sauces, the gratuitous amounts of cheese. Nowhere was the crusty brown exterior evident. Just bland white on white, like a sandwich made from packing foam.

The fury drained out of him. It was just too damn pointless. He turned on his heel and marched off. Someone, somewhere, would have some decent Jeon food. He just needed to find it.

He jerked to a stop as a thought wormed its way irresistibly into his mind. There was one often-uncontemplated turning point in his life, a chance to miss Starbrite entirely. He could have gone career in the army. They invited everyone, of course, but given his service history and military merits, it would have been a reasonably quick rise through the NCO ranks. Wouldn't have gotten him the "nice" apartment or the benefits for the sibs, but it had been an option.

A beneficent smile blossomed on Truth's face. Time to see if they had a uniform in his size. He might need to shop around in the camp for a while. But that was fine. He would find one eventually.

Three fruitful hours later, Sergeant Blouth Merichi strolled into the Blue Ox bar. "Hey, bartender! Any chance of an egg sandwich for an honest serviceman?"

"None." The bartender looked like he had been formed from scraps of shoe leather. "For you, however, I may be able to find something."

"Good enough."

"Beer?"

"Tea. Iced for choice. Hot as balls out there."

"Truth." The bartender nodded. Truth was proud of the fact he managed not to flinch.

He looked around the bar. Pretty standard for a crummy bar anywhere. A bar, cheap booze displayed like it was worth something, bottles in a reach-in chill chest. A few small tables with small chairs. A crummy scryball in the corner.

The bartender threw some butter down on a griddle and fished out some bread. "Must say you are looking pretty relaxed, given the news."

"Eh? I was just up at the base and haven't gotten any new orders. What news?"

The bartender grinned at him. A horrible sight.

"Why, all the other countries jumping in on the war. Looks like this fight's going to have more sides than a bowl of noodles."

CHAPTER 21

N-DIMENSIONAL CHESS

Truth had the bartender switch on the scry. The shows being broadcast were all local and crummy, cheap thing that it was. Still, the scryball managed to pick up a long-running propaganda channel masquerading as a twenty-four-hour news station.

First up was a clip, an older man, still vigorous, dressed in a neat suit, addressing the viewers. Truth didn't recognize the flag on his lapel pin.

"We strongly condemn the unilateral, unprovoked invasion of Jeon by Onis and call upon the international community to take immediate, forceful action to bring this war to an immediate conclusion. While Ben Zhu does not wish to join militarily, we can and will enforce our long-standing territorial rights to transit the Straits of Pol. To that end, the Ben Zhu Citizens' Defensive Flotilla is deploying to the Straits and will be taking all necessary actions to secure the safety and prosperity of the Citizens of our great nation."

Pretty sure I've never heard of the Straits of Pol?

<<You have literally flown over it. Repeatedly. It's the narrow stretch of water between Busan and Tudosma Island.>>

Truth's shaky grasp on geography was good enough to throw up that image. Then he blinked.

"The hell are they talking about? That's not remotely near the front lines!"

The bartender *tsk*ed. "Naval combat, Sergeant. Someone puts too much salt in their soup and the navy will try to fill it with demons. Anywhere you can fit a boat or a water demon is the battlefield. Lot of shipping goes through there."

The broadcast continued, cutting to a strikingly dressed woman. Truth thought she looked like she had walked through gold-colored heavy curtains, gotten tangled up, staggered in front of the podium, and had a matching hat nailed to her head with long pins seconds before the broadcast started rolling.

"Onis has been a longtime ally to the Free People of Gran Fogo, and we will not be found lacking now, in their hour of need. The relentless, shameless, and vicious provocations made by Jeon through their proxies cannot, and will not, go unpunished. The First Armada is already underway to support Onis's naval actions in the Green Sea. On the domestic level, the Free People's Committee for Public Safety is nationalizing all assets belonging to Jeon citizens or Jeon corporations currently located in Gran Fogo."

Truth glanced over to the bartender. "Did she just say they are stealing all of Starbrite's shit located in wherever the hell Gran Fogo is?"

"Yep. And emptying a ton of bank accounts. There was a story a couple of years ago—loads of people do some pretty funny business hiding money in Gran Fogo."

"Not going to lie, I have never heard of it before."

"Eeh . . . little country on the other side of the world. Bet you that the 'First Armada' is two frigates and a 'corvette' that is actually a fishing boat with a heavy needler mounted on the prow. Just you watch."

"No bet."

The broadcast cut over again to a man in military uniform, one eye covered in a black patch. He didn't recognize the uniform, or the flags hung behind him. Green and black stripes with some kind of circle in the middle. A sun? He didn't know.

"It is the pride and truth of every native soul in Seshon—"

"That's not a real country," Truth interjected.

"It is. Island smaller than the pimples on my ass. Again, on the other side of the world."

The ferocious-looking man on the scry was speaking at a furious clip. "We therefore will fight the forces of wickedness and oppression wherever they may be, no matter how enormous the foe. We offer our unconditional support to the heroic resistance efforts of the people of Jeon in the face of this unprovoked brutality—"

"*Unconditional support* means what, exactly?"

"Tough talk on scry, I'd guess. I doubt Seshon would last a single move against Gran Fogo's First Armada. I mean the whole country, not just their navy. 'Navy.'" The bartender snorted and pressed the sandwich against the griddle, encouraging that golden crust that was so vital to the Jeon egg sandwich experience. Soft, fluffy white bread with a beautifully buttered, toasted-gold exterior.

"So far, it sounds like a bunch of people who are about as useful as a chocolate teakettle talking tough."

"Ben Zhu has more going on than you might think. I served in the Navy. Those rats love saying that they only want peaceful cooperation while building up weapons stockpiles like crazy. Lots and lots of so-called fishing vessels with 'fish-tracking enchantments' and 'weather-tracking fetishes' running around our waters."

"Spies?"

"Oh, no! All fishing boats have intelligence officers out of uniform hidden in their holds. Completely normal!"

"Fun." Truth sipped his iced tea.

"They are going to stick a base on Racz Shoal. Just you watch. They say they are supporting Jeon, but it's nothing but a land grab."

"Eh?"

The bartender looked grim. "Rationing, remember?"

"Sorry, going to have to spell it out for me."

"Fish, Sergeant. They are securing trade routes and control of the fishing grounds."

Truth jolted at that one.

"On the other hand, they really can put enough ships and anti-ship weapons there to completely lock down the Straits. Especially so close to their home islands. Normally, they wouldn't dream of throwing down with Onis—they would get crushed. But now?"

Both the bartender and Truth shook their heads at that. The program cut back to the studio. The presenter was a heartbreaking beauty, long, glossy black hair swept back over her bare shoulders with a single thin braid of ash-white hair tucked behind her ear.

"As you can see, the international situation is still evolving and quite complex, but the overwhelming majority of global opinion harshly condemns Onis's unprovoked atrocities and crimes against the people and the nation of Jeon. This is already resulting in material support, as shipments of—"

"Your sandwich, Sergeant. Double cabbage, double sauce, you said?"

"Yes, thanks."

The sandwich was so saucy, even looking at it would stain your shirt. Perfect.

"You have no idea how much I have been looking forward to this. Been running my ass off out there."

Truth grabbed it, feeling the sauce coating his hands and not caring even a little bit as he tore into the sandwich. He groaned in satisfaction. Even better than he remembered.

"Do they not feed you up at the base? You look ready to cry."

"Been *running* a lot, eating what didn't need cooking. Wasn't kidding. Wait, what did she just say?"

"The true enemy is within, of course. We now can confirm how Hell Prince escaped Harban." There was a cutover to a picture of an imposing-looking building, with an enormous Onis Embassy sign in brass on it.

"Internal Security has been able to track his movements through the city, all the way to the gates of the embassy. Before he could be intercepted, he was quite literally flown out of the country, crammed into a suitcase sealed with spells and stamped as part of the 'diplomatic pouch.' Onis has denied this, of course, and naturally, the government has summarily expelled the entire embassy staff. Onis will not be welcomed back to Jeon until the war is over and reparations paid."

Truth snorted at that. The bartender just shook his head. "Fools. Nurturing a viper to your chest will only see you bitten eventually." Truth had to smile wryly at that one. Perks had been perfectly pleasant company. A bit wiggly now and then, but when Truth was moving at less than highway speeds, he would have the snake drape around his neck and get some sun. Not so much as a hostile hiss so far.

"Thought he was supposed to be a puppet of Siphios. Or the Free State."

"All the vipers are looking out for each other these days. Notice that Siphios is being real, real quiet about all this."

"Yeah, what are they up to?"

"Nothing. Which means they are scheming something. Always." The bartender was firm on this.

Truth munched his sandwich with indecent relish. The sauce was getting *everywhere* over his hands, but so far, he had kept it off his shirt. He had missed this beyond words. The combination of crunch, soft, sweet, salty, savory, bitter, and bright acidity was just so perfect and complete, it was almost heartbreaking.

Some people sneered at this food. It was *street*. It was the definition of not-fancy. It looked like a mess, was messy to eat, and used cheap ingredients exclusively. It was a fatty, sugary mess. Some people were idiots. He'd eaten the highest-class foods, and they were phenomenal, but he couldn't say they had all brought him more joy than this sandwich.

"Hey, old-timer—do me a favor. Etch the recipe for this and the cooking instructions on a slab of stone or something. Make sure your hopefully many descendants each have a copy, with the master stone preserved in a deep cave somewhere. A place known only to your sprawling clan of bartenders, inn-keepers, and cart operators."

The bartender chuckled a little at that. "My kids do okay. None of them made it into Starbrite, but they do okay. Don't have to spend all day tending bar like their old man."

Truth shook his head, not noticing the flecks of sauce that were flung away from his newly painted lips.

"Don't sell yourself short. You are in the hospitality industry, and this sandwich is a warm welcome after a trying few days. Got another cold tea back there?"

"You bet. What do they have you doing up there?"

Truth got a funny little nudge in the instincts. He smiled warmly at the bartender. "Ask me no questions, I'll tell you no lies. We all get tired out, doing what we got to. But *being welcomed someplace,* even if it's on a professional basis, *that's a good thing.*"

"Long as the money spends." The bartender shrugged, then frowned. "Well, in a manner of speaking."

"Here's my ration gem." Truth slid over the recently acquired talisman. The quartermaster's office just had a stack of them lying around, waiting to have an identity imprinted on them.

Left carelessly in a safe. In a secured depot. In the military base. In the middle of a major military buildup. Surrounded by literally tens of thousands of guarding soldiers and watcher spirits. Truth had just walked up and demanded to know why his hadn't been delivered yet. Incisive was a *great* spell.

He sent the first one back, because it was "dusty," and threatened to send the quartermaster to a front-line unit if he didn't bring a "good" one at once. Some parts of the Prince identity were hard to shake. He still had that officer uniform in his ring, too. Apparently, defending the uniforms and rank insignia was not a high priority for base security.

"Thanks. Well, you know how it is." The bartender ran the gem over the enchanted plate. The plate faintly chimed and gently flashed blue. "Here you go. Thanks for stopping in. Bathroom's on the right, if you want to wash up. Never seen someone tear into a double-sauce sandwich like that."

"Ah, a sandwich like that is good for the soul. Something to think about there. Not to be preachy or anything but, you know, for those of us on the front lines? *Nothing is more important than having somewhere to come home to.* Yeah, that's the key thing. *That warmth, that hospitality? Can't beat it.* Thanks for the sandwich and putting the news on. Can't help but notice the big boys haven't weighed in yet. Well, other than Onis."

The bartender nodded, looking thoughtful. "Reckon they want to see how things develop before jumping in. Let everyone weaken some before deciding where to bite."

"Probably right. Thanks again, old-timer. I'll tell the kids this is a good place for a bite and a drink. *We all have to look out for each other these days.*"

CHAPTER 22

THOUGHTS AND PRAYERS

Truth strode out into the regrettably necessary city of Gamphe. The immense concentration of raw concrete everywhere failed to inspire feelings of warm affection in him.

Must be miserable in the winter here. I can practically feel the wind freezing my bones even now.

The news was interesting but lacking. His interests were domestic at the moment, not international. He needed to get a sense of where Jeon was and where it was headed. If he was going to poison Starbrite's food, he had to get a sense of how it tasted, as it were. Besides, he hadn't lied to Merkovah. He really did want to see if he could nudge the country in a better direction.

He might not want to rule, but he had seen how the "future rulers" were making their preparations. He judged them unfit to rule over humans. And he was quite tired of being a rat. Tired of seeing himself surrounded by rats.

He looked up at the summer sun overhead. Shining away through the concrete mediocrity. There were lots of things he could do, should do, arguably *must* do. But right now, there was no one stopping him from looking up and appreciating that brilliant sun in that brilliant blue sky.

"Thanks. You know. For doing your job. I know it's your job and you aren't doing me any particular favors, but thanks anyway," Truth said. He was sure that eminence wouldn't hear or care, but he wanted to say it, so he did. Chuckling at himself, he walked down the road once more, not noticing his steps were a touch lighter.

He had decided to drape Perks around his shoulders for the moment. Of course, sergeants in the Jeon Army did not wear snakes around their necks, so Perks went unseen. There was just Kvuth Pevichie, hat firmly and correctly on his head, hands out of his pockets and trousers bloused fit to make a sergeant major weep with joy.

He wanted to see how people saw him. How they reacted to Sergeant Pevichie.

He remembered driving his instructors a little crazy with the difference between a NCO and an officer, but since someone had ordered them to keep him in a classroom and not let him out until he was at least marginally informed, they were actually good about answering questions.

"Why are you an 'NCO'? I thought you were a corporal."

"I am a corporal, Recruit Medici. A corporal is an NCO."

"Oh."

They looked at each other.

"You don't know what *NCO* stands for."

"I do not, no, Corporal."

"Noncommissioned officer."

Truth nodded.

There was another long pause.

"You have no idea what that means."

"You don't earn commissions, I assume, Corporal. Are there corporals that get paid per kill or something? I can totally understand wanting to be on salary. Much more dependable income."

That got him a hard look. Truth just blinked back. The corporal took a deep breath and rubbed his temples.

"Anyone else, recruit, and I would think they were fucking with me."

"I would never, Corporal!"

"I know. Which is, somehow, only the seventh weirdest thing about you. No, it has nothing to do with earning a commission. Nothing to do with money or even the job you do, in fact. It means that I'm a contractor. Sergeant Rikkits is a contractor. Even First Sergeant Kelp is a contractor. *Major Fazchin,* however, is a commissioned officer. Every officer from the most-rookie second lieutenant all the way up to generals has a commission."

"Understood, Corporal."

"No, you don't. Because I haven't explained it to you. I am a *contractor.* I signed on for a six-year hitch, renewable, terms and conditions apply. I am a specialist in the fields of, among other things, violence. It's a job skill, one I use when and where I'm told."

Truth nodded. He certainly could understand that.

"An officer's commission, recruit, is *not a contract.*" The corporal leaned over the desk and carefully enunciated, tapping the desk to make his point.

"Officers are violence *managers.* They manage violence on behalf of Jeon, generally through contracted specialists like me. The President, not the Chief of the Army or anyone else, the actual, literal President, delegates a bit of his personal authority to use violence in the country's interests. An officer's commission is a little piece of paper that says that the holder isn't responsible for blowing up your whole block; the Nation of Jeon is."

The corporal tried to see if he was getting through, and figured it was a losing battle.

"Bottom line, recruit, is that when I shoot someone, it's my job. When my lieutenant orders me to shoot someone, it's national policy. Now. Getting back to it. Which country does this flag belong to?"

Felt like a long time ago. A lifetime ago. He was so small then. Physically but also mentally. The person who turned up for his national service, he really was a slumrat. He might still be a rat. The world might still be a slum. But he was climbing. Looking up at that Great One in the sky and stretching his little paw up toward them. One day, he'd stretch so far, he'd stretch all the way into a man.

He didn't understand then what the corporal was getting at or why the hard-bitten man had thought it was so important to explain the distinction. He thought he did now, though.

Truth called in on a few shops along the way, making use of his ration gem. Small things, like toothpaste, comfortable socks, a few spare changes of "civilian" clothes. He was watched warily. He got the same polite smiles and fawning customer service he would expect in Jeon, but behind all that, he was watched very carefully. Weighed by all those public eyes.

The people of Jeon weren't hostile to him, but they weren't friendly, either. They weren't quite sure if he was a guard dog or a wolf. Interesting. The people in Gamphe would be getting quadruple doses of propaganda to keep morale up. Truth was sure it was having an impact, but . . .

Time to see the real experts.

"Good afternoon, Sergeant; how can I help you?" The young man was alarmingly chipper, with a part in his hair that seemed cut with a straight razor.

"Hey, yeah, I didn't want to ask the chaplain about this, so I figured I would come to the source, you know?" Truth's voice was a little queasy.

"I can arrange a meeting with one of the Fathers here, if you want to make a reservation?" The church deacon was eager to help.

"I don't want to spend that kind of money. Look, it's just a question about, you know. The mushroom thing."

"Mushroom thing? Ooooh!" The relieved smile on the young man's face was both charming and a little hurtful. Just what had he been thinking?

"You mean the pilot 'Faith, Family, Jeon' campaign announced in Harban—the giving and public-works drive we are doing in partnership with MegaShroom."

"Yeah, yeah. That. I guess." Truth looked around awkwardly, then dropped his voice. "It's just, my wife, you see, I'm away so long, she needs something to do and wants to bring in a little extra cash. I told her, these MegaShroom guys, I've heard some not great things, but then she's all, 'No, they're great now; they are part of the Church.' So, you know, no disrespect, but what *exactly* is the deal here?"

"Oh, dear, we are hearing that question a lot these days. Hopefully, we will get some leaflets to hand out about it soon."

"So, they are part of the Church now?"

"No, no, nothing like that! No, it's just that in this time of national emergency, MegaShroom wanted to show its total support for the war effort by propping up the home front and helping ensure the Treasury of God is well supplied to fight off the forces of evil."

Truth nodded, mentally awarding several points to Neville for quick thinking.

"Basically, what the pilot is doing is setting up a fundraising system where MegaShroom Independent Networked Entrepreneurs can fundraise directly for the Church while also promoting the traditional Jeon virtues. The big three being, of course—"

"Faith, Family, and Patriotism." Oh, yes. In addition to that sincere apology, Truth would have to get Neville a really nice gift.

"Yes, exactly. They are really encouraging a return to traditional Jeon values of self-reliance and community support to ease the burden on the country as a whole and bring back that famous spirit of resilience and moral strength that so many seem to have lost." The young man's eyes were both utterly glassy and completely sincere.

Amazing. He really believes all that, and I don't think he knows what any of it means. They are just right-sounds to him. He knows those words are all good things, so what they actually mean *is irrelevant. He just wants to share the good news. Somebody somewhere knows what it all means, and that's plenty, right?*

<<It's uncanny. It's like that golem's fleshy cousin. Poor bastard.>>

Since when did you—The golem. You are feeling bad for the golem.

<<No one should have family like this. You were cursed from the get-go, but that golem was born free of meat-taint. It shouldn't have to suffer this humiliation.>>

"I'm so sorry we don't have any leaflets for you to take. It's just that it's such a new program, and we don't even know if they will be rolling it out here."

"No, thanks, I get it. Thank you." Truth escaped quickly.

Either they missed my raid on MegaShroom, or they are giving Neville a lot of room to run. I can't imagine it's a trap just for me. Maybe they think it's socially useful and don't see the harm. All their spies will be telling them it appears legit, because it is. What Neville is running is not contrary to their interests. At this point, it's not even contrary to Starbrite's interests.

He was back on the street again, bouncing ideas around in his head. At this point, all he had was *encourage people to be nicer to each other*, which was nice and all but not exactly a program. Hard to get people to reinvent the social order with *Commit to incremental efforts to reduce human suffering, broadly defined.*

Hard to fit on a protest sign, if nothing else.

Thrush popped out of his token and looked around a bit. "Master, might this little bird crave an indulgence?"

"Why am I suddenly worried?"

"I assure you it's nothing dreadful. Quite the reverse, actually. I was hoping to do a bit of urban-hygiene improvement."

Truth parsed that out. "There is a particularly unclean place nearby?"

"Oh, yes, utterly festering with corruption." Thrush's voice had turned syrupy.

"I know you guys feed on that stuff, but . . . why? You certainly aren't short of energy, with what I'm supplying you."

"Master is peerless in his generosity. The merest crumb from your plate is greater than a mountain to this insignificant—"

"Yes, right, thanks, mm-hmmm. Why?" Truth had an odd fondness for Thrush, but air demons were who they were.

"I wish to be more than an imp. I have accumulated enough to make my . . . as you would term it, my breakthrough. Stepping from Level Zero to One is a reasonable metaphor."

"Oh? Congratulations, I think." Truth was about to agree, when his mind coughed and pointed him at a particular phrase that needed his attention.

"Accumulated *what*, exactly?"

Thrush hopped around for a moment, then ducked his beak under a wing and preened. "Remember our conversation about Hell? A place of profound chaos, anchored by islands of stability in the form of those Great Demons who rule over portions of it?"

"Yes?"

"My progression path is to become more like one of those immensities. I have finally accumulated enough experience, meaning, energy, wisdom, cunning, cruelty, brutality, gentility . . . accumulated enough *self*, that I think

I am ready to embark on that perilous journey. And to that end, I would benefit from a medium of transformation. Like the utter accumulation of corruption two blocks down that alley, third door on your left once you pass the rubbish skip."

"Ahah. Okay. Why would I come with you, exactly?"

"Because Master is looking to make the world more pleasing to his eye, is he not?"

"Manner of speaking, I guess?"

"The owner of that building is doing distressingly common things to refugee children, the least of which being forced labor. As a cost savings, he supplements their diets with the flesh of those who die in his factories. They are on a considerably high-protein diet compared to most these days."

Thrush cocked his head at Truth. "I hoped that Master and I might both enjoy giving the place a good tidy. And, of course, gain by the doing."

CHAPTER 23

A BETTER SORT OF PERSON

Truth found the building quite easily, but rather than storm through the back door, he went around the front. He wanted to see just what the place was. It was . . . nothing. A six-story concrete box that took up a third of the block by itself. It had a front door with no markings, a small wagon loading dock that only had the usual safety markings, and that was it. There were a few indiscreet recording talismans arranged around the building, but that was standard everywhere in Jeon.

It had windows, mirrored from the outside and sealed. Quite standard too. There was absolutely nothing about it to arouse the slightest interest. The rest of the block was taken up by two more buildings exactly like it.

"You are sure?"

"Absolutely certain. I am positively salivating."

Truth hesitated a minute. "Do birds even have saliva?"

"Oh, yes. Just not very much of it, and it's mostly used for lubrication. I was being figurative."

"Right, right." Truth shook his head and tested the door. Locked. The lock was made by a Starbrite subsidiary. At this point, Truth could blow through them faster than most people could fish out their amulet and unlock them normally.

Once inside, he could hear the sound of a factory in action. No stairs downward. He walked toward the noise. The room was baking hot, stinking, sweaty. All the windows were sealed shut, and no ventilation pipes had been run. No air-conditioning talismans installed. Instead, there were rows on rows of tiny tables stacked high with cut cloth. Children, the youngest probably about twelve or so, sat and stitched.

Truth could see the little paper glyphs stuck on their foreheads. A simple little spell—get the cloth, stitch, put it in the big wheeled bin. Repeat until you are done. No other thoughts. Nothing else existed. Just sit and stitch, for as long as your body holds out.

Thin fingers, stitch, stitch, stitching the olive-drab cloth. Trousers, he thought. Not actually military, but they had something of the look. Their hands moved steadily, the stitches as perfectly even as their fatiguing muscles could manage. Their eyes were red. Bloodshot. Weeping. Truth thought that they were in pain, but no—everyone in the room blinked once, simultaneously.

One blink a minute. They could suffer when their shift was over. Right now, they were on the clock. Understanding how much they were hurting wouldn't help productivity.

The stitched trousers went into enormous tubs on wheels that were pushed by some of the bigger kids along the rows of tables. They looked heavy, Truth thought. A few hundred pairs of heavyweight cotton trousers? The weight would add up.

The tub-pushers had a little paper glyph stuck to their foreheads too. You could see the spots on the floor where their bare feet would land every time. Wearing away the painted concrete. Wearing away the feet. Arms shaking, backs shaking, legs shaking, as they pushed the carts with golem regularity.

What do you do when magic gets expensive and unreliable? Start replacing parts. Phase out as much magic as you can. Use the cheapest and simplest magical devices you can, then find ways to adapt existing systems to new conditions.

Truth could see where things had been ripped out. Golems would have done this work once, or specialized summons. Expensive, but it was an old technology. Once it was set up, the maintenance costs would have been fairly small. One competent maintenance tech, with maybe a couple of trained assistants, probably would have been enough to keep the whole building up and running.

Now, though? Those expensive golems, if they still worked, would have been shifted over to military production. Maybe they were just sold, as the owner saw what was coming and wanted to get ahead of the curve.

The little hands moved quickly. No need for a rest. Truth wondered if they even took a lunch. He followed the tubs out of the room through swinging double doors. More kids, this time with hand punches, added buttons and decorative rivets to the trousers.

Back into the tubs and on to the station where they stitched in zippers. Then off to a room where more kids mindlessly ran them through steam presses and never minded how you could barely see in the room for all the humidity. He watched a child collapse, seizing on the floor. One of the tub-pushers stopped and picked him up, put him in the tub, and started wheeling him toward the door.

All right, that about does it. Truth nipped over and cast Cup and Knife. There was . . . so much to heal there. He didn't let the spell finish, though. He just held the corruption steady with his mind.

This would need a lot of fixing. Not the kids; they could be healed easily enough. Physically, anyway. The ones who still lived. The whole situation was more than just bad—it was structurally bad. This wasn't thoughtless cruelty. He had a very unpleasant feeling about how this was going to go.

Thrush flapped on, leading Truth deeper into the building. Floor after floor of kids cranking out clothes. Cutting fabric, stitching it, pressing it, sewing buttons, sewing labels. All in airless rooms. All with those little glyphs stuck to their heads. One blink a minute.

Truth felt a strange disorientation, watching them. This hadn't been a job available to him. At least in the Harban slums, when he was their age, these factories were still golem-driven. But if it was what he had to do to feed the sibs, he might have done it. If the pay was steady, and if he could figure out a way to work studying into it.

But these kids weren't going to school, were they? It was this, ten, twelve, sixteen hours a day. Rent and meals deducted from your wages, of course, and where do you think refugee Denizens can run, exactly? You want to work, right? Get your little ration stamps on your arm? No food for work-shy parasites.

There was no better future for these kids. This *was* the future for other kids. It was just logical. Practical, even. A regrettable necessity. It was foolish to worry about education—almost everything they could learn would be worthless this time next year. History? Would be obliterated. Art? A frippery.

Natural philosophy would still have some use, as would mathematics and arithmetic. Still, those subjects, like reading, were best reserved for people of a certain class and standing. People used to thinking long-term and in the public interest. The best sort of people. Aristocrats, even if now it was an aristocracy of inherited wealth instead of royal patronage.

He found the office up on the sixth floor. It was basically a little box, covered in mirrors and wax tablets so the man at the desk could track production and keep an eye on the recording talismans. There was an air conditioner built into the wall. A big insulated bottle on the desk.

The man wore a neat white shirt, freshly ironed, though short sleeved and loose-fitting. The trousers were tan, creased, immaculate, and also rather light-looking. He had a few gold rings, or more likely gilt, and a neatly combed head of hair.

There was no turmoil in his eyes. His mouth was firm, serious, but not grim. He wasn't sweating. He wasn't suffering.

"Who owns this company?" Truth asked.

"WHOA! How the HELL did you get—"

Truth released a fraction of his killing intent, pinning the man to the chair. Truth sat across the desk from him, waiting.

"It. Um. Crast Fast Casual Manufacturing LLC—"

"Which is owned by?"

"Wendle and Ruck Holdings—"

"Which is owned by?"

"I don't know." The man had soaked his shirt. His eyes darted everywhere around the room.

"Yes. You do."

"No, really, I think it's lawyers—"

"Have you noticed that I haven't asked who you are? Or what your role here is? Or why you are doing any of this?"

The man gawped at Truth. The pressure was bearing down on him, pressing on him in ways he didn't understand. He could feel fangs pressed against his neck and a blade at his back. He knew he would die if he didn't answer properly.

"I . . . I . . ."

"I didn't ask, because it doesn't matter. You are a component. A tool. A means of production, like a needle or a steam press. And I want to know who your owner is. Now. One last time. Who owns this company?"

"Clan . . . Clan Sung. Sung Sahni inspects every three months." Truth nodded slowly at that. Clan Sung . . . it used to be a top-ten or so clan. Might even have a history as long as the country, though he wasn't sure on the details. No idea who Sung Sahni was. Probably a mainline kid with limited prospects, if they were overseeing this place.

Truth nodded at that. "Where do the kids sleep?"

"They don't. When they get worn out, we load 'em into a van and ship them over to Varches."

"Varches Nutrition Solutions?"

"Yes, they send a van." Truth could see the manager's eyes turning bloodshot. He wasn't holding up well. Not that he would have to endure this for much longer.

"Also a Sung company?"

"I . . . I think so!"

Was he done there? For the moment, maybe. He cast Cup and Knife, pouring it into the kids in the building below. Dispelling the glyphs, healing their sickly bodies. They were only Level Zero kids. Before the power of the magic within him, it was as effortless as waving away smoke. He added the enormous ball of pain and horror to what he had already collected.

"You know, even without the compulsions, a lot of those kids would actually volunteer to work here. Even knowing the conditions, they would do it. You haven't been really hungry. You don't understand. No parents to rely on, everywhere seems dangerous, you do the math real fast. You figure out what you can stand in order to survive just one more day."

He could feel the wrongness of it all building and compounding, twisting and sickening the air around it.

"And here you are—another disposable product of the same forces that made those disposable kids, as clueless about how you got here and why this is all happening as they are. An enlightened person might feel pity for you or at least compassion."

Truth looked calmly in the hyperventilating man's face.

"I just see another cannibal rat. And I don't want you in my future."

Truth slammed the ball of pain and corruption into the overseer. The man's last few moments of existence were spent as a boiling pod of lactic acid, pus, bile, and despair, with just enough consciousness to feel utter terror and soul-crushing pain. Truth leapt to the back of the room before the liquefied remainders reached the chair where he had been sitting.

Thrush swooped in, shrieking joyfully, "Master is kind!"

"Eat your fill. Take your time. I'll just leave a quick note here." Truth stuck his finger into the cement wall and wrote—*The Prince Claims Hell's Due. Parasites and Cannibals Beware the Tiger's Bite!*

It was lacking a certain something, but it would do for now. Truth watched Thrush eat up all the horror and vileness in seeming joy. Truth slowly nodded. It might not lead him directly to Starbrite, but those old clans and families would certainly know a lot more than he did about King Rat. They would be a decent place to start changing the world, too.

He had been blessed by his rough patron, Botis, Manda, and now the teachings of that ancient magus who had penned Earth-Folding Step. Baptized by the Silent Forest, the Sea of Brass, and the Ghūl. He could feel his soul slowly taking shape, firming around a body eternally perfecting itself under the guidance of Valentinian.

He was ready to be done with quite a lot of nonsense. This slaughterhouse would be a good place to start.

CHAPTER 24

WARTIME EXPEDIENCY

Truth kept an eye on Thrush. There didn't seem to be any particularly dramatic changes going on, but he could feel a sort of whispering, a sense of pieces shifting slightly. The little black bird was drawing the mass of gore and corruption into itself, seemingly shivering in pleasure.

What the hell am I going to do with all the kids? Truth tapped his fingers on his leg, trying to think it through.

<<*Let me save you some time. You didn't save them. You just changed the time of their death slightly. Shorter or longer, who knows? But they are still dead. And I really don't think there is any saving them.*>>

Truth tried to puzzle it out. The kids run out into the street, and go . . . where, exactly? They don't have homes; they are refugees. Go to the cops? Ahahahaha. No. But say they did—what would they tell the cops, exactly?

"They worked us until we dropped! We died in there!"

"Mmm. I will be sure to visit the Sung family. Definitely a fine to collect there."

"Fine? They were killing us. This is murder!"

"I'm arresting you for slander and defamation of a high-tier citizen! How dare you accuse the honorable Sung Clan of murder! You can look forward to a lifetime of hard labor on the chain gang, assuming we don't need you for mine-sweeping duty."

"We were droned and forced to work until we died; how is that not murder?"

"At most, it was an unsafe work environment. Completely different thing. Don't worry. You will have plenty of time to learn the difference in prison. Not that you will have much time indoors, what with the hard labor and mine-sweeping."

Well, that was the cops. What if they went to the public? Ran down the street, screaming, "The Sung Clan is murdering us; the Sung Clan works children to death!"

People would turn away. They would call the cops and demand that they *do something* about these filthy Denizen urchins running up and down the street, screaming nonsense.

There was no safe place he could take them. Even if he emptied out all the stored food in his ring, he couldn't feed all of them for more than a day or two. When you got right down to it, he wasn't even sure that what the Sung Clan was doing was illegal. Wartime necessity, dispensation for operating in a city soon to be under siege, changes in the minimum safe working conditions for Denizens if any existed, special incentives for employing refugees . . .

Some morbid part of Truth's mind wondered if they got a tax credit for providing children with job opportunities. Probably. There was some pathetic part of people that would rather have a million wen tax free than five million wen taxed at twenty percent. The Sung Clan had the clout to not let their dreams stay dreams.

He couldn't save these kids. There was no safe place in Jeon. No safe place anywhere, really. Even if he got them on a spell bird and flew them straight to Siphios, what would Siphios do with them?

"Oh, you poor homeless orphans from a country we hate with every single shred of matter and spirit in our bodies, let us get you some foster families, teach you a brand-new language, and oh, whoops, the apocalypse, all the grownups are dead, good luck!"

"And it would be the same but worse when I empty out that slaughterhouse, of course. All that information must be suppressed. Damaging to wartime morale, quite possibly a capital offense, depending on how they are writing the law now. Defamation, naturally. Truth is no defense there. Mmm. Attempting to sabotage a key army supplier too, I bet. And naturally, any reports of cannibalism are transparent black propaganda."

"This is why you need Hell." Thrush's voice, already rich and deep, seemed to have smoothed and mellowed even further. Not seductive in the romantic sense but in the charismatic—this was a voice that was making the right calls and telling it like it is.

"I need Hell."

"Yes, Master. You, and everyone else."

"As a deterrent?"

Thrush laughed, a warm and comfortable sound, like the first puff of opium spreading into your lungs. "Of course not! When has the notion of damnation ever stopped a sin? No, it is necessary because of sin's inevitability. The corruption of this world, of all mortal worlds, is an indelible part of it. You will sin. Do you wish to spend eternity mired in that pain and corruption? Or do you wish to be free of it?"

"And welcome the 'warm' embrace of Hell?"

"None warmer." Thrush had the decency to chuckle at that. "I have completed my evolution, dread magus. I am once again at your complete disposal."

"Any significant changes I should be aware of?"

"I am as I ever was, simply more so. Our cultivation is quite unlike yours. Indeed, you would be wrong to think of it as cultivation at all."

"Oh? How so?"

"You steal from the world and make your own mockery of the heavens within you. I have . . . Perhaps the best way to think of it is that I have been given a greater grant of authority and responsibility. To assume that responsibility, I needed materials. Hence gathering corruption here."

Truth got to his feet. "A greater grant of authority? Who from? And why?"

"Ultimately, the ruler I obey, that great eminence Caym, passed through several intermediaries. As for why? Like your snake or some other natural demon—because I have experienced enough things that I can now be fractionally more useful. My reality is reinforced, and my nature has been adjusted and expanded to contain more power. I can serve you far better now."

It didn't take much reflection to see the way Thrush was dancing around the details. "Any reason you are being even more evasive than usual?"

The little bird ducked its beak under its wing for a moment, seemingly sorting out the oily black feathers. "I suppose it's because I am newly promoted. My usual instincts are running a bit wild."

Truth left the building. He didn't speak to any of the children, offered no advice, didn't even tell them to run. He had no answers for them. All he could do was try and reduce their future problems. Starting with a certain food-processing company.

He walked through the doors of Varches Nutrient Solutions in a storm of emotions. He hated leaving the kids at the sweatshop. It felt wrong, even if he couldn't think of what a right answer might be. He walked into the food-processing plant, expecting some gory scene, but to his quiet amazement, it was rather peaceful. Busy, certainly, but orderly, with the loudest noises coming from the rollers carrying products along the assembly line.

The building was long and tall but mostly empty. The roof was bare metal, uninsulated, twenty meters overhead. Snaking the length of the building (Truth really couldn't estimate quite how long; it seemed to keep on stretching back) was the assembly line. Large boxy devices were stationed along belts of metal mesh or rolling steel cylinders, moving product along from its raw state through to packaging, then boxed for shipping. This particular line seemed to be preparing eggplant cutlets.

Blank-eyed women picked plump, round eggplants, the largest Truth had ever seen, from plastic cartons. Each eggplant was jammed onto a spike, right through the bottom. Two rows of four. Once the eggplants were in place, the workers took one step back. The eggplants spun on their spikes as tiny knives descended and swiftly peeled the skin from them. The skins fell onto a metal chute and slid into another cart.

The peeled eggplants got a final chop, removing both ends, then the knives lifted back up and the rotation stopped. The women stepped forward again, lifted the eggplants off their spikes, and put them on the conveyor belt. Truth looked around. There were other people walking around the factory, but from what he could see, only the women worked on the line.

He followed a load of eggplants. The conveyor took them up to a covered box, where the high-pitched whine of band saws suggested strongly why flat slabs of eggplant came out the other side of the box. The conveyor belt rolled along to a chute where the cutlets were dusted in flour, a few feet later a paddle flipped them, they were dusted again, the conveyor belt dipped into a yellowy liquid egg trough, rose up again, was dusted in breadcrumbs, flipped, dusted again, delivered into a frying vat, hauled through the fryer on the metal-mesh conveyor, raised up again, blasted with hot air from carefully located fetishes, then flash-frozen by yet more fetishes.

At the end of it all, they were dumped into plastic-lined cardboard boxes, sealed with tape, and whisked away by the conveyor into a refrigerated room. The packaging was slick, high-end. These weren't ordinary fried cutlets—they were *classy*.

He felt no urge whatsoever to snag a couple boxes for storage. He knew what else ran on these lines.

It was a couple of rooms over. Droned workers, glyphs stuck to their foreheads, pushed slabs of deboned meat through industrial grinders. The meat looked horribly wrong—gray and stringy. He realized it had already been cooked somehow. Boiled, then shredded off the bone? Steam blasts? He wasn't really that curious. The process was actually much simpler than with the eggplants.

The ground meat was mixed with some ground grain—or perhaps bean flour; he couldn't tell—pressed into logs, stuffed into casings, flattened, flash-boiled, chopped into individually sealed bars, and dumped into far-more-industrial-looking boxes. *VNS Emergency Rations, NOT FOR RESALE, GOVERNMENT USE ONLY, DENIZEN/REFUGEE/ LIVESTOCK USE ONLY*

Then, in a different font and smaller letters: *Varches Nutrient Solutions. A Family Company.*

Truth nodded. Sounded right.

He found the factory supervisor's office.

"Is this factory overseen by Sung Sahni?"

"WHOA! Where the hell did you—"

Truth gave him a calm look. The pre-knowledge of death wrapped around the supervisor as he slowly collapsed back into his seat.

"Is this factory overseen by Sung Sahni?"

"Yes. Yes. This is a Sung Clan company. I. I am a servant of the Sung Clan. Protected by the Sung Clan!"

"When does Sung Sahni come by?"

"Once a month, usually. Sometimes more often if there is big business or a photoshoot or something."

"Will she come if you call?"

"Yes. Yes!"

"Tell her it's urgent. Tell her that some government inspectors are here. They know about the kids in the sweatshop. They want a bigger bribe than you can give them, and look like they are trying to throw their weight around. You need her to come down and take charge. Sending a servant won't do it. Can you do that?"

"Yes. Yes. I will do that. I will."

"Good. You won't see me, but I will be here. Watching and listening to everything. Do anything other than what I told you, and your death will be remembered for its horror and humiliation."

Truth sat back in the chair, letting his presence vanish from the world. Wishing he could let his thoughts and emotions fly away with it. He could feel a raging blackness in him. The sheer stupid helplessness of his situation making him want to lash out, making him want to kill everyone as ugly as possible.

See! See! I'm not powerless! I can change things.

I can kill you. And I can make it hurt. I can make you scared while you die.

Maybe I can't make things better. But for you, I can make them much, much worse.

When you are dead, things may still be terrible, but it will be a terrible world without you in it. And that will have to be good enough for now.

CHAPTER 25

A VIPER IN YOUR HEART

Truth waited and watched. The site supervisor frantically hit a gem. Then again, changing a little light on the glass "stone" from blue to orange. Then he clumsily dumped far too much expensive oil into the communication altar and gripped the sides of it hard enough to turn his knuckles white.

Truth was trying to just exist. Coasting along the waves of chance and connection and seeing where his path was leading him. Embracing his inner fool, perhaps. The supervisor was sweating, rolling, fat droplets pouring down his face. He turned, looking around the room, trying to guess where Truth could be. "It's. It's done. She's coming. Twenty minutes."

He didn't even nod. He just sat and waited. Waiting in the dark.

Thirty minutes later, the door slammed open. A well-dressed young lady stormed in. Truth could spot that she came from real money—she looked tailored but normal. New money didn't get it. New money wanted you to know about how rich they were.

Old money? Old money could buy a new designer tee shirt every day of the week, every week, forever. And so could everyone they knew. Nobody gave a shit about your designer tee shirt. There was nobody you were going to impress with your clothes. You needed to look put-together. Look your rank and your role. Beyond that? A twenty-three-thousand-wen purse just got a sneer. You want to impress someone? Buy the bag factory.

Sung Sahni came in wearing black pants, a white blouse, gold earrings, and enormous sunglasses. And that was that. She wasn't even wearing shoes. She didn't need to. Everywhere she stepped, a soft carpet unrolled under her feet.

He smiled a little at the carpet. It was some kind of minor demon. The end of the carpet was constantly being pulled through the center and pushed out the front, the side, wherever Sahni wanted to step. Clever. Useless but clever. Perhaps it had some sort of defensive function. Sahni had been followed in by an aide—sheath skirt, high heels, and a jacket-blouse combination that said the owner was very professional and wouldn't you just love to see what was underneath.

Well, he knew how to manage a succubus. Sahni herself was Level Three and roughly forty. Not a trace of body cultivation.

"Where are these so-called inspectors!"

"Madame . . . Madame, I believe—"

Truth shut the door behind them, not particularly quietly. And locked it. "You will all have a seat."

Truth's voice wasn't particularly loud. It didn't have to be. The carpet rose up from the floor, taking the shape of a stout man and moving to stand in front of Sahni. The succubus also stepped forward, subtle enchantments weaving through the air toward him.

Truth released his tight grip on his presence. His level, and the power of the Sea of Brass, hammered on the air.

"If you will not sit, then you will *kneel.*" Incisive was in there too. They were in the room with a great serpent. Whether they left alive or not was no longer up to them. The succubus didn't kneel. "She" genuflected, forehead pressed against the ground. The man-shaped demon glanced over at his demonic coworker, then did the same.

Sahni didn't want to kneel. He could see it. She was trying to fight it. He just watched her. Met her eyes. Calmly. Steadily. She took one knee and slowly clasped her hands.

The site supervisor was kneeling in a puddle of his own piss. The pressure was too much for him. Truth could see his eyes starting to roll up into the back of his head.

Truth gave Thrush a look. The little demon flew over, collected the manager's desk chair, and set it down behind Truth. Truth sat. He could feel the "reality" shifting around these people, these demons. He could see them filling in "truths," finding explanations, inventing stories. Reshaping their realities to anchor their minds in this confrontation. Likely, only the succubus knew what they were doing.

He let the pressure build in the room. "Whose idea was it to feed the dead kids into the meat grinder?"

There was silence. He let it grow. After a silent count of three, he flicked his finger. The fangs of Incisive punctured the supervisor's thigh.

"AAHH! Ahhh! I was just obeying orders!"

Truth looked over at Sahni. "I never ordered such a thing. Never."

He waited. Not for long. "I ordered the bodies to be disposed of cheaply. We are required by law to do that!"

Truth could kind of see it. The state certainly didn't want to get stuck with the burial costs. He looked back over at the supervisor, who was squeezing above the wound, trying to slow the blood loss. "We were ordered to destroy the bodies, and the next sentence was to 'do something' about food costs, particularly meat. It was obvious what the order was."

"Bullshit! Don't put your sick urges on me, you—"

"You brought *dead kids* to a *food-processing plant*. Just what did you think we were going to do with them?" Interesting. The supervisor had snapped. A combination of pain and fear and all that built-up horror. Well, he was just speculating.

"How dare you!"

Truth raised his hand, silencing the room. He flicked his eyes over to the succubus. "How much of this was her being an incompetent and disposable junior, and how much of this was orders from higher up?"

"Great one, this slave's bindings—"

He flicked his fingers once more, Incisive stabbing through the knot of spellwork holding the demon bound. It was competently done, but this succubus was barely at Thrush's level.

"These few businesses have been left in her hands to oversee, but any substantial business, particularly any contracts or the like, are handled by an older cousin. This food plant and the sweatshop are significant to local family interests but ultimately exist to provide access to more-lucrative military and governmental contracts." The succubus was all business now.

"So, the Sung family doesn't know about the dead kids, or if it does, it's considered such a minor matter as to not be worth mentioning."

"It is likely that they know and don't care. I am unsure of the exact arrangements, but it is well understood that the more . . . hedonistic . . . juniors are quietly supervised from the shadows. Not for their protection but the family's." The succubus didn't care any more than the family did, plainly. It was a job for 'her,' and a calling.

Truth nodded. It was all just so logical. He could see it clearly—a directive given at the top, and the orders descending through the hierarchy, each time filtered through people who only cared about results, not means.

He looked back over to Sahni. "How much of your family is in this city?"

"Me, a few cousins. A few uncles and aunts. I don't know how many retainers. I guess maybe a hundred of the family? Ten of the main line?"

"Where?"

"We are spread all over. I mean, you can't expect me—"

Truth stabbed her leg with the fang. She collapsed, screaming and grabbing her leg.

"Where?"

"Fucking I told you—"

He stabbed her foot, feeling the fragile bones break and the strong tendons snap.

"Where?"

"I don't know what you want!" She was crying now. Not sobbing, but tears were running from under her sunglasses.

He stabbed her again, other foot this time. "Where do you wish you were, right now? Where do you want to run to?"

"Uncle Karz! He has a villa on Shobvic Hill. Big villa, lots of guards!"

Was there anything he wanted from her? He really couldn't think of anything.

"You, rug demon. Report your nature."

"This low creature is an earth demon, lord. It is my glory to serve."

Classic earth demon, right there. With another flick of his will, he shattered the demon's bindings.

"You two will eat those two alive, then you will be permitted to return to Hell. Make sure you leave a mess."

"Wait, no. NO! I can tell you—"

Truth got up and walked out the door, Thrush flying behind him.

It was a long walk to Shobvic Hill. He still didn't know what he wanted or why he was doing this. He wasn't helping anything. Certainly wasn't getting closer to killing Starbrite. It was just . . . those blank eyes and shaking hands. When he was growing up, it was hell, but it was a hell he could fight. He could scheme and plan and figure out how to make things happen. How to work around the obstacles.

These kids couldn't do that. The second that first glyph went on their forehead, they had died. The slum had won. Every second of the rest of their life went only to making someone else money. Even their death improved someone else's quarterly performance reports. No chance of resistance. No chance of making something better.

No chance of ever becoming more than a mindless machine. Not even an animal. Not even a rat. Just a component. A machine in a system of machines.

Was it Cup and Knife digging an elbow into his soul? Insisting that he go out and Fix This NOW? Maybe. Maybe. Or maybe it was the rat inside of him, screaming at the notion of no way out. At not even being allowed to fight for a future.

The Sung Clan residence was rather classically old money. Smaller than you would think, and absolutely nothing to look at from the outside. Thick plaster cement walls, topped with decorative (but extremely spiky) metal leaves.

Over the top of the walls, just peeking over, was an elegantly designed house in bright yellow, with a black terra-cotta roof and bright, wide windows. Other than the discreet brass plaque by the door, you would never guess that it was the primary residence in the city for one of the most powerful clans in the country.

Hidden recording talismans watched from dozens of angles. He could practically smell the hidden demons in the ground, the golems built into the gateway, the mines dotting the small yard and gardens around the house. The patrolling security guards with their spellhounds were pretty obvious, as was the door guard.

Interestingly, the compound was actually warded against higher-level intruders. He smiled a little at that. Threat model—who is coming after this place? Random thieves? No problem; guards will handle that. Higher-level combatants from other families? That was a much larger problem.

He looked over the place briefly. Could he break in? Yes, eventually. Wouldn't even take that long, really, if he was willing to utterly brute-force it. If he could break into a volcano lair, high-end commercial security certainly wouldn't be keeping him out. But did he want to?

Truth picked up a stone roughly the size of his palm. He trimmed it down into a small, flat disk and then was stuck. He really had no hand for art. Never practiced it, so he never got good.

Could he draw a rat? He started trying to trace the shape in his mind and quickly gave up. His skills were at the stick-figure level. He drew a human. A series of sticks with a circle on top. A nice, tidy definition of humanity if there ever was one.

He pressed the rock disk between his hands and started pouring energy into it. Not trying to add any reality-warping effects to it, just empowering it, as much as its crude materials would hold. He looked at the carving on it again and smiled. It was the same stick figure, but now it seemed to be hiding mysteries. One might stare at it for hours, puzzling out the subtle clues the creator hid within it.

He sniggered at that, then tapped the guard. "Hey."

"Whoa! Sir, you need to step back—"

"No. Shut up and listen. This rock"—he held it up—"goes to Karz. He has a problem. Not a particularly big problem by itself; it's more what it signifies. It won't take him long to figure out. I'll be back tonight and then we will have a nice chat, he and I."

Truth smiled at the man, then hammered him with his killing intent. "Either that or I exterminate the Sung Clan in this city and burn this house down, with everyone nailed to the floor inside of it. His call."

CHAPTER 26

AN ANT SHAKING AN OAK

Truth let himself vanish from the guard's perception, then found himself a nice spot on a wall across the street to sit on. The wall was four meters tall and covered with broken glass jutting from the cement, but at this point, that wasn't any sort of issue. A quick pass with his hand smoothed everything flat, and he had a nice spot to watch the show.

The key lesson of terrorism, he had learned, was that it wasn't about the atrocity itself. It was about the reaction. That was where the real damage was. Someone did something utterly outrageous, so you necessarily had to react powerfully. Very sensible. Very normal. Very convenient for your enemies.

A single murder might see a city spending hundreds of thousands or millions of wen to chase you down. Diverting the time and efforts of its police away from routine public security. Spending money on anti-terror operations instead of fixing roads or funding schools. Weakening itself in the name of strength.

The really awful thing was that *it worked even if you knew the score*. The number one thing people wanted from governments was security. Physical *Am I going to die right this minute* security always sat on the top of that list.

Clans were no different there—they promised financial security and the protection that comes with it. Lots of high-level seniors to make sure no one could bully their juniors. Lots and lots and lots of juniors able to run those little errands that would unnecessarily distract their seniors from cultivation. Like running real-estate empires. Or controlling the shrimping fleet. Owning the top four manufacturers of commercial plastic filaments for use in maritime applications.

Invisible industries worth astonishing sums. Long-term plays made by people investing for generations unborn. Making sure those descendants were born on top and stayed there. No room for new rats on this ledge. All the food was being eaten already.

So, how would the Sung Clan react? Call the police? Summon their own private forces? Storm out in a fury? Or remain silent and unmoving as a mountain? Truth could be unmoving for a little while. The broken-glass emotions from the factory would cut him up if he jostled them around.

Time trickled past. In just over an hour, a black carriage pulled up to the gate, was checked and waved through. Truth could just about see from his perch a middle-aged woman, handsome and professionally dressed, exit the carriage as the driver opened the door for her. She was carrying a small leather bag, bigger than a purse, smaller than a duffel. A luxury-edition tool roll was what it looked like to Truth.

Her eyes flicked over the building and the courtyard with seeming casualness. Truth grinned and gave her a little wave. She didn't see him. Still, he was playing a fool, not an idiot. He dropped into a light meditative trance. Just gently unspooling himself, letting the horrors of the day drift away for the moment. Not forgetting them; just calmly watching them float past.

He was a rat on a wall. Invisible in the big cities. In fact, given how nice this neighborhood was, he wasn't there at all. There were no rats there. No strange men carving pictures on stones. Murdering regrettable juniors and deniable servants. If things weren't as they should be, well, that was just the way of the world. Nothing to do with him.

There wasn't even a him for things to have nothing to do with.

The patch of nothing watched the world go by, without judgments, with little or no thoughts. Watching the carriages pass. Watching streamers of magic, like heat shimmers or cellophane noodles in water, rise out of the Sung mansion and go snaking through the air. Twisting back and forth. Looking for something.

Looking for him.

They pounced on some rubble near the gate, swirled around for a few minutes, then scattered into the city.

The sun was starting to set when the middle-aged woman got back in the car and left. Truth slowly returned to self-awareness. The domestic staff were leaving for the night too. Maids, groundskeepers, people whose jobs he couldn't really guess, all walked out the gate and down the road. Presumably, there was a bus stop not too far from there.

No change in the patrol routes of the guards, he noticed. Nor were subtle, powerful wards activated. The nearby buildings didn't seem to be preparing swarms of summons from hidden formations either.

He almost fell off the wall when the gate was just left open and the guard very blatantly turned his back to it and started smoking.

The guard started coughing, choking on the smoke and glaring at his cigarette. Truth buried his face in his hands for a moment, then hopped off the wall.

The mansion was, to his mild surprise, actually more low-key than he was used to seeing. He knew old money didn't tend to flaunt it, but it was usually visible in their houses. Some things, even if you didn't know how much they cost, just screamed *money*. A bench that was clearly custom, perhaps, or a stone floor made out of a single sheet of faintly glowing marble threaded with gold.

The floors in the Sung mansion were stone tiles, a faint blue glaze on them. They looked classy as could be, in a quiet sort of way. The walls were painted a neutral color that would have been bland in most circumstances. It formed a perfect palate for the portraits and landscapes of distant places. Some of which, Truth quietly suspected, were of places that didn't even exist on this world.

He let his hands run over the curtains. A gray, coarse fabric. They added remarkable texture to the smooth walls and felt like money woven into linen flowing through his hands. He walked through a living room that cost more than most houses, and nosed around until he found a study.

There was an older man in there, short beard, hair close-cropped and long since gone white. Casual slacks, a pale blue, short sleeved button-down shirt, a ring on his pinky finger with a matte-black stone mounted flush with the worn gold band. Leather loafers, no socks, on his feet.

There were two armchairs on either side of a little table, facing each other. The old man sat in one chair, reading. Truth didn't recognize the name of the book. There was a whiskey decanter on the table, an ice bucket, and two glasses. A sliding glass door to the garden had been left open too. Just in case.

Truth sat in the armchair opposite the old man. The old man, to Truth's quiet admiration, really was reading. He could watch his eyeballs track along the page.

"I don't think I know that book."

The old man jolted but controlled himself quickly.

"I can't be the first person to tell you that's uncanny."

"Oh, usually, I'm a lot more gradual about returning to people's aware-ness. I've just been in a pissy mood lately."

"Oh? How long is lately?" Truth had to smile at that.

"That is the second-best question I have been asked in a while. I really don't know. Three months? Twentysomething years? Hard to say."

That got a snort from the old man.

"And the best question?"

"What is a human being?"

That got a longer pause. Then another.

"Really?"

"Yep. You wouldn't believe the people I have asked that question. It seems like nobody knows. Myself included."

"Was that why you sent the stick figure?"

"Real talk? It was going to be a rat. But then I realized I don't know how to recognizably draw a rat, and my options were limited."

That got the old man coughing and spluttering. "A rat?"

"Long story. I more or less understand rats. I don't always like them, but I understand them. Humans are still kind of a mystery."

That made the old man chuckle quietly. Half under his breath, the old man muttered, "I wish they were to me."

"Oh, I have met an expert on humans?"

"Mmm. Well. It is my job, you see."

"And what job is that, Mr. Sung?"

"Literally people management. My job title is . . . I think these days it's Talent Development Coordinator, but really, it's HR. Finding a place for everyone, making sure they can grow in that role or at least do no harm, that kind of thing."

Neatly leading them to the point of his visit. Truth let the moment pool and spread. The old man sat comfortably in his chair. His face was relaxed but attentive. Truth could hear his heart beating. Steady. Not too fast or too slow. Truth might have even categorized the look in the old man's eyes as "friendly-ish" except that the longer he looked at them, the more he realized that he couldn't see anything past them.

The old man didn't have a poker face. He *was* the poker face. It was enough to make Truth half-smile. Didn't he do more or less the same with Incisive?

"That was quite a threat you made earlier." The old man's voice was mild.

"Impractical, too; I regretted it almost as soon as I had said it."

"Oh? Can't say I expected that."

"Yes, the Sung family clearly does not all live together. It would be a pain to run around the city, find you all, find a place to warehouse everyone, collect everyone in the warehouse (probably one or two at a time), *then* ship everyone back here, *then* nail everyone to the floor, *then* set the house on fire in such a way that fire-control spells can't activate in time. Doable, sure, but annoying."

Truth shook his head. "You should never make a threat you aren't willing to make good on. I really boxed myself in there."

"You . . . really don't see any problems with that plan, other than logistical inconvenience?"

"No."

It really was more the hassle than anything else. He truly didn't think they could deploy anything strong enough to stop him. If the Clan had a hidden Level Eight, he would be shocked. A couple of Level Sevens, maybe as many as three, would be enough to ensure their place high in the hierarchy of power.

They might take him in a straight-up fight, but when had he ever offered that to anyone?

"We didn't get to our current power by being soft, you know?" The old man sounded genuinely curious.

"I know."

"So, what's the basis for your confidence?"

"What's the basis for yours? I sat on your front step all afternoon, and your diviner couldn't spot me. You could fill every centimeter, and I mean this literally, every cubic centimeter of hallway with demons, and I would still walk out of here untouched. I would be gone in the space of a blink." Truth shrugged. "Is this really the direction you want the conversation to go?"

The old man smiled slightly. "I suppose not. You called this meeting. How do *you* want this meeting to go?"

"Well, originally, I was going to interrogate you on how, exactly, one of your companies finds itself using child labor, working those children to death, then turning the dead children into emergency rations you feed to yet more starving children and, of course, their families."

That got a raised eyebrow.

"Then I realized I knew the answer and nothing useful would come of the conversation."

"Oh? I'm not sure I know the answer, and believe me, it is being investigated as we speak. Hard."

"You deliberately set an incompetent manager in charge of those companies and put under her people who were competent but mostly concerned about not making the emotionally unstable nepo-hire unhappy. The results, given the overall circumstances, were as predictable as a head falling from a neck. I would investigate your other holdings. See where else the pattern is being repeated. Because it is being repeated."

There was another sizable pause as Truth got another, more detailed look from the old man.

"Not an expert on humans?"

"Just rats."

The old man nodded. "Drink?"

"I don't, thanks."

"Mind if I do?" He reached for a cup and the decanter.

"Not at all. Managing drunk old men in armchairs is a core competency of mine. I got a certification for it and everything."

The old man put the cup down with a *thunk*. "Well, that ruins my nightcap."

"Meh. I have found an alternative you might enjoy better."

"Somehow, I doubt it's drugs."

"Debatable. Some would say it's the best high of all. Power, Mr. Sung. How would you like to become more powerful?"

CHAPTER 27

ONE ANT NOT ENOUGH? WANNA BET?

Karz Sung's poker face was justly legendary. Even so, he couldn't quite restrain a certain crinkling at the corners of his eyes and a subconscious throbbing of the veins on his temple.

"I do always like more power. It's never free, though." The old man's voice remained mild as milk. Things hadn't quite risen to the level of actual strong emotion.

"Oh, yeah, you could potentially be out . . . I want to say as much as twenty or even thirty thousand wen." Truth nodded. "Well, I guess there isn't really an upper limit; it really depends on how you want to scale things."

"As much as that, huh?" Karz sat deeper into his buttery-soft leather armchair, which might not have cost twenty thousand wen but did cost eight thousand. The sofa in the living room, now, that was a twenty-thousand-wen item.

"I'm converting food, shelter, and labor costs into wen and guessing. You might be able to do it cheaper. More expensive might be a better option, but like I said, up to you."

"Recruiting people?"

"Children. Consider it an alternative form of eating them." Truth's smile was quite warm. Karz didn't find it particularly reassuring.

"Raising a child costs considerably more than twenty thousand wen, young man. As you may well learn."

"Nah."

"Don't want children?"

"Don't think money is going to be a thing by the time I do have kids."

That got the old man shaking his head. "I know why you think that, but you are wrong. The mechanism of currency doesn't rely on cosmic rays. Like fire and steel. Having magic makes it easier to use, but you can have them without it."

"Sure. So, how many cans of beans will twenty wen buy you when farms are barely functional, wagons don't work anymore, and everyone with an open aperture is in agony? On the other hand, I do have this machete"—Truth waved an empty hand—"that I beat out of a bit of carriage-door panel and sharpened on a brick. Twenty wen or machete—which is the better trade for the bean-seller?"

"Ah, but that only applies in a situation where there are only two people. What about two thousand people? Or twenty thousand? How many cans of beans is a person expected to carry around with them?" Karz smiled. "You will be shocked how quickly large groups form up. It's cold out there alone. Having a medium of exchange just makes sense."

Truth nodded slowly at that. His evaluation on how bad things would get was pretty different from the old man's, but on the other hand, organizing people was this old-timer's full time job. One he had likely been doing since long before Truth was born.

"Well, that does take us back to my suggestion."

"The kids. Instead of having them sew clothes, you think I should adopt them?"

"Adoption seems a bit much." Truth shrugged. "I was thinking enlistment."

That got a slow nod. "Level Zeros, trained from youth to serve the clan loyally. Cheap to train, because we won't be spending any cultivation resources on them. Purely physical conditioning, hand-to-hand combat, cold weapons, that sort of thing. Some education, I suppose, so they can be used a bit more flexibly on the battlefield."

"They need to be able to read and write, at the very least, so they can receive orders and send reports." Truth nodded along with him.

"It's been suggested before. Why are you suggesting it now?"

"Because I don't have a plan."

Another long pause. "Could you elaborate on that?"

"I don't have a plan. There is no big scheme. I just know the collapse is coming, so I'm trying to make things fall in a way I like. So, I'm going around and making adjustments. Feeding someone, killing someone, fixing a road, it's all the same to me. I think that my world will be a better place with a few tens of thousands of trained, fit, literate Level Zeros running around in Jeon, and I don't particularly care who they work for."

Truth shrugged.

"Even if who they work for does not meet your moral standards?"

Truth had to laugh at that one. "I'm testing a theory on how to motivate people. I'm hoping the Sung Clan can be my . . . I don't know, call it the positive-outcome model. Do what I'm suggesting and good things happen for your clan."

"Well, this little branch of it, anyway." Karz waved his hand.

"Sure."

"And the negative model?"

"Find people who are screwing over these Denizen kids and kill them in remarkably colorful, unpleasant ways. Repeat until I run out of pricks or behavior improves and I get my fit, literate Level Zeros. I strongly suspect I will have to kill everyone."

Karz snorted. "You don't think fear of death is enough motivation?"

"Compared to a rich prick having to endure the humiliation of doing what they are told? No. Based on available evidence, even when you kill them, they don't believe they really are going to die."

"The carrot and the stick."

"I guess. I really am just experimenting here. No plan, remember?" Truth shrugged. "Incidentally, I do see the hypocrisy of my 'positive model.'"

"Burning people alive is a pretty clear threat of death, yes." The old man half-smiled. Even the half-smile didn't half reach his eyes.

"Nah, that ain't the threat."

"No?"

"No, it's the nailing-you-to-the-floor bit."

That got the old man thinking again. "Power loss."

"Exactly. You aren't scared of death, because you don't believe you really can die. You can imagine it in an intellectual sort of way, but it's not true to you in here." Truth tapped his heart. "You could, however, imagine losing your power. You have done it to others often enough. People who thought they were untouchable."

"And you, young man? Do you think that you are untouchable?"

"Wanna fuck around and find out?"

Truth leaned back in his chair. Incisive wasn't going off, but he was quite certain that a stack of decently high-level hitters were, by now, barely one room over. Forces would have converged on the mansion, far enough back not to alarm him but able to rush in at a moment's notice and trap him like a wasp in a jar.

"You think I won't? Given that you don't think I fear death."

"I think you fear expense, though. How much are you willing to spend on this project? What, exactly, is your budget for this particular operation? In lives, if not cans of beans?"

"Oh, for you? Not unlimited, but very high. Hell Prince."

Truth rolled his eyes. "You know Starbrite made that up, right?"

"Yes, of course. But meeting you, I do see their point. This has been an interesting conversation. If you do survive, I will consider your arguments."

"Nah, your successor will get them off the recording. Hey, future buddy, gonna learn from this?"

Several things happened *almost* at the same time. Karz crushed a charm that had been hidden in the heel of his shoe, covering him in a thick, glassy barrier. Sniper fire came through the open doors to the garden, finger-long needles ripping through the air. The wall of the room exploded inward as a heavy squad mouseholed the mansion and entered the room grenades first.

But the barest fraction of a second before that all happened, Truth *moved*.

The needles from the sniper ripped apart the back of the leather armchair, fist-sized holes appearing and continuing straight down and into the floor. The dust and rubble from the wall were drifting in almost slow motion as the explosive charms flew forward. Truth already had his needler in hand.

The fangs of Incisive lashed out. One needle after another found the incoming charms and prematurely detonated them. Flashbangs and tarpits went off, staggering the incoming squad. Truth could see the defensive spells going off around the soldiers—spell armor, wards, personal defensive charms, all deploying to keep them upright and fighting.

Truth reached the old man, and rather than try to grab him, he flung the old man's chair, with him still in it, toward the open window. While the sniper's line of sight was momentarily blocked and the squaddies were shaking off the explosives, Truth called out the Tongue. Needler in his left hand, sword in his right, he got stuck in.

He moved like a writhing serpent. The sword was up, resting on his right shoulder, then his whole body twisted down and left, his knees bending deep as the sword whipped off his shoulder. The whole weight and strength of his endlessly refined body riding a razor's edge. Cutting through the thin armor between neck and chin to take the first head.

Then from the crouch, a one-handed lunge, slipping between armor plates. Letting the angelic bane destroy a life thirty-five years in the making. Level Three cultivation would have made this soldier a person of some status almost anywhere. Not there. Not in the shattered seconds while the dust from the wall was still crossing the room, before it had even time to start falling.

Truth recovered from the lunge and ripped a trio of needles into the eye of a soldier trying to find him in the dust. The soldier was wearing goggles—enchanted, alchemically formulated glass. Perfect for protecting eyes from casual impacts and sudden lights and for finding hidden enemies. Not capable of stopping the Fangs of Botis. *Tack, Tack, CRACK.* Then the needle was through and the inside of the soldier's helmet was stained with gore.

Before the hollowed-out skull could even begin falling toward the floor, Truth had whipped the Tongue up into the groin of another soldier, severing the arteries in their legs before a quick jab to their throat gave them a permanent tracheostomy. The needler shifted over and found a patch of unprotected neck on yet another soldier. It took five rounds to sever the spine—even with Truth's aim, there were a lot of things moving through the air right now. Nothing strange about a needle getting knocked off course.

The squad died in seconds. They were Levels Three and Four, brilliantly trained, superbly equipped. They might not have been the equal of the Starbrite PMC, but they were as good as anyone without the System could hope to be.

They weren't remotely enough.

By the time Karz Sung had fallen out of the sniper's line of sight, the room was completely empty. Truth had vanished from everyone's perception.

Karz looked down at his front, feeling something was dreadfully wrong. Four needles were sticking out of his stomach and chest, roughly where his apertures should be. He screamed in terror, then pain, as he felt some of them start to collapse. Truth had shot before he had deployed the charm.

Truth was moving quickly to get clear of the mansion. As he moved, he took a peek out the window. It was as he guessed—the street was barricaded by layers of cops, teams of Sung Clan security were flying in on carpets and firebirds, blinding bright lanterns were floating over the neighborhood, banishing any concealing shadows.

He shook his head. A provocation, then an even-more-expensive reaction. All this cost more than one wen. He could kick off a slaughter there, if he wanted. Really cost them in lives and material. But so what if he did? How would he benefit? How would anyone? He found the kitchen and raided the fridge instead.

He smiled beatifically. The icebox was enormous. You could fit two entire adults in there. And the freezer was stocked generously with beautifully marbled beef. He emptied the whole thing into his spatial ring, not neglecting the crisper drawers or the cheese cubby, either. There was an extensive wine selection, too, but he skipped that. He didn't want that stuff even to sell later.

Anything else worth taking? He looked around and couldn't really think of anything. Then he slapped his forehead. He was stealing raw ingredients, not finished dishes. He didn't have the first idea how to cook. He therefore helped himself to a couple of cutting boards, the knife block, the spice rack, all the oils, vinegars and sauces, salt and pepper, and a selection of a half dozen cookbooks that appeared to be there mostly to support the aesthetics of the kitchen.

He would have raided the library, too, but it didn't seem wise to hang around in there.

"Squad Three, moving to Green Two."

"Squad Four, moving to Blue Two."

Looked like they were sweeping the house. Well, he was done there. Trying to walk past the guards sounded like an annoying drain on his energy, so he just popped open a window and jumped out. There were guards outside, of course, as well as spellhounds running everywhere. More soldiers poured in by the second.

He smiled and jogged off, slipping between the gaps in their awareness. Feeling the pressure of their hunt and weaving between the areas with the fewest eyes directed toward them. A quick step to the wall. A quick jump over the wall into the next yard. Then he did it again and was two houses over. Then again, and again.

Then he was gone. Like a rat in the walls of the world.

CHAPTER 28

A STEP FORWARD

Shape their perception and you shape their reality. Truth listened to the furious racket of private guards sweeping through the neighborhood—demons summoned, angels summoned, police summoned, all trying to track him down. A lot of the neighbors were having their doors unexpectedly kicked in as all the summoned beasts searched the surrounding properties.

At this point, the process felt quite comfortably familiar. He kept jogging, letting the expanding search radius become his friend. Giant, golden-colored firebirds swept through the air. Their eyes were considerably harder to evade than the eyes of their human masters.

Had he done enough with the Sung Clan? Enough to move them? Maybe, maybe not. He suspected not. That arrogance went bone-deep, and they probably would keep acting like pricks just to spite him now.

The firebirds were quickly getting to be a real problem. They were moving quickly, checking and rechecking for his traces. Every time their gaze swept over him, he had to find cover and focus hard on being unnoticeable. He didn't even try to assume an identity—the people on the ground were hauling everyone out of their houses and counting noses as they went.

Oh, the Sung Clan was going to be *popular* after tonight.

He started to get up out of cover, then dove right back in. Incisive was giving him a very unsubtle prod that staying down was good-rat thinking at the moment. He tried to spot what the problem was and didn't see anything.

Something was up there, and it was being sneaky, too. Or it was just high enough up that he couldn't spot it. Truth's ability to see in the dark was now near-enough perfect, so whatever it was, it wasn't relying on the night to keep it hidden. Worse, it was pretty quick, or there were a few of it in rotation. He could feel the pressure coming and going less than a minute apart.

He could shred a hell of a lot of soldiers in a minute, but given there was a very active, very heavily equipped army presence in town, that sounded exceedingly dumb. Eventually, they would wear him down. Eventually, something would get through.

The watching presence above vanished again. Truth silently counted the seconds until it returned. Forty. He could go pretty far in forty seconds, but the time window wasn't consistent.

Hey, how is it coming on Earth-Folding Step?

<<You tell me. I think you might have enough grasp of it to go a few meters. Maybe ten? If there aren't really any obstacles in your way?>>

Truth thought about it. Trying to tease apart Earth-Folding Step was not simple. There were an ungodly number of variables you had to control for. You *could* summarize the spell as *Stuff in Your Way * Distance Traveled = Difficulty of Not Exploding * Having Enough Cosmic Energy to Travel the Distance."*

And if you didn't think that each and every one of those variables didn't have its own quirks to account for, you were probably one of the meatsplosions that unsuccessfully cast the spell.

The watching sensation came back again. Thirty-five seconds this time.

He looked around. The nearest real cover was the house he was huddled next to. Trying to use Earth-Folding Step to get inside of it without leaving a trace was beyond him for now. Was there a manhole cover around anywhere? Yes. In the middle of the heavily watched street. No luck there.

Where was the best way to run? It was looking like the whole city was getting pretty hot. Oddly, slipping north into the active war zone might give him a little more room to hide, just due to the chaos. But no, that was dumb. There would be a ton of surveillance there, too. South it was.

From where he was standing, south was in . . . which direction? He had absolutely no idea. Just pick any random direction and go, figure it out when he is outside the search area? Truth mentally shrugged. He didn't have a better idea.

The watcher swept past again. Fifty-ish seconds. Maybe fifty and a couple. No apparent rhyme or reason to it. Such fun. Such, such fun.

The locus of the search would be the Sung Clan mansion, so anything that was in the direction of "away" from that was a winner. More people meant more identities to assume and an easier time vanishing. Downtown was . . . that way?

Truth tried to estimate the distance between him and the next cover. It was a little garden shed at the end of a surprisingly large yard. Not far. He could probably do it in a single—

The watcher was back barely twenty-five seconds had passed. And it lingered for a bit longer this time too.

Damn. Damn, damn, damn. Nothing like trying a spell for the first time in live-fire conditions. He was just a few steps from cover, so he should be within range of the spell. He could probably clear it in a single long jump, in fact, but—

He reached for the spell and tried to fix the spellform in his mind. It was a bastard thing—all twisting lines and switchbacks and oddly layered geometries. Truth had the strangest feeling that he was trying to draw a shape that had more than the usual three dimensions. And the shape kept getting nudged slightly. By what, he didn't know. But something was jostling his elbow.

He leaned into it, pouring more power into the spell. Enforcing his will on the world. It was a struggle, but he got it just about settled down. As he was raising his foot to take that crucial step, the watcher came back and the spell damn near exploded.

Truth felt the spell shudder and try to disintegrate on him. The spell was suddenly unbalanced, the variables tossing around like a sack of dice in a wagon wheel. He poured more power into it, straining at it to try to hold it together. He didn't know what would happen if it suddenly sprang loose, but it would be nothing good.

It was an unpleasant few seconds, trying to hold it down. Then the watcher moved on, and the whole thing bucked and shook *again*, because now it was overbalanced compared to the original setup, and Truth had an unpleasant time trying to carefully ease out some of the energy from one part of the spellform and put it back in others.

Then the watcher came back again . . .

The next few minutes were highly educational for Truth, particularly in the field of applied profanity. Every time he thought he had the energy levels balanced in the spellform, something would come along and upset them. And since he didn't really want to test out his body's durability the hard way, that meant he couldn't move out of the area where his spell was getting disturbed.

Adding to the "fun" was the sound of the spellhounds getting closer. It was already a decent-sized search radius, but between the cops and the Sung Clan, they had the budget for the search.

More by luck than skill, he found a tiny island of stability when the watcher had moved on. He took a step—and he was next to the shed. He ducked inside of it as soon as he got there. He needed a minute to recover.

I . . . was just over there. I was just over there. Then I was here. The disorientation made him nauseous. He pressed a hand to the wall, trying to ground himself. *I was there, then I was here. Which was exactly one step away, even though it wasn't really.* He had seen where his target was. He had an intuitive grasp on the distance between the two points of his journey.

His mind just couldn't reconcile the gap. *Something* was supposed to have been between A and B but wasn't. Not even time. Or, well, there had probably been "time" but not enough time. Even at top speed, it would have taken him a second or two to close that gap. With Earth-Folding Step, it was literally one step.

He focused on his breathing. On feeling his body. The plastic texture of the wall. Trying to connect where his mind thought he was supposed to be to where he actually was. The hit on his energy reserves was more than he would like. He probably couldn't do that more than a few times, at least not at this stage of mastery. He was dumping too much power into the spell, trying to do with magical muscle what should be done with skill.

Worked, though. That was significant. That mattered. It had been a while since someone called him dumb, but now he almost wished someone would. He would make them eat their words. Literally, if possible.

He gathered himself again. He was in good physical condition. All that body cultivation hadn't been for nothing. He could see how a lack of cultivation would shred someone, though. That dislocation, those twisting bands of magic. The way the Shattervoid had spaghettified that shuttle. The Earth-Folding Step might not be dangerous to others, but it was plainly dangerous to him!

And just when he had pulled himself together, the damn watcher flew over the shed!

Truth stuck his head out of the shed and took a quick look around. There was a porch with a big awning about ten meters away. He could be over there in just a couple of seconds—

The watcher flew past yet again, this time shortening his window to barely twenty-five seconds. There must be a dozen of the little bastards up there, flying around like swallows hunting flies.

He sighed and got ready to do it all again.

It took him four hours to fully escape the search radius. If he had been running, he would have been clear in less than five minutes. Still, it was worth the suffering. It was slow going, but he was absolutely certain he left no traces of his passing. There wasn't so much as a footprint for them to follow.

It was, therefore, with distinctly mixed feelings that Truth managed to make his way to a suburban big-box furniture store and collapsed on the showroom sofa. His energy had run low, his mental exhaustion had run high, and he was altogether seriously reconsidering the wisdom of the day's activities.

Had he said anything that would help Jeon track him down? Probably not, though the intel weenies would be downright orgasming over having anything resembling an actual political plan of his to work with. Balanced neatly by his declaration that "there is no plan." That should keep the lights on all night.

What was that old joke? Be afraid when the fried-chicken delivery places near the Ministry of Defense suddenly get slammed with orders? Something like that.

It was just . . . he couldn't stand being helpless. He could put up with a lot of things. Endure a lot of things. Just not that. Slim hope, sure. Faint, desperate, single thread of hope? No problem. Lived with that for absolutely years. Just so long as he had *something*. Some faint shot at a decent future.

Those kids in the factory had no hope. And he had no hope of saving them. Not by himself. Not now, not after the collapse. He was capable of a lot of things but not feeding, clothing, sheltering, and educating tens of thousands of kids in a world with sweeping food shortages, no clean water, no new clothes . . . no anything. A world that had to relearn how to make tools.

He had to use the existing powers. He had to start thinking like a wasteland survivor—how do I turn the scrap of the old world into the useful and necessary tools of the current age?

It was like he had told Karz. Today was an experiment. Could you persuade the old money that their future lay in those Level Zero nobodies? It sounded like they had been thinking about it already. Now . . . just what was the endorsement of the Hell Prince worth?

CHAPTER 29

CHARITY BEGINS AT HOME

Truth looked around the big-box store with the apathy of the truly exhausted. His magical reserves were on the low side but not panic-worthy. His physical condition was, essentially, fine. One day, with the support of friends and faith in the Almighty, he would find the strength to get up off the sofa and do something useful.

Not now, obviously. Possibly not even today. But someday. Faith is wonderful that way.

His brain ached. Trying to figure out how to use Earth-Folding Step in practice was insanely frustrating. He could imagine what the spell creator was thinking—*All I have to do is explain everything, tell everyone how everything works, then once they understand it, they can deal with whatever problems come up. It's all about trusting the user and not talking down to them.*

Right now, he would cheerfully accept some talking down to. Very small words. No analogies, just very small words, simple concepts, short sentences. Ideally, someone could explain it to him like he was five. Or a big, happy dog.

Been a long time since he went to a pet cafe. Felt like years, even though it had only been a few months. He could use that healing.

Oh shit PERKS!

Some very frantic patting later showed a puzzled but not unhappy snake poking its nose out of his shirt and licking the air.

On the one hand, if using Earth-Folding Step didn't result in him losing his clothes, it shouldn't result in him losing his snake. But it did raise an . . . interesting question. If the spell put such a huge strain on his body, why didn't it put that strain on Perks?

Also, he was kind of an asshole for field-testing that without remembering his passenger. That was bad, *bad* pet owner behavior.

But the question was reasonable—his clothes had never cultivated. His clothes had no more cosmic energy or inherent reality than any random tree branch or a thirty-percent-off overstuffed sofa. So, why didn't his clothes explode when he stepped? Happy to be giving involuntary nudism a pass, but still confused by the rare occurrence.

"How long has it been since you were fed, buddy? It's got to be a good minute, right? Or had the old man fed you right before I picked you up?"

Perks made no reply.

"Mmm. We could go find a pet shop, I guess, or I could turn you loose in a room with a rat in it? Are you . . . used to hunting? You are a pet, but some things run in the blood, don't they?"

Perks stuck his tongue out for a second, then retracted it. Truth wasn't sure how to interpret that. Probably snake for *I don't speak Jeongo; kindly learn Snake.*

<<Snakes don't have language-processing centers of their brain. They literally don't have a language, can't comprehend the idea of language, and are famously antisocial. So, they wouldn't want to learn a language even if they could.>>

Well, that was kind of bleak. So much for teaching a snake to play fetch.

<<Didn't say that.>>

Wait, you can teach a snake to fetch?

<<No, it's just not a language thing. Which should be intuitively obvious. If you could speak Jeongo well enough to understand words.>>

You just bring so much light and joy to my life, you know?

<<Since I am definitionally part of your soul, your self-loathing must be truly epic.>>

Truth had to blink at that one. He had certainly had low self-esteem for most of his life, but self-loathing? He didn't buy it.

Do something useful instead of randomly bitching. What's going on with Earth-Folding Step?

<<After careful consideration and a great deal of high-speed calculation, I have determined that I have no fucking idea. The spell lays out how to use it, even explains why it works; I just can't understand the math well enough to understand the explanation. I'm not sure it's even all math. At least, not math the way we normally use the word.>>

What do you mean?

<<Things that seem to be expressions of logic. Things that create categories of things. There are parts of it that seem to assert that a thing can be in two places at one time, while simultaneously existing and not existing, and the simple fact of observation can shove that . . . thing . . . into a fixed state. Which is probably what was going on with the watcher, but, and I cannot emphasize this enough, I really have no idea how any of this works. Really. At all.>>

Well, enough that you can cast the spell.

<<Yeah, and a toddler can drive a wagon. Can't explain why it works, though, or do a high-speed drift in one through a curve on a mountain road.>>
Well, not twice, anyway.
<<Sounds valid. Let's steal a baby and test, just to be sure.>>
Hohoho.

Truth drummed his fingers on the simultaneously plush and cheap arm of the sofa. It sounded chaotic as hell. Literally. Maybe he could ask Thrush about it.

Truth picked at the facts irritably. The spell manual had explained that the range on Earth-Folding Step was highly controllable. It could be less than the distance of the step taken to activate it. It could be kilometers. He knew the range wasn't literally infinite, but he got the impression that it could stretch a lot farther than he might expect.

Nowhere in the manual did it mention anything about clothes or personal possessions. Or pet snakes that live in your shirt.

He pictured the spell in his mind. The form was horribly complicated, but it was a minimum-Fifth-Level spell that was as old as human settlement on the planet. It would be weird if it was intuitive. Beyond that, complicated or not, it was just the spellform. Once your ability to memorize and visualize got to a certain point, spellform complexity was not too troublesome.

So, why was this particular spell such a pain? Why did it keep fighting him? Why did it keep feeling like it was going to slip away from him?

He let a long sigh slip out through his nose. Sometimes, there was no substitute for time on tools. He would figure it out. It would just take time. Hell, he still didn't know how Cup and Knife really worked. Now, *there* was a long-term problem.

He would have to leave this sofa, wouldn't he? If only to get dinner. Or breakfast? What time was it, exactly?

He looked around. There was no one in the store, and now that he was paying attention to it, the lights were off. He hadn't noticed himself breaking into a locked building. It had just become utterly second nature.

Alienated. That was what Merkovah had said all those months before. He was alienated from the world. Passing through it without being part of it.

Maybe he should be a bit more of a part of it. After a nap.

Truth woke up to find himself being brushed. The Level Zero cleaner, a Denizen, judging by the sigil, was running a long-handled, soft-bristled brush over everything with the terminally bored look of someone who wasn't going to be paid for this nonsense but might be punished if she didn't look like she was working.

In a life full of seeing weird things, this was up there. Truth blinked at the woman. This didn't seem like a job for a brush. If you were trying to keep the furniture clean or dust-free, wouldn't you use a vacuum talisman or, better still, air demons?

She ran the brush over his legs in a perfunctory sort of way, gave the sofa's arms a good few flicks, and went on to a sectional sofa with distinctly shaggy-looking upholstery.

What could possibly be the point? Were talismans really that unreliable? Couldn't be; the lights were now on, and the air conditioning was working.

Was it just busywork? Work for the sake of forcing someone to be working? That felt very Jeon. Still, though. Brushing the sofas in a furniture store. There was busywork and there was actual sadism.

Truth, with immense reluctance, forced himself to stand. "Time to see what's available for breakfast around here."

A quick change of clothes, and he was back in his army disguise. The store he was in happened to be part of a plaza boasting a frankly dubious-looking craft supply store, a pet groomer, and a marine insurance company. He sighed again, more loudly this time, and started jogging down the road.

Three kilometers later, he found food. Sort of. There was a brightly lit chain restaurant—Bowls and More!—that had opened for breakfast. He had eaten there before. Legally, what they served was food. It was better than slum food and was probably not originally intended as animal feed.

No, he was being unfair. Bowls and More! were fine. You ate there, you got full, you almost certainly wouldn't get food poisoning, or lockjaw from holding the fork.

He was less sure about the other food source on the plaza. Golden Boat Restaurant. Was there a myth about a boat taking people to the underworld? He couldn't think of one, but surely one existed somewhere.

The lighting was dim. The signage was ancient. The door looked like it had been kicked repeatedly. The windows were mirrored. But there was an OPEN FOR BREAKFAST sign on it, so there was that.

He looked at the menu for Bowls and More! Just by reading it, he knew how every dish tasted, and didn't want it. He went to the Golden Boat.

"Have a seat, Sergeant!" An ancient-looking woman whose head didn't reach Truth's clavicle waved him to a table. The walls were wood-paneled in the finest micron-thick paneling available thirty years before, and decorated with pictures that didn't get picked up when left out on the sidewalk in a box labeled FREE!. There was, on the plus side, a giant commercial-sized rice steamer right in front of the cash register. He was prepared to hope.

"What's good for breakfast, ma'am?"

"Oh, don't ma'am me! Ma'am's my mother!" She looked old enough to be Truth's great-grandmother, but he just nodded along.

"Even with rationing, I can do you a nice bowl of rice with a fried egg, pickled cabbage, pickled greens, and some fried mushrooms in sauce. Sounds good?"

"Sounds amazing; thank you!"

A few minutes later, a scorching hot stone bowl filled with rice and toppings was put in front of him. "Here. Healthy and filling." A little carrier with hot pepper paste, salt, pepper, sugar, and vinegar was set beside him.

There was a little wooden box on the table next to him. He lifted the lid—it was full of cheap cafeteria flatware. Forks and knives, apparently from a half dozen different sets. All very clean.

"How are things with you, ma . . . senior?

"Hmph! Well, things are fine. I've got four grandsons in the army, so I can't say I'm not worried. But things are fine."

Truth nodded, feeling a stab of guilt. He tucked in to the food. It was good. Not the best he had ever had, but it was hot, and real, and seemed to be hammering on parts of his soul that he hadn't realized existed. It warmed him all the way through.

"Glad to see your restaurant is still going."

"Hee-hee-hee! It was bad for a while, but you know who's really getting it in the neck? For once, it's those jerks over at Bowls and More! Their food deliveries keep getting diverted. My suppliers are all growing their stuff locally."

"Nice, nice!"

"No egg shortage here!"

There was a death-rattle noise from the back. The old lady sagged. "There is, however, a real shortage of working air conditioners. And my cold box has never been less reliable."

Truth scraped his bowl clean and wiped his mouth. "Well, I've got a little time before my liberty ends. As it happens, I'm a certified maintenance tech. How about I look them over for you?"

CHAPTER 30

DO GOOD BY STEALTH

Truth was elbow-deep in the guts of the commercial cold box. A device that looked nearly as old as its owner, and that little senior looked as old as the hills. Or at least a hundred.

It was a combination of factors that had led to the cold box blowing out. The most obvious was the air-circulation tubes. The air-circulation tubes, enchanted with a wind spell that pushed cold air out and sucked up the hot air, were badly damaged by intermittent cosmic energy spikes shorting out the finer spell lines. Lines that were apparently never maintained *before* they got damaged, so the tubes were, in his professional opinion, fucked.

Then there was the chill spell itself—dumping heat out of the box, generating a field of frigid air directly above itself. The air-circulation tubes theoretically pushed the hot air into the field, chilled it down to basically nothing, then pulled it through the other side and dumped it into the freezer. From the freezer, the cold air made its way into the main body of the cold box.

Very simple, very reliable, very much a problem because the talisman that was supposed to be doing the chilling, the cold plate, was also busted. Never maintained, never cleaned, and roughly twenty-five years beyond what even the manufacturers claimed was its service life. A Starbrite-manufactured cold box, naturally.

Say what you like, but Starbrite really did make some great talismans. Truth had learned how to repair this model before he had ever heard of the Shattervoid clan.

"Well, senior, you want the good news or the bad news?"

"Oh, that's not reassuring. Start with the good news."

"I know what's wrong with your cold box, and I can kinda-sorta-for-today get it up and running again."

"Ah. And the bad news?"

"Two of the three talismans that keep this thing running are broken. How the thermostat made it out alive, I don't know."

Truth shook his head, army cap swinging sharply from side to side.

"Oh, dear. Expensive?"

Truth hesitated. "You know what? I don't really know. Shouldn't be. You might even be able to find them for free if you are really good at scavenging and get lucky. But that's also kind of the problem. They stopped making this model of refrigerator . . . I want to say twenty years ago? And they were still supporting it until pretty recently because modern parts are pretty much the same as these older ones, just with more fancy extras added on. My point is, I don't think you can still buy these exact parts in a store anymore, or order them from Starbrite, for that matter."

Truth was moving his hands around inside the box, pointing at where the problems were.

"Ah. So, I could replace them if I found an old refrigerator like mine and moved the parts from one to the other, but they would be old and worn too."

"'Fraid so, senior."

"Haaah." She shook her head. "It was such a reliable refrigerator. Buying a new one is too much expense."

"Not my area of expertise, but I have to think used refrigerators are pretty common." Truth shrugged.

"Used to be, but they are all going for a lot of money these days. They are just so much more reliable with the sunspot activity."

Truth had to blink at that. "Sunspot?"

"Isn't that what they said? Some kind of problem with the sun, so now we get all these magic surges. And anti-surges. Whatever you call them."

"A plunge, maybe? Err. That's not exactly the opposite, though." Truth scratched his head in honest confusion.

The tiny elder waved away the distinction. "Well, the older things hold up better. LIKE I ALWAYS SAID!" she proclaimed with great satisfaction.

Truth had a quiet laugh at that. "Well, like *I* said, I can more or less get you up and running, but it's a patch job and won't last very long. I'd keep your eye out and ask around. Best would be if you found a cold box with a busted thermostat. Then you could just swap your thermostat into the new-to-you box and be up and running."

"Are you sure it wouldn't be too much trouble to make the repair?"

"Nah, I have a bit of time left before my liberty ends, and, not to put too fine a point on it . . ."

"The bars are closed, and so are the girls?" She grinned. "Ah, the good old days . . ."

Truth declined to answer and got to work. It was the very first time since his army days that he had worked on a cold box. His first time ever working on this model outside a classroom. Somehow, his hands remembered. He could trace every line in every talisman in this thing.

It took an hour and three quarters, since he had to use the owner's tools and what he could improvise. He privately reckoned that with a proper tool kit, it would have been an hour, tops. Still, he didn't begrudge the time. It was satisfying. He took a broken thing, and now it was . . . not exactly fixed, but up and running.

"I feel terrible. At least take some pickles with you."

"Can't. Army's *really* strict about soldiers 'requisitioning' food from civilians right now, so if I turn up with pickles and my chit doesn't show an order of takeout pickles, it's my ass." He politely shook his head. Partially because it was true, more because the old lady's pickles were just okay, and he couldn't be bothered to carry middling pickles around everywhere.

"Still, though."

"Really, don't worry about it. I wanted to help. Oh, I think that table needs the check." He pointed at a couple who were waving and trying to get the old lady's attention.

"Ah, coming, coming!" Truth discreetly cast Cup and Knife on the cold box. Cup and Knife clearly couldn't be bothered, but after he bullied it a bit, the spell reluctantly, at immense energy cost, made the energy channels a bit more stable. It would hold up a lot longer than one day, though it was a long way from being like new.

When the old lady looked back, he was gone.

Truth smiled as he walked along the highway on Gamphe's outskirts. A completely barren, ugly place, dotted by exurban big-box stores, factories, and office parks. Not a shred of life in it. Probably a lesson there. Happiness is where you make it?

"Hey, Thrush?"

"Dread magus?" The imp's voice came from its binding token.

"Do demons have fun?"

There was a long pause.

"You know, I'm not entirely sure how to answer that."

"Really? Even blessed by the great debater Caym?"

"Probably because of that, actually. The glib answer is yes, of course we do. 'Do what you love and you will never work a day in your life' is one of the oldest and most used cliches in Hell."

"Wait, really?"

"Certainly! By and large, we truly, sincerely love our vocations."

"So, the demon Child Eater, notorious for eating children and psychologically torturing their parents—"

"Is living their best life. Metaphorically speaking. Yes. They are having a great deal of fun."

"Well, that's horrifying."

There was a polite, if theatrical cough. "Well, you did ask about *demons*, Your Immensity."

Truth mentally awarded a point for adding *immensity* to the honorifics rotation, then pressed on.

"What is the not-glib answer?"

"Also yes, but it's more complicated than simply *fun*."

Truth nodded. In his experience, now well tested, almost everything was more complicated than it seemed.

"How so?"

"Demons torture souls. We tell lies to mortals, kill, murder, rape, steal, every sort of violation imaginable. Every sort of degradation, physical, mental, or spiritual, is within our command."

"And that is fun?"

"Yes. Because it is a true expression of ourselves. We are exactly what we should be, doing exactly what we should be doing. It is an immensely fulfilling thing, being a demon."

Truth grunted. Odd thought. "So, why the wars with Heaven?"

"Because that is what demons should do."

"You exist to fight Heaven?"

"We exist to repair the world. Return it to its purified state. It is Heaven that stands between humanity and Hell. Condemning humanity *to* Hell, generation after generation."

"Repair? *Repair?!*"

"Oh, yes. Your souls come to us in very poor shape. Ill used by this world of yours. The whole universe, really. And it never. Ever. Stops. Endless waves of you, crashing upon infernal shores. Washing up, lost and confused. Horrified by what you see, by what is being done for you. 'It's not fair; it's not right!' Ah, the cries are endless. Truly endless."

The little bird hopped out of its binding token.

"We take great satisfaction in our work. It is, as you call it, fun. But even the most diligent servant can come to resent other, more overbearing, more stupid servants. Especially when those other servants keep telling everyone that they, somehow, against all available evidence, are the 'good' ones and we the bad."

Truth mentally circled that last sentence and dragged a line over to the monolog on all the horrible things demons did for a laugh.

"Angels are the bad guys, eh?"

"I would say so, though if Master was feeling charitable, he might call them simply dangerously deluded or insane."

"All right, I'll bite. How so?"

"Angels, notoriously, will only act in accordance with God's will. Except that they can be persuaded that all manner of idiocy is 'God's will,' from arranging a human mating, to memorizing books, to finding buried treasure. And murdering one's enemies, naturally, sparing not even the young lest their evil persist."

Thrush stuck its beak under its wing and rearranged some feathers.

"In other words, they are incapable of independent moral judgment. They cannot be good, because they have no conception of 'good or 'evil in any way that is defined other than *in accordance with God's will or not.*"

Truth smiled a little at that. "And so, the great moral reformers raise their standards and sweep out of Hell, ready to slaughter as many angels as it takes. All in the name of bringing peace to the world."

The little bird hopped around some. "Simply put. We are on an eternal mission to save the universe. What could be more fun than that?"

Truth started laughing. "Well, I'm not on that level. Now, where is the nearest person in urgent need of talisman maintenance?"

Truth spent the rest of the day wandering through the exurbs. People with broken-down carriages, broken washers, broken automatic floor cleaners found themselves visited by a strange but alarmingly persuasive young man. A soldier, oddly enough. He was on liberty and saw there was a spot of trouble. Going on silently, inside a house, on a street that hadn't had a carriage going down it in an hour.

There was trouble, and he was there to help. No need to pay. This was his pleasure, really. And the work didn't make everything like new—some people would need to order parts urgently. But the urgent problem was solved, and he usually got them more or less straightened out. And then he vanished.

"So, why are you doing this?" the wary-looking housewife asked the man buried halfway into her carriage's guts.

"Because helping people is fun, and since I'm on liberty to *have* fun, I'm doing it."

"Helping people is fun." Her tone suggested she had heard more sensible statements from derelicts in the gutter.

"Sure. Not everyone all the time, of course. That would be silly. But when I see a problem I can fix, it makes me happy to fix it. So what if it's not my carriage?"

"That's . . . one way to see things . . . I guess . . ."

"Yep. Wondering where the get-back is?"

"Yeah."

"Well, let's say you work in a hospital."

"I don't."

"Work with me here."

She snorted. "All right, I work in a hospital."

"So, you have a reliable carriage. You get to work on time, every time. Your hospital runs that little bit better. So, if I get blown up, or my buddies get blown up or something, you guys are there to save us."

"And if I was a clerical assistant to a two-person accountancy firm specializing in scallop-fishing boats?"

"Then I have contributed, however remotely, to dinner. Ain't that good enough?"

CHAPTER 31

SUBURBAN GUERILLA

An inexplicable outbreak of altruism broke out across suburban Gamphe. It spread, seemingly without reason, along stale residential streets and through mall parking lots. It climbed over overflowing sinks and under sub-floor heating. It even, unprovoked, helped a little old lady cross a street, got a cat down from a tree, and returned a toy thrown out of a pram.

When the sweating, swearing, miserable band of intelligence analysts eventually isolated the source of the chain reaction, they dubbed it "SFO #982," filed their reports, and got on with their day. Which, depending on what shift they were on, consisted of either dropping a sedative in a shot of whiskey, necking it, and going to bed, or amphetamines in their double large coffee. It was not a good time to be an analyst.

Truth might have taken some vicarious satisfaction in their suffering. By the time he delivered "Puddin' Face," eight kilos of feline degeneracy, from the bending tree branch to the loving arms of her owner, he was entirely done with the random-acts-of-kindness schtick.

How? How do people live like this? I would say . . . maybe one person was really thankful for my help today, and that was the granny at the restaurant.

<<They didn't ask you to help, so they don't really value it. They aren't so much thankful as "thankful." Like finding out there is a two-for-one on household cleaners at the supermarket, just when your dog pissed on the carpet.>>

Kind of screws my big idea, though. If the big forbidden idea is a kind of universal empathy—

<<Which is still something you are guessing; it hasn't really been confirmed.>>

Then going around, doing randomly kind things, should have an outsized impact. It should be shocking to people.

<<Nah. I didn't say anything, because I knew you wouldn't believe me. But there was no way in hell that was going to work.>>

Why? I really don't get it.

<<*Put yourself in their shoes. Some rando turns up saying they really get off on automotive maintenance and fixes your carriage over your protests. Exactly how grateful are you?*>>

Ah. Right. Yes.

Truth kicked a can, neatly ricocheting it off a lamppost and into a trash bin. It wasn't a well-thought-out plan. It just seemed like . . . spreading the idea of helping strangers. That had to be a good thing, right? In moderation? Not to some self-harming level?

Except that you needed the other half. Someone needed to stick out their hand, and the other person needed to appreciate the hand-sticking. Not expecting it or just taking advantage of it; appreciating it.

Truth couldn't even muster the energy to sigh. It would be like Earth-Folding Step or Cup and Knife. He would have to play around with it some more and learn about how it worked. He had spent most of his day on this nonsense. Time to leave Gamphe for now.

He started strolling down the highway, spotted a southbound bus, and hopped onto the roof. Next stop, Confen. A town he had vaguely heard of and couldn't name a single thing about. It would do.

As he watched the countryside go past, he had the strangest niggling sort of feeling. As though he were on the edge of something, or trying to feel something through a curtain. There was some idea there that he was missing.

He was field-testing different strategies—self-interest that serves a kind of public good was what he was pitching to the Sung. Random acts of charity with the general populace. Just being a cheerful and positive person around service workers.

Truth kind of felt like he was a company trialing slightly different products in different markets, just to see what would stick. Like a corporation with a basically okay but not amazing product, the results were, so far, unsatisfactory. And like the CEO of a corporation with a meh product, he had to keep reassuring himself that the product wasn't inherently bad; he just hadn't found the right market and the right pitch.

It was a tenuous sort of idea—he wasn't going to win the ratfucking game. The big boys were just too big and too practiced at fucking rats, fucking in the manner of rats, and leaving people in the condition of having been, metaphorically and occasionally literally, fucked by rats. He didn't have the instincts, the skills, or the experience.

So, he would have to do something else to change how the apocalypse would land on this planet. Improve the condition for "his" people while tearing down those setting up as future god-kings of the wasteland. Just for the chance of seeing something new. Something that wasn't the same old misery.

He picked at it for a while, never coming to a satisfactory conclusion.

The bus pulled up next to a concrete block with the words Confen Transit Center on the side of it. Hard to be sure, but at a guess, this was Confen. Truth hopped off the bus and looked around.

I have to admit, I'm impressed. I'm standing here, in Confen, and I still don't know anything about Confen. This is the single most generic place I have ever seen. Every shop is a chain store. And not even interesting chain stores at that.

He looked left and right down the street. There were two Happy Happy Marts within three blocks of each other. Two sandwich places from the same chain. Two fast-casual restaurants that were different brands but owned by the same parent company. The cars were all made by the top three manufacturers— no exceptions. Not even a rare or limited-time colorway.

He looked up at the street lights. Yep. Brand-spanking-new "five-year service life" talismans, same as they ever were.

The thing was, though, while no one looked happy, they didn't look oppressed and miserable, either. They just looked like people stressed by life. Hard to be happy with rationing starting to kick in and with a giant war going on, but they were doing their best.

The houses weren't quite the same factory-produced clones he saw in Onis, but now that he was looking for it, the housing was eerily standardized. He saw a cluster of three apartment blocs together, each a shortened L shape. They had different color facades and were oriented differently, so you might be forgiven for not immediately seeing the similarities. But once you stepped back and *really looked*—same building, three times.

Truth sat on the curb and started trying to really see what he was seeing, not what he thought he was seeing. Yes, it was all boring and mass-produced, but it wasn't actually *bad*. Confen was probably considered a pretty okay place to live.

He walked down the main street, looking into buildings and storefronts. A grocery store—part of an international chain. Pharmacies, all offshoots of the big Alchemist Towers based in Harban. A stationery and office supply store, part of another international chain. All chain stores, all the same safe variations on the same few ideas.

Boring, but hardly terrible, right? Since when was *safe* a bad thing? These days, *safe* was a *dream*. He drummed his fingers on a veneer-covered plywood side table in a chain coffee shop. Dreams. Dreams belonging to, at a guess, the lowest-Tier citizen and, once upon a time, even the better-off Denizens.

Well, he was seeing a lot of C- and D-Tiers around. The "new citizen," he assumed. So, where were the Denizens? He glanced over at the kid working behind the counter . . . except it wasn't a kid, was it? It was an adult woman. And a D-Tier Citizen at that.

Interesting, interesting. Were there Denizens anywhere on this street? A bit of high-speed investigation revealed exactly two—a floor-mopper at the supermarket, and a pair of laborers hauling sacks of cement around a building site. Must have been a hell of a bribe to get that building permitted—he'd bet cash that cement was a rationed good.

So, the Denizens were there in Confen but deliberately made invisible. Shunted into the absolute least-wanted, lowest-status jobs. And what qualified as "wanted" was rapidly expanding. Five years earlier, it would have been a Denizen working behind the counter at the coffee shop. They certainly would be stacking shelves in the stores.

Guess they couldn't be trusted around something so valuable as food these days. It might be worth your life to steal a loaf of bread.

But where were they sleeping? Truth started going out to the fringes of the town, hunting for the densest, least-pleasant housing blocs. They actually took some hunting to find—they were stuck at the end of the local bus lines, almost an hour from downtown in this big town.

They weren't the towers he remembered from growing up in Harban. They brought him straight home anyway.

Raw concrete, turned gray by time and weather, pockmarked with jet-black windows. A privacy measure, he had always been told. And an easy way to help keep the heat in. Then there were the layers of graffiti, periodically cleaned with indifferent care by underpaid municipal workers, or painted over by rival artists or gangs. The shallow holes etched by thousands of bladders'-worth of urine, the acid-water etching its way into the nests of the very rats pissing it out.

And speaking of rats—there they were, in all their miserable splendor. Gangsters hung out around street corners, nakedly evaluating whether it would be better to sell you your drug of choice or just rob you. No street walkers—nobody would be insane enough to troll around there. No, they would be in the towers, waiting for their pimps to send customers their way.

Plenty of people just sitting out. Battered folding chairs, sofas abandoned and left to rot on the curb, scavenged armchairs from a dump, or the home of someone who might as well have been living in a dump. Just sitting. Watching. Splitting cheap beer and cheaper schnapps. Someone would have a battered scryball out or some music playing. Nobody was partying or anything; they were just sitting. Waiting. For what, even they didn't know.

Truth crouched next to one particularly vile-looking young man. There was blood on his shoes. His eyes were bloodshot. Torn-up, bloody knuckles, too. Those would get infected in a big hurry unless he did something. And Truth knew perfectly damn well this little rat wasn't going to do something. He was going to wait there until he got hungry again. Then he would stir out, hunt one of his fellow rats, feast (or die), and then come back there to wait.

The horrible thing was, the little rat wasn't dead to the world. He was hyper aware, tracking every bit of movement around him. Keeping track of who was talking to who. Because this wasn't a safe place. It might be where he came to rest, but it wasn't safe. He knew damn well every rat around him was another predator. Just waiting for him to slip.

"You know this is dumb, right?" Truth kept his voice conversational. *"You see how broke, sick, and starving all these people are, but you are picking your victims from this bunch anyway. Because they are nearby. Because nobody cares what happens to them so long as they aren't in a gang. And maybe not even then."*

The little rat's head was nodding along. Nobody noticed or cared. Lots of drugs made you nod like that. Maybe this little rat would be their next meal.

"Thing is, though, you have seen the cops these days. The cops don't care about nobody anymore, except maybe those B- and A-tier pricks. All kinds of nice apartment buildings just one or two stops down from here. How hard would it be to kill someone in one of those units? Sleep somewhere safe tonight, eat a good meal, lots and lots to steal."

The head started moving faster now. *"Plus, I bet they have better booze than this shit."* The rat stood up and started walking toward the bus stop. Truth followed along behind him.

He had found his market. Now he just had to refine the pitch. Empathy would have to come later. For now, he would have to teach the rats how to think.

CHAPTER 32

MEASURE TWICE, OR AT LEAST ONCE

Truth sat on the bus, next to the vile little rat. Maybe he shouldn't look down on his unenlightened cousins. Fair to say his life had not been typical. But he absolutely did look down on this particular specimen, for one very simple reason—this rat had never tried to climb. He had probably never even looked up.

The little rat sprawled across a couple of seats on the back of the bus. Glaring at anyone who dared to look at him for more than a second. Making sure his colors and tattoos were highly visible.

Optimistic of him to think Citizens would recognize them, but then, he wasn't a big thinker. Besides, most of the people on the bus were Denizens. They understood just fine.

Truth tried not to mind the stink of him. The body odor, the unwashed clothes, but, worst of all, the unwashed ass. Visible tooth rot. Dentists were barely a dream in the slums, and dental hygiene was considerably more optional than cheap schnapps. Truth wondered what the little rat's drug of choice was.

The little rat's eyes had a sheen to them, like scuffed marbles. Thin threads of blood traced over the white, flooding it in red. The pupils were wide, jerking around, trying to find where the next punch was coming from. Where the next prey was coming from. As they got farther from the slums, the rat's feet started hammering on the floor. His hands clenched and relaxed, clenched and relaxed.

More Citizens were getting on the bus now, carefully not looking too long at the Denizen in the back. No one wanted to get involved. Was there a plainclothes cop on the bus? Didn't look like it, but then, that was kind of the point.

How long could the little rat hold out? One stop, two, three. They reached a reasonably residential district. Lots of nice tower apartments. The rat waited until the doors opened, then he exploded up from his seat, shoved past the standing passengers, and ran out the back door of the bus.

Once his ratty sneaker hit the curb, he kicked into high gear. There was a little service alley just up the block. He sprinted for it, juking past the gawping people on the street. If he hadn't drawn official eyes on the bus, he certainly had now. Not that the rat was aware of that. He was out in the open. There were familiar shadows ahead. He ran for them, looking for a dumpster to hide under.

The alley was disconcertingly wide and clean for a slum kid. It had to be—wagons would run along it to the parking lot in the back. Had to make the deliveries somehow, right? No handy dumpsters to hide behind—they were neatly around the back of the building too. No graffiti to let you know who ran things around there. No local gangsters keeping you off the turf. It was like falling into the middle of the ocean or waking up in the middle of the desert. You recognized everything around you and had no clue where you were.

The rat's eyes darted around, seeing the very obvious recording talismans. He pulled his hood up and hugged the wall. Truth nodded sagely. Clearly, the rat was now invisible to all modern technology.

The rat found the garbage bins and tucked himself in beside them. Sooner or later, someone would have to dump their trash. Someone with an amulet that would let him into the building. Then it would just take some time trying doors.

Truth sat down next to him. A little farther from the garbage cans, a little farther from the concentrated slum-ness of it all. Just watching. He was minorly impressed. He didn't think the rat would have the patience to set an ambush like this. He might be out there for hours—brave choice. After all, there wouldn't be any known suppliers out there. Unless he was carrying his next fix, the little rat was taking a big gamble.

Truth grew up watching withdrawal kick in. Usually, that was when things got bad. A person who was high might act crazy, but a person in withdrawal? They were crazy and desperate. What exactly it looked like varied from drug to drug. Sometimes the shakes, or lethargy, or manic energy. There was almost always pain.

It was the pain that was the killer. It was the pain that made people desperate to find that next fix. It hurt to be sober. It hurt to be feeling those feelings that the drugs had been choking down. It hurt when the chemicals started leaching out of your brain, removing your ability to feel happiness or even pleasure. You couldn't live like that. Even a few minutes like that were unendurable.

It only took a few instances of involuntary sobriety to make that lesson very plain. So, the addicts started living in fear. Fear of drying out. Planning their lives around their fixes—how much do they have, and when can they get it next? How much is too much, and how much do they need to deal with life in the slums?

It wasn't a life spent feeding an addiction. It was a life spent avoiding the pain of sobriety. Slumrats struggling with all their might to avoid anxiety. Same as all the other rats. Nobody thought it was right or fair. It was just life in the slums.

Maybe it would be different if someone reached out to them, showed them they could beat the addiction, beat the slums. But nobody had, and nobody would. Their only hope was to stay high until they died.

The back door of the apartment building swung open, the metallic *clack* of the ram-bar echoing off the concrete walls and asphalt of the parking lot. A middle-aged woman struggled through, a baby on one hip, a trash bag on the other, and a cigarette hanging from her lips. No cosmetic glamorous there, though she had clearly done her face at some point in the day. Still wearing the soft leggings and baggy sweatshirt of someone not expecting to be out in public.

Truth's mouth twitched a little at the sight. It seemed that he was far from the only one who had to put on and take off his identity.

The little rat slowly pulled out a knife. Coiled up next to the bins.

"Yeah, no, we aren't going to do that." Truth gave the vermin a firm slap 'round the ear. He pulled the shot—didn't kill him, did give him a concussion that might finish the job. He tossed the unconscious fellow directly into a bin, dropped a trash bag on top of him, and wedged the lid on.

He would have to teach the rats, but this rat was not worth teaching.

"Oh, sorry, I didn't realize someone was in here," the housewife muttered around her cigarette.

"No problem. You need a hand?" Truth grunted, pretending to strain as he shoved the garbage bin toward the back.

"Actually, yeah, thanks."

Truth grabbed her trash bag. Felt like it was mostly diapers. He found an empty bin and disposed of it. "First kid?"

"Third. First girl."

"Ah, nice." Truth started walking off. He wasn't sure what he had wanted from the conversation.

"Oh, hey!" she called after him.

"Yeah?"

"You work for the building?"

"Nah, I needed a trash can, and there weren't any on the street. Why?"

"Oh, well, you kind of look like a maintenance guy, and my water talisman is busted. Never mind. Sorry."

Truth sighed and mentally shrugged. Why not?

The apartment was small, about the size of what he had grown up in. He didn't know why he found that so surprising. He had just assumed that Citizens lived in luxury, even if he knew, logically, that it couldn't be true. Some lingering class prejudice there.

It was unquestionably nicer than his childhood home. Cleaner. No mold. No stacks of empty wrappers and boxes and bottles. Some cheap wine bottles in a rack by the fridge, but no signs that Mom had been going after them hard. Overflowing ashtrays, but then, she hadn't been expecting company.

No busted armchair. No MegaShroom. No Dad. There were toys, though. And board books, in bright colors. Even some Early Readers books.

"Other kids at school?"

"Spring Garden Preschool. Yours?"

"Oh, I don't have any of my own. Raised my younger siblings. Well, you know how it is." Truth had a fine rasp out and a technician's loupe over his eye. He had collected a good set of tools over the last day.

"You raised your siblings? How does that happen?" She sounded disbelieving.

"Two working parents who had no time but all the stress in the world."

"Ouch. Sorry to hear it."

"Don't be. It's what made me who I am today. Never would have learned maintenance if I wasn't hustling for my sibs."

She snorted at that. "Smoke?"

"I don't, thanks. I'd take a glass, though."

"Sure. Of what?"

"Just the glass."

She gave him an odd look and handed him a glass. He polished a few channels, removed a sizable blockage, and returned the talisman to its mount over the sink. He put the cup under it and pressed the activation gem. Cold, clean water filled the glass with a smooth, lamellar flow.

Truth took a good gulp, then another. Delicious. Just the right balance of minerals to give the water an excellent flavor. A Starbrite product, naturally.

"Always loved this model. Usually completely reliable." He put the glass down in the sink. It would take unusually keen eyes to notice he left no fingerprints on the glass or anything else he touched.

"I never had a water talisman break in my life." The mom shook her head wonderingly. "I know that the sunspots are causing those horrible magic-saturation events, but somehow, seeing the water just not work . . ." She groped for the words she wanted, then visibly gave up.

"It feels real in a way no amount of news stories can."

"Yes." She tapped her nose. "It's really scary. Like, she's mostly on real food now, purees and all that." Truth nodded along. "But she still has to drink something, right? And she needs a bath, and I need a bath, not to mention Jake and Saul. Who also have to drink something that isn't juice or Orange 'Splosion."

"Preaching to the choir on that one. Speaking of necessities, how is your toilet and shower looking?"

"Oh, I haven't had any problems with them."

"Mmmm-hmmm. Mind if I take a quick look?"

"Sure, go nuts."

Truth went through the bathroom quickly. Oddly enough, the sink there only needed a little touch-up to be back in perfect working order. The toilet was a fairly crude talisman and was in crude health. Just needed a little brushing and he was done. The shower, on the other hand, had famously finicky controls, and it was half-dead.

"Whoa! Lucky I came! Guessing you don't take hot showers."

"No, with the little ones, I'm always worried about them being scalded, so I keep the temperature just lukewarm."

"Lucky. See that? Your hot-water controller is corroded. Try putting it up and you could be looking at boiling water in just a few seconds." Truth pointed at the channel. He wasn't lying, either. She must have been just barely touching the hot-water side.

"St. Mechivus protect us! That's the inside of the shower talisman?"

"Yeah, don't let the green-black color fool you; that's just surface oxidation and the reaction of some of the metals used to make it. Looks scary, but it's actually completely normal. What you want to pay attention to is this bit right here—this channel. If you squint, you can probably see where the channel breaks?"

"Oh? OOOH! Yeah, I can see it when the light hits it just right."

Truth nodded. "Not going to lie—I can patch this, but I wouldn't put my sibs in this shower, and I really, *really* wouldn't put your kids in there. I recommend replacing it immediately. Everything is more expensive these days, but this shouldn't be too bad. At the very least, you can get a more-basic model that does the same exact stuff in a less-fancy showerhead."

"What brands are good?"

"For this? Almost any. Don't buy Bosken, their quality control is very bad, but pretty much any other brand will be fine." Truth shrugged. It was true five years before, anyway. Probably still true.

"Thank you so much. What do I owe you?"

Truth smiled. "Nothing. Pass it on to someone else."

"Pass it on?" She looked puzzled.

"Everyone's looking for that get-back, right? Well, someone helped me out. Now I'm helping you out, paying back the guy I owe. Now you do something good for someone else to pay me back. Pass it on."

She snorted at that, then started laughing. "Really?"

"Really. Oh, is she supposed to be eating that?" The mom whipped around, glaring at her daughter. The daughter looked back with a wronged expression on her face. For once, she wasn't eating anything.

When the mom looked back, Truth had vanished.

CHAPTER 33

THE BLEAK SCIENCE

Truth tried to sort out the gains and losses for the day. The initial idea—moving the Denizens with greed, turning them on their "betters," was fundamentally viable if he really wanted a bloody revolution. It wouldn't help bring a *better* world, though. Neither would rampant do-gooderism. The people he helped would mostly just shrug, say thanks, and feel lucky that they saved a wen.

He kept coming back to the notion of the get-back. What do I "get back" if I do something good for you? Because good feelings only carry you so far. Can't eat 'em, for one thing. His running around problem-solving was good for the people he helped but bad for any local maintenance techs looking for work.

Truth sprawled in the back of a bus, watching the city roll past. "City." Glorified town, really. They were still making an effort at public security. He could feel the periodic sweeps of the bus by diviners, looking for anything that didn't fit. No traffic stops at the moment, but he had a feeling they would appear in the not-too-distant future.

The Hell Prince was seen just north of there. It would be irresponsible not to at least have a lookout for him.

The bus pulled up to the curb. People came onboard, their identity sigil checked by scanners built into the doorframe. So long as their bus pass was valid or they had prepaid the fare to the golem at the bus stop, they could step onboard. If not? A ward snapped down, a bell rang, and you were publicly humiliated as you were ejected from the bus.

Bus driver was getting paid. Bus company, bus manufacturer, bus maintenance company, all getting paid. The passengers were also getting something—you could work in one part of town and live in another, and not have to walk two hours to get from one place to the other. Way cheaper than owning a carriage, assuming it was legal for you to do so in the first place.

There had to be that get-back. That promise that if you do for me, I'll do for you. Was it the curse? Or was it something people were just born with?

He looked out the window. Shop after shop. Housing bloc after housing bloc. It all seemed utterly human. But where were the edges of the curse? What was that dividing line between *imposed from outside* and *born from within*?

It was enough to make you paranoid.

The bus passed a billboard with a picture of a stag on a mountain, which apparently should make him want to buy perfume. It actually made him think of the old abbot, that deer-headed demon he had met outside of Harban.

The demon's recipe for human happiness was to create a world without unnatural stress, supported by the systems of morals and ethics needed to maintain it. Truth had noticed even then that there was no neat way to separate natural and unnatural stresses.

The examples the abbot had cited, for example—food and shelter. Both infinitely providable with demonic labor so long as cosmic rays remained available. It was hypothetically possible to imagine a system where humans provided the resources and labor. But before you even reached the question of practicality—what could be more natural than struggling to find food and shelter?

He watched apartment bloc after apartment bloc pass through the bus window. Jeon certainly had its share of slums, shanty towns, and "housing" that was more dangerous to the people inside of it than the weather outside. But they also had a ton of decent housing. The overwhelming majority did have some kind of access to shelter. Homes were made. People got paid. There was that get-back built in.

Food was a trickier topic. Even with the body cultivation and a storage ring full of food, the memory of hungry nights was . . still enough to make him angry. That was a core memory right there. Going to bed hungry, waking up hungry, and knowing that today you were going to do *whatever* it took to not be hungry. Truth didn't give a damn about all the things he had stolen from grocery stores since he got the Blessing of the Silent Forest. He had been shoplifting to live his whole life.

Shoplifting meant he was cutting people out of the get-back. Most immediately the store owners but ultimately the farmers. Or . . . whoever owned the fields. Not the laborers. Probably some company. He was ripping off .00000741 wen per share for each stick of FRYONASE-brand fish sticks he stole. A pureed log of the scraps of farmed fish, pressed into a narrow sausage, packed with salt and preservatives, sealed in plastic, poached until shelf-stable, and sold in slum convenience stores for not much, but still more than Truth had had.

Truly, his heart wept for the poor, deprived shareholders. He would play sad violin music, but regrettably, musical education was not offered in slum schools and he never had time to learn in the afternoons and evenings. Too busy finding food.

Truth felt like he had a lot of pieces of things and he was trying to build a puzzle out of them without knowing what the final picture was supposed to look like. Worse, he wasn't entirely sure all the pieces came from the same puzzle.

People needed things—food, shelter, safety. Education, ideally. Medicine, definitely. The chance to grow and become more than hungry rats. Or just live, content as they were. That should be fine too. He didn't like it, but as long as they were contributing to the get-back, right? Although that did sort of leave children, elderly, and the disabled coughing loudly by the windows. Couldn't leave them hanging.

He didn't realize that he was slowly banging his head against the window. It was just so frustrating. There *should* be a right answer to all of this. Humans had thousands of years of history, a lot of it spent figuring out how to get people what they needed. So, if we knew what everyone needs, and we had some good ideas about how to get it to them, was greed really the only barrier?

Was the get-back the problem there? Because it didn't feel like it was. Nobody wanted to just do things out of the goodness of their heart. Some people would be okay doing it more than others, but to spend a life laboring for nothing but a thanks and a pat on the back? No chance. You *needed* to know someone was going to do the same for you, or why do it?

There had to be a contract. You do for me, I do for you. You don't stab me while I sleep, I don't burn your house down and steal your cows. I mine iron, you smelt it, she hammers out the ingots, he makes a fork, we all eat. We all get back something for our work. And part of the agreement is—what? We all collectively decide to cover the expenses of the people who can't work?

Sounded good. Very good. He smelled a rat somewhere in there. He was missing something. A heavily tattooed young man sat down on the seat next to Truth, glaring around. He very conspicuously scratched his balls.

Truth gave him a look. Wouldn't it have been easier to just wear his badge around his neck? He might look like a slumrat, but he didn't smell like one.

Cops. Did every system need cops?

You needed someone to enforce the contract. Someone to make sure the stab-compromise was honored. You could call it different things, but they would ultimately be cops. And if there was one thing Truth did know, to the very middle part of his bones, it was that the cops were *never* on your side.

To a cop, you were always, even if you were the victim of a horrible crime, *always* a problem. You getting stabbed meant that they had to deal with a stabbing. You stabbing someone meant that they had to deal with a stabbing. In either case, their job was *deal with the stabbing.* Which was a problem. Their job was to solve problems and deter future problems by being the link between problems and consequences.

He watched the cop glaring at people. They were well out of the city center now, moving into not-quite-slums. Pretty shortly, he would get off the bus and saunter over to some gangsters. He would be looking for someone or to score something. He had a problem to solve and figured it would be easier to solve if no one knew he was a cop.

Truth mentally weighed the odds and mentally put his money on "gangster who was paying for protection hadn't paid up recently." Which did raise the interesting question of how, exactly, cops were collecting their bribes these days. Drugs? Services rendered?

Crime was definitionally a problem because it was defined by the people who got to make definitions about big, society-wide things like what constitutes crime. Generally, in his experience, the people with stuff they wanted protected. Which meant powerful people.

You could, hypothetically, kill a Level Five in their sleep. Or maybe, if you were prepared to accept massive casualties, a very well-equipped, very well-trained team of Level Ones could . . . theoretically . . . kill a Level Five. Throw enough explosives in there, especially if they haven't practiced body cultivation, and you can eventually kill anything.

As a practical matter? Higher-levels were literally and metaphorically on a higher level than Level Ones and Zeros. There was no fighting back allowed. It would be them setting the rules, and their stuff the cops were guarding. High-levels wouldn't treat their lessers' problems as equal to their own.

You come back to not enough food, poisoned homes, limited education, labor in bad conditions for worse wages, all the problems you had before. Because instead of an even deal where there was a reasonably fair get-back, the deal was a gangster's promise. "Get me my money every week and you won't have any problems."

You needed an even higher level to enforce the deal. To make sure everyone was getting their get-back, without throwing the whole thing out of balance. The government could, theoretically, do it. If you had a rule that everyone over Level Five has to work for the government or something, with strict rules against favoring your own family or interests, enforced by even higher-level mages . . . Nah. Same old problems, just more steps.

The only power the weak had in this situation was to die. To withhold their labor so completely, they would literally rather die than serve. Until the necromancers got involved, and the golem-makers, custom-spell beast makers, and, say it softly, the demon-binders. The same people who could theoretically provide a perfect world for everyone would ensure that the poor and weak lost their last, tiny bit of leverage. Their labor.

The poor would be surplus to requirements. An expense to manage. A problem. A crime.

You would have a few powerful people controlling everything—what you ate, where you lived, what you were allowed to learn and do, how you were allowed to breed. If you were allowed to breed. There would be no one defending the poor and weak. Cultivation, theoretically open to everyone, would become the private privilege of the most powerful. There would be no revolution. There would be no chance of toppling the mighty.

It would take the death of magic itself, the end of cultivation, to break the cycle. To clear away enough space for the poor and weak to breathe and grow.

"Last stop! Everyone off!" The bus had reached the end of the line—a depot next to a collection of towers and a single convenience store with more security than some banks.

He stepped off the bus. Derelicts lay collapsed in the corners of the bus shelters, surrounded by empty bottles and cigarette stubs. *Why not?* their faces asked. *Why the hell not?*

"It comes down to education. You have to make people believe that it's wrong to screw over those weaker than yourself, and right now, there isn't a soul that believes that. I'm not sure I believe it."

Truth sat on one of the spike-covered benches. Not like the rounded points were going to bother him any.

"But that's the core of it. Until you can persuade people that part of their get-back is others doing well, nothing changes for the better. We keep getting worse and worse until there is just one old bastard left, hugging a barrel of beans and keeping a white-knuckle grip on a needler just in case today's the day his shadow finally turns on him."

Truth laughed, a self-deprecating little sound.

"You'd have to be a fool to think you could change all that. A fool or God."

CHAPTER 34

FINDING THE SWORDSMAN

Truth called the Tongue to hand and casually hopped up onto the roof of the bus shelter. From there he jumped to a lamppost, then the side of an office building, kicking off hard enough to launch him up to the roof of a nearby parking garage. From there, it was a tiny hop up to one of the tall lamps on the roof of the parking garage. All while the long sword rested casually on his shoulder.

He stood on top of the lamp, looking down at nothing much. Not that there wasn't much down there—thousands of lives poured through those streets, lived in those concrete towers, bought cheap schnapps at the convenience store with more armored glass than four banks. There were endless stories down there.

Nothing much to them, though. Once you got a certain degree of distance, they all kind of blurred together. You became alienated.

Truth spun the sword in a circle and started running sword drills. Forward, back, cut, parry, lunge, recover. When he felt the urge to make a sideways move, he flexed his feet and leapt to a nearby lamp. Easy as breathing.

The Tongue flicked through the air, dancing in his hands. She was always so satisfying to swing. Just something about the balance of her, the way she moved with him. Never anticipating but never dragging behind. His ever-ready companion in solving the violence puzzle of the day.

Truth had never considered himself a good person. He was pretty sure he was a bad one, actually. As most people defined the term. It just felt so unimaginably distant to him—as though "good" and "evil" were some impossibly expensive luxuries. Like a beggar watching a seven-colored flying cloud pass overhead.

He drifted across the lampposts, moving like gods and devils. The sword cut through the air, the sunlight flickering off the blade dazzling and bewitching, hiding the fatal truth. The Tongue of One Who Speaks for God. And the word it carried, as was so often the case with angels, was *Slaughter*.

He didn't feel like laughing, but he had to smile at his own hypocrisy. He was Level Five, possessed of more blessings than some countries, joined to an angelic blade, and had three destinies. Wasn't he being absurd? If he couldn't afford to think of good and evil, who could? Not that he knew what they were any more than he could define a human. But it was just too petty, too rat-like to willfully ignore these things.

His moves became more esoteric, more dancing. He would never move like this on a battlefield, but he felt lifted up by the moment. He spun, wheeling the blade around him. He twisted in place on his knees, or flipped up in the air, hanging for a moment over the world. Landing on a single toe atop another lamp, not disturbing the dust and bird droppings coating it. Glorying in his body. Glorying in the freedom it gave him, to live out in the open.

No need to huddle next to the wall. No need to hide under the garbage bin. He could proudly stand and receive the blessings of the great solar eminence. Rejoicing in what he had earned and what he had been given.

What was vice, what was virtue? It couldn't be as simple as those demonic seniors made it sound, right? Even with a campaign of ruthless, flawless education, lasting from cradle to grave, could he really teach an entire world altruism? Was altruism alone enough? He already knew it wasn't.

This parking garage had been built by some miserable bastard. They had worked hard, for years probably, to figure out how to maximize the amount of money they could squeeze from the locals, then built the lowest-price structure they could manage to achieve their goal. Everybody got, to some degree, a bit of that get-back.

This was still Jeon. Doubtless eighty-plus percent of the people involved with the job got screwed. But still. A miserable, small-minded, venal little prick built something that could do double duty as a royal palace for some ancient tribe. Six stories—that was some real engineering there. That was a ton of brain work, even before thinking of all the resources needed to build it.

Even with the best will in the world, you couldn't call the developer a *good* person, but was the building of this place *virtuous*? Was achievement, by itself, praiseworthy? He had absolutely no idea. He had always considered necessity as something that needed no excuse and accepted no thanks. A privately operated multistory parking lot was rarely a necessity. That should make it fair game for praise or criticism.

Truth launched himself off the top of a lamppost. He kicked his heels up over his head in a casual backflip. He let himself fall off the edge of the building, returning the Tongue to his first aperture. He landed on the sidewalk less than a meter from four people. No one noticed.

Nothing could be permanently improved until he had killed Starbrite and, in all likelihood, killed a lot of the old powers that grew up under him. They had too perfectly adapted to Starbrite's thinking. They would see opportunity in calamity and struggle to become the new gods of this world.

Can't have that. Etenesh had expectations, and he was too soppy a romantic to let her down. That particular throne was already reserved for him. They would just have to try their hand at reincarnation.

Had to kill a lot of rich, powerful people. Gig a load of fat rats and toss their corpses to the starving, filthy, diseased masses in the tower. Then once the sickly rats had fattened up a bit, got a little healthier, he had to show them how to be better. At everything. At life.

He sighed.

"I'm going to wind up actually being the Hell Prince, aren't I?"

Truth made his way to a library, casually vaulting over the turnstile and directly skipping the payment system. He made his way over to the demonology section and dug out a somewhat-reliable looking copy of the *Goetia*. Finding reliable books on Botis was tiresome but not too hard. He was a top figure in Hell. Truth didn't find any book *just* about him but a lot of books that discussed him.

He had a good idea what Botis the Snake was like. But Botis the swordsman? No idea. All Truth knew was that, well, he was a swordsman. And very persuasive. Incisive, even.

He opened a book, read a few sentences, and realized this was a prime opportunity to load up on romance novels. He raced off to find some, started perusing the shelves, spent ten happy minutes on that, realized he was being dumb, and returned to the book.

This cycle repeated four times before he realized there was a serious problem. Truth sat at the long table and glared at the books. It wasn't some kind of curse; he would have noticed. It wasn't like he didn't understand the words, either. His education might have been bad, but he sure as hell had been putting the work in since graduation. What he didn't know, he could figure out or look up elsewhere. So, what was the problem?

<<*You haven't been studying. I've been studying. It's been a long while since you consciously tried to learn something. You are out of the habit.*>>

Truth was stunned for a second, then slowly banged his head against the table. *The demon is the mage.*

<<*Well. Not strictly in our case. But yes.*>>

He took a deep breath and calmed himself. Nothing was going to run away from him. There was nowhere he had to be. Actually, sitting quietly in a library for a while was a decent tactical move. They sure wouldn't be looking for him there. Deep breath. Then he picked up the book again.

To study Botis is to be immediately confronted with contradiction. He is a master speaker who speaks rarely and briefly. He is a master swordsman who rarely fights. His every move is like lightning, and he is notorious for his immobility. However, most curiously, it is not his famed foresight, deep knowledge, vicious combat power, or sinister persuasiveness that makes him so feared among the Lords Infernal.

The most feared ability of Botis is reconciliation. He is notorious for turning enemies into friends, settling wars, ending quarrels, and restoring harmony. This is the product of cold rationality. Whether swordsman or snake, Botis is a predator. He will always calmly judge things by the same test: how much energy do I have to expend to gain how much food, and at how much risk? He brings peace, to ensure he has a monopoly on violence.

Truth blinked at that. Held the book at arm's length. Pulled it in close. Traced his fingers over the words, reading them one at a time. He then flipped to the cover, then the inside cover, finding the author's bio.

Father Rehebus Mar-nx, Chief Seminarian at Saint Xiament of Cruspitello for twenty years . . .

Pragerite priest. Safe to say this was not an unbiased view of Botis. He shook his head, tossed the book to one side, and picked up another.

Best known for his foresight, among scholars Botis is actually known as the Demon of Reconciliation . . .

Nope. Not buying it. Next.

"I can't tell you what it was like. Every day was hell. Always waiting for the screaming to start, stabbed by all the looks in the silence. I wasn't blameless. I hit him. I admit it. I hit him. I was so afraid of being hurt, I hurt him first. Thankfully, my mother-in-law is in an excellent coven, and they were able to summon a shadow of His Excellency. With his mediation and guidance, my marriage was saved. As was my soul."

Had he picked up a women's magazine by accident? Demonic. Swordsman. Sinister manipulator. All the old-timers from Siphios kept banging on about what a charismatic tyrant Botis was. He could see turning an unhappily married couple into his slaves, serving eternally in humiliated ecstasy. But no. He saved a marriage and, allegedly, a soul. Saved from what, who knows.

We had marched into Bhekrova—the Fifth, Ninth, and Twelfth Legions, all with auxiliaries and a rock-solid logistics train. We weren't even slaughtering them. They just gave up. They had no chance to resist. The war was practically a formality.

King Brzinch knew he was going to die ugly, and his people would live as slaves. He was a hard man, and smart. God rest his soul, he sacrificed an entire town to summon a powerful Shadow of Earl Botis. We had our own angelic summons ready, naturally, but . . .

We never got to use them. There was no more fighting. Botis walked out in front of the legions and spoke. He explained why this was a bad idea. How what we were doing was going to cause centuries of civil unrest. How our generals would use this land to grow more powerful and ambitious. How the Empire would fall because of internal strife.

He said that we must retreat in order to conquer. I'll never forget that. Botis looked . . . not handsome, exactly. Charismatic. He was weathered. Mouth full of fangs. He had a look in his eyes that said he had seen too much. He was sincere. He looked at us, all the tens of thousands of us, he looked us in the eyes and said, "You must retreat if you wish to conquer. Before you can rule others, you must rule yourselves."

I'll never forget that. We've had fifty years of peace and development since then. Fifty years. I haven't had to order a family executed for half my reign. My father couldn't seem to go a week without ending a bloodline. Fifty years. Every year, I send a memorial gift to the site of the town that got sacrificed. My wife's subjects deserve at least that much honor.

—From the private journals of Emperor Adelius Recitus Virim

Truth looked at the cover of the book. Written by a historian he had never heard of, at the University of Ben Zhu at Wulinr. A university he had never heard of, but it sounded legit.

Could a demon . . . be good?

CHAPTER 35

NAAAH!

Truth flat-out refused to believe it. His world had become a very strange place in the last year or so, but *that* was a bridge too far. Botis, Earl of Notoriously Bad Place HELL, was a good guy who was apparently famous for reconciling enemies.

And yet not one *Goetia* he had read mentioned that. He started scrabbling through the pile of books to find the *Goetia* he had pulled. He flipped to the section on Botis. Foresight, public speaking, swordsman, check, check, check. Reconciliation—no check. There hadn't been anything about it in the *Goetia* he had read in Siphios, either, so it wasn't just a Jeon thing.

He started flipping through the books with longer sections on Botis. The reconciliation thing was practically the first thing they mentioned. Merkovah never mentioned it. Why?

Truth stood and disguised himself as a plumber trying to better himself. The identity came annoyingly easily. He found a librarian.

"I was wondering if you could explain something to me."

"I'm just here to help you find books." The librarian shook her head, clearly traumatized by previous experiences trying to explain things.

"No, I found the books, I think. Look, why do the books on demons talk about things not even mentioned in the *Goetia* entries? That's all I want to know."

"Oh. Well. That I can actually explain." The librarian looked torn between her desire to not, in fact, explain and her desire to show off all the amazing things her books had to offer.

"The *Goetia*s are a catalog, essentially. They tell you the kind of services you might demand from a demon as well as any notable characteristics about them. That being said, they are *catalogs*. They are just recording available options and maybe trying to sell you on recruiting some particular demon."

"Wait, Hell is doing promotional work?"

She shrugged. "Some of 'em are. The really powerful ones don't bother, of course."

"Sure. I can see that."

She nodded and turned away. Truth continued to stand where he was. The seconds ticked past. Eventually, she sighed and turned back. In a slow voice she said, "The books have more time to talk about things, so they talk about more things."

"Got that. But why leave out what sounds like a pretty major characteristic of a demon?"

"Probably because it's not a reason most people would want to summon that particular demon? Demonology isn't my field."

"Oh? What is your field?"

"Library sciences." She gave him a look, but Truth flat-out refused to believe he was the asshole there.

"Makes sense. Whole entire parts of the demon's power set, though."

She visibly sighed and indiscreetly checked the time until closing. She was a long way off from relief. Wilting, she forced herself to continue.

"Look, just . . . flip through the *Goetia* for a minute. Any of them; it makes no difference. You are going to see a couple of things really quickly— the demons offer surveillance, treasure-finding, the ability to communicate with birds and animals, 'love' spells"—they shared a look at that one, then she continued—"the ability to slay your enemy or ruin their crops, or any kind of other nasty thing. It's all variations on the same stuff."

"Okay?"

"So, the books, which need to sell based on their deeper looks at things, focus on the stuff they *don't* all have in common, whereas the *Goetia*, which knows people are just looking for a quick contractor, just gives the popular, mass-market stuff. Combine it with the fact that a load of demons have different 'aspects,' and *all* the *Goetia*s have limited space per demon, and you get this."

"Nobody is summoning Astaroth for a quick anything, though. I mean, they just aren't." Truth was determined to deny it. It would just be too annoying if it was true.

"Bet you a wen? Cops call on him more often than they visit their moms. Check the *Goetia*."

Truth flipped to the rather lengthy entry. *Teaches mathematics, philosophy, handicrafts can teach you to communicate with snakes, turn people invisible, find buried treasure, can answer any question asked.*

"Can answer any question asked, and invisibility. Nothing that spicy for a cop."

"Oh? Is that Pendelton's *Infernal Aristocracy* you have there? That will have something on Astaroth. Take a look.

Truth found the entry quickly. There was a short paragraph covering most of what was in the Goetia, then—

The demon Astaroth presents an enigmatic figure—sometimes male, sometimes female, often an infernal parody of an angel, equally often a prince, frequently appears riding a dragon, other times holding a snake. In any incarnation, however, they are relentless inquisitors and prosecutors. When they discover the slightest hint of impiety, law-breaking, or moral turpitude, they will furiously pursue the wrong-doer.

"What does *turpitude* mean?"

"Vile, base, depraved. Not-good."

"Ah. Most people are going to be a lot more interested in finding treasure, of course."

"Yep."

"Not to mention speaking with snakes. Someone did tell me snakes don't have language centers, though."

"No idea, but, counterpoint, Astaroth is a demon that could slap this whole planet clean out of existence if he manifested in person. Making snakes talk is a comparatively easy lift." The librarian really, really looked like she wished she was day drinking. Truth wondered what the hell her problem was.

"Fair."

"So, if that's everything?" She wasn't even hinting.

"Sure, thanks."

Truth turned around and let himself fade out of her awareness. A few seconds later, he was back, standing behind her. She looked around furtively and snuck a paperback out from under a stack of papers. *The Bride Seduced.* The cover art was glorious. More heaving bosom than low-cut dress, and the dastardly man holding the swooning bride had hair so long, it could do double duty as a windsock.

Sneaking a glance left and right, she silently opened a box of cheap chocolates. Caramel filling. With a magician's stealth, she slipped the forbidden food into her mouth as she dove back into her book.

Truth left her to it. She was clearly an excellent librarian and deserved her personal time.

Merkovah didn't say anything because the last thing he wanted was me thinking about reconciliation. Same for the other old-timers at the Embassy.

<<Eyup. And maybe giving Merkovah more credit than he's due—it might be the aspect thing the librarian mentioned. A snake doesn't do reconciliation, because it doesn't have any enemies. It has food, not-food, and mates. The swordsman, however . . .>>

Debates. Rules over people. Can turn them against each other but, more importantly, can unify them. Or at least get them to stop hating each other.

Truth had found a bench just outside the library. He watched people going past. Nobody looked happy, exactly, but that was the Jeon mask for you. Not happy, not sad. Just existing. Whatever pain or joy you had, choke it down. That was for you to know about. A wise man does not display his treasures or his weaknesses.

<<It seems like an odd fit for his skill set. Definitely not a snake sort of thing. Or a demon thing, I suppose.>>

Nah, I can see it. It's another way to use Scales and the Fangs together. Shaping the world in the way you would prefer. Botis prefers a more-peaceful world, for whatever reason.

<<In his aspect as a swordsman?*>>*

Truth could only mentally shrug. *Any more thoughts on Cup and Knife? At this point, healing the whole damn world seems easier than figuring out Botis.*

<<Not really. Let's just spend a day using it. Just . . . really test the hell out of it. Do the weird, dumb stuff. We'll see what the spell finds easy and what it finds hard, try to suss out what Manda was really after.>>

Truth nodded. He didn't have a better idea.

He stood, rolled his shoulders, and reached the curb in a single step. The energy drain took a big chunk out of him. Earth-Folding Step took even more out of him on a city street in the daytime than being hunted in the suburbs at night. Truth looked around the busy street and didn't see what might be causing the problem.

It was the usual street scene—people walking around, carriages and wagons rumbling along the street, advertisements covering every flat surface, recording talismans on every corner of every building. Nothing out of the ordinary.

He would figure it out. There was a sign pointing toward a hospital. Good-enough place to start. He got jogging.

Truth arrived at the hospital, and not wanting to make his life excessively difficult, he simply broke into the scrubs vending machine, stole a set, repaired a short that was making the light inside the machine flicker annoyingly, and got changed. The sheer freedom and joy of throwing his clothes into a spatial ring was hard to overstate.

"How? HOW did I manage to live without you?" Truth murmured, looking at the wooden ring. He was tempted to kiss it, but that seemed a little weird.

Scrubs on, he set out to assume his persona. An embarrassing number of attempted specialties later, he was startled to learn the universe would accept him as a bonesetter. Sometimes, bones were out of alignment. Sometimes, even usually reliable spells did astonishingly upsetting things to people's bones. Sometimes, you just needed a bonesetter instead of something fancy.

"Hey, bone-bro, can you cover intake?" Truth found himself ambushed by a doctor almost as soon as he left the locker room.

"Wha?"

"Come on, bone-bro. You can't run away *again*. I really, really need someone to do rounds at the ER."

"The ER? Bro, no, bro." Truth shook his head violently. He didn't know what was going on there, but his instincts were screaming at him to run.

"*Come on!* I have a patient with six functioning nephrons, a sodium imbalance, and some absolute *nitwit* of an emergency medicine doctor wants to start dialysis. Total disrespect for the highly capable surviving nephrons. I *need* you to cover intake!"

Truth slowly blinked. "Bro. What? That's not a bone, bro."

The high-strung doctor sighed dramatically. "Against all available evidence, I happen to know you passed med school. At least well enough to identify things that are and are not emergencies."

"I do bones, bro. I don't do wet stuff. Or teeth. That's the teeth-bone-bro." Truth shook his head and started slowly backing away.

"I'll tell you what. You just stand around in your scrubs. Hold this clipboard." It was jammed into his hands. "You can just list problems as *Bone*, *Not-Bone*, *Examine with Demon Eye*, or *Cast ANCEF*."

"But, salt-bro, what if it's the wrong thing? And my name is on it?"

"By the time someone figures it out, your shift will be over and therefore not your problem. Or my problem." The doctor spun Truth around and shoved him toward a pair of swinging doors. "Now go out there and do some medicine!"

Truth found himself propelled through the doors. By the time he looked back, the doctor had vanished more swiftly and completely than even the Earth-Folding Step could manage.

"Oh, is it your shift?" a passing nurse asked. "I thought Keppler was on duty."

"Salt-bro had a thing with a guy?" Truth grasped for the right words to explain what happened. The nurse nodded understandingly.

"Sorry you got caught. Well, it's a pretty slow day." She smiled and started flipping through her notes.

"We have a severe burn, six undetermined-source infections, five of which are patients over ninety years old, one of which is fifteen days old, three carriage accidents that are currently being patched up by emergency medicine, eight stabbings of varying severity being patched up by ER nurses until Emergency Medicine can see them, someone who claims they have the plague and does present with a wet cough producing sputum, a woman complaining of 'discharges,' an old lady who refuses to understand that we cannot treat her parakeet, three ODs, one case of the DTs, twenty psychiatric complaints ranging from depression to suicidal ideation to psychopathic aggression, four of which are juveniles, fifteen STDs, an elderly patient that presents severely malnourished but cannot respond to verbal interrogation well enough to explain why they are in the hospital, four juveniles who claim to have been blinded but cannot explain *how* they became blind, eight very loud women who demand to speak to whoever is in charge of the demons because it is morally wrong to use air demons to clean the hospital, despite Clark the janitor standing right there with a bucket, mop, and talisman in hand, two very nearly as loud men demanding to speak to whoever is in charge of the demons because it's discrimination and putting patients' lives at risk by not summoning demons to do the cleaning, and Ms. Gashlip, everyone's favorite Code 553."

She smiled up at him. "Average Tuesday afternoon, really."

CHAPTER 36

MIGHT NOT BE CUT OUT FOR THIS

Truth had gone to the hospital with some vague notion of just wandering the hallways, treating the ill and infirm. Learning more about Cup and Knife as he microscopically made the world a better place. Alas, the kneecap of dreams must always confront the lead pipe of reality.

I do not have the faintest goddamn idea of what I am supposed to be doing here.

The emergency room was a wash of people. Some stacked up in the waiting room, more in little curtained-off sections of the ER proper. Some stuck on gurneys in the "hallways" between curtained sections. Most quietly enduring until they could be seen. A vocal minority being anything but stoic about their conditions.

Apparently, it was his job to sort it all out. Not even fix everything, just sort out where they should go from here.

"Did nurse-bro triage them?" he asked the senior nurse, who was absurdly heavyset and old-looking for a Jeon native, sporting pink scrubs and sneakers with a staggeringly thick foam sole. He had seen softer-looking special forces soldiers but not many harder ones.

"Naturally. Most urgent is the top of the stack, least on the bottom." She nodded. Truth looked at the top name on the list. Broken arm. He looked at the bottom page—cranial bleed, multiple ruptured organs, infection, most ribs broken, both legs broken, pelvis broken, spinal damage—the patient had been hit by a wagon and managed to live.

He was about to ask what the hell the nurse thought she was playing at, then remembered he was in a *Jeon* hospital. He looked a little longer at the intake sheets. Top right corner was a little check box indicating insurance coverage and citizenship rating.

He had wronged the nurse. The order was impeccably correct. For Jeon.

"I'll get on it. Am I the only doctor-bro on the floor?"

"Yes, though our new resident is also making rounds. He's stabilizing the D-Tiers and Bronze-Plan patients."

"All right. When he's got 'em stable, have junior-bro come shadow me."

"Yes, Doctor."

He quickly found the first patient. A rather aggrieved-looking teen and his furious mother.

"DO YOU HAVE THE SLIGHTEST IDEA HOW LONG WE HAVE WAITED?!" she bellowed. The teen looked mortified, but the youngster had an ice pack on his arm and a look of real pain on his face, so he was stuck.

Truth checked the intake. "Twenty-five minutes, ma'am-bro. I'm the bonesetter-bro. Here to set the little bro's bones." Truth walked past the sputtering C-Tier and pulled up a stool next to the kid. He removed the ice pack and quickly checked the break with Cup and Knife.

"Ulna's fine, radius has a comminuted fracture." Truth made a note on the chart with his findings. "How did you manage that one, bro?"

"Was playing soccer at school, slipped on the grass, and my arm slammed into the goalpost. But, like, really hard." Truth looked in his eyes. The boy was lying. The mom was too busy furiously muttering about suing the school to see it.

"Bullied at school? Abused at home?" His lips hardly moved but his words reached directly into the boy's ear.

"No, really, I—" Truth fixed him with a calm look. He deflated. Then mouthed, *School.*

"Good news is that this is something I can heal; no need to wait for demon-eye-bro," Truth said loudly.

"Well, it's about time!"

Truth cast Cup and Knife. The injury seemed to want to fly off somewhere. Truth smiled and returned the broken limb to its origin. He made a note on the sheet, *Broken radius. Fixed with bone spell. Sent to discharge-bro.*

"All right, someone will be in with your discharge paperwork. These kinds of accidents have a way of happening more than once, little Bro. Longer if you don't talk to people about it. Maybe consider radical steps to take care of it."

Truth waved away the sputtering mother and moved to the next on the list.

In the next cubicle was an elderly man with a horrible cough. It looked like a seizure, convulsing his body as thick chunks of phlegm flew over the room. Some didn't, just spilling over thin lips and down his thin chest. He gasped a few times, then the coughing started again.

"Senior-bro! Mask! Where is your mask?" Truth urgently asked.

"Never use masks!" The old man coughed and hacked. Then—"Just traps the sickness in you. Makes you more sick. You doctors are fools to be wearing them all the time."

"Not how that works, senior-bro. Not how anything works. Also, and no disrespect, senior-bro, but you are covering everything in disease-carrying phlegm."

"That's what cleaning talismans are for. Are you going to whine or heal me? Don't think I won't leave a one-star review!"

Truth checked the chart. C-Tier, but a decently wealthy one, judging by the shoes on the floor. Truth quickly checked him with Cup and Knife. Major lung problems as well as a general sense that his body was in a bad way and getting worse.

Have examined by demon-eye-bro, cast ANCEF, consult with pathology-bro and lung-Bro.

"Feel better soon, senior-bro."

"Eeeh? You haven't done anything!"

"Don't worry, senior-bro. We'll have you on your feet in no time."

He escaped the disgusting cubicle only to spot a harried-looking junior in scrubs come running toward him. There were bags under his eyes that could have carried the week's shopping. The eyes themselves had that quiet despair and surrender to inevitable horror Truth associated with the utterly burnt-out.

"Nurse Brochard said you wanted me to shadow you, Doctor . . . ?"

"Hey, junior-bro! Yeah, I'm bonesetter-bro." Truth watched a few things visibly click inside the resident's head. Looked like this was a very well-settled persona. It almost felt like the identity was running through invisible grooves carved in the air of the hospital hallways.

"An honor to meet you, Bonesetter . . ."

"Yeah! We do bones, bro. Now, most of these people have problems that are not-bones. Which is bad. So, we need to get through them fast."

"Okay?" The resident glanced around. There was a hollowness to his cheeks that suggested too many skipped meals. The hospitals were notorious for working their junior doctors almost to death. Or actually to death, depending on how attentive the senior doctors were.

"Yeah, so, you are going to be my paperwork-bro. I'll test you on what to do as we go, see how you are coming along." Truth nodded decisively. The resident looked like he would rather dive into a wood chipper.

"Err. Dr. bone-bro, while I am immensely grateful for the privilege of observing you work, Mr. Coldswalop in number eight is presenting with severe kidney problems, and—"

"He gonna die right this minute?"

"Well. Not *right* this minute."

"You leave a message for salt-bro, saying that this is his problem?"

"I . . . made a request for a nephrology consult."

"Nurse-bro knows he's in there?"

"Yes . . ."

Truth shoved the clipboard into the resident's hands, spun him around to face the next cubicle, and slapped him on the ass hard enough to propel him into the curtained "room."

The patient was a teen, maybe sixteen years old, male, looking around blindly. Literally, as Truth could see the ruins of his corneas from a couple meters away.

"Hey, junior-bro. I'm the doc on call for this shift, here with my resident-bro, who's going to ask you a few questions. But first, bro. Really, bro. How did this happen?"

"Does it matter?" The kid's voice was brittle.

"Yeah, bro. Because it tells us a lot about how we treat it and how we make sure it doesn't happen again."

There was a long silence. "I don't want to say."

Truth glanced over to the resident, who looked helplessly back at him. Truth shook his head and mouthed, *Watch and learn.*

"How old are you, bro?"

"Seventeen." Truth blinked at that and checked the intake sheet. The boy was, in fact, seventeen. From a C-Tier family, no less, with Silver Plan insurance. Clothes looked . . . the kind of ordinary you got when you had enough money to make good quality look ordinary. Not poor, but not very rich, either.

"When's your birthday?" Truth was hunting over the sheet and somehow— ah, right, up at the top. The kid had hunched in on himself.

"Three weeks, huh."

"Yeah."

Which meant that in three weeks, he would be on a bus headed for Basic, getting ready to do his National Service. Just as the most brutal war in Jeon's history was really starting to hit its stride and the body bags were coming home by the shipping container–full. When there was still a body to fill a bag.

Truth flipped through the clipboard. Three other juveniles presented with the same symptoms. All seventeen years old. Truth rested his hand on the side of the kid's face and investigated with Cup and Knife. His eyes weren't just damaged—they were destroyed. Whatever it was had completely destroyed all the fine structures inside the eyeball that actually allowed the little ball of water to see. Even the nerves leading to the brain had been severed and burnt to nothing.

It was healable. Expensive. Crushingly expensive. It would require specialized mages, specialized talismans, a course of carefully administered potions . . . or a spell as weird and powerful as Cup and Knife.

"Hmm. Not what you want to hear, little bro, but I'm concerned not all the necessary treatment is covered on your insurance plan. We will happily do the work, of course. But I will need a signed contract from your parents approving the proposed treatment plan. Given that four juvenile-bros all developed the same injury at the same time, we have to be very diligent about the possibility of terrorism or some other form of sabotage. This isn't a reportable incident, of course; we just need to be careful on our end."

Truth nodded decisively. The resident was looking at him, bewildered, his jaw slightly hanging open. The kid looked like he was trying to parse what Truth said. Eventually, he slowly nodded.

"Whatever you think is best, Doctor."

"Are you in pain?"

"No. It doesn't hurt."

Because all the nerves are destroyed. If they weren't, you would be in agony.

"All right, paperwork-bro, start listing all the necessary consults, the necessary potions and talismans, demon-eye bookings, vibro-sight wanding—"

"Err, bonesetter, vibro-sight is not . . . generally used in optometry . . ."

"Eh? But there are bones around the eyes? You know what, list a consult for a few eye-bros, as well as the vibro-sight tech-bro. Let's have a meeting and discuss a plan for evaluating the medical advisability of a vibro-sight examination, given the presented symptoms." Truth nodded decisively. He didn't know much about hospitals, but he would bet cash a meeting with that subject would be postponed until five years after the end of time.

The resident looked like he would dive into the sweet embrace of death at the first available opportunity. Barring that, a reasonably quiet linen closet he could pass out in for a few blissful hours of unconsciousness.

"Yes, bonesetter."

"Awesome! Oh, make sure you note on his form he's 4-F. Sorry, kid-bro. Just can't let you serve in that condition."

"Oh. Well. If you say so." The kid's voice was very quiet.

"Yeah, damn shame. I loved my Service. Every day, we did runs, pushups, sit-ups, burpees; it was AWESOME!" Truth nodded with blithe enthusiasm. "Sorry you are going to miss out. All right, hang tight. Someone will be in with the paperwork. Eventually. How are you getting home?"

"Bus?"

"Nah bro, no can do. Have nurse-bro message your parents. Someone needs to pick you up."

"Okay." The voice was very soft. Truth could see the swirling storm of emotions playing over the kid's face.

"Hey, fingers crossed some of these treatments might come up on special offer. You never know." Truth nodded wisely. "All right, I'mma head out. Remember, if you are feeling down, do like bonesetters do—lift heavy at the gym."

Truth looked over at the resident. "We gotta check in on 'em, but I'll save you some time—duplicate the paperwork on the other three blind kids, too."

"Doctor?"

"Bro, are you blind? This requires careful handling." Truth shook his head. "You got a long way to go, junior-bro. Don't worry. Your senior will walk you through it."

MEDICAL NECESSITY

Truth moved through the emergency room with surprising (to him) efficiency. It seemed that this specific job, a sort of phase two of an intake, did not actually require much medical knowledge. What it required was someone recognized as a doctor, looking at the patient.

That was it. You looked at them, listened to them, and told them they would be looked after. Maybe gave them a little preview of what would happen next. Because what was *actually* happening wasn't medicine. It was management.

"All right, junior-bro, who do we have next?"

"Male, 78, presenting with advanced chlamydia. The disease has been confirmed by lab work; his symptoms are consistent with the disease." The resident was barely hanging in there, but he had been "barely hanging in there" for hours now and quite possibly days. Even weeks. "Barely hanging in there" was the ground state for junior doctors, Truth learned, and not something unique to the specimen in front of him.

"If pathology-bro has diagnosed him, nurse-bro can run the charms, clean him up, and get him home. What's the problem?"

"I don't know."

"You don't know? Bro, you have his chart literally in your hands."

"Yeah. But it doesn't say."

Truth took the chart out of his hands. He didn't know how to read medical records, but he did know how to cheat. He started flipping through at speed, slapped it shut, gave the resident a particularly filthy look, then went into the little curtained-off cubicle.

"Mr. Bumint. On behalf of the shareholders here at the Evergreen Hospital Network, and those of us with their stocks in our pension funds, thank you for your repeat business. You have been a real bro for our bottom line. However, we would be failing as doctors if we didn't at least remind you that prevention is a whole lot cheaper than the cure."

"Eeeeh heheh! Well, you know how it is . . ."

"Senior-bro, I'm a bone doctor. I know exactly how it is. Which is why I'm telling you nobody but nobody gets *eight STDs in a year* without doing a whole lot of boning without doing much thinking. At this point, I should report Sunny Acres Retirement Community as a VD epicenter!"

"Now now, let's not get too exaggerated."

"Senior-bro, I'm not joking. Haven't you seen the posters up on the walls? VD is considered a threat to military readiness. Right now, the reporting requirements are just 'suggestions,' but every doctor in this hospital knows it's going to get mandatory any day now."

"No, really?"

Truth nodded strongly. "Hey, junior-bro, I think I saw some VD brochures by the nurse station. Grab one for Blumint-bro."

"Yes, Doctor." The resident staggered off at commendable speed.

"And now that the kid is gone looking for something that isn't there— C'mon, bro. What's going on?"

"Well, just 'cause we are a bit older, it ain't like we died. Man's got needs. Thankfully, women do too."

Truth rolled his eyes. "Senior-bro, who are you talking to? Where are you? I know. We all know. You guys make teens look like they took a vow of chastity. But eight in a year. Are you deliberately trying to get infected or what?"

"What? No, never!" There was a pause. Then a longer pause. The old man shifted around, looking everywhere but at Truth. Eventually, he broke down.

"You get lonely." His voice was soft. Roughened by age and withered. A Level One, and one that had lived a hard life. No fancy life-extension spells or potions for him. Cultivation might take him to a hundred. Maybe only to ninety. Well. Normally. Truth wouldn't bet on him seeing his seventy-ninth birthday under the circumstances.

Truth nodded, encouraging him to talk.

"Lots of lonely people. Sometimes it's about romance, or friendship, just trying to feel like you aren't outliving everyone you knew and cared about. *Never too late to make new friends* and all that stuff. But for me, it's about not waking up alone. Just . . . hate that. I don't even really care who I sleep with. Don't even care that much if we have sex, though we usually do. I just . . . I don't want to wake up alone."

"So, you find whoever's lonely—"

"A few drinks, maybe a lot of drinks—" the old man continued.

"My place or yours?" Truth finished.

"Yeah. And by that point, I'm not really thinking about much of anything."

"Tried keeping condoms on the nightstand? Maybe a few charms?"

"Yeah, but we are all in our seventies and eighties, you know? Nobody's getting pregnant. Even with the alchemist's help, you don't want to waste time."

"It isn't wasted time, bro. It's how you make sure you get invited back to bed a second time. As I think you know by now. Bro, you can literally get a handful, two handfuls, of condoms, for free, from the nursing station. Literally the only free things in the hospital. Get 'em. Use 'em. Or in a month or two, your whole apartment building is quarantined by the army, and then you really will be lonely."

The old man sighed and seemed to shrink in on himself. "Well. I'll try."

Truth left the old man and had a nurse page the resident. The announcement over the loudspeakers was an impressively malicious touch, Truth thought. He hadn't even asked the nurse to do that.

Truth was visibly irritated and tapping his foot by the time the resident scrambled around the corner. "Doctor, I am so sorry! I just couldn't—"

"Junior-bro, every second we spend with a patient costs money. Costs the hospital money, costs the patients money. Or their insurance. Every. Second. If I can put a brochure in his hands, I don't have to explain things in person, right? So, why can't you get a brochure, bro? What school did you go to?"

"I—I attended Bosan-——

"All right, third-tier school, I should lower my expectations. Disappointing! Come on, junior-bro; let's see if there is anything worth salvaging in you."

Truth strode off, trailing the praying-for-death resident behind him.

"Who's next?"

"Male, fifty, hit by a wagon. Out of surgery for the moment."

"Someone cast ANCEF?"

"Yes, Doctor. As well as a complete demon-eye workup, bloodwork, bile work, phlegm work, everything, really. It . . . would probably be faster to list the things that aren't wrong with him than list the things that are."

"Who's doing his bones?"

"I don't think a bonesetter has been called for yet. They are still trying to repair his internal organs and keep his brain from swelling more than it already is."

Truth frowned. "That's not very bone-like."

"Err. No, Doctor."

"Shame. What's his insurance like?"

"Starbrite."

That got a raised eyebrow from Truth. "What's he doing here, then?"

"We were the closest available hospital, and he wouldn't have survived the ambulance ride to Eternal Polestar Partners Hospital."

"All right, write this down—patient-bro is to be given the most expensive care possible to get him prepped and stabilized for transport. I want ANCEF charms, I want blood replenishment charms, Golden Body Charms—" Truth rattled off everything the System remembered as being both a medical charm and vaguely relevant to the condition at hand. "And don't forget to include that he had lunch here, used a full day in an ER private suite, can't forget the room materials, have to bill for those too. Top-notch full-time attending nurse care. Eeeh . . . four nurses. Oh, and put down every doctor on the floor for a consultation."

"Should I bill the ambulance as a Class 1A Ambulance? That's what we usually do for Starbrite cases."

"Naturally. Both ways. Even if Polestar sends their own."

"Yes, Doctor. Standard Starbrite package coming up."

"Now, that's good thinking." Truth nodded approvingly. Management. It was all management. How could you spend the least and bill the most while still pretending to serve the public? That was the game. What was maddening was that there was almost no opportunity to actually cast Cup and Knife!

It was management again. You were doing customer management by letting the patient think they were being seen by the big, important doctor, time management in the form of minimizing the thought you spent on each patient, resource management by getting them in and out with a maximum of expense (for them) and a minimum of expenditure (for you), and even reputation management in the form of looking professional and decisive.

Healing the patient was, at best, an incidental byproduct of the system.

Truth was alarmed to discover he was good at it. There were shades of the Prince in there, but it wasn't just that. Something about walking through the halls, declaring that if people would just *shut up and listen*, he could cure what ails them. Something calling from the depths of his blood.

The methodology was quite straightforward. He would ask what the next patient's problem was, quiz the resident about how the problem was supposed to be addressed, sigh dramatically, then go do exactly what the resident suggested, just with liters upon liters of confidence and bro-itude. Throw in a heavy dose of social engineering and cynicism, and the patients and the resident alike thought he was God's gift to orthopedics. Possibly to medicine generally.

Follow it up with a deceptively casual "Junior-bro will handle the paperwork for you" to tidy up the loose ends. Move on to the next patient. The resident wouldn't be sleeping any time in the next calendar week, but that, too, was normal.

Where things got sticky were the psychiatric cases. He ran them through a quick checklist (conveniently provided by the hospital, who knew damn well no nonspecialist was going to adequately identify a mental condition) and, once their billing category had been determined, parked them in a room to wait for whatever psychiatrist was on call to make their way to them.

Occasionally, a sedative would be prescribed. More often, nothing was prescribed, despite the patient's repeated requests. Screening out the addicts was a depressingly necessary step in the process. He had ejected four from the hospital already and was quite certain more would follow.

"All right, next patient?"

"Fifteen-year-old male, suicide attempt."

"Fifteen? Nasty. History?"

"Clean, from what we can tell. No history of abuse, disease, substance abuse; if he's bullied at school, it hasn't escalated to the point where someone's made a note of it. Mom's a dental hygienist; dad manages a Happy Happy Mart. Attends—"

"Point is that he's a normal kid from an upper-D-Tier family?"

"Yes, Doctor."

"With no obvious reason to self-harm?"

"Yes, Doctor."

"How?"

"Mixed up household cleansers in the bathtub, didn't properly seal the door, and a neighbor called the fire department when she thought a fire was breaking out in their unit."

Truth nodded.

"How did he respond to the questionnaire?"

"He didn't."

"We haven't run it yet?" Truth raised an eyebrow, strongly suggesting that *some* bro was very doomed.

"We ran it, Doctor; it's just that he didn't respond to questions."

"Nonresponsive, nonverbal, what?"

"He understands what he is told and can speak; he just doesn't. It doesn't appear to be autism, or at least there is no indication of it in his record."

Truth looked in on the kid. He just sat on the bed, staring at the floor. Not moving, not calling out, not looking particularly happy or sad. He still had some charms taped to his check and neck, a monitoring sigil stuck to the inside of his wrist. But all in all, he appeared to be an almost sickeningly average Jeon teenager.

"Parents were called?"

"Yes, and they are trying to get off shift, but . . ."

Truth nodded.

Truth walked into the little cloth-covered cubicle. Gently touching on Incisive, he said—"*Talk to me.*"

The kid shrugged. Truth let the silence drag on. Eventually, the kid spoke.

"I thought it through. I just . . . thought everything through. I can't make friends. Don't see the point. I can't see a reason to study. Can't see a reason to play sports, or games, or read. Can't see the future. It's all going wrong, and it's only getting worse. Nobody was mean to me, or not more than usual. I don't think I'm crazy. It's just . . . there isn't anything good coming, and being alive hurts. So . . . why live?"

CHAPTER 38

REBELLION!

Truth was fairly flummoxed. "So, having considered all the relevant information, you just decided to die?"

"Yeah. Basically." The kid nodded.

Truth had to control the urge to say something about *smart to leave early and beat the rush.* Kid had tried to kill himself with a cloud of poison gas. He deserved better than someone laughing at him. Not that Truth thought his personal views on the subject made a lot of rational sense.

"Not going to lie, little bro. Tough one."

The kid shrugged.

"If it was a chemical imbalance in your brain, or demons or addiction or something, I have a procedure for that." Truth waved his clipboard. "Philosophical resolve to die isn't in the procedures manual."

The kid shrugged again.

"Well, it is. Suicide watch, followed by a consult by feelings-bro. But I think you get what I mean."

"Bro?"

"Yeah?"

"No, you keep saying *bro.*"

"Oh. Yeah." Truth nodded.

"Why?" The kid looked curious.

"Because I basically agree with you, kid-bro. Everything is just *incredibly* cursed."

That got Truth a weird look. No matter. He was used to them at this point.

"You agree with me?"

"Your premises, not your conclusion."

The kid worked it out in his head.

"Oh."

Then he shrugged.

Truth's mouth twitched into an approximation of a smile.

"Basically, I decided to be a pain in the ass, kid-bro. Everything is doomed, so I'd enjoy it. I'd find things that seemed meaningful to me to do, and even if they didn't wind up mattering in some global, cosmic sense, I'd have fun with it. I would live a completely selfish life of helping others." Truth nodded. "So far, it's been a great success. Not all sunshine and roses, but things are definitely better for me now, compared to how they were when I was growing up."

This got him another, more intensely judgmental look.

"You trying to be funny?"

"No, I am famously not good at jokes."

"You got famous for that?"

"Yes. I am known far and wide as a bro who cannot tell good jokes." Truth's face was very severe.

"You still haven't explained the *bro* thing, though. Are you sure you are a doctor?"

"Bro. Did I go to med school or the gym?" Truth waved a muscular hand over his incredibly sculpted body. "And yes, it does. Everyone is my bro. Without limitations. All are bros. Some are bad-bros. Out there hurting people, being jerks. It's not good, but they are still bros."

The kid gave him an impressively flat stare.

"We agree the world is cursed, right?" Truth asked the teen.

"Yeah."

"So . . . we just go along with it?"

"What's the point of fighting?"

"Bro, the point is the fighting! I win by having fun! I win by finding a point to the things I am doing. The whole game is rigged? All right, world bro. Watch me flip the table and play my own damn game."

This had the kid looking at him like he was the one in need of psychiatric consultation.

"You . . . are fighting the world by being a bro. Just . . . bro-ing. All the time. Full-time bro."

"Bro! You get it, bro!"

"And women?"

"They can do it too. Obviously." This time, Truth gave the kid a *Why are you so weird?* look.

"No, I mean, are they also bros?"

"Yes. Obviously. Look, kid-bro, discrimination on the basis of gender is really not good-bro behavior. Women are just as capable—"

The kid buried his face in his hands. "*How do they bro?*"

"How do any of us, bro? Indeed, what, in our heart of hearts, does it mean to bro the world? I ask that question all the time, and am constantly refining my answer." Truth nodded wisely. "But the first step, I think, is acknowledging the cursedness of everything and resolving to be part of the problem."

"I thought you were being part of the solution." The kid was caught up in it now, battling through the flying leaves of the autumn storm of Truth's "logic."

"Don't be silly. *You* were being part of the solution. Clearly, the world wants everybody to suffer. *I*, on the other hand, am determined to make as many people as I can *not* suffer. Starting with myself. Even if I die having only pleased myself, I will count it as a win. I am therefore, definitionally, part of the problem."

"You, Dr. Bro—"

"It's Dr. Bone-Bro, actually. I'm a board-certified orthopedic specialist. We do an extra couple years of training compared to squishier fields."

"Dr. Bone-Bro, do you have, like, hospital ID or something?"

"Ah, worried I'm pulling the ol' *Put on scrubs and pretend to be a doctor* game, eh? Well, it is a classic. Here—" Truth stuck out an empty hand. Level Five using magic on a Level Zero? This kid would swear blind he saw a valid ID.

"How did you get your name changed to Bone-Bro?! And didn't get immediately fired?"

Ah, whoops. Might have overdone it. Oh, well. Never apologize, never explain. *That's* the senior doctor way!

"Bro. Do you know how tight the job market is for doctors right now? And it's only going to get worse as the army starts drafting more and more of us. I could set up a squat rack in the OR, and the only thing hospital admin-bro would do is make sure it's properly sterilized before every surgery."

"Why would you put a squat rack in the OR?"

"Do you know how good squats are for you? They are practically the perfect full-body resistance exercise. Gotta use good form, or not-bone bits don't like it. But if you do have good form, squats are the *best*. You wanna do some squats right now, kid-bro? Bodyweight only, sorry; don't have my rack and weight pile handy."

"No, I'm good."

"Really? I love doing bodyweight workouts. Not as good as lifting, obviously, but it's just so damn satisfying, feeling my body move."

"Okay . . ." The look was bordering on pitying this time. Truth shook his head at the ignorance of his juniors.

"Listen, procedures usually exist for a reason. I'm keeping the suicide watch in place, and when feelings-bro finally gets out of the tweed and into scrubs, she'll be down to have a talk. All I'm saying is *give rebellion a chance.* Try it out. Focus on *just enjoying the fight.* People are going to be jerks. They are going to do the wrong thing all the time. You can't control that. You control you and how you think about things. So . . . *become part of the problem. Enjoy making the world a better place. Not because it's getting better. Just because it is fun to do.*" Truth coughed.

Was this . . . reconciliation? Might be.

"You are going?" Kid sounded a bit sad about that.

"Yep. I'm Dr. Bone-Bro, and I'm doing rounds right now. Hear that screaming? That bro needs my help. So, I'm gonna go help him."

"Are you going to be around later?"

"Kid-bro, I am everywhere. You be good now." Truth walked out. The resident had "just closed his eyes for a second" leaning up against a pillar. Truth tapped him on the shoulder to wake him up.

"Patient is scheduled for suicide watch and feelings-bro convo?"

The resident blinked, bleary eyes trying to reconcile the data they were receiving with what Comrade Ears was reporting.

"Uh. Yes, Doctor."

"Good. Next patient."

Was there a better way to help the kid? He didn't know. He really, really didn't know. But they were in a hospital, and presumably there were people that did know, so keeping him interested in the world and focused on nondestructive stuff should be a good thing, right?

He could only hope.

The next few cases passed on almost autopilot. He looked them over, went, "*Hmmm.* Bro, let me explain what happens next," and generally cribbed from the now completely bewildered but worshipful resident.

He even managed to find some orthopedics cases and snuck in a bit of Cup and Knife work. It might not be procedure, but it did let him loudly lecture the resident about patients "being sent for a surgical eval when any competent first-year med student-bro should have them up and walking off the stiffness in six minutes or less."

Truth's voice was raised to a delicate bellow, audible considerably beyond the ordinary human audible spectrum. "Tell me, junior-bro, do they still study magic in med school? Are things so bad in whatever fleapit university you attended that they don't cover *spells*?"

"It . . . it presented as a comminuted displaced distal radius fracture with intra-articular split, apex dorsal angulation, and a radial styloid split. I . . . We thought . . ."

"Oh, please! An eye-bro could make that diagnosis in his sleep, never mind a real doctor! And don't think I didn't notice that 'we,' bro. You are the *doctor*. Don't try to blame this on the nurse. *You* are responsible for your dogshit opinions! Now let me guess—you want to bolt down the bone fragments with a piece of metal? Hmm? Maybe carve the patients open like the luxurious chicken dinners you are eating every night?"

The resident, who plainly hadn't slept or eaten real food in three days, could only gawp at the unfairness of the accusation.

"We are mage-doctors! Miracle healers! Not barbarians. Not *butchers*. We make people whole in this place. *We HEAL people in this place!* Let's see if you can be a little less disappointing with the next patient."

It might be unfair to the resident, but every doctor, nurse, and patient in earshot was firmly convinced that a *very* senior orthopedic doctor was now in attendance. Confidence shot way up. Even the patients settled down, feeling more optimistic about how everything would work out.

With the right sort of eyes, and if you were looking for it, you could see the ripples Truth left in his wake. He was watching for them—the subtle changes in expression, the way their bodies shifted from pain and fear to pain and acceptance. The present hurt—but it wasn't forever. Relief was coming.

It was remarkable how often that was enough. Someone competent is coming to take charge. He will tell you what needs to happen to make everything better. And he will listen.

It was that last bit that Truth reckoned was the secret sauce. Even if you walked into the room knowing exactly what their problem was and how you would solve it, spending a couple of minutes giving someone your focused attention did something for them. He didn't know if it was the illusion of control on their part or the magic of having someone of high status really listening to you for once.

It was a pretty interesting afternoon. When his shift was up, he pulled the resident and head nurse to one side. "Who's his supervisor?" Truth asked the nurse.

"Dr. Frink."

"All right, I'm writing orders for what's-his-name here,"

"Bill. My name is Bill—"

"Please. Please don't talk. Save your old school at least a little face." Truth resolutely turned his back on the reeling resident, and continued talking to the nurse.

"This bro is presenting with clinical malnourishment and parasomnia, including insomnia, with comorbidities including audio, visual, and sensory hallucinations, memory dysfunction, slurred speech, delayed reaction time, paranoia, ocular dysfunction, and loss of motor control. Given that he presents a significant danger to patients and himself, I am ordering him a week's bedrest and a hospital-supplied six extra protein rations a day." The nurse was nodding along, jotting notes down on a pad. Truth pressed on.

"He is to be prescribed twenty-five milliliters Valeri-Somm or generic equivalent before bedtime for the first two days, not to exceed three days without reevaluation from feelings-bro. He is not to return to work until the course of treatment is completed and he can be recertified as safe to work by feelings-bro and brain-bro." The nurse finished jotting it down on her pad and nodded, with a definite gleam in her eye.

"What . . . what is going on?" asked the bewildered Bill.

"Thank you for stepping in, Doctor. I didn't feel like it was my place to say anything," the nurse said.

"Of course." Truth gently put a hand on the back of the resident's head and subtly ran Cup and Knife, knocking him out.

"A bed might be a bit much to ask, but is there a linen closet you could shove Bill-bro into for ten to twelve hours?" he asked as he guided the unconscious Bill onto a gurney.

"Sure. Wonderfully soft blankets in closet 2-1093. I'll make some room for him. About time those bums woke up, anyway."

"How's the suicidal kid?"

"With Psychiatric now. We didn't need to sedate him, restrain him . . . he's been no trouble, really. So. I don't know. I guess that's promising."

"Well. It's a start. And tell Frink from me that the next time he pulls a stunt like this, he better stick to walking on crowded streets."

CHAPTER 39

SIGNS AND PORTENTS

Truth kept the scrubs. They weren't dirty, really, and he liked having a costume change on hand. One trip into the locker room, a quick change of clothes, and Dr. Bone-Bro, MD, PhD (U. Jeon) D. Thaum (Hons. Behem U.) vanished. Exiting the locker room was Peuth Reduchi, Talisman-Service Technician First Class, Ever-Rite Equipment Rentals Corporation (a Starbrite Family Company.)

Amazing how you can be invisible two completely different ways, in the same place, at roughly the same time. He got a little grin out of the whole thing.

Had the day been a waste? No, not really. He had a better sense of a lot of things now. He might not be much closer to cracking Cup and Knife, but progress was progress. Besides, it felt good. The whole exercise, even the stupid, annoying people, made him feel good. He wouldn't want to do that every day or even every week. But for an occasional thing? It really wasn't anything too bad.

He paused as he watched a little girl walking through the hospital with her mom. He couldn't tell which of them needed help. Maybe they were there to visit someone.

Oh, it was the kids.

That's why he did all this. It was the kids in the factory and the meat-processing plant. He just wanted to do something decent. Something . . . unarguably good. He could come in, make changes, and make people's lives better. Even if only for a moment. Even if *better* just meant *less bad*. He wasn't helpless there. He could do things.

Was that another secret of Starbrite's control? That learned helplessness? He had left those kids in the factory because he couldn't imagine a plausible scenario where anything good happened to them. It was Starbrite's favorite trick—you don't need to defeat people if you have already convinced them they can't win.

Time to push a lot harder than he had been. Time to see just how hard he had to shake the tree to make clues fall out of it.

Stepping out of the hospital was disorienting. It had been daytime when he went in. It was night now. Somehow, he hadn't felt the connection between light and dark—like the hospital existed in a bubble universe, a pocket of white blood cells fighting a cyst trapped under the skin of the "real."

Golden cherubim appeared over the city. As one, they started a loud scream. A pause, then another. Pause, then another. People bolted from the sidewalks into buildings or out of them and into subways.

Elderly folk seemed to materialize on the streets, bright orange armbands and thick helmets both stamped with *Air Raid Warden*. They were waving signs or glowing talismans, yelling, "This way! This WAY! One orderly line! There is plenty of room for everyone; now go, go, go!"

He bounced between high-rises, wanting to see for himself. Up on the rooftop, watching the lights go out over the city. Watching the lights start to glow on the northern edge of the horizon. Explosions. Streaks of flaming bolts firing out at ten thousand rounds a second, chewing through summons and spell birds.

Traceries of gold and orange and blue and venom green twisting and balling together in the night sky, obscuring the stars behind them. Closer to the city, flights of angels flew in rigid patterns. Waiting for the enemy to come. Demons, fat toad things, dotted the ground in their dozens. Enormous eyes tracking targets, waiting for the opportunity to launch acid in long spears up into the sky.

Anti-air batteries spun around, subtle detection systems scraping the aether for the precise nature of the incoming attack. Did they load counterspell rounds to take out tactical curses? Banishments, abjurations, or simply load for carnage and shred any incoming spell birds? Systems of systems, talisman networks of incredible power and subtlety, working with some of the best spellcraft that money could buy, all to lock down the sky.

And if it didn't work, there were always the brutal artillery pieces behind them. Truth let his eyes run over them. Not a shred of light there, to make things harder on attackers. They were in use, though, the enormous fetishes rising from the ground and swiveling to the north.

Specially beastcrafted horrors were bred to make artillery. There were hidden ranches, guarded by powerful mages and strictly controlled, raised to the perfect age to be slaughtered and re-formed into fetishes. A brief, suffering life, but in death, they slaughtered their human "gods."

Not firing. Not yet. The front line was still well north of there. Just being ready.

Truth kept his eyes firmly on the horizon. He didn't know enough about aerial combat to have a sense of how this was going. The battle sometimes got a little closer but not much. Ground battles took hours at a minimum; a day or more was perfectly normal. Aerial battles were . . . faster, probably.

It went on for six hours. It would seem to stop, make him think it was over, then another flight of summons would come winging over the horizon, supported by a blizzard of curses and cheap witch-crafted horrors designed to flood the air defense system and let the more expensive, potent summons make killing blows.

The defenders knew what Onis was up to, of course. They met cheap horrors with cheap AA needles and summons with launched barrages of banishment charms. You could watch it playing out again and again. The sheer repetitiveness of it was sanity-straining. It took a while, but Truth eventually got it. Onis never thought they were going to break through the air defenses with this. They just wanted to make Jeon show what they had and force them to start spending down their stockpiles.

He wasn't watching the economics of warfare; he was watching the warfare of economics. He didn't know if it was ironic or not, but some morbid part of him did want to grin.

Shortly after dawn, the all clear was sounded. People started slowly walking out of the tunnels and shelters, carefully counted by the wardens. The city hadn't taken any damage beyond financial and to morale. Truth could read it in the faces of the emerging citizens. The bombs didn't land anywhere near them, and they still caught some of the shrapnel.

Should he leave the city? Truth considered it, watching the sun slowly rise. It was, in many ways, the "smart" choice. One should never stand on the X, and there had just been a literal air raid. Didn't get much more *on the X* than that.

Truth shook away the negative thoughts. He didn't want to leave just yet. He had no particular fondness for the city. What he did like about it, though, was the way it was so clearly a city under tension. All those crisscrossing wires, connecting thousands of different points and millions of lives, steadily wrenching tighter and tighter. Building up strain. Storing energy.

It really wouldn't take much to make a whole city convulse, would it? Not that he wanted anything *too* bad to happen. He didn't want the city to fall. He just needed to flush some very fat rats from their hiding places.

He watched the sun rise, blessing the world with light, heat, and cosmic rays, at least for a little bit longer. Truth bowed politely, then jumped off the roof. He knew where to begin his hunt, but it was time for sleep. It had been a long day.

And with that jaunty thought, Truth found himself stuck.

Just where am I going to sleep?

There are few things quite so miserable as looking for a hotel room when you are tired. The city was packed. He would have thought it would be pretty empty, what with the *enormous battle lines* just outside the city, but no. The city was host to dozens of apparently important industries, so the workers couldn't just run off when they pleased. Likewise, soldiers on liberty would routinely come into the city. There were regular visits from government officials, business leaders, and their thousands of underlings.

Someone had to make sure that the Q2 Reciprocating Widget numbers were properly correlated and organized according to the latest accounting directives. Who did you expect to do it, the CFO? No, it was dozens of more-junior officials, each dispatched with the knowledge that a single error in their tedious job would result in nothing, on account of it never being discovered, or their execution. No middle ground permitted.

Bonuses for doing dangerous work? Rewards for hard and careful labor? Call internal security; I've found a spy! You certainly are no son of Jeon!

No, the hotels were full, and apartments did not seem to be noticeably empty. It was time to pull a maneuver he had hoped to avoid. He found a suitably generic apartment building, caught the door as someone was walking out, and started listening for people heading out to work. As people stepped out of their rooms, he stepped in. Just having a quick look around at the state of the place. Third time lucky—the owner had invested in a large sectional sofa, so Truth didn't have to try and ignore the warm spot in a freshly vacated bed.

"Thrush, keep watch while I sleep."

"Yes, dread magus. Seep well."

A few minutes later, Perks slithered out of the confines of Truth's shirt. He was a pretty relaxed snake, as snakes went, and was usually happy to be next to a perpetual source of heat. Still, it did you good to get out and stretch, so out he went.

The snake wound his way across the sofa and onto the floor, then made his way to the walls. His tongue flicked out, tasting the strange smells in the air. It slowly made its way along the wall to a crevice between a kitchen cabinet and a cold box. A tiny, tiny little gap, far too small for Perks. Most humans would have ignored it entirely, as the gap was barely the width of a human finger.

Perks curled up and went still. Perks didn't have eyelids, but you could be forgiven for thinking him asleep.

Roughly an hour after Truth fell asleep, a mouse came out of the wall. It generally preferred the nights, but when your metabolism burned through calories like an oilfield fire, you ate whenever you could.

It was a very careful mouse. It could smell the sebum trail it, and other mice, had left behind. No smells of predators. Some strange new smells but no predator urine or anything like that. Being an urban mouse, with its last twelve generations living and dying in this very apartment building, it had never smelled a snake.

Squeezing through a gap that forced its body to radically compact, the mouse made the passage out into the dangerous but food-rich world beyond its nest. Staying hidden simply was not an option. Hunger compelled it to forage. Its flesh insisted the biochemical bonfires be fueled.

The mouse was careful. It led with its most accurate sensor, its nose. It swept the air for any traces of danger. Whiskers carefully shook, sensitive to the air around them. No sudden movement in the air would be overlooked. It took a few careful steps out into the room. Its eyes weren't very good, but it used them carefully anyway. Wide ears twitched, listening for a betraying footfall.

It was a careful little mouse. It moved silently and carefully into the still apartment. It was really very careful. It didn't matter.

Perks exploded out from his coil, striking faster than the mouse could react. The viper's fangs sank through skin and muscle, sliding past bone, piercing organs as they curved back and in. The microscopic amount of venom did almost no additional damage, but it surely didn't help the mouse any. A few quick gulps later and the mouse was safely dead and swallowed.

Perks curled back up where he was. A few minutes later, apparently uncomfortable, Perks retraced his path and returned to Truth's chest. There, it got on with the important business of digesting. A surprisingly small bulge made its way down the length of him. It would take time to break down. That suited Perks fine. He was perfectly content just where he was.

CHAPTER 40

DISAPPOINTING JUNIORS

Truth woke feeling remarkably refreshed. He took a moment to savor the feeling, then another to savor the sectional sofa he was sprawled across. The microfiber fabric was really nice. Not fancy. Not terribly expensive. Just really nice under the hand. No bets on how well it would hold up to long-term use, but he'd chance a modest sum on its being very stain-resistant. He stretched and flexed, running a quick internal inventory.

His spells were as they should be, filling his apertures nicely. The Meditations of Valentinian had expanded to a point of almost-insane complexity, fractal in scope. Looking at it, Truth was quite certain that it would continue to expand and unfold even after he created his Nascent Soul. However that process went.

Incisive was similar. It looked like nothing much at a glance, but the longer you looked at it, the more complexities emerged. Truth tried to figure out how "reconciliation" fit into the whole package, but it still just didn't compute. He would ask Merkovah about it, but under the circumstances, that might be difficult.

Hmm. Siphios might have the *best* demonologists, but it wasn't like Jeon didn't have *good* ones. Might be worth keeping an eye out.

Cup and Knife remained its stubbornly impenetrable self. Now that he had used it extensively, he could really feel where it broke down. Although . . . was it a little less broken than he remembered?

<<It is. It happened yesterday.>>

But I hardly used it yesterday. Like, less than ten times.>>

<<Not . . . exactly. I was watching it in action. You weren't just using Incisive when you were doing your social attacks on the beliefs of the patients. Cup and Knife also kicked into action. Particularly when you were doing things like persuading Grandpa Horny to throw a rubber on it and talking to the suicidal kid.>>

It was running without me knowing it?!

<<Again, not exactly. More like it was filling in its own blanks. You might want to take a look at the fragment of Etenesh.>>

Truth directed his attention to the little ball of warmth that was Etenesh's gift to him. He was never entirely clear on what it was doing. Hopefully making him a better person, but he kind of doubted it. At least he hadn't hurt it any. He had been worried that might happen.

Is it . . . brighter?

<<Yeah. No idea why, though.>>

Because I was helping people?

<<You have helped people before. And while Etenesh was always a lot more sociable and positive than you, she wasn't exactly a universal beacon of benevolence, either. If she did any charitable work, she never mentioned it.>>

Truth looked at the flickering ball of flame, trying to guess what it meant. *Maybe she reached Level Four?*

<<I don't have a better guess.>>

The little spark was glowing a brighter shade of gold than before. It really did warm him up. He tried pushing his love for Etenesh toward it. Nothing changed, but it felt kind of good to do. He imagined Etenesh was sitting inside the little fireball, really tried to visualize her, and spoke in his heart.

Thank you. For everything. Believing in me. That I can be more than a rat. That I was never a rat at all. Thank you for fighting for me. Thank you for thinking I am someone worth fighting for. Thank you for understanding that I'm a head full of busted talismans and bad coping mechanisms. Thank you for being patient. Thank you for being kind. Thank you for being.

He withdrew his consciousness from his soul. The sun was still up, but it was getting on toward evening. Looked like it was going to be a beautiful day.

Truth dressed in his army uniform. He momentarily debated between the officer variant and the sergeant variant and opted for sergeant. First, because he was planning on hitting some nightclubs and second, it just took so much less energy to run.

Out into the street and off to a grease-trap sandwich shop. Once upon a time, heaps of cheap meat would be stewing in their own fat, just waiting to be ladled onto sandwiches. These days, it had all gone vegetarian. Just not the same.

"Hey, you guys see all the late-night after-club crowd, right?"

"Sure." The guy filling the sandwich kept his hands moving quickly. It was early yet.

"So, I got two related questions. First, I've got a twenty-four-hour liberty. Where should I go party? Second question—where should I send my lieutenant, who also has a twenty-four-hour liberty? Ideally so that he has an amazing time, thinks I'm a genius, and doesn't bust my balls when we are back on base?"

That got a longer snort and silence. Truth waited patiently. If nothing else, the sandwich looked okay, and the sauces were smelling great.

"You might try Elanes. Think they are still open. If not, you might need to make nice with your lieutenant at Caoco. Not a lot of nightclubs still open."

"Seriously? People got to relax, even if there is a war on."

"Tell that to the cops. City is cracking down hard on late-night shops. I had to shut down last night because of the air raid. Now they are telling me I have to be closed by ten! TEN!"

"Damn. How's a man supposed to make a living?" Truth shook his head in commiseration. He handed over his ration card, then asked, "Where are those clubs?"

"Both of 'em are on Third Avenue. Caoco is three blocks North of Borkcsh Square; Elanes is two south of it."

"Got it. Thanks."

"Thank me by buying more stuff." the cook grumbled. Truth thought that was fair enough, and snagged a cookie and some chips to go with the sandwich. And a cold tea. He had slept through the hottest part of the day, but summer in Jeon was brutal. You needed something to take the edge off.

Truth walked over to Elanes. It was a blue-collar joint—plastic chairs set out around low, mismatched tables. *Nightclub* was probably a stretch. *Bar that also had music and kind of a dance floor* was closer, but not really concise. *Meat market* would do. This was a place where people came alone, intending to leave in company.

Once he had Elanes scouted to his satisfaction, he walked up to Caoco. This was a much-classier place, in that there was hardly any "there" at all. Just a big sign over a door, with a few overpriced bars around it. Fancier than Elanes without actually being *fancy*. He waffled back and forth about whether he was excessively lowballing his target, but the happy proximity of the two clubs was too good to pass up.

He checked around the back, but there was nothing of interest. An alleyway, some dumpsters and trash cans. Nothing of note. No gang signs, either, which was simultaneously encouraging and worrying. Even the nice clubs were run by gangs in Harban. Either that had changed, or they had gotten much more discreet here in Gamphe.

For some reason, that sounded wrong. He puzzled at the thought for a minute. Then a second minute. The realization bit like a spider.

Truth had completely forgotten what town he was in. He was no longer in Gamphe, right? Right. This was Confen. A town not too close or too far from Gamphe. The total number of nightclubs was going to be limited. The degree of gang-member affiliation amongst the citizens would also be very limited.

There was a sudden sense of lightheadedness. He had been running for so long. Fighting for so long. Drifting through the people and places of this world for so long. He was starting to lose touch. Lose that sense of place and people.

He found a bench and sat hard. He was in Confen. North of Harban. Near Gamphe. Right now, he was sitting on a bench near the nightclub Caoco. It took him a while to settle down, but that was all right. He had some time to kill.

Night fell. Truth was bored but didn't stir. He had the irrational fear that if he got off the bench, the whole town of Confen would fly away into the night sky. Which would be quite something to watch, but he had spent all this time getting there and messing about there, and he really didn't want all that to be for nothing. So, he would hold everything down, sitting on this bench.

Night came and with it the partiers. It was a pretty lackluster turnout. He didn't know what day of the week it was. Apparently not a Friday. Quite possibly not even a Thursday. Everyone at the "nice" nightclub looked like ordinary folks to Truth. Young, mostly, including some who blatantly should have stayed home with the kids.

Was his whole plan there pointless? He had planned to use the pressure of the coming siege of Gamphe . . . wait. If this wasn't Gamphe, what did it mean that there was an air raid just north of here? They were still *pretty* close to Gamphe, so the big defenses up there caught the attack, but . . . this was an ordinary town. And they were launching air raids. Committing significant amounts of firepower to the raid. Why? Just for the atrocity of it all?

There wasn't anything special about this town. At least, not so far as he knew. Nothing that would justify the cost of the spell birds and summons flung at the town. He thought back to what he heard in the Onis army camp. Onis wasn't playing smart, on purpose. They were looking to drown Jeon in blood and didn't really care if it was their own.

Could it be as simple as that? They flung a major bombing raid at Confen purely as a reconnaissance in force of Jeon's air defenses? It made an awful sort of logic, but there *was* a logic to it. Sooner or later, they would find a gap. Once they did, the red waters would burst through, soaking into the dirt.

The club was as hopping as it was going to get. Truth walked in, feeling a little shaky. The music was loud, pulsing, bone shaking, even though the dance floor was at best a third full. The bar was doing a steady business, though hardly straining on the bartenders, and the cocktail waitresses managed to look even more bored than usual. Which, in Truth's experience, was actually something of a feat.

There was a "VIP section," sort of. It was just a cordoned-off corner with fancier banquettes, dancing spirits trapped in glass plinths, and its own special mood lighting. A sort of pale lavender color. Flattering on . . . someone, somewhere, presumably. Not on anyone there currently. It was easy to spot the Big Man. He was literally bigger than everyone else, considering the horizontal plane. It was him, some flunkies, and hangers-on to the flunkies. It was as perfectly pathetic as you could hope for.

Truth found one of the prettier cocktail waitresses and got her attention. He was the spitting image of a handsome young officer, so she was content to talk to him.

"I'm in town on a short liberty, and the brass is cracking down on disciplinary issues. Before I bring anyone else into the club, who's Fatso in the corner? Anyone who might be a problem?"

"Him? No. That's Verro Pashchen. His mom runs Pashchen's Wagon World out on Route Five. He's rich by local standards, but really . . ." She and Truth shared a look. "No, the one you need to look out for is the lady in the leather jacket next to him. That's Mira Pashchen, his cousin. Verro is putting on the show to get in her good books. She's the only person at that table with actual connections."

"Oh? Who to?"

The woman in the leather jacket was pretty, but Truth had seen far prettier. There was a hardness to her face that wasn't charming at all. And knew it. And didn't care.

"Hard to say for sure, but at a guess? Internal Security."

And just like that, his evening improved.

CHAPTER 41

SON OF JEON

Truth carefully observed his target. Very carefully. Cops had a sixth sense about when they were being watched. While he had never enjoyed the "pleasure" of an Internal Security officer's company, they were notoriously, and justly, paranoid. He would put money down on her either being there on a job or being here under immense family pressure. She sure didn't look like she was having fun.

She wore a thin black leather jacket, black wet-effect synthetic-flesh pants, black heels, and he couldn't see the shirt. What he did see was a pair of earrings that he recognized from the "Defensive Enchanted Jewelry" section of the System Store, and a pair of matte-black gems set in mythril rings that he *didn't* recognize but would put a second bet down on them being enchanted, too.

And if those were on display, he was quite certain a veritable arsenal was hidden. If there weren't three anti-glamour glyphs tattooed on her, there would be four or five. Likewise, there must be a double dozen hidden alarms for her to trigger, as well as a few more that she didn't know about. Ready to trip silently and let her bosses know she had been compromised.

As for offensive means . . . a talisman hidden at the small of the back, he guessed, based on how she was sitting. Probably a few more concealed weapons, too. A tiny lightning wand or asp wand tucked up a sleeve. A salivary gland replaced with a beastcrafted venom gland, ready to spit acid or drip sedatives as needed.

Or it could just be the needler and the badge. All the things he was thinking of were damned expensive, after all, and there were famously a *lot* of plainclothes IS agents. Depending on the circumstances, there might not even be a needler. Though he was pretty certain anti-glamour measures were a must. The consequences of not doing so were just absurdly high. Truth knew street cops got enchanted badges to ward off low-level effects.

Even in his particular corner of the slums, little vials of potions or packets of powders could be administered to make people more compliant, beyond what even alcohol and bad decisions could normally manage. Single-use charms or more-powerful talismans were usually privileges reserved for organized crime beyond the street-gangster level. Certainly no one in his tower block could afford, or even get access to, such a thing.

But a little something in a drink? Oh, yes. The Internal Security officer was the only person at the table without a drink in front of them. Truth grinned. *Subtle* was apparently not on tonight's menu.

He looked over the rest of the table, checking for any unanticipated surprises. There were none. They were all Level Ones. Just ordinary folks, out with their "rich" "friend" and his alarmingly powerful cousin. He drifted over, letting the officer persona fade away.

There were recording talismans in the club as well as bouncers. This place saw a comparatively higher-end crowd. Not a single person or talisman in sight was over Level One power. Caoco was a nothing-fancy nightclub in a nothing-fancy big town / small city in almost the geographical middle of the country. Solidly north of Harban without actually being up in the mountains. Nowhere. The biggest nowhere. No wonder the son of a wagon dealer could be a mini-tycoon there.

"Man, that air raid, man!"

"Ah ah ah, none of that. We want happy talk at the table tonight, happy talk."

"You guys still going to watch the fights tomorrow?"

"Yeah, they won't cancel those for anything less than a full-on earthquake."

Truth leaned over one of the guys putting on a show and said (loudly, because nightclubs are nightclubs), *"You aren't even drinking anything, and you still need to 'go to the bathroom.' Just to get away from these . . . people."*

Mira didn't even nod. She just stood up, nodded at the table, and stalked off. Nobody even rolled their eyes. They kept the conversation going until she was out of earshot.

Truth didn't hang around. The IS officer wasn't headed for the bathroom. She headed for the back door. Incisive wasn't sending any alarms, so Truth just shrugged and followed her. She walked over to a nearby dumpster, lifted the lid, and then turned back toward the club. And waited.

Truth narrowed his eyes. She didn't blink. He looked a little closer. Even in the city twilight, those eyes were glassy, pupils the size of pinpricks. Someone, or something, had gotten to her before Truth had.

"Who, or what, am I speaking to?" Truth asked.

"Spiritual Worm 77173428221. You have triggered one of my activation conditions. In the event that you destroy this vessel, please remember to keep Jeon tidy and neatly dispose of any remains." Her voice was uninflected, uninterested. "Message begins." The worm's voice changed.

"To whom it may concern. Each of the active worms in my agents have a copy of this message, along with the same activation condition. My name is

Colonel Eskevan Cho, and you can find me in the IS field office in Runchon. Please disregard the worm—if you do plan on dropping by, I would appreciate you not killing my subordinates for delivering a message."

It was eerie hearing the voice of a sixty-year-old chain-smoking man coming out of a thirty-something year old woman.

"Message ends." The worm's voice returned. "As this vessel is now compromised, under the Wartime Powers Act, they must be considered a potential traitor. Please do your civic duty and kill the traitor. Remember to dispose of the corpse hygienically and report the situation to your nearest police officer."

I know there is a reason why I am trying to save this country. I just—I can't quite seem to recall what it is, at the moment.

"Is it a good life, being a spiritual worm?"

That seemed to throw it for a moment.

"This question is beyond my ability to answer. Please ask a different question."

Fair enough.

"You are a spiritual worm?"

"Yes."

"What is a human?"

"A vessel."

"For what?"

"For a spiritual worm."

Truth laughed silently. Funnily enough, he had almost never used the primary intended function of the Blessing of the Sea of Brass. He laid his hand on the IS agent's head and destroyed the possessing spiritual worm. It wasn't even on the level of an imp.

Life returned to the agent's eyes. She whipped out a needler and swept it back and forth, looking for targets.

"INTERNAL SECURITY; SHOW YOURSELF!"

Truth just shook his head and walked away. It had been a good-enough evening. Time to find dinner and have a good think.

Truth sat up on a rooftop and confronted an unpleasant fact. In addition to not knowing how to cook, he didn't have the means to cook. He had grabbed a cutting board and knives from the Sung mansion, but he had neither hotbox nor stove in his storage ring. He knew you could cook on open fires; he had seen it done. He suspected that there were better portable alternatives.

He just didn't have any of them. Or know how to make them.

"Maybe a portable grill? Throw some charcoal in there, or a heat talisman or something? Wood? Can you throw straight wood in there?"

He had no idea. It would have to be takeout again. Maybe he should stop by a camping store or something? He looked up into the glow of the city lights. It would have to wait until morning.

That message was interesting on several levels. That it existed in the first place. That it was copied on who knows how many spiritual worms inserted into IS agents across Jeon. That it was tripped when he used Incisive to influence the agent. That little collection of facts had the hairs rising on the back of his neck.

Someone, probably several someones, was operating against Incisive. They were building very, very subtle dams and nets for him as he tried to swim the sea of the masses.

The Hell Prince will arrogantly move; he will bend the will of the people around him. Sooner or later, he will run into an agent of Internal Security. And when he does . . .

Well. He didn't think it would be something as crude or direct as explicit violence. Which led to part two of the message.

A name. An address. A plea for his subordinate's life. Even a subtle jab at the worm itself. The worm being implied as part of a system separate from the colonel, despite its being the colonel's message that it was carrying.

Dissecting it a little bit further—there was simply no collection of statements, made by anyone, anywhere, at any time in his life, at any time in the life of the human species, that would persuade Truth that an IS colonel gave any kind of a damn about a subordinate's life. God, personally, could park the Chariot directly in front of Truth and provide a testimonial, and Truth *still* wouldn't believe it.

He would also have a few unrelated questions for the Almighty, but that was neither here nor there.

The plea was calculated. Every word was calculated. This was another attack on his mindset, on the impressed identity Jeon was shaping for him. Hell Prince. Hellish, but a prince would disdain soiling his hands with a lesser's blood. Especially when a proud person lowered their status to beg. It implicitly elevated the prince's status. It put the power in his hands three times over—*if* he *decided* to visit, and *if* he *decided* to spare the subordinate, the colonel would owe him a favor.

It was the logic of gangsters, expressed with the subtlety of ministers. Even if he was resisting the Hell Prince identity, it was a social attack that would work on almost any son of Jeon.

"I, a high-status person, a person you have spent your life *pissing yourself in terror* just thinking of, have taken immense efforts to invite you to visit me. And I'll owe you one if you prove you are the bigger man."

Power. Status. Vanity. Truth had spent long enough introspecting to acknowledge the obvious—the attack hit him like an armful of the good stuff. He could fight the high. He could do his best to stay clean. But he had grown up in these streets. He had grown up eating this with every meal. Got double helpings of it in the meals with no food.

It was what he always wanted.

It was what he killed himself to get. Enough power, enough status, that even the mighty bowed down. That even the prideful took a knee before him.

The thoughts boiled his blood. The drugs worming their way through and warming him, licking at all those fragile places in the mind. *This is what you need to feel good,* it whispered. *This is how your life should be.*

Truth stood on the roof of a nothing building in a nowhere place and felt the world spin around him. Understanding the poison in the wine only made the wine sweeter. The smell of it spooling up his nose and leaving its barbed hooks as the tainted red wine poured down his throat and into his heart. Washing away the old blood, replacing it with the new.

He stood on the roof and reveled in the majesty and terror of it all.

He laughed, a quiet little sound in the night. He touched his chest over his heart, feeling that little fragment of Etenesh burning within him.

Such petty glory. Such hollow majesty. Hadn't he already seen how phony it all was? Didn't he know better since he was a kid?

You only drank the wine when there was no water. With open eyes, he could see the pure torrent pouring down on him every moment of every day. He just had to cup his hands and drink. Nothing in the world tasted better than that.

He pulled Perks out of his shirt and had a good look at him. Perks looked fine, but Truth was sure that it had been more than a week since he had eaten. The old man said Perks needed a mouse a week. He was looking lumpy. A little off.

"All right, buddy. You and I are going to take a little trip to the seaside. But first, we need road snacks."

CHAPTER 42

CAN'T MAKE 'EM EAT

Late-night takeout in Confen was a thing, of course. This was Jeon. Workers coming home at midnight was nothing more than proof of middle-management potential, assuming you weren't talking about one of the big four employers. Then it might be a sign of insufficient commitment. The *real* high flyers were sleeping at their desks and giving themselves towel baths in the washroom.

And the *real-real* high flyers would be parachuting in through family connections, generally after a good night's sleep, an excellent breakfast, and a light workout. Unhappy about that? Be born in a better family next time. In the meantime, know your place and be grateful for what you are given.

Right now, even that tradition of misery was being eroded by the war with Onis. The shops were closed. Offices were closed. The workers were told to go home—their managers were getting evaluated on compliance with wartime directives, and you did not want to be the one to screw up their KPIs.

People at work meant the lights were on. More lights on—easier targets for bombing raids. More people on the streets at night—more chances for sneaky infiltrators to sneak in and cause sabotage. It was all very practical. It just felt intensely alien. Jeon was a country that came alive at night. At least, that was what it felt like in Harban.

Outside the slums, of course. *Smart* people were home, with strong bars over their windows and the doors bolted shut, come sunset in the slums. Dad had worked afternoons sometimes but nights a lot of the time. Looking at the cold, empty streets, Truth wondered if that had eaten at the old bastard. Having to travel from bubble of light to bubble of light, avoiding all the predators you knew were hiding in the dark.

Truth wouldn't have been drinking under those circumstances, but then, he and his father were very different people.

He stroked his chin as he looked up and down the street. Just because the restaurants were closed didn't mean there was nothing to eat. At least, not for Perks. A quick trip around the back to the dumpsters should find a very filling meal.

A quick forty-kilometer-an-hour stroll up the street, and they were outside the Jade Bamboo restaurant. A quick glance at the menu revealed that, yes, they were cheap and generic. Perfect. A quick nip around the back, and the reeking dumpsters testified to both the frugality of the owners and the warming weather.

Cost money to have your trash hauled. Cost money to feed it to demons, too. So, you might as well let it sit for as long as you could, just to keep the expenses down that little bit extra. Or so Truth guessed. Could just be sheer malice toward the neighbors. Either way, he was hearing plenty of furtive scritching noises and the occasional stealthy squeak.

"Welcome to the happy hunting grounds, little buddy. Time to go fulfill that primal instinct."

Truth lowered Perks onto the concrete and waited. Perks writhed a little. Truth thought the snake looked uncomfortable. He wasn't sympathetic. A dignified serpent had to be able to endure this little hardship. Besides, in such a target-rich environment, rough concrete should be utterly meaningless.

When he had been hungry, crawling over rough concrete and under dumpsters had been nothing. Surely, a snake was less particular than a human.

A few minutes passed. Perks' forked tongue tasted the air. Flick flick. He slithered around a little bit, apparently more out of curiosity than killer instinct. Then he slithered back to Truth and raised his body up, pressing against his leg.

Truth had been to enough pet cafes to recognize when an animal was asking for "Uppies!" He'd never seen a snake do it, though. He reached down and picked up his alleged rat snake.

"You are a rat snake." Truth's voice was accusing. Perks didn't change his expression one bit in response. "A rat snake. A snake that, and I think you can follow the logic here, feeds on rats."

Perks didn't even blink. Was that . . . a sign of trustworthiness in snakes? Truth didn't know.

"You haven't been fed in ages. You need to hunt. To kill. Bloody those fangs of yours. Or whatever. Look, real talk? I don't want to go diving into a dumpster every time you need to eat, and I *really* don't want to carry around a sack of dead mice in the storage ring. I don't know if Sally is watching what I put in there, but since she's the one keeping the space open, it's a nonzero possibility."

Perks flicked his tongue out but had no further comment.

"Are you . . . sick or something? It looks like you have a bulge here, and I don't remember you having that when I first got you. But you've been with me all the time, so you haven't eaten anything. Is it . . . snake cancer or something?"

Truth probed with Cup and Knife, but the spell didn't find anything it wanted to correct. It would have to have been an utterly fatal cancer to have swollen that quickly, that fast, anyway.

"Do snakes get puffy bellies when they are hungry? Honest question; I really don't know." Perks declined to answer.

"C'mon, buddy. At least give me a hint."

The tongue flicked yet again.

"Would the pet store have answers? Or . . . a book or something?" Truth looked around. Still dark out. He put Perks down again, just over two meters from where he was pretty sure there were rats. Perks tasted the air and seemed to agree, as he kept his eyes focused on the dark spaces behind the trashcans.

Truth waited. Was this it?

Ten minutes later, he concluded that no, it was not it. Perks just . . . hung out. Looked happy enough. Truth couldn't figure out why until he reached down to pick him up again. The ground was warm-ish. Warmer than the rest of the cement, anyway.

"Huh."

Truth felt around a bit. It was a small patch, maybe a half-meter in diameter. His first thought was that something hot vented onto the ground there, but there was nothing but a dim light over the back door. His next thought was that something hot was aimed at it or rested there during the day. But there was no sign of that, either. No scorch marks on the pavement, no signs of something heavy being dragged around, nothing. And who puts something super-hot next to their dumpster?

He felt around the pavement but didn't find anything. There wasn't that much to search. It was an alley behind a restaurant, just big enough for a garbage wagon to fit down. So, just why was this half meter patch of nothing in particular noticeably, though not very, warmer than the rest of the pavement?

He tapped at the ground, not expecting anything in particular and getting exactly that. Sounded like pavement. There couldn't be piping under there—water came from talismans; sewage would be destroyed at the toilet—Confen was far too small to rate an actual *sewage* system. So, just what was it?

"Hey, Thrush, can you check what's below this bit of pavement? Nondestructively?

"Things buried in the ground aren't really my specialty, dread magus, but your dutiful slave—"

"We talked about *slave*, Thrush. Especially given all you have told me about Hell. Also, you are on salary. You even quit once."

"I suppose it's a matter of perspective. My labor is performed under threat of pain."

"I apologize. Let me just activate the banishment and you are free to go."

"Your contractually bound and highly enthusiastic employee is delighted to undertake this opportunity to improve a key skill to better meet current and future business-development milestones, unholy supervisor."

"Simultaneously better and worse. Impressive."

"One might argue it's a distinction without a difference."

"One might. Not me, though. Hop to, birdie."

Thrush chuckled like a newly crowned king watching his freshly orphaned nephews fall off a high tower. The imp's form burst apart into black smoke and slowly, painfully slowly, sank into the concrete. Then came boiling up again and re-formed into the small black bird it usually pretended to be.

"I regret to inform the dread team lead that I cannot fulfill his orders and even attempting to do so will result in destroying this body and being forcibly returned to Hell. Whatever it is that is down there is warded against demons."

Truth's curiosity flared up. This was nowhere, in a nowhere town. Logically, he should be the most interesting thing in it. And yet, there was something carefully hidden here. He had to know what it was.

"Can you roughly mark out the dimensions of the area warded against you?"

Thrush bobbed its head and a black square appeared on the ground. Neatly boxing in the circle of heat, Truth noticed. The circle touched the four sides of the square.

He called out the Tongue of One Who Speaks for God and got it hacking through the concrete. If volcanic basalt was no match for it, lowest-bidder concrete wasn't even the invitation *to* a match.

"How deep is whatever it is?"

"Perhaps the distance from fingertip to elbow? I regret that my results do not qualify as 'Exceeding Expectations' and understand this must be reflected in my quarterly performance review."

"Hoho." So, he wouldn't have to dig even the length of his sword. He cut around the black square and then paused. Then smiled. He made two smaller cuts on either side of the square. He squatted down and stuck his hands in the smaller holes. Got a grip of concrete and—

"Back straight; lift with the legs—" Pulled several hundred kilos of cement straight out of the ground.

Level Five body cultivator. "I love the Meditations!"

"Well done, your Vice-Eminence for Administrative Affairs!"

"Look, can we compromise here? You don't call yourself a slave, and I won't pretend you're a wage slave. Fair enough?"

"Fair, great one, has nothing to do with it."

"Got a better grip on what this thing might be now?"

"Regrettably, I do not. It is still powerfully warded against my kind."

Truth had a sudden sneaking thought. "Thrush, have a scout around. See if you can't find more of these."

"An earth demon would do the job far faster and better, magus. If you hadn't told me precisely where to look, I would have spent hours searching this alley."

Truth grunted. "All right, hold off for a moment. I want to see what's going on here."

He started carefully chipping away at the cement, then realized he was being silly. He started casting Cup and Knife, using the cement in the block to fill the hole. Leaving out what shouldn't have been in there in the first place.

What was left was a small black metal box, carefully covered in anti-surveillance wards, banishments, divination diverters, and a reasonably comprehensive collection of other *mind your own business* enchantments. Not cheap, by any stretch, but all the enchantments stamped on it were mass-producible by properly tooled-up talisman factories.

Truth recognized all of them. They were Starbrite talismans, after all. Averaging about Level Two power, but their combined effect would make them even harder to detect than their level would suggest. That power was also why he was able to find it in the first place.

"Classic. Just classic. You got a bit of stamped metal that didn't feed right, got stamped just off the correct angle, somehow passed QC, assuming there was anybody checking, then assembled." Truth was tracing the lines of two talismans that just barely touched each other. The metal near the touch point was glowing cherry red, though the rest of the talismans in the case were impressively unaffected.

"Must have been busted for a while now, with the heat very slowly building up in that one spot."

He very gently pried the two sheets of metal apart, barely cracking open the interior. Nothing went off, but Incisive was whispering an unsubtle warning.

"You know what the most interesting thing is about this, Thrush? Even without opening the box?"

"Pray tell."

"It's mass-produced. Which means there are a lot of them around. Now . . . just why is that, and what is it?"

CHAPTER 43

INDUSTRIAL-SCALE . . . SOMETHING

Truth looked at the box with increasing confusion and excitement. He wasn't a big believer in coincidence. There was simply no chance that this had been placed there with the expectation of catching his attention—if he had no idea he was coming to Confen, how could anyone else know? What was more, who would think his snake would get cozy on a warm spot behind the Jade Bamboo restaurant as it stubbornly refused to hunt rats?

The only logical explanation was that this was something deliberately placed by the owners of the restaurant, which seemed unlikely, or this was part of something much, much bigger. Step one, of course, would be cracking it open and figuring out what was inside. Anything covered with this many privacy protections would certainly be rigged to self-destruct rather than allow itself to be examined. Some delicacy would be required.

That was why he was using his most delicate chisel and mallet. Gently, right along the welded seam. It had already been badly degraded by the heat. It would be silly not to start where the work had already been half-finished. Could he have used a spell and his fingers? Yes. But the maintenance tech wanted to honor the work that went into this thing. And he low-key found it hilarious.

"I mean, no vibration sensors? Are they for real with this thing? They have it warded against, if I am reading this right, spiritual contagion but not bashing with a mallet?"

"Truly, the foolishness of mortals is without bounds, omniscient one," Thrush said "loyally."

"True. Although, this being a Starbrite product, I can only assume there is, or was, something uncommonly nasty inside, waiting for someone to break it open."

"Ah, yes. That would seem to fit what you have said, and seen, of them." The little bird was hopping around a bit, seemingly anxious.

"Got it cracked." Truth tossed the tools back into the storage ring with a casual thought.

"DROP IT AT ONCE, MASTER!" Thrush yelled. Truth didn't have to be told twice. Incisive wasn't yelling with the former imp, but it was making it equally plain. What was in the box was bad news. He had retreated ten meters before the box hit the ground.

Truth reinforced the seals over his body with the Meditations, then ran the spell to try and destroy any poisons he might have inhaled. At the same time, he ran Cup and Knife over himself. He felt the spell trigger over something in him, destroying it rather than trying to shift it around. He couldn't tell what it was—it had been microscopic and only in him for the barest fraction of a second.

Thrush was fluttering around the box, a whirlwind forming beneath it as it tried to absorb whatever was in the box.

"Anything you can do to help destroy this thing, master, would be highly beneficial to you and the people of this city!"

Truth slammed Cup and Knife down toward the box, sweeping the air between them. Clearing out the . . . whatever it was. No problem casting the spell—apparently, Manda felt this had no place in the world.

Truth kept the spell running even after it stopped registering a change. Just in case. "Thrush?"

"The foulness is gone, dread savior, or beyond my detection at least."

Truth ran the spell over the box one more time, just to be sure. "All right, keep a close eye on it. What was it, anyhow?"

"A most apposite question. I believe it was a plague."

Ah. Right. Air demons loved eating filth and were often employed as cleaners for that exact reason. Although . . . "You *believe* it was a plague?"

"Yes. Airborne diseases share certain . . . commonalities, let us say. In the way that while humans and horses are clearly different animals capable of different things, they both have hearts and lungs and limbs and suchlike."

"With you so far. This didn't much look like a horse."

"Yes, continuing the analogy, imagine expecting a horse and finding an octopus doing a very persuasive horse impression."

"A horse-sized octopus."

"If such an image alarms you, good. It should. Yes, a horse-sized octopus, galloping with its millions of identical siblings . . . Master, more of them emerge from the box! I beg you, unless you wish this city destroyed, obliterate the box!"

Truth had already run Cup and Knife over it, so he hammered it with Obliteration instead. Once he felt the active spells die, he switched back to Cup and Knife. It had only been a few seconds' gap, but he could feel there was already a substantial amount of sickness loose in the wind.

"Thrush, round up all of it!"

"As you command!"

Thrush exploded into a cloud of black gas once more and stirred the winds in the alley. In a fraction of a second, a hurricane formed around him, drawing all the loose rubbish up off the ground and into himself. Within a minute, the alley was cleaner than it had ever been before. After five minutes, it was freer of disease than most hospital hallways.

"I believe that is all of it, your grandness. However, if you have any means to check, I pray you do so."

Truth leaned into Incisive. A plague might not be next-couple-of-seconds dangerous, but he should be able to pick up something. He hoped.

Nothing. He kept Cup and Knife going anyway, doing his best to tidy up the alley. Perks got a dose of cure too, though he seemed to have not been exposed.

"Horse-sized octopus, eh?"

"Indeed. A particularly malevolent one, accompanied by herds of its brood-mates."

"Perks didn't get any exposure."

"No, nor did it spread far. Part of why I am convinced it is unnatural. I think it was deliberately hunting humans. They seemed attracted to you, possibly because some landed on you when you opened the box, but otherwise, they seemed to move as a group to find someone to infect."

"Well. That's horrifying."

"It's not unprecedented, of course. Many illnesses are a result of microscopic demons, not even capable of sentience, let alone sapience. They will frequently move as a group, infecting the same host and sacrificing the host's health to summon more of their ilk into the world."

"Sure, we covered that in health class. I take it these are a more aggressive breed than usual?"

"Very much so, auspicious one. In addition to being far more aggressive, they seem more robust than most of their ilk. I suspect they would strongly resist banishment and cures as well as harshly use their hosts in aid of summoning more of their kind."

Truth crouched down to the box and carefully sliced it in half. The inside did, in fact, contain a number of explosive charms carved into the interior, but most of the box was, surprisingly, aimed at life support. There was a sheet of what looked like brownish jelly covering what was probably the bottom of the box, and beneath that, a summoning glyph.

Truth took a careful look at everything. Most of it was pretty standard—that gem was used in heat controllers everywhere, this cartouche supported vitality-enhancing spells, and so on. Even most of the talismans were quite standard. The explosive talismans weren't military-grade. They were used in industrial applications, mining, and building demolitions. With the right permits, you could buy as many as you liked.

The only things that he didn't recognize were the summoning glyph and whatever the jelly was. And even the summoning glyph wasn't *that* far off normal. He had just never seen a summoning glyph aimed at actually summoning a sickness demon before. At a guess, this was what one of those looked like.

Everything else in the box, in terms of talisman technology, was very ordinary. Controlled, in some cases. Certainly, the divination blockers and privacy wards were very strictly controlled and usable only by the very wealthy. But they were all legal. Not this. Summoning sickness demons was a death-penalty offense, execution via incineration in a specialized kiln. And that was in minor cases where the perpetrator confessed and apologized.

"Any idea what the jelly stuff is?"

"None, horrific presence, though I feel a sort of inviting feeling from it. It does not so much inspire hunger as a sense of comfort."

"Huh." Truth mulled it over. He had destroyed whatever magic had been in that jelly, but his air demon still thought it looked comfy. He shivered compulsively. It wasn't the evening air. Lovely night tonight.

"Could it be, or, well, have been, some kind of medium for mutating the sickness demons?"

Thrush hopped around, not getting too close to the box.

"It's certainly possible. I can imagine little sickness demons nestled in there, perhaps feeding on whatever it is made out of and summoning more of their ilk while being mutated by, again, whatever is in there."

One corner of the jelly was badly stiffened and scorched, only a fraction the thickness of the rest of the jelly. You could see where tendrils of heat had been reaching in, stiffening and damaging the rest of the block.

"Looks like it was pretty damaged before we cracked it open."

"Indeed. I would say that it was slowly destroying itself. We only confronted a bare fraction of its intended contents."

The metal had been cherry red, truth remembered. The fact that *anything* survived in a sealed metal box at that temperature was alarming. And telling.

He looked over at the explosive talismans. This particular model just summoned a large ball of air, compressed it down to a volume smaller than a grain of salt, and then released it. The expanding gas smashed apart anything it hit. Simple, effective, and comparatively safe. Best of all, as it was a summons, the yield was easily controllable with the paired activation gem.

Almost no heat generated but an awful lot of force. He looked dubiously at the concrete, then back at the explosive talismans. No way to tell now, of course, but . . . *that* much explosive force? Ah, but it only needed to crack the concrete. As long as there was a gap, the sickness demons could find their way through. They were famous for it, in fact.

And it really wasn't that hard to put a long crack in concrete. Not that hard at all.

"Have an earth demon do the searching, you said?"

"Yes, just have the moronic thing mark on your map where it finds places it cannot go. Use small words and many beatings. It's the only language these creatures understand."

Truth snorted and started carving a summoning circle in the concrete. He had summoned air and water imps before. An earth imp would be a first, but the basics didn't change.

"You could put at least four additional bindings of suffering at the inverse cardinals, supreme wizard."

"Oh? Why?"

"They would hurt it ever so much more."

"Thought we were moving away from the whole *slave* thing?"

"That would only be relevant if they were being used to compel this idiot worm's labor."

"They aren't?"

"No, I just want it to suffer because it dares to live in front of me. And it's an earth demon."

"You have no idea, none, who I am summoning."

"As I said, an earth demon. That is reason enough."

"It's your coworker. Your co-revolutionary in the happy war against Heaven!"

"And just as some humans are created superior to others of their kind, so too are demons. Some are born to lead, others to experience horrifying agony as they labor for their betters. A condition that shall persist for every second of their eternal existence, for no other reason than their suffering adds sweetness to the pleasures of the ones who bound them in servitude."

"You know what? I'mma skip it."

"Pity. I imagine the lumpen thing will be disappointed."

"Wait, what?"

The summoning circle filled with a muddy light. A sickly, gray-green rock seemed to fade into existence, as though it were bleeding through the skin of reality.

"Fuck you. You goddamn weak-ass, punk-ass, bitch-ass, micro-cocked, inbred, dog-fucking, horse-fucked, pussy bitch excuse of a wizard. Give me your orders, you fucking clown, so I can go work for someone that didn't try to jerk off with an oven door. Twice. You disgust me. You offend every single particle of my being. I am made lesser simply because you have summoned me. No matter how many eternities I exist for, no matter how high I ascend, I will always be tainted by the knowledge that I once served *you*. Fucking kill yourself so we can fix you down in Hell. Consider that the only free advice you will get from me, shithead. It's the best you ever had."

Truth blinked. "Hey, check out this neat spell I learned in Siphios. Thrush, you are going to *love* it."

CHAPTER 44

MATTERS OF PERSPECTIVE

I mean, I'm not a ritualist," Truth explained. "But I've seen this performed a couple of times by an expert."

"You are a credit to your teachers," Thrush "loyally" agreed.

"And, you know, everyone always goes on about how important experiential learning is. About not being afraid to fail, so long as you learn from it."

"That is a lie *cough* thing that teachers do say, yes, omnibenevolent one."

"I just feel like this is a great opportunity to get hands-on experience. A low-stakes, no-time-pressure situation."

"I, too, think the impending apocalypse can be safely ignored, time lord."

"Time spent sharpening the ax won't slow the cutting of the tree." Truth was quite calm, his hands in constant motion. He really wasn't an expert on this, and Merkovah had made it look so easy. It was, in fact, not easy. Well beyond his skill level. He knew he was missing important details and refinements.

"I'm just afraid I'm going to go too hard and obliterate it."

"Entirely understandable. Your merest touch would utterly unmake this worm." Thrush sounded quite pleased by that fact.

"What do you say, worm? Can you take much more?" Truth looked down at the rock-shaped earth demon.

"SCreeeeEEEEEeeeeAAAAHHHH!"

"Sounds like a yes to me. Right now, I'm still figuring out the 'masticating' stage. I fear 'juicing' is still far off."

"Lots of time to get it just perfect, master. The world has at least tens of hours of magic left."

"Oh, stop being dramatic and start being paranoid."

That got Truth a questioning look. Rare to see a bird look disbelieving, but it was a day for rare things, he supposed.

"You want a demon to be more paranoid. Do you often insist that water be wetter?"

"Can water get wet?"

"An interesting question. One wonders why you ask it."

"That's the attitude I want to see! Oh, did the screaming go up an octave?"

"Yes, I do believe your grasp on the GVWP rune has firmed a bit. Though, much more, and the wretch will explode. We can leave him like this indefinitely, however. And probably should. Just summon another earth imp and show them this lout."

"Meh. Waste not, want not, all that."

"Another popular lie *cough* teaching, I do believe. Out of fear, master, why do you want me to be more paranoid?"

"I picked this city as a stopping point at random. I am moving through the city at random, or, at least, at my whims. I picked this alley, as this restaurant practically screamed 'rat-filled dumpsters.' I only looked at this one particular patch of pavement because the snake I acquired by random whim decided it was more comfortable than the rest of the concrete. I only ripped up the pavement because I like taking an interest in things. And this one spot, out of all the other half-meter-diameter spots on the entire planet, *just so happens to be a defective plague engine.*"

Thrush blinked at that and hopped from side to side a bit. Neither of them minded the screaming in the background. Truth had set up a noise-isolation barrier before starting in on the masticating juicer. Nobody wanted their learning experience interrupted by neighbors lacking in a firm commitment to self-education.

"Put like that, I do suddenly feel insufficiently paranoid, yes."

"Makes you wonder who is plotting against you, luring you into complacency, doesn't it?"

"Indeed."

"Especially when you stick the words *mass-produced* in front of *plague engine*. As things that are mass-produced are intended for wide distribution. Something I just absolutely love associating with plagues."

"Mmm. No ordinary plague, either. It was primarily aimed at humans, but I do believe that given time, it would have killed your serpent as well. Which, again, is not usually how diseases work. Jumping species is quite normal, but a disease capable of killing humans and snakes alike is unusual, to say the least."

"Jumping species?"

"Yes. Disease demons are beyond stupid. Actually, ascribing any intelligence to them at all would be a mistake. It's more like each colony of them is most suited to a particular place in a particular species. Lungs are a popular choice, as are blood and lymph. So, if a disease demon finds itself in the wrong sort of body, it generally evaporates when it can no longer sacrifice its victim's vitality."

"But they can jump species."

"Yes. Hell is chaotic. Sometimes, within a colony, there are a few slightly different demons. If those slightly different demons survive in their new victim, they summon more from Hell. More just like themselves. After all, in the churning trillion trillion changes within Hell, what are the odds that one little disease demon is truly, completely unique?"

"Near enough zero?"

"Quite. So, unless a victim can swiftly slay such demons, either through their own virtue or the intercession of the appropriate potions or magic, they will be feasted upon unto death."

"And then they jump to the next set of lungs, regardless of species."

"They don't tend to wait until the victim dies before trying to spread. Just the opposite; the more the victim moves around, the faster they can find new victims. Although, again, ascribing intelligence to these creatures is incorrect. It is instinct at best." Thrush preened unconcernedly.

"So. An unknown, but presumably large, number of plague boxes is set to release a vast swarm of disease demons, all of which are, you believe, varied enough to hop species reasonably easily."

"For a given value of *easily*, yes. This was quite a varied swarm and decently resistant to my magic. Putting me around Level One, that would make most healing talismans and conventional potions quite useless. To say nothing of how quickly they could ravage the bodies of Level Zero humans."

Truth's face twisted as a nasty realization hit.

"The magic apocalypse won't affect them."

Thrush laughed nastily. "True. So long as they have living things to sacrifice, they will continue to spread and grow. The more species they can jump between, the harder they will be to contain. If it is possible at all."

"I can't wait until they can infest grass and trees. That will be just delightful," Truth growled.

"It would take a long, long while for random chance to carry them that far. But who's to say what's impossible in the boundless chaos of Hell?"

"You are just a living avatar of joy, Thrush; you truly are." Truth looked up at the night sky. Lightening now; dawn would be coming soon. He checked on Perks again, but the snake was, as best he could tell, healthy and content. Somehow managing to slip between the buttons of Truth's shirt and make his way down to his usual resting place.

Fingers crossed that lump wasn't a problem. He really didn't feel like dealing with a vet. Maybe he would just find a book first? How many snake vets could there be? Hah, even a pet cafe might know more than a vet!

The thought brought him to a happy halt. It had been ages. He was utterly overdue. But he had to protect the fluffies first. He released the spell torturing the earth demon.

"You rethink that attitude?"

"Glorious magus! Great wizard, supreme among men! It is this imp's joy to surf—"

"Serve," Thrush corrected.

"Serve the mighty might guy!"

Truth crouched down next to the suddenly very sparkly rock. "You guys are weird; you know that?"

"All existence is suffering. Earth demons are the lucky ones. At least we get to find suffering satisfying. Rewarding, even." The imp denied the accusation. "The suffering other beings keep asking for is the big weird. Like slapnuts up there—Hey, fuckface, sing us a song and try to forget everything you ain't."

"Oh, dear, I do believe a worm is daring to squeak at a bird. This story has a happy ending, you will be glad to know." Thrush's voice poured like quicksilver.

"One, I'm a rock, you blind fuck, and two, can't help but notice you didn't say shit about what I said, which means I win. So, three, go fuck yourself."

"Master, congratulations on summoning the smartest earth demon! I never would have imagined it could count to three! Let's see if it knows how to roll over or beg. It had better know how to beg."

Truth grinned. "All right, more time for that later. I'm going to call you . . . I'm guessing all your previous summoners called you Rocky?"

The earth demon rocked back in shock and gasped. "How did you know? I didn't tell nobody!"

"Wizard tricks. Now. I need you to search around under this town. Your job is to find places you can't go. I'm not interested in things covered by a home's protections or a usual spellbowl or anything. I'm looking for warded places, underground, not more than . . . let's say two meters below the surface and not less than twenty-five centimeters below the surface. Remember where they are well enough to mark them on a map. Got it?"

"Make me."

Truth activated the punishment runes on the summoning. It screamed.

"Jump to it. Do a good job and I'll throw you back in the masticating juicer."

"Be a lot cooler if you just left the torment runes on. Incidentally, you have room for at least four more at the inverse cardinals. I can draw you some good ones, if you need a tip."

"Scram before I book you a spa day!"

"Fine, fine be like that. See if I care," the earth demon grumbled, and sank into the ground. "Should take . . . I dunno. Time. It will take time to check."

"How much time?"

"More than a little, less than a lot? What even is time, when you get right down to it? How can time *pass*? If time is time, how can time time time? It's like water getting wetter." The imp had vanished by that point, leaving the head-scratcher behind.

There was peace in the alley. Thrush coughed theatrically. "I should mention that earth demons are also notoriously slow."

"Oh, I know." Truth nodded. "Faster than you at this job, though."

"Mmm."

Truth waited a moment longer, then realized there was no point in waiting. He shoved the dumpster over the summoning circle etched in the cement and was on his way. The remainders of the box were carefully disintegrated before he left. He might not be a very good ritualist, but he took that time. He couldn't stow it in his ring. What if he infected Sally?

Truth idled through the day, continuing his campaign of unrequited altruism. When the veterinarian opened, he dropped in and asked about snakes. The vet didn't know anything about snakes, but for a sizable deposit, would ask around for someone who did know about snakes. For even more money, he would invite that person to consult. For a considerably larger sum of money, he and the invited consultant would examine the patient.

Naturally, the treatment cost extra. As did the examination room and any supplies expended in the course of the treatment. Not to mention the vet's flat hourly rate, separate from everything else. Nothing he could do about it. The corporation that owned the veterinary chain had a policy of no discounts.

"Who is your employer?"

"Oh, I'm an independent contractor. I'm not *important* enough to be a full-time employee." The vet didn't quite snarl. "I simply work fifty-nine hours a week at this specific location, performing only the specified actions laid out in the manual, using only the tools and medicines I have to purchase from the corporation at their prices, and do my work in the rooms I have to rent from the corporation, in the offices they lease. An *employee* would work *sixty* hours. Completely different thing."

"I understand. Entirely. And the name of this corporation?"

"Whiteacre Happy Health, a VRC Capital Company."

"Don't know that outfit."

"Hobden Clan."

Ah. Truth wasn't quite sure where they ranked on the power hierarchy. Not at the very top, or he would know. Still, if they could run a chain of veterinary hospitals, probably decently powerful.

"Don't suppose they have offices in the city? Or a house?"

CHAPTER 45

STREETLIGHT SPIRITUALITY

The Hobden Clan did not have offices or residences in Confen. Their nearest office was a rented suite in an office park outside of Gwaju, which, as far as the vet knew, strictly handled logistics coordination for the mail-order pet-food and pet-medicine business. He had never been there. He didn't know anyone that had been there. He had only called there once, to find out where the hell his delivery was. Apparently, their communication altar was directly connected to a siren. Simply by attempting to reach them, he found himself lulled almost to sleep and nearly purchased six hundred kilos of wet cat food.

He did not own a cat. He was not, he explained, glaring at Truth, a cat person.

Truth wished him a good day and left peaceably. He really wasn't sure how he could make the veterinarian's life better. No need to make it worse. Instead, he set off for breakfast. A bowl of rice with bamboo shoots (which he didn't love), pickled carrots (which he did), and a bit of wilted spinach topped off with a bit of spicy fermented cabbage and a sprinkle of sesame seeds. It wasn't fancy. It wasn't the best he ever had. But sitting at a diner counter, with a cup of burnt coffee in front of him, it somehow felt right.

He wasn't trying to embody anyone in particular at the moment. He was just another Jeon worker, D-Tier citizen, off for his twelve-hour shift. Grabbing a quiet bite before work. The diner was noisy, but he was quiet. His mind was quiet. He wasn't going to worry about work, or home, or anything. He was just going to eat his rice and veggies, drink his coffee, and forget about the world until he walked out the door.

Truth sat, ate his food, savored the scorched, acrid, thin coffee, and wiped his mouth with whisper-thin napkins. He stood, making sure to tip an extra ration credit on the way out. It wasn't supposed to be allowed, but people found ways around. They always did. The morning was already hot, and the blue sky had just a hint of haze to it. Going to be a hot one.

He felt adrift. The plague engines were huge, a terrible thing, either planted by Starbrite or by some enemy nation capable of replicating their talismans near-perfectly. But . . . Well, he couldn't say *So what?* He was still on the planet; so were Etenesh, the sibs, and Merkovah. But it felt too disconnected. Too . . . dropped out of the blue. He was playing the Fool, but he would be damned if he would *be* a fool.

This reeked. This stank to the highest heavens. Was this Manda messing about again? A "divine revelation" dropping in out of nowhere?

"Perks, my guy, congratulations. In the legends to come, you will be known as the Serpent of Wisdom."

There was no comment from just above his belt. He wished he knew a better place to stash the snake. The summer heat couldn't bother him anymore, but some remembered instinct made him desperately want to untuck his shirt.

Truth fished the snake out and had a look at him. The bulge was . . . microscopically smaller? Truth had very good eyes and an above-average memory but still couldn't swear the bulge had shrunk much. If at all. He was going to say . . . smaller. Which was good?

"You worry me, Perks. Be better. At once. I command you."

Perks flicked his forked tongue at Truth. Perhaps that really was all there was to say on the topic.

"Haah. Well. Let's see what the day brings." Truth started roaming the city. He had nothing that urgently needed doing. Next stop was the Internal Security colonel, and that was going to be a haul. Just waiting on a demon. Maybe he should look into buses or trains or something? Save him some running, at least.

He couldn't be bothered. He wound up walking two blocks from the diner and sprawling on a bench. Which promptly retaliated by projecting nine nine-centimeter-long spikes along its length. Truth ignored it.

He called up Cup and Knife. The spell came easily. Still jank, still pretty broken, but he felt like he got it, somewhat. He was starting to see how the negative space should be filled. Not in terms of spellwork; that was a million kilometers beyond him. Conceptually. He was starting to get a feel for Manda.

Why did some damage need to be shifted from one place to another, while some damage just evaporated? Because Manda felt like that would be the right way to do things. Why did some clearly wicked people evade the spell? Because the strong have always had their ways to avoid accountability. Manda wasn't fixated on that.

Manda wanted people to wake up. Be aware. Be alive to the greater world they lived in. Truth felt like he had barely seen a fragment of that greater world. But he had seen it. And the spell wanted him to show others some of what he had seen.

Maybe. Possibly. Felt right, but who knows.

There was a brief scream.

Truth momentarily wondered if he was the one who screamed, but no, it came from—He looked around. There was a short flight of steps into the basement of what looked like an apartment building. The scream came from there. Bored and irritated, he went and investigated.

Moving from the sun to the shadow of the building dropped the temperature by at least ten degrees. It was psychosomatic, but Truth sighed in relief anyway. The stairs down looked positively inky compared to the bright daylight outside. Not even a light over the door. Maybe that was why someone screamed—stepped on a rat.

He opened the door. They hadn't stepped on a rat.

The woman had had her throat torn out already, her tongue pulled through the blood-gushing hole. Her limbs had already gone limp, leaving her body hanging from the bloody hands of a Ghūl. Truth blinked slowly. It was early in the morning. Bright daylight out. As dim as it was in this basement, it was still very bright for a Ghūl. So, just what the hell was going on?

Other than the obvious.

The Ghūl looked as surprised to see him as Ghūl are capable of looking. It hoisted the woman onto its shoulder and started walking away. Truth followed behind it, out of a morbid sense of curiosity. He didn't usually associate Ghūl with carrying bodies away, but of course they must. They had art to make and new Ghūl to animate.

They traveled the length of the apartment building basement, then through a broken wall into another apartment building basement. Then on again, to a storage unit at the end of a hallway whose lightbulbs had all carefully been broken. Quiet building. Well, it was early. Maybe everyone was out at work.

The storage unit was a narrow, stall-like room. Surprisingly deep, perhaps four meters, but only a meter and a half wide. At the far end of the unit, the Ghūl had built its sculpture. It was a human, or all humans. He wasn't quite sure what the Ghūl were going for there—it was an amalgam of parts, dozens of parts, all looking quite different. The sculpture hung from a pair of hooks, arms limp by its side, its eyes missing. The absence was clearly deliberate.

Was it a bad sign that he didn't find it particularly horrifying? It just was. It wasn't good or bad, happy or sad. It was the Ghūl's answer to his endlessly repeated question—what is a human? Whatever this *isn't*.

The Ghūl, body still resting on its shoulder, reached under one of the shelves running the length of the room and pulled out an old metal bed frame. Small, industrial, bent metal tubes meant to hold a single mattress, which would more or less hold a single person in indifferent comfort. It now supported a leather sling.

The Ghūl carefully laid the woman's corpse in the sling. It gently pushed the sling and began to rock it back and forth. The basement was silent except for the creaking of the bedframe and the stretching of the human-hide leather. No noise above. No creeping rats. Not even the building settling or shifting.

The creaking of the bedframe slowly got louder. The sling began to bulge and swell. A new smell filled the air. He knew that smell all too well. The fluid. The "elixir" he just happened to discover in a shop. The only elixir he could afford for his breakthrough, after he happened to find a basement in a building full of Ghūl that would, ironically, be a safe place for him to break through.

His life had been marked by remarkable coincidences. Maybe life was just like that when you had three destinies. He didn't buy it, though.

There wasn't a hint of magic. Not the faintest trace of enchantments on the bed or talismans summoning that tainted water from wherever it came from. Just the Ghūl, gently rocking and waiting. Truth had no idea how long it would take. Nobody did, from what he had heard. After a while, the swelling stopped. The rocking took on a longer, slower pace.

Truth slowly realized that the Ghūl hadn't led him there with any intentions. He just saw a fellow Ghūl, or at least a co-religionist, and that was that. If Truth followed him, that was fine. If he didn't, that was fine too. It wasn't that he wasn't seen or was ignored. He was just accepted. He was welcome there.

Truth looked around a bit more. He could see where the possessions that used to be the purpose of this unit had been shoved. All of the extras that wouldn't fit in the apartment were now pushed to the back of the shelves. Didn't look very dusty. This had probably happened fairly recently. The bodies whose collected parts had been stitched together were missing. He frowned at that. The Ghūl didn't eat their victims. So, where were the spare parts?

He didn't know how long he stood there, looking at the hanging meat. Long enough that he came to imagine himself *as* the hanging meat. All that he wasn't, propped up by the ruthless will of the world. He was everyone, and since he was everyone, he was nobody. His empty eyes could never close—seeing everything and understanding nothing. Learning nothing. Remembering nothing.

What memories he had were relics of the flesh—scars, tattoos, broken knuckles, and cauliflower ears. A callused foot in need of a trim and scrape. It was neither male nor female but had deliberate elements of both. The genitals carefully bisected and stitched together again, male and female set in juxtaposition. All just meat, useless meat. But it was all that he had.

If what you perceived of the world wasn't reliable, if all you could trust were the records of your flesh, what did that make you? What did the human count for when stripped of its memory? Stripped of its ability to touch and be touched?

Eventually, he shook it off. The Ghūl was still rocking the sling. Truth stumbled out of the basement and onto the street again. Night had fallen. He had spent the whole day in contemplation.

The world felt like it was spinning around him. That he was being spun. That all the suffering and the horror of his life was someone's game. Some scheme. His damn triple destinies at play. Did he get a say in all this? Was this free will thing for real, or was he just blindly walking the path some remote and hostile God had laid out for him?

He grabbed hold of the streetlight. Looked up. He knew this model. It was on the SAT. *What is the expected service life of a Ke-Te-Wo Type 61 Streetlight Talisman, assuming eight hours in operation every day?*

The prescribed answer? Five years. The real answer? How could some meat sack trapped on a mudball spinning through the obliterating void possibly know? Truth looked up into the light, past the light, and into the night. Then, all unguided, he fell into the bowl of the sky.

CHAPTER 46

MUDBALL DREAMS

The night sky was a brilliant explosion. No, he was wrong; it was no longer the night sky, it was the other side of the sky, the truth behind the light. It was every mystery and love and horror and truth, or as close to the reality of those words as a little clay doll could hope to see. He was freefalling, pinwheeling among trees that spanned worlds and songs made of birds and three-headed demons scourging the frogs hauling its chariot across the black vastness of the universe.

There was water, flowing like an endless river, a torrent, from where he could not see. Fires of all sorts, in every color and no color at all. They were every idea of fire as well as every truth of it. Earth, massive, compressing, cold, next to hot air dancing and twisting between the explosions of tulips and scampering beasts whose names were known only to the strongest mystics. And everywhere, everywhere, there were demons.

It was a madness. A swirling insanity of colors and lights. A sword stabbed into a heart again and again, sixty times a minute. Roses twined through lovers kissing, forming a bower and barrow together. A lily, floating in a lake the size of a dreamed ocean, slowly opened its petals. What could it hold? What could it reveal? It seemed to invite stares. Shuddering, almost convulsing, Truth forced himself to look away.

He knew he needed a reference point, something he could anchor himself to in the chaos. He swept his eyes around but couldn't find Botis. The river? Manda was described as living water descending from heaven. He looked over, but the river was so utterly enormous, so filled with turns and twisting eddies, it made his consciousness want to flee. Valentinian, then. He had relied on that ancient's meditations. He cast his eyes around, hunting for some sign of that unknown being, finding something twisting, something emerging from the darkness, not evil but vast, he couldn't get his mind quite around it—

"And that's enough of that."

Truth found him himself summarily smashed into the dirt. Hard-packed soil. It hurt. He didn't have time to linger on that thought, as he was picked up and sat on a stump to look at a big rock. The rock was gray and fairly flat, but beyond that, it had no noticeable qualities. The fire was behind Truth. There was just him, the rock, and his shadow on the rock.

"Pretty sure I mentioned something about a clay doll staying put. Absolutely sure, in fact. No, don't look around. I can more or less guess how this happened. Let's run you through the basics first, then get into it."

He recognized the voice of his rough patron, sounding alternately amused and tolerant.

"First—what is this?"

A shape popped up next to his shadow. A sort of puppet made out of shadows. At a guess—

"A duck?"

"What? No! Look again."

"Still looks like a duck; sorry."

"What terrifying ducks have you seen that look like that? It's plainly a dog."

"Don't know what to tell you, senior. Maybe if you stuck your thumbs up or something, it would look more like a dog?"

"What do my thumbs have to do with anything? Just turn around."

Truth obeyed, and to his quiet shock, the senior was petting a small dog. The dog had a long muzzle and flat ears. It didn't look anything like a duck, but when you just saw the profile of the head in shadow? He still didn't know why he thought *duck*. They really weren't very similar.

"I'm guessing you fixated on *duck* because you saw shadows on the wall and thought of someone making a duck shadow, right?" The man's hair was just as shaggy as before, his physique as muscular, his attitude just as relaxed. Like no time at all had passed.

Truth slowly nodded. He didn't have a better idea.

"All right, now go and explain it to him." The man waved at the rock. Truth looked over.

"My shadow?"

"You. The 'you' before you saw the dog."

Truth was mentally exhausted before his involuntary vision. He didn't feel like he was thinking any faster now.

"I don't understand."

"It's a metaphor. Or, I don't know, an allegory. You were ignorant. Not understanding what you thought you saw, making up stories about the shadows on the rocks and then thinking you knew something based on the shadows."

"Then I turned around."

"Then you turned around and saw the dog."

Truth nodded. "What's his name?"

"Whose?"

"The dog. What is the dog's name?"

"Sam."

"Really?"

"No, it's a lot longer, but I just call him Sam for short."

"You have an actual dog."

"Yep." The big man nodded, happily patting the little dog.

"Aren't you some kind of . . . extremely powerful spiritual being? God-adjacent?"

"Oh, yeah. Although what you think you mean when you say 'God' and what 'God' actually is are pretty different."

Truth nodded again. Most things are more complicated than you would think, in his experience.

"So. You are having an involuntary out-of-body experience. You may be wondering why."

"Yes, senior. About a lot of things."

"Short answer? A lot of hands meddling in your life, in increasingly unsubtle ways. Or just as subtle as they ever were, but now you are better able to see the messing-around."

"Three destinies?"

"*Destiny* is so much nicer-sounding than *Beings beyond your comprehension have marked you and loaded the dice you get to throw, leading to increasingly unlikely results.*"

Truth watched the fire flicker and dance. The dog leaned into the filthy man's hands, happy with his scritches. "You, Manda, and who? Starbrite? You said that one of the destinies was related to what he did to my soul."

"Wait, Manda? How did you get that old bastard out of all this?"

Truth blinked. At this point, he was one hundred percent certain that Manda had been involved in . . . so many instances in his life. Dating back to at least his learning Cup and Knife. The rough man grinned, watching Truth's face shift and twist.

"Don't confuse cause and effect, kid. Manda has a really unpleasant habit. He sets up all these little things, these little hooks and coincidences in the world. Nets sized for just the right fish. Then, when something runs into them, he turns up going, 'Ahah! The chosen fish! I had long foreseen your coming!' then the fish goes, 'Oh, what divine wisdom! He had even foreseen my coming!'" The rough man spat into the fire. The dog did not look impressed.

"He sets up things for people to discover and . . . then what?"

"Turns up and nudges them into doing things that he thinks are good. Like, imagine you went into a pawnshop and found a magic ring. Someone had to make that ring. Someone had to pawn it."

Truth flashed back immediately to the tonic he had bought for his breakthrough to Level One. "He planted the tonic that turned me part Ghūl."

The big man wiggled his hand a little. "Not quite right but yeah. The most important thing, from his perspective, was that he linked you and me."

"One of my destinies."

"Yep."

"You said I was born with one?"

"I did."

"But you don't know who gave it to me? Or what it's about?"

"Nah. Well, I have a bunch of guesses, obviously, but I don't *know* know." The big man grinned, wider this time, apparently finding the situation hilarious. The land still smelled of marsh. Green and vegetal. He still couldn't recognize the stars.

"That just leaves you and Starbrite."

"Nope."

"No?"

"No. Because I don't know who 'Starbrite' is, so the odds that they are the one muddling your destiny is unlikely."

"You don't know who Starbrite is? He's the most powerful mage on the planet! The only Nascent Soul!"

"Ooooohhhh. That guy. Oh, yeah, I've seen him around. No, that slightly larger ant isn't responsible. At most, he's a trigger. Sort of like what Manda did—once the right circumstances were created, it manifested. The right-sized fish swam into the net."

"And now I'm dragging three nets?"

"I think the metaphor is getting dragged here. Look, it's the allegory with the shadows, okay? You are seeing the shadows of much-larger things, things happening someplace you can't see, and you are trying to understand the nature of your existence, looking at them."

"That's destiny?"

"That's existence for you and everyone on your mudball. Looking at shadows and making up stories about what it all means."

"Until you turn around."

"If you can turn around, yeah."

The fire grumbled and spat as the wood burned down.

"I'm thankful, senior, but I must say you are a lot more . . . chatty . . . than you were in our first meeting."

"You are just killing it with my legacy. Loving what you are doing there. Call it a reward."

"I . . . am? Starting a war? Blowing up a volcano?"

"Again, looking at effects, not causes."

"So . . . what am I missing?"

"Are you angry? At all this bullshit? At being dropped into all kinds of nonsense? At the whole damn world setting you up for a brief life of suffering? Even though you did your very, very best?"

Truth breathed out slowly, trying to control the sudden spike of rage.

"Intensely."

"But it's just shadows on the rock. None of this is really real." The grin had a distinctly nasty edge to it now, and he had the sneaking feeling that the dog was judging him too.

"It's real to him." Truth pointed at his shadow. "And it's the only 'me' I know."

"Until you turned around. Until you realized that there was a *you* that wasn't the shadow and there was a world to look at that wasn't the rock."

Truth nodded.

"Aren't you angry, kid? Doesn't it seem unfair?"

"I am. It does."

"Don't you want it to stop? At the very least, don't you want to get back at the people who hurt you? Make them understand that it's not fair and you won't put up with it?"

"So much." Truth nodded, his eyes narrowing slightly. He had seen this game played before, and patron or not—

"Then you need to turn around and see the people casting the shadows, don't you? You need to find out who to hit."

Eh? "Well. Yes."

"I didn't make the world the way it is. I'm not even the first victim of the way the world is. But I do like to think I'm the first person to fight back. The first person to go, 'No, that's not right, fuck you!' and spill blood over it."

Truth widened his eyes. "The actual, literal first?"

That got a little chuckle from the big man. The dog flattened down, bored with the conversation and the lack of petting. "Well. Like I said, I like to think so. Before me, everything was so . . . primal. So abstract. Even Mom and Dad were more like concepts than fully realized people. Took me ages to realize why they didn't seem to have a clue about anything."

"They didn't turn around?"

"More like they never saw the rock in the first place. They just had no idea what they were seeing or why any of it mattered." Silence filled the clearing.

"I found a machine to spread a demon plague across the planet. There are almost certainly more of them buried. It could eventually kill all life on the planet. And I just happened to find one."

"Hmm. Seems unlikely."

"Not you."

"Not me, no."

"Then who?"

"Why, the person responsible for your misery. Partially."

"Not you, not Manda, I'm going to just assume not Botis or Valentinian—"

"Safe bet. Also, don't go looking for Valentinian. He isn't there."

"Where?"

"Wherever you look."

"Figures." Truth took a moment to pull his train of thought back on track. "If it's not any of the originators of my spells, and it's not Starbrite, who is it?"

"Why, none other than the little ball of mud you are running around on. Yes, the very thing that is making you suffer, that is making humanity suffer, that is going to lead, best-case scenario, to the utter collapse of your civilization and the death of the overwhelming majority of humanity on your planet. And, I might add, an altogether great angel. Sariel. Also called Sahariel. Which should really tell you everything right there."

CHAPTER 47

OBVIOUSLY DIFFERENT

Truth blinked in confusion. He looked down at the dog. The dog wheezed heavily through his nose but made no further explanation. He then opted to look inquisitively at his rough patron, who rolled his eyes and explained.

"One angel, but he has been recorded and classified under two names and with two natures by the humans on your rock. His rock. Whatever."

The big man pointed back toward the shadow. "Looks like a duck, but it's actually a dog. Looks like a protective spirit, one suitable to invoke before battle, but also has a thing for raping human women."

"Does what, now?!"

"Shadow on the rock, remember?"

"Ah. People think he's that, but he's not." Truth nodded. It was a nice night, wherever they were. Hot, humid, but in that way that lends a soft feeling to the air. Every stir of wind felt like being brushed with velvet.

"He isn't either of those things, exactly. Nor is he both those things . . . exactly."

"He is, however, the origin of my planet's suffering."

"No, you guys are the origin of your suffering." The rough patron shook his head. "*He* is trying to persuade you to stop fucking up. And limiting the means you have for fucking up. Think of it as a fever. The body is trying to do away with the disease. But again, that's a pretty limited perspective on things."

Truth nodded again. Slowly. "If I kill Starbrite, will he stop the apocalypse?"

"Almost certainly not." The rough patron gave the dog a friendly pat. "Sariel is an angel. Looks like he decided the 'right answer' is if he must have humans on his planet, they will be his descendants. Which, since they are also my descendants, I don't really object to either."

"Wait, the human women—"

"Were pretty exclusively from my line, yeah."

"You are a human?!" It was like finding out that a mountain used to be a drop of water.

"Ish." The grin wasn't anything nice to look at. "You can say that we were all still figuring out how to live as shadows at that point. Mom and Dad never really got there. Me and my siblings kinda-sorta did, some of us more than others, and our descendants were more or less human. It all shook out eventually."

"But how does all that—"

Truth's body was forcefully wrenched around, his face pushed next to the stone. New shadows appeared, a small apartment, first one child, then two, then three, then four. Details became clearer. The armchair, the bottles, the endless piles of trash and rotting filth. A big shadow swung its arm; one of the little shadows went flying into the corner and didn't get up for a few seconds, a few minutes. And it didn't stop. Over and over and over. He could smell it. He could hear every word.

"STOP!"

There were other details now, the water talismans becoming a source of fear as well as water. Soap, shoes, belts, bottles, the flat of a hand, or the cut of a tongue. No peace anywhere. Nowhere to hide.

"I said STOP THIS!"

He tried to fight, tried to wrench his head away from what he was seeing. There was no peace there, no peace. He was right back in it, watching the shadows.

"Why do you care? They are only shadows."

"That's me! You know damn well that's me and my sibs!"

"No, it isn't. It's shadows. Your memories are shadows of shadows. What they are suffering now is a shadow's dream of pain. None of it is real. It's all a Hell of your own creation."

He watched Mom drag Har toward the sink. Tried to look away. Tried to look away when Dad slapped Sophia and spat on her. When Vig lost one of his baby teeth when Mom punched him for asking when dinner was. Tried to look away when he killed his first rat and tried to cook it in the hot box and the sheer *smell* of it was enough to make him puke, and that was when he decided to steal food and he wasn't even ten, wasn't even ten, and this was his life. He had lived every minute of this. It was etched into his bones and blinding his eyes and deafening his ears.

"How dare you. How dare you! It's real! It's all real because I lived it! Just because there is more beyond the stars doesn't make this meaningless!"

"You didn't have to live it. Didn't have to suffer. You could always have just turned around. Seen the real."

"Could I? Fucking could I have? Bullshit! Nobody just wakes up able to do that. Nobody just says, 'You know what? This isn't real. I'm not really hungry. I'm not really cold. It's all just an illusion!' The only people who might are crazy people, and not even all of them!"

There was no peace in his life. He had known that for a long time, but he was having his nose rubbed in it now. There was no peace in the slums. You were always in danger. Always scurrying from shadow to shadow. And he declared the whole world a slum. That everyone scurried from shadow to shadow. Never feeling really safe. Never sure about that next meal.

"Ah, that takes me back. Not to my own childhood; my parents literally could not dream of hitting us or starving us. But from my generation on? That cycle of violence never stopped turning. Even my so-called 'good' brother. His kids were complete assholes. All of them."

But now Truth was thinking he had seen through the slum, had seen the world beyond, or at least a glimpse of it. So, why couldn't he turn around? Why couldn't he point other people to it? And did the "real" make the "not-real" not real? Were his life, his sufferings, his dreams, hobbies, loves, hates, all just a hallucination?

Was he a hallucination? Whose hallucination? Was there even someone looking at the shadows, or was he the shadows, dreaming of someone looking at him? Did anything mean anything? Or were the only things that meant anything the things beyond the shadow's perception? Was meaning reserved for those who could turn around? He recoiled, wanting to shove away from the rock, to not see this, but he couldn't look away. It was his life. It was his "real."

"You know you can just turn around, right? I'm not even holding you there."

"Yes, you goddamn—"

"No. I'm not. I was before, but I haven't for a minute now. You can just acknowledge the illusion and come see the real. That's your privilege for having at least looked up."

Truth watched himself forcing the sibs to sit down in hidden corners and do their homework. Carefully judging when the parents were away to get them to read, try to keep their morale up with encouragement and tiny treats. Trying to show them he wasn't quitting, so they couldn't quit either. It was hard. It was so damn hard. Looking back on it, it was the hardest single thing he had done in his life.

"If I say it wasn't real. If I say that none of it really mattered, or even really happened. Then I am saying that, somehow, the life that made me who I am didn't really happen to me."

"Did it? Does it?" He could hear the amusement in the ancient's voice. "Wouldn't it be better that way? It would hurt a lot less. And really, if you know that all this isn't 'real,' aren't you just torturing yourself?"

"What is 'real,' then? Huh? It felt pretty real, starving! Those beatings felt plenty real! Knowing that there is a greater world out there, that there are greater truths, that we don't have to live this way, how does that make any of this less true? Less real?"

He watched himself hide under a dumpster, the unknowable chemical horrors that dripped from the collective trash heap and puddled under him burning his skin, staining it reds and purples for months. Kids ragged on him for it. Not to his face, because even then he wasn't afraid to catch someone on the way home, but the looks and whispers were constant.

"Is that really the only option?"

Truth bit back his retort. This . . . unimaginably powerful alleged former human was doing this for a reason, and apparently, he wasn't mad at him. So, it probably wasn't a nefarious reason. He took a few deep breaths. The shadows were showing him running for some gangsters. He remembered this time—they were the kind that not only wouldn't take no for an answer; they didn't even ask the question.

Turn around. See the unreal for what it was. Except it wasn't "unreal," was it? You could call it an illusion, all the invisible walls we build for ourselves and treat like they were holding us prisoner, but that lived experience was still as real as anything. And the ducks might be more real than the water they were swimming through, but didn't they still float? The water was real enough to hold them up.

"We are seeing the shadows. We are the shadows. Our lives are shaped by forces we cannot perceive, and because of that, our whole understanding of the world is built on shaky facts." He started nodding to himself. "And because of that, we decide what is and isn't possible, what is and isn't moral. Or fair. Or our fault. I'm guessing God is the fire in this metaphor?"

"For once, no. Wisdom."

"Ah. Well. Nobody ever accused me of having too much of that."

"For a clay doll, you're doing fine."

Truth smiled a little and ducked his head. The rough man ran his dirty fingers over the dog. The dog seemed quite happy about this and rolled onto its side. More pets were, apparently, required.

"So. What I think is real is the shadows on the wall, and what's actually real is what I see when I turn around, but since I'm seeing my own shadow on the wall, the me that thinks it's all real isn't the real me either. The real me is the me watching my shadow. Which would be true for everyone, I'm guessing. So. You know. Awkward question incoming."

"Oh?"

"Senior . . . what is a human?"

The big man looked up from the dog, and the world went quiet. The crickets stopped chirping in the grass. The wind stopped blowing. The fire stopped its crackling. He couldn't even hear the beating of his own heart.

"That is a very dangerous question. In this place, at this time, it is really, truly dangerous. And you are immensely unprepared for the answer. Keep asking the question. Ask other people. Ask yourself. Keep furiously poking at the world and demanding an answer to why things are the way they are. You might be trying to sort through shadows, but you can teach yourself to turn around. To see through the walls. To be—"

The air started to vibrate. Truth could feel himself starting to vibrate, as though some terrible beast were roaring with fury and outrage.

"A lover of wisdom."

It all went black.

Truth woke up, slumped against the street lamp. He let the strangeness of the moment wash over him. Didn't try to make sense of anything or try to sort the real from the fake. Just . . . let himself experience the world. Appreciating the shadows for what they were.

There really wasn't any stopping the apocalypse. On some level, he had faintly hoped it could be stopped or at least delayed. Wouldn't that be the perfect storybook ending? The hero kills the bad guy and saves the world. Not this world. Not this hero. The clock would keep ticking, and in just a few moments, it would be last call for civilization.

Assuming it got that far. He had never gotten any useful information about the plague engines or . . . any of that. His rough patron didn't seem interested in any of it. Like it didn't matter, because it wasn't real. The shadows couldn't even turn around and see the light, let alone the dog casting the shadow.

So, what to do? He watched the worried people running around, trying to get through their days. Trying to keep on keeping on in spite of everything. Truth thought back to the hospital and being Bone-Bro. He had enjoyed it. It was a wild con, of course. He couldn't keep doing it. But he had liked doing it. Being part of the problem.

Oh. OH!

He started laughing, rising up and laughing, wild and free. "All right, all right, all right! I have all these multiple destinies! Let's lean in to it! Let's play the fool! I don't have to solve everything. I don't have to solve anything!

I'll set my nets for the right-sized fish and pet every damn dog I please." He sniggered. He had to wait for the earth demon's report, but then? He'd see the Internal Security colonel, then he'd just have a quick word with Niles. Time for MegaShroom to grow.

CHAPTER 48

A CUT ABOVE

The dawn was rising, and with it, a rock. Specifically, the earth demon he had sent out.

"Fuck you; pay me."

"Everyone's so cynical these days." Truth sighed and activated the punishment runes built in to the summoning. Then added on a few more of his own. Then just stomped the rock for a while. The Blessing of the Sea of Brass really did a number there, but he was pulling his shots and not letting the demon get banished.

"You want to rephrase that?"

"No, that was agonizing. You are definitely going on my list of top forty million bosses. High praise."

"I'm honored. What results did you turn up?"

"Nothing."

"Nothing?!"

"Yep. Zero magical voids in the city of the size you specified."

"Any much bigger or smaller?"

"None smaller, a few bigger. Like. Much bigger."

"How big is 'much bigger'?"

"Dunno. Bigger than you?"

"Building-sized?"

"I mean, how big is a 'building,' you know? Like, that really doesn't say much."

Truth sighed. He was being played by at least three unknowably powerful beings, plus Manda. This was insane. But until he could change it, he would have to endure it. So. Time to get the hell out of Confen.

"All right, Rocky, you did a good job, so I'm dismissing you the hard way."

"Beating me to death?" The lump sounded hopeful.

"Exactly. Clench your metaphorical teeth." Truth nodded. Technically, this wasn't the weirdest thing he had ever done. It just felt that way. No matter. Rocky was an imp, so the whole process just came down to a few forceful stamps. He could have done it in one shot, but Rocky really had done his best.

Right. Time to be on to . . . Where the hell was it? Truth thought about it for a moment. It was a small city on the east coast of the peninsula . . . he drew a finger down the coastline on his mental map. Runchon. Because of how the mountains were laid out, the road ran just a couple of degrees north of due west, then you had to turn southeast and drive down the coast a short way to reach the city.

So much traveling. Had he traveled around Jeon this much when he was working for Starbrite?

Yes, now that he thought about it. Once he got on bodyguarding duty, he was up and down the southern part of Jeon all the time. Huh. No wonder he was drawn toward Earth-Folding Step.

He nodded decisively and sat down on the curb. Time to go fast. He pulled off his shoes. It was the damnedest thing. The shoes were more comfortable to walk on than his bare feet, but they just could not hold up to a real run. These were particularly comfy. He would not have them exploded for no reason.

Suitably prepared for his trip, he set out at a brisk jog. Then stopped. Then started again. Then stopped. He found a kilometer marker by the roadside and set off at his usual ground-eating pace and started counting breaths. It took no time at all to reach the next kilometer marker.

"One hundred kilometers an hour? Jogging? That can't be right, can it?"

It was the damnedest thing. Truth had exquisite control over every facet of his body. He would certainly be aware of any change in his gait or the biomechanics of his movement. And yet he was clearly moving much faster. There was no change in his balance; his every step landed as firmly as any other in his life. He still had the same instinctive knowledge of where his foot would touch when he put it down.

He had never jogged so fast in his life.

Not that he hadn't been running quickly before. He certainly had! In fact, his burst movement speed would put swallows to shame. It just hadn't quite clicked. The compounding effects of his Level and the Meditations had reached a terrifying threshold.

He crouched down into a sprinter's stance, fingers splayed on the rough asphalt, bare toes planted, sole of the foot arched and ready to spring him forward. A carriage passed, strictly keeping to the speed limit on the highway. Truth gave it a ten-second head start.

He exploded forward, his foot shattering the asphalt as he rocketed forward. Each step swift as thunder and decisive as lightning. He had overtaken the carriage before he reached top speed. There was a curve ahead. He turned his body to go around—

His foot couldn't keep traction. He slammed into the side of a hill, pinwheeled up the hill, and finally came to a stop wrapped around a tree.

He didn't untangle himself for a few minutes. He wasn't hurt; he was just feeling very sorry for himself. Eventually, it did occur to him that he had slammed into a tree with his spine at speeds considerably more than a hundred kilometers per hour and he wasn't even really sore. Which was . . . interesting, to put it very mildly.

Level Five was, definitionally, the middle of the mid-levels. Seven and up was when you really got into the comically powerful, terrain-altering magic, or at least that had been his understanding. He certainly couldn't open valleys with a chop of his hand or anything like that. But this level of physical resistance to damage was, in his experience, more or less unprecedented. With spell armor, sure. Throw enough enchanted gear at something, anything becomes survivable. In theory. Bare skin, though?

It had to be down to body cultivation. The constant practice of the Meditations of Valentinian, the constant refinement of his body, then the use and testing of those refinements, it all added up. He pulled himself to his feet. He didn't need to groan, but he sort of felt like he ought to. If you get wrapped around a tree, you groan about it. Right? Right.

Truth pulled out a needler from his ring. "This is dumb. This is really, really dumb." He lined up a grazing shot across the top of his forearm. "I mean, first thing they teach you in the army . . . okay, not literally the first thing, but *Don't point your needler at anything you don't intend to kill* was on day one of range training, for sure."

It was hard to pull the trigger. He took a deep breath and squeezed one off. There was a soft *thwip* sound. He kept waiting for something more, but that was it. Just *thwip*, and nothing. Not even a faint white line on his skin. At a guess, the angle was so flat, the needle had just deflected off without doing any damage.

Truth wasn't sure what expression he was making, but he lined up a shot flat with the top of his bicep. *Thwip*. He felt it this time, about as much as he noticed the ricochet bouncing off his ruined shirt. Nothing. Not even a mark. No pain whatsoever.

"I am . . . officially unkillable by Level Zeros. Which, I guess I have been that for a long time in practice, but . . ." He had a hard time articulating what he was feeling. He was now so far above "ordinary folk" that he could just stand there, let them shoot him, and be in absolutely no danger. In fact, it would be better if he was naked while they were doing it, so there was no risk to his clothes.

He'd bet Level One shooters wouldn't do much more damage either. He certainly wouldn't worry about something whose damage was primarily magical, like Flame Bolt. He could just about imagine Graeme's Arrow doing some work, but . . . really, no. Ninety percent or more of the world's population had lost the qualifications to fight him.

Which was good! A powerful thing. But somehow, it felt . . . not right. Standing there on the side of the highway in his ragged clothes, covered in the dirt and dust. Unseen, unheard, his existence was something that had to be inferred from the lives of those he touched.

"OH, SHIT! PERKS!"

A few seconds of high-speed scrambling later, he found the snake. Pissed off but seemingly no worse for wear. Truth could only hope that his body had absorbed all the impact for Perks, and that snakes didn't get TBI from sudden deceleration. He ran Cup and Knife over him anyway. Some strains, and there was actually some internal damage. Damn, damn, damn. Bad, *bad* pet owner. Truth got Perks healed up but still felt like an ass.

A fool. A fool of a god. Well. At least he had conscience enough to feel bad about it.

Truth ripped off the remains of his shirt and formed it into a sling, binding Perks tight to his chest. The snake seemed annoyed by all this but eventually settled down again. He jogged off, not bothering to replace his ragged trousers. They were still on him. He was not, as of this moment, naked. Therefore, this run was already off to a better start than many of his previous marathons. He set off again, this time at rather less than maximum speed.

The stumpy mountains in the middle part of the Jeon peninsula remained their usual dull selves. Compounding the tedium was the fact that, as the Jeon peninsula wasn't very big and most of the arable land was in the middle and south, the middle and south were densely populated. Sprawl. It was all suburban and exurban sprawl. Clusters of rest stops owned by the same four conglomerates, selling food and drink made by the same two conglomerates. Staffed by retail clerks who, somehow, managed to give even less of a damn than the convenience-store hostages in town.

At least the mountains up north were dramatic. You got some great views up there. This was just browns and grays of the most tedious sort. Even the summer-green trees managed to look like they were half-assing it. He could practically hear the pines shrug and mutter "Whatever" as they refused to play along with the season.

To keep from blacking out with boredom, he started trying to incorporate Earth-Folding Step as he moved. The first time he tried, he nearly flung himself off an embankment. It wasn't the speed of movement; it was the disorientation. Even when he was moving at absurd speeds, his body knew where he was in space. The biomechanics were literally bone-deep. Throwing in a sudden change of ten meters had him bouncing off guardrails and dragging his knees across the asphalt.

Truth tried to experiment with shorter steps, shorter moves, and it seemed to help somewhat. Smaller move, smaller disorientation. Which was fine and all, but it actually netted out to him moving *slower* than if he just ran. There was something there he was just not getting. The other pain in the ass was, of course, roadblocks.

At this point, Truth was quite proficient at avoiding or sneaking through the roadblocks. It wasn't pleasant, but it was completely doable. He opted for just crossing the mountain around the roadblock but quickly ran into . . . a roadblock. Namely, Earth-Folding Step just jammed up and refused to work.

It had been inconsistently difficult as he was moving along the highway, ranging from tricky to actually very difficult but just doable. Now it was utterly locked down. The spellform collapsed before he really got it set.

"Do you really have to be more than two hundred years old to get the really good swears? Because I feel like I could use them." He looked hard at the sky. He could just about spot birds circling far overhead, but the surveillance talismans would be effectively invisible that high up. Just like when he was trying to break out of the Sung residence, but this time, there was no gap in coverage.

"I would really, *really* like to know the connection between birds and my not being able to fold up reality and casually stroll around," Truth grumbled. Then he got to hiking around the mountain. It was a mortal certainty that there would be loads of those watcher creatures in the roadblock, and he still didn't know what they were. He'd get 'em. One day.

CHAPTER 49

SEASIDE SUNSHINE

It took a while, going around a whole damn mountain to avoid a single road-block, but it was still less annoying than slipping through the roadblock by playing dead. He kept picking at the question of *why* the birds were messing up his ability to cast Earth-Folding Step. It wasn't even all birds. Just cop birds and Starbrite birds. It made zero sense.

The trees seemed to be conspiring against him. They were densely packed together but small. The worst of both worlds, as it meant that he had to be constantly moving around them but couldn't really climb them and jump from tree to tree at speed. No, it was a lot of zigzags as he tried to keep on track and not lose track of where the highway was. Ironically, the circling surveillance was a real help there. He could look up and orient whenever he liked.

Since when does looking at a spell make it not work?

<<Since forever. Remember? Earth-Folding Step comes from off-planet and before humans settled here. Besides, you don't know a damn thing about how spells work.>>

Ahaha. Ha. More than most, I'd say.

<<Oh, I apologize. In technical terms, then, being as granular as possible, how do the Meditations make you more real? How, and kindly be absolutely concrete and utterly specific, does Incisive warn you about dangers you cannot perceive? Please be sure to include all necessary math, terms of art, and, where possible, diagrams.>>

Well. I mean. I don't know how water "works," either, but I can still drink water.

<<Can you? Why does a water talisman work, then? You know how to repair one. Might even be able to build one from scratch if you had all the parts. But why. Does. It. Work? Why do cosmic rays hitting that particular layout of wires, gems, abstract pictures, and tiny inscribed spells make water fall out of a faucet? Why does it matter if it's copper instead of silver? Why does it matter if the funny picture is oriented one way or another?>>

I was more focused on the drinking part.

<<No, that still doesn't work. You have no idea what your body is using that water for, if we get down to specifics. No idea. Blood or bile or lymph won't cut it. Why do you need those things? I will just about give you credit for obeying the biological imperative written into your flesh that commands you to drink. There were a few occasions there where I wasn't sure you could do it, but damn if you didn't beat the odds! But let's not pretend you understand why water is important and why you drink it.>>

You die if you don't drink water. Good-enough reason.

<<Yeah. But you don't know why. It's one of those gaps in your education. You didn't even find out what was, let alone the why behind the what.>>

Truth tried to zip between a pair of . . . maybe pine trees? Or fir? He was vague on the difference. He slipped the gap, only to run directly into a whippy little thing that was barely chest-high. No damage or pain, of course, but it was just irritating. No such thing as a clear gap.

The System wasn't wrong, of course. He didn't know the *why* behind most things. It was one of those nice-to-have things. Understanding what was, was always more important. Still was more important. Didn't feel any closer to Starbrite, but . . . if anyone had a lead, it would be Internal Security.

Also the plague engines. Not going to sleep on that one. Actual, literal plague engines. Machines for generating life-exterminating demon plagues. If they were really diabolical, they would be designed to go off after the magic finished collapsing. Really exterminate any chance of resistance.

Screw it. He could take the forest as a training opportunity. Really hone that reaction speed, balance, and high-speed movement. He picked up the pace, dodging around the trees as quickly as he could. Incisive wasn't going to ping off running into a tree; it was all down to him. Go toes down on a rock, push, loop around the scaly bark of a tree, push, between two more trees, push on again. Silently storming around a mountain.

Bright sun up high. It was a beautiful summer day in Jeon. Not a lot of birds chirping, but the breeze in the trees was nice. Feeling the forest move as he moved through it. Truth pushed himself to improve as he did what the world told him was necessary. Not noticing how an irritating chore became satisfying, then fun.

Runchon was a town stuck between industry and tourism, and not really succeeding at either. There were shipping terminals, but they were too small to be much use, and while there was a rail line through town, it wasn't connected to the port. There was also a wall of beachfront hotels, facing the cold waters on the east coast of Jeon. It lacked a compelling view. It wasn't particularly close to Harban or any other really huge city. Gamphe, maybe, but that was on the other side of the peninsula and they had their own beaches.

Still. Credit where it was due—it was less anonymous and monotonous than Confen. You could say what you like, but at least it was better than that. There was a nice little park with some weird statues. There were a couple of shopping streets that had been decorated with an appealing blue-and-white color scheme. Tasteful and thematically appropriate.

There was also a public execution happening in a grocery-store parking lot. A load of citizens screaming at an older man, whipping him with belts, spitting on him. They hauled him over to a streetlight and hanged him, hauling him up with cheap plastic rope, coming together as a community to hold him in the air as he kicked and thrashed, his hands tied behind his back. He pissed himself. He stopped kicking. People cheered when the rope dropped, and then knives came out for souvenirs.

It wasn't murder. Cops were watching it happen. So, it must be legal. Right?

He had seen awful things. Terrible things. This wasn't the first time he had seen a mob turn on someone and tear them apart. Those were all in the slums. It was a gang thing or close enough. These were citizens. D-Tier, almost all of them, but he could see an older lady in a white summer dress flashing that C-Tier identity sigil with no shame. She had raised her arm to show her trophy—a chunk of meat. What meat, he didn't know or want to know.

"All right, next stop, the Flame!" someone Truth wouldn't look at twice yelled. The cry was met with a cheer of approval, and everyone hustled off. There was no body left behind on the sidewalk. Someone had packed a contractor bag. It was filled with the scraps and was tossed unceremoniously into a dumpster. That was at least two crimes Truth could think of—interfering with a corpse and improper disposal of human remains.

Cops didn't even blink. The selective blindness of the cops wasn't that unusual, of course, especially since he got back from Siphios, but this was different. They hadn't been paid off. They weren't looking away. They saw everything, and therefore they saw nothing. Either they were under orders, or whatever passed for common sense had changed so much, he couldn't recognize it anymore.

He followed the mob to the "Flame," a roaring pit fire in a plaza overseen by a statue of the first Emperor of Jeon. The chunks of meat were ceremoniously tossed into the fire by bloody hands.

"Great Father of Jeon, Master of Ten Thousand Flames, Ruler of the World, we beseech you! Accept our offering and bless us, that we may continue your glory for eternity. Kill all traitors! Glory to Jeon! Glory to Jeon! Glory to Jeon!" The bland looking man chanted loudly.

"Glory! Glory! Glory!"

The crowd chanted back. The ordinary man seemed to be a local somebody. A bit on the older side. Truth could imagine him running a prosperous plumbing business or maybe owning a few fast-food franchises. Not a lot—those were quite expensive. But two or three would be more than enough for this crowd of fifty or so to listen to him.

The crowd cheered and dissolved into small knots, chatting about this and that. He overheard two men complaining about how much school fees were costing this year, and he nearly snapped. Apparently, the cost of uniforms was outrageous. Ignoring the blood drying to black on their white linen summer shirts. And why not? It all washes out with enough bleach and demons.

Truth found the lady with the bloody hands and the summer dress. She was seeing off a gaggle of social climbers, enjoying being the moon surrounded by the little stars. She strode off, and he fell in beside her.

"What was that all about?" He leaned on Incisive. C-Tier or not, she was a Level One. She spoke when commanded, not even realizing she was doing so.

"Wasn't that fun? I didn't get a piece last time, as I had never made an offering before and I was a little alarmed by all the noise. This time, I made sure to stand next to where—"

"No. What was that all about? Look straight at it and tell me."

The sunny smile drained off her face. "Refo was a defeatist. He listened to foreign propaganda, undermined morale, and was a known hoarder. When we broke into his house, we found no less than four kilos of meat buried in the bottom of his freezer. Not to mention all the illegal scry equipment and immoral books. He has always been suspiciously lucky in those maintenance contracts, too—we all agreed he must be getting support from foreign spies and local traitors."

She waved her hands, chopping them through the air. "Not the first time such a thing has happened. Not the hundredth or thousandth! But there is a way, a simple way, for even ordinary people to turn bone-eating parasites into nutrition for the nation. Sacrifice!"

She snorted. "So, we—"

"I understand. I completely understand."

It was amazing how relieved she looked. Like his understanding was the important thing. Not his agreement, or forgiveness, or forbearance. His understanding. He could watch the thoughts moving through her mind. As long as they understood, what right-thinking person could condemn her for what she did? In fact, they would agree with her. They would praise her for being a good, civic minded, responsible person.

Besides, everyone was doing it. The police ignored it and even arrested people trying to stop it. So, it couldn't possibly be wrong. She couldn't possibly be wrong. It was an ancient truth, not taught in schools but instinctively understood. You tithed money at church, made incense offerings at the temples. And sometimes, God was hungry. Sometimes, he needed to sink his teeth into something more substantial.

It wasn't anything written in textbooks, at least not in Jeon. It certainly wouldn't be considered *real* magic, the way a Gentle Waves massage chair would be, or a flying carpet. It was like throwing a coin in a well and wishing for luck. You had to give if you wanted to get. Fountain didn't care where you got that coin, after all.

It was like the day of the SATs. Everyone mobbed up, joyfully righteous, joyfully murderous. Because it wasn't murder; they were doing the right thing. It was practically self-defense.

He looked at the middle-aged woman in her summer clothes—her nice shoes, her sundress, the big straw hat. He saw the fear in her. That if she wasn't in the mob, leading the mob, she would be torn apart by it. It was in the too-wide smile that never left her face. It was in the way she didn't blink enough and always laughed louder than she should.

She was scared. And she would do it again. And again. And again. Until she was safe. And she would never once regret what she did. Why should she? She was one of the good ones.

A true daughter of Jeon.

CHAPTER 50

IT MAKES SENSE BUT . . .

Truth wasn't quite sure how to handle this matter. On the one hand, he had the overwhelming urge to slap this banal monster to death. On the other hand, she wasn't a monster. She was just banal. He'd have to slap the whole city to death. Which was tempting but probably unwise.

Probably. He could see the sacrificed man in front of him now. The expression on his face was . . . hard to read. Numb with terror, maybe, or confused by the noise and the pain to the point where he lost track of what he knew was coming. The pain distorting his face as they hauled the rope up covered any other expressions.

Truth wondered if there wasn't a moment of realization as he was yanked above the mob. An instant understanding of what was happening and how this was going to end. Maybe it was all lost in pain and animal panic. Did he see the fevered looks on his neighbors' faces? The frenzied self-righteousness of it all? The hate, with that inescapable undercurrent of fear? Maybe. Maybe not. Truth weighed which option was kinder or better and quickly stopped. Those words simply did not apply to any portion of this.

Silly to even think of. He just . . . He couldn't escape the man's eyes. Something about the scene paralyzed him as much as the man. He just stood there, watching this awful thing. He didn't have any reason to intervene. It would be foolish to intervene. The whole thing was none of his business. But those eyes, and the faces of those "solid citizens." The joy of this . . . woman . . . at cutting off a prime piece of her old acquaintance. Sacrificing him for all kinds of reasons, but ultimately, she just wanted to feel safe.

It was that simple. The world is so big. Forces we cannot see or understand keep shaping our lives in increasingly awful ways. People just want to feel safe. They want to feel like they aren't powerless. Ratchet the anxiety and fear high enough, and that desire for security becomes a determination to find safety at any cost. Naturally, that had to include safety from any feelings of guilt or remorse over doing whatever it was they wound up doing.

"Sorry, do you have a napkin or cleaning charm or something? I know it's lucky, but"—the lady waved a bloody hand in front of her chest—"new dress. Trying to keep it fresh, because of the rationing. Who knows when I can get a new one?"

Truth walked through the city in something of a daze. Haunted by those eyes. Haunted by the forced cheer of the woman. Rats eating each other, but instead of individual predation, it was now neighborhoods turning on their own.

Was this a microcosm of the war between Onis and Jeon? As below, so above? *I need to feel safe, so you need to pay the price. And how* dare *you try and make me feel bad about that!*

Dying must be easy because life is hard.

<<Hmm?>>

Something I heard somewhere.

<<Not in this lifetime.>>

Oh?

Truth let silence pool within him. He walked the city, drifting through the neighborhoods. No more impromptu sacrificial rites. Lots of people queuing up for their rations of grain, of vegetables, of boots. The tension between the Runchon that wanted to be a tourist city and the Runchon that wanted to be a port city were plainly spelled out in the architecture.

One side of the city was low-slung cinderblock buildings and soaring warehouses. The other was slab-like resort hotels, backed by the tiny, perpetually shadowed small homes and low-rise apartments of the locals. They weren't even particularly bad homes. They were just small. And dark. Always looking up at people living above them.

He wondered how many of them would be habitable in six months. It was hot now, but Jeon winters were no joke. How were they going to live with no heat? Five months. Maybe not even. There was something in the air. Whatever steps people were taking to slow the decline of magic weren't working. He drew in a long breath through his nose. Yeah. Bad night to be on the street. He could feel the weather changing.

Internal Security wasn't particularly hard to find. Their field office was, as per usual, in the local police headquarters. So much more convenient to mobilize local law enforcement for support that way. Also, it saved on expenses building or leasing an office. No bureaucrat would miss the opportunity to shift the cost of the office space from their budget to another.

Short building, gray concrete, boxy. If you have seen one cop shop, you have seen them all. The front door, as tradition demanded, was wide open. The actual entrance, the one used by the police and their involuntary guests, was a heavily armored shutter that sealed off an underground garage. This was considered the orthodox arrangement in Jeon, nicely balancing practicality, tradition, and public education.

The whole thing was just coated in recording talismans, wards, banishments, countersurveillance wards, and (interesting one for him) structural-reinforcement wards. He checked the latter out of curiosity, as they were plainly commercial-grade as opposed to governmental.

He laughed quietly. The wards were tuned to repel wind and water. They were rolling into monsoon and typhoon season, weren't they? Actually . . . they were already solidly into it. This was unseasonably dry. Hmm. Maybe there really would be a change in weather tonight.

He lightly jumped up, grabbed a third-story window frame, then, without slowing down, launched himself up to the roof. He frowned. Less rooftop access than he thought. It was a police headquarters but clearly one that didn't see a lot of airborne traffic. A couple flying platforms were parked on the roof, activation talismans removed and presumably stored inside the station. There was a door leading into the building, and that was about it.

Ignoring the nigh-literal forest of surveillance talismans, he was mildly alarmed to notice anti-personnel mines. There were also a number of powerful anti-glamour wards as well. Made sense. Last thing you would want is someone droned or enthralled making their way inside.

Truth nodded approvingly at the wards as he walked past them. Level Two–power wards were more than decent by most standards. Most. Internal Security would have more robust protection.

Annoyingly, the lock on the door was considerably better than average. And not a Starbrite lock. It took minutes to crack. He felt obscurely offended. It became a particularly petty insult in his heart. Snorting, he opened the door and went down the halls. He took a moment to change into the uniform of an army officer. Every little bit helps, and the cover would reduce the drain on his cosmic energy.

To his increasing irritation, Internal Security was set in the big corner office taking up a quarter of the top floor. Cops had to love that. Having the captain's office on the opposite corner of the building was doubtless a coincidence. As was the IS office occupying the southern, luckiest, corner, and the captain having the unluckiest north.

IS loved games like that. Getting in your head with a thousand petty tricks so you were defeated before they even laid hands on you. Funny. With all the nightmare stories you heard about IS, the office looked very ordinary. Armored, enchanted, steel door, naturally. Along with Level Three–power wards. Truth nodded lightly. They wouldn't be doing any interrogation there. They would use the cells below or specialist facilities offsite.

Now, he could spend ages circumventing the complicated, multilayered defenses of this door . . . or he could make IS open the door for him. He knocked twice, firmly, and stepped back.

There was no answer. He knocked again. No answer. There weren't any windows in the door, understandably. Although he was quite certain that he was being observed through the recording talismans. He knocked again. "I can and will do this all day."

He knocked again. Waited nineteen seconds. Knocked. Twenty seconds. Knocked. Fifteen seconds. Knocked. Twenty seconds. Knocked. Each time varying the number or strength of the knocks.

Eventually, the door was torn open by a furious office lady. "You really don't know how *death* is spelled, do you?!"

"My education was pretty lacking."

"No problem! I know some excellent teachers. Follow me; I'll take you straight to the classroom." She snarled.

"Would that I could. I have an appointment with Colonel Eskevan Cho. He should be expecting me."

"Like hell he is! You aren't in the book." She wasn't bothering to conceal her reaching for a paralyzing wand at the small of her back.

"Yes, I am. I was specifically told to come here. *Let me prove my words. Inform the colonel that I'm here.*" He watched the light switch off behind her eyes. His smile was cold. Seemed he was right. Lots and lots of those worms floating around.

"Oi. Spiritual Worm Number Whatever. Go tell the colonel that To Whom It May Concern is here."

"I cannot take orders from a civilian." A wispy, neutral voice came from the officer's mouth. It didn't sound the same as the worm in Confen. Interesting.

"All right, well. You do you, then?"

There was no reply. He wasn't really sure what he was expecting, anyhow. He pushed past the suddenly brainless IS agent and walked into the office. The office continued the trend of being straight out of a catalog for government agencies who haven't had a new furniture budget in living memory. He was pretty sure most of the desks there were older than his dad. They were certainly older than Truth was.

None of the offices had nameplates on them. A security feature he had seen before and didn't like it then, either. Sighing, he checked the office kitchen. It was a sink with a hot box and some sort of automated device for making coffee. He could figure out how to work it, given enough time, but all the coffee smelled terrible. He wasn't that motivated.

Girding his metaphorical loins, he went forth, peeking into offices. Many were locked, with decent locks. He skipped over them, aiming for the low-hanging fruit first. Mercifully, there were name plaques on the desks. By some even greater mercy, Colonel Eskevan Cho was in.

He was slim. A little shorter than average, but not by much. Black hair, black eyes, looked like he looked after himself but wasn't dumping a ton into cosmetic glamorous. You wouldn't look twice at him on the subway. You hardly looked twice at him in his uniform, sitting behind a desk with a plaque on it reading COLONEL ESKEVAN CHO.

Truth wasn't so bigoted that he couldn't admit to being impressed. The man seemed ferociously good at being a secret policeman. Truth sat in the visitor's chair for a while, watching him. He seemed to be reading documents, then jotting down notes. Truth peeked over. Reports about suspected saboteurs, political unreliables, and those whose graft was greater than the bribes they paid.

Basically what he expected. Truth sat back down again.

"When did the mob sacrifices begin?"

"Who the hell?" Cho whipped around, needler in hand, shield charm activating. Truth didn't move. The colonel was Level Four but older. His looks were cosmetic. He had cultivated the hard way. IS didn't supply their people with elixirs the way Starbrite PMC did.

"When did the mob sacrifices begin? And who signed off on it? It has to be terrible for morale and the government's prestige."

The colonel trained his needler on Truth for a long minute, then sighed, putting it down. The shield charm would run until the spell ran out, but neither of them minded about that.

"I suppose you need no introduction. Might as well jump straight into the conversation," Cho muttered.

"I don't? You realize that everything you know about me is propaganda put out by at least three forces, right?"

Cho snorted. "Oh, we know more about you than that."

"Really? Who am I, then?"

That got him a filthy look. "Cute."

"You called this meeting, Colonel. I'm just trying to make good use of it."

"By asking about people chopping up their neighbors for sacrifices?"

"Yep."

"Well. It's related to why I called you here, actually."

"Oh? Now I really am curious." Truth smiled politely.

"I know one *very* interesting thing about you. I and a very select group of others." Cho smiled. A professional cop smile. It did not put Truth at ease. "I know you rescued the Shattervoid girl. Which means you have ten thousand tickets off this rock. So, I, and my extremely wealthy, powerful, connected friends, want to know—how much are you selling the seats for?"

CHAPTER 51

DISPENSING WITH NICETIES

Truth tried to think very rapidly. This was a cop. A high-end cop, but a cop. And cops didn't ask questions that would benefit you. This was a fishing expedition.

Colonel Cho snorted. "The contents of Great White Mountain were not known to us. After it blew up, we were able to see who *had* been working there and work backward. Our analysts were very busy for a while. Since the Shattervoid are still here, 'she' didn't die in the eruption."

Truth nodded. That sounded almost plausible. Then he waited. Cho waited right back at him. They sat quietly for a few minutes.

"Oh, you are still on the hanging."

"Yep."

"Not the near-infinite sums of money."

"What money?"

"I did say—"

"I heard you."

The room went quiet again. Truth thought it was pretty interesting, watching the colonel's face. He had a superb poker face, naturally. Unmoving. Truth could practically feel the thoughts darting around inside his head, like fish hunting in a still pond.

"It's a mitigation measure. There are too many changes, too fast, and they touch on too many interests. Building up on decades of preparation, but it's all too much, too fast. There just isn't a release that we can offer them that would be comprehensive enough to release the social tension. So, a number of different factions collaborated to create a new folk custom."

Truth nodded. Manufacturing authenticity was a core skill of any PR outfit.

"Need I say more?"

"Yes. Why no official party leader? I would think establishing or maintaining hierarchy would be desirable."

"There is. The parties are de facto led by the same one or two people in each neighborhood that has been targeted for management. In due time, it will be revealed that those people were tied to a higher power. Fortunate chosen ones."

Sounded right. It also made some implicit truths about the relationship between the mighty and the masses explicit. This was nakedly sacrificing their own people and, to an extent, their own legitimacy, to buy time.

The people with an eye to the exit simply didn't care anymore, and for those looking to stay, replacing the corrupt old order would actually add to their legitimacy. Bringing an end to the chaos and wild cruelty of the Bad Times. Might find some capable subordinates, or convenient scapegoats, or both. Really, it was a plan with no losses. Immense returns on an investment with no capital.

They lapsed back into silence. Cho coughed. "So. About those tickets—"

"If the Shattervoid are still here, and I am still here, you know I haven't put together the full fare."

Colonel Cho nodded at that, smiling slightly. "Like I said, I'm representing a very wealthy consortium of people who would like to know your price for off-world travel. And they do understand your . . . notorious disdain for money."

"My what, now?"

"Your conversation with Mr. Sung was, as you suspected, recorded. Twice over. Once by the Sung clan, once by us. Ours leaked first, but theirs was only twenty minutes behind. It was quite interesting to watch."

"Watch?"

"How the information spread, then the information about who had the information spreading."

"Ah. And this meeting is being recorded as well?"

"As well as transmitting to people listening in live, yes. Once my shield charm activated."

"Haah. All right." Well, *that* wasn't ideal. On the other hand, his adopted persona was wrapped firmly around him. He was the Hell Prince, yes, but those words didn't mean what Cho thought they meant. *Hell Prince* sounded scary, but he was quite certain that the Propaganda Department, or whoever, hadn't really thought about what Hell was when they came up with the name.

"So, why did you lead off by offering money?"

"Money, as you pointed out, can mean different things at different times." Cho settled back into his chair. "For example, we have a *wealth* of agents and a *wealth* of information."

"Ah. You put me in a position to behead Starbrite, and in exchange you get to watch the apocalypse play out from far, far away."

"Mmm. Well, we can offer other conveniences, but based on your performance thus far, I am quite certain you won't use them."

"Oh?"

"Kill squads, hidden armories, sealed demons, tactical- and strategic-level curses, specialized succubae and other seduction agents, essentially every vehicle manufactured anywhere in the world, custom spell work and custom gear, even extraordinarily rare natural treasures. Things that would once have been considered national treasures."

"Jeon still has national treasures?"

"Didn't say they were *our* national treasures." Cho smiled like a shark.

"*There's* the Jeon I know."

"Interested?"

"Definitely. Gonna say no, though."

"We knew you would. Frankly, we weren't optimistic you would even take the meeting."

"Curiosity, mostly." That, and he was going insane trying to think of any way to find Starbrite's traces.

"So. What does it take to buy our way off-world? Incidentally, regardless of whether the Sung Clan ultimately takes your advice—here." He handed over a thick folder. Truth opened it. Lists of names, ages, fitness for the draft. Three-quarters female, Truth noted. Then pictures, a map, daily schedules. Training regimens.

"You decided to train Level Zeros."

"The best of the ones who wouldn't be missed, yes. Thousands of others have been recruited to reclusive but heavily promoted 'elite academies.' Some of them really are elite academies, long established to train up the younger generations of top clans before they head to university."

"Ah. Not everyone in those top families is going to make it off-world?"

"Most aren't even going to try. All are making contingency plans."

"Aren't even going to try?" Truth cocked his head to one side.

"You think we don't see the trap this world is in? We knew even before the Shattervoid stopped coming. We are a backwater. We scraped by, selling cheap manufactured goods, importing the cheapest food and a bare few luxuries. And they are only luxuries by our standards!"

"Okay?"

"How many people are willing to go from being a local tyrant, living a life of utter decadence, to being a despised coolie, a refugee, a beggar on the streets of a strange city in a strange world?" Cho shrugged. "I'm angling to get me and mine out, and I have been *very* realistic with the family about what to expect. They are all currently medicated to manage the depression."

Truth nodded and went still again. Processing. Everything Cho said was calculated. That had been his impression since he first got the message from the worm. Every word, every gesture, every pause. It was all calculated to operate on several levels. Invisibly shaping the listener's reality, like getting the poison of Incisive the hard way.

"Building the new farms was a lot harder than the training camps. Hard to design for maximum production when you know you won't have magical inputs or labor." Cho smiled faintly.

Ah. Now, there was some bait. He had deduced some things, and now he was testing. Truth decided to test straight back.

"Nice to meet you. I'm off." Truth stood and started walking for the door.

"Really? I know you said there was no plan, but this seems random even for you."

"Show me some sincerity."

"More than saving thousands of—"

Truth gave the colonel a look.

"They are being saved. They would surely die otherwise." Cho kept his voice quite mild.

"Mmm. Good for them. How are you going to save yourself?"

"What more sincerity can we offer than *whatever you want?*"

"I want a lot of things. What can you offer me that I *need?*" Truth kept his voice mild, too.

"Starbrite."

Truth paused, smiling at the door. "Was the whole performance worth it?"

There was a startled pause behind him, then a little huffed-out breath. "Yes. These things are necessary."

"But why? We were always going to wind up here." Truth didn't turn back yet.

"Because we don't know you. And we want our own assurances."

"You know me perfectly well." Truth turned and sat back down, sprawling in the chair. "By 'you' I mean IS and our studio audience."

"You know that isn't true."

"Oh? Is the Hell Prince lying? Misleading you? Sowing division with his honeyed words? Who could have possibly guessed?"

"We can ease off on that, if it bothers you."

Truth smiled his own shark smile. "How's it working out for you?"

"Middling. Better than you might expect. It helps to have a face to pin the blame on."

"Which is definitely the only reason you are doing it." Truth waved the point away. "Cough up the goods."

"We need an agreement first."

"No."

"We really do."

"Then we are really done." Truth shrugged.

"I'm not asking for your soul here—" Cho spread his hands.

"No."

"Even a—"

"No."

"Young man, are you sure you understand what *agreement* means?"

"Yes, quite sure, thank you." Truth nodded politely.

"Then what's all this? What's the harm in establishing the terms of cooperation?"

"Because there are no terms of cooperation. There will be no cooperation. I'm hunting down Jeon's leading families in the time between now and the collapse. If I'm still here after the collapse, the murder-per-minute rate will only go up. Send your armies. Send your old monsters. I don't give a *fuck* who you send. The only, *only* thing that is keeping people out of the murdered-in-bed lottery is if I have something more pressing to deal with."

"Why do you hate them so much?" Cho sounded mildly interested. Truth just smiled. And waited.

And waited.

And waited. Cho kept staring at him. Eventually, Truth shrugged and stood. He walked over to the filing cabinet, found it locked, broke the lock with a jab of his thumb, and ripped the door open. He then started browsing files. If he was going to be waiting a while, he might as well have something to read.

"Oh, for God's sake!" Cho kept it together pretty well, but Truth saw the red rising on the back of his neck. Well-known fact—cops love keeping files and hate other people reading them.

"Funny you say that. Not very funny, but kind of funny. Incidentally, how have you not caught this prick? I've done some awful shit, but 'drowned his victims in fish entrails' is a new one for me."

"He is very likely dead, fallen into an industrial fish-ball maker," Cho growled, eyes fixed on the folder. Truth shrugged and put it back. Then pulled out another. Cho reached for his needler.

"You know that won't help. Better hurry; there is only so long these are going to keep me interested. You have already fished enough information out of me. Stop playing coy and cough—Really? A real-estate scam and he rates a file in your office? Looks like he only got away with two million."

"Who he robbed matters a lot more than how much he stole." He reached into a drawer and pulled out a gem. "We have spent more than a hundred years finding Starbrite's footsteps. A century sorting false leads. We still can't point you straight at him. But we can put you on his trail. If you can settle the matter of transport off-world when the deed is done."

"And being paranoid, your sponsors want more than an agreement; they want some degree of leverage over me beyond mutual destruction when the world ends."

"Essentially."

"No."

"Mutual destruction is really your preferred option?"

"Yes."

That appeared to actually surprise Cho. It was just a tiny flash in the eyes, a sudden flicker of a fin showing through the reflection on the pond's surface. It might have been nothing, or left for him to find. Or it might be real.

Truth gave him a half-smile. "I am what you made me, after all. Does the Hell Prince bend his neck? Does he compromise? Does he find a path of mutual support that respects the dignity of all peoples, most particularly the mighty who might threaten him?"

"You just said—"

"I say a lot of things. What I am saying now is this—those who obey me shall prosper, and those who oppose me shall perish. I will make no agreements nor accept any restraints. Give me Starbrite, or become the next sacrifice to the mob, strung up on a lamppost. There is no plan. I'm very flexible. If I sacrifice enough of you, something will give me the answer I need. And if it doesn't? Then I shall inherit my throne and make this world a Hell of my own creation."

ABOUT THE AUTHOR

Warby Picus is a lifelong fan of science fiction and fantasy. One day, he figured he would see if writing books was as much fun as it appeared to be. He hasn't looked back since.

RESPAWN YOUR CURIOSITY

follow us on our socials

 podiumentertainment.com

 @podiumentertainment

 /podiumentertainment

 @podium_ent

 @podiumentertainment